国際俳句歳時記 秋

国境を越えた魂の震撼

向瀬美音 企画・編集・翻訳
中野千秋 翻訳

International Saijiki : Autumn
Saijiki international : Automne

The Shaking Souls Across Borders

Planed, edited, translated by
Mine Mukose
Translated by
Chiaki Nakano

コールサック社

向瀬美音 編

国際俳句歳時記　秋
国境を越えた魂の震撼

International Saijiki : Autumn
The Shaking Souls Across Borders

Saijiki International Automne
Secouer les âmes par-delà les frontières

Planed, edited translated by Mine Mukose
Translated by Chiaki Nakano

序

向瀬美音

　私は国際俳句に関わって8年になる。

　その間に様々な発見があった。

　初めは、海外から投句される作品にひたすら五感を刺激された。実作の結晶に触れて魂を揺さぶられた。

　そのうち、季語を紹介してはどうかと考え、国際歳時記を作成した。

　今回は計画中の春夏秋冬の最後に編集した「秋」の出版である。

　歳時記形式にすると読みやすいし、なんと言っても同じ季節に同じ対象を愛で、一体感が増すのである。

　今回の秋だけが少し厚くなってしまったが、これは外国の俳人の季節への関心の深まりと秀句が多くなったためである。勿論秋には共有できる季語が多いというのも背景にある。

　海外の俳人は特に天文が好きで、月、星、天の川、流星の欄には多くの句が集まった。また彼らは鳥が好きで、渡鳥は海外でもよく使われる季語である。

　宗教的にも、哲学的にも、地理的にも地政学的にも世界の俳人は興味の幅が違う。例えば刈田、秋の蛇などはアジア系の俳人に好まれる。同様に紛争の続く中東では北アフリカの俳人がたくさん社会詠を投句してくる。さまざまな宗教に関する独自の季語も顕著である。

　国際俳句とは英語俳句であると思っていたが、これは間違いである。

国際コンクールでは英語が使われているが、日々の句会ではイタリア人はイタリア語圏で、フランス人はフランス語圏で句会をしている。それぞれの言語は音節も違うし、リズムも違うし、切れの表記法も異なる。季語に関しては多少のずれも生じる。
　しかし、俳句にとって大切な「切れ」と「省略」と「具体的なものに託す」という点においては全世界共通である。
　そして、「取り合わせ」が成功しやすいという点でも同じである。「取り合わせ」によって生まれる調和、二物衝撃によって生まれる響き、世界観は同じである。

　俳句ガーデンは昨年、俳句コラムから独立して今や3,500人を超えるメンバーを抱えている。8年前からずっと投句を続けている俳人も多い。これらは会員間にある信頼と尊重と向上心によるものである。

　私は毎日句に目を通し、今ではライフワークの一部になっている。
　30カ国を超える俳人がインターネットで毎週句会をやっており世界は広いようで、世界を一周していう感覚にも陥る。最近は地球儀を眺める時間が多くなり、世界の紛争にも敏感になった。閉塞感、矛盾、混沌、世界的な自然災害も彼らは俳句に詠んでいる。遠い島国である日本人が社会詠、戦争句を読むとしばしば「人ごと感」がするが、当事者の俳句には心に迫るものがある。俳句は四季を愛で、子供を慈愛するとともに、社会の矛盾にも迫ってくる。しかし、これらは季語を使ったり自然と組み合わせているので、十分詩に昇華している。

　「国境を越えた俳句」毎日の実践でこのことを痛感している。

世界は広いが人の心はとても近いと思うのである。

原句に関して、1行、2行、3行のいずれの俳句にするのも、俳人の自由だと私は思っている。

この国際歳時記は2022年、2023年、2024年の秋に投句されたものを季語別にまとめたものである。初めは4,000句にも及び、どうしようかと困っていたがどうにか約2,160句にまとめた。毎日の投句で秀句は全て保存してあるので後世に残していきたいと思っている。

主宰である私と英語の俳句を素晴らしく17音に収めるバイリンガルの俳人、中野千秋氏の俳句は全ての季語の最後に載せてある。

preface

Mine Mukose

I have been involved in international haiku for eight years now.
Various discoveries were made during that time.
At first, the works submitted from abroad stimulated my senses. I was touched by the crystallization of actual works and my soul was shaken.
Eventually, we thought it would be a good idea to introduce seasonal words, so we created the International Chronicle.
This time, the publication is for "Autumn," the last of the Spring, Summer, Autumn, and Winter seasons.
The chronological format makes it easy to read, and, what is more, it increases the sense of unity by loving the same object at the same season.
Only autumn is a little thicker this time, but this is due to the growing interest in the season among foreign haiku poets and the number of excellent poems. Of course, this is also due to the fact that there are many seasonal words that can be shared in autumn.
Overseas haiku poets were especially fond of astronomy, and the moon, stars, Milky Way, and meteor columns attracted many haiku. They also like birds, and migrating birds is a common seasonal term used abroad.
Another new discovery is that we now know which seasonal words are favored by foreign haiku poets.
Religiously, philosophically, geographically, and geopolitically, haiku poets around the world have different interests. Karita and Autumn Snake, for example, are favored by Asian haiku poets. Similarly, in

the Middle East, where conflict continues, many North African haiku poets submit social poems. The unique seasonal words related to various religions are also remarkable.

Those who think that international haiku is English-language haiku are mistaken.
English is used in international competitions, but in daily haiku meetings, Italians meet in Italian-speaking countries, and French meet in French-speaking countries. Each language has different syllables, different rhythms, and different notations for breaks. There can also be some discrepancies with regard to seasonal words.
However, the important aspects of haiku, such as "cutting," "omission," and "entrusting to something concrete," are the same throughout the world.
And it is also the same in that "assortment" is more likely to succeed. The harmony created by "assortment," the resonance created by the impact of two things, and the worldview are the same.

Haiku Garden became independent from Haiku Column last year and now has over 3,500 members, many of whom have been submitting haiku for the past eight years. This is due to the trust and respect that exists among the members.

I look through the phrases every day and they are now part of my life's work.
Haiku poets from more than 30 countries hold weekly haiku gatherings on the Internet. Recently, I have been spending more time looking at the globe and have become more sensitive to world con-

flicts. He and his colleagues also write haiku about the sense of stagnation, contradiction, chaos, and natural disasters around the world. When Japanese people in distant island countries read social or war poems, they often feel as if they are reading about "other people's business," but the haiku of those who are involved in these conflicts are very moving. Haiku poets love the four seasons and children, and they also approach the contradictions of society. However, because they use seasonal words and combine them with nature, they are sufficiently sublimated into poetry.

I am acutely aware of this in my daily practice of "haiku across borders."
The world is a big place, but I believe that people's hearts are very close.

As for the original text, I think it's up to haiku poet to decide one-line or two lines or three lines Haiku.

This International Chronicle is a collection of poems submitted in the autumns of 2022, 2023, and 2024, grouped by season word. At first, there were as many as 4,000 poems, and I was at a loss as to what to do with them, but I managed to compile them into 2,000 poems. I have saved all the excellent daily submissions and hope to preserve them for posterity.

Haiku by myself, the lead haiku writer, and Chiaki Nakano, a bilingual haiku poet who wonderfully captures English haiku in 17 syllables, are included at the end of all the seasonal words.

Preface

Mine Mukose

Cela fait maintenant huit ans que je m'intéresse au haïku international.

Au cours de cette période, j'ai fait diverses découvertes.

Tout d'abord, les œuvres envoyées de l'étranger ont stimulé mes sens.

J'ai été touché e touchée par la cristallisation des œuvres actuelles et mon âme a été ébranlée.

Finalement, nous avons pensé qu'il serait bon d'introduire des mots de saison et nous avons créé la Chronique internationale.

Cette fois-ci, la publication porte sur « l'automne », la dernière des saisons printemps, été, automne et hiver.

Le format chronologique facilite la lecture et, de plus, renforce le sentiment d'unité en aimant le même objet à la même saison.

Seul l'automne est un peu plus épais cette fois-ci, mais cela est dû à l'intérêt croissant pour cette saison parmi les poètes de haïku étrangers et au nombre d'excellents poèmes. Bien entendu, cela s'explique également par le fait que de nombreux mots saisonniers peuvent être partagés en automne.

Les poètes de haïku d'outre-mer aiment particulièrement l'astronomie, et la lune, les étoiles, la Voie lactée et les colonnes de météores ont attiré de nombreux haïkus. Ils aiment également les oiseaux, et le terme « oiseaux migrateurs » est un terme saisonnier couramment utilisé à l'étranger.

Autre découverte, nous savons désormais quels mots saisonniers sont privilégiés par les poètes de haïku étrangers.

Sur le plan religieux, philosophique, géographique et géopolitique, les poètes de haïku du monde entier ont des intérêts différents. Karita et Autumn Snake, par exemple, ont la préférence des poètes asiatiques. De même, au Moyen-Orient, où les conflits se poursuivent, de nombreux poètes haïku nord-africains soumettent des poèmes sociaux. Les mots saisonniers uniques liés à diverses religions sont également remarquables.

Ceux qui pensent que le haïku international est un haïku en langue anglaise se trompent.
L'anglais est utilisé dans les compétitions internationales, mais dans les réunions quotidiennes de haïku, les Italiens se rencontrent dans les pays italophones et les Français dans les pays francophones.
 Chaque langue a des syllabes différentes, des rythmes différents et des notations différentes pour les pauses. Il peut également y avoir des divergences en ce qui concerne les mots saisonniers.
Cependant, les aspects importants du haïku, tels que la « coupe », l'« omission » et le fait de « confier à quelque chose de concret », sont les mêmes dans le monde entier.
Il en va de même pour le fait que l'« assortiment » a plus de chances de réussir. L'harmonie créée par l'« assortiment », la résonance créée par l'impact de deux choses et la vision du monde sont les mêmes.

Haiku Garden est devenu indépendant de Haiku Column l'année dernière et compte aujourd'hui plus de 3,500 membres, dont beaucoup soumettent des haïkus depuis huit ans. Cela est dû à la confiance et au respect qui existent entre les membres.

Je consulte les phrases tous les jours et elles font désormais partie du travail de ma vie.

Des poètes de haïku de plus de 30 pays organisent des réunions hebdomadaires de haïku sur l'internet. Récemment, j'ai passé plus de temps à observer le globe et je suis devenu plus sensible aux conflits mondiaux. Les Haijins écrivent également des haïkus sur le sentiment de stagnation, de contradiction, de chaos et de catastrophes naturelles dans le monde. Lorsque les Japonais de leurs îles lointaines lisent des poèmes sociaux ou des poèmes de guerre, ils ont souvent l'impression de lire « les affaires des autres », mais les haïkus de ceux qui sont impliqués dans ces conflits sont très émouvants. Les poètes haïku aiment les quatre saisons et les enfants, et ils abordent également les contradictions de la société. Mais parce qu'ils utilisent des mots de saison et qu'ils les associent à la nature, ils les subliment suffisamment pour en faire de la poésie.

J'en ai une conscience aiguë dans ma pratique quotidienne du « haïku transfrontalier ».
Le monde est vaste, mais je crois que le cœur des gens est très proche.

Quand au haiku original vous êtes libre d'écrie une ligne ou 2 lignes ou 3 lignes Haiku.

Cette Chronique internationale est un recueil de poèmes soumis au cours des automnes 2022, 2023 et 2024, regroupés par mot de saison. Au début, il y avait jusqu'à 4,000 poèmes, et je ne savais pas quoi en faire, mais j'ai réussi à les compiler en 2,000 poèmes. J'ai conservé toutes les excellentes contributions quotidiennes et j'espère les préserver pour la postérité.

Des haïkus de moi-même, l'auteur principal des haïkus, et de Chiaki Nakano, un poète bilingue qui capture merveilleusement les haïkus anglais en 17 syllabes, sont inclus à la fin de tous les mots saisonniers.

目次　　Contents

序　向瀬美音　〈preface　Mine Mukose〉················ 2
私が考える俳句とは　ナディン・レオン
　〈Qu'est-ce que le haïku selon moi　Nadine Léon〉················ 20
私にとって俳句とは　デニス・カンバラウ
　〈Cosa è per me lo haiku　Dennys Cambarau〉················ 29
俳句の概要　ポール・カルス　〈Haiku at a Glance　Paul Callus〉········ 38
俳句の道　愛　タンポポ・アニス
　〈THE HAIKU PATH I LOVE　Tanpopo Anis〉················ 44
アラブの舞台における俳句　モハメド・ベンファレス
　〈Le Haiku sur la Scène Arabe　Mohammed Benfares〉················ 55

時候（じこう・jiko）season ／ saison

立秋【りっしゅう・risshu】the first day of fall ／ premier jour de l'automne······ 64
秋初め【あきはじめ・akihajime】begininng of autumn ／ début de l'automne···· 68
九月【くがつ・kugatsu】september ／ septembre················ 82
残暑【ざんしょ・zansho】the late summer heat ／ dernières chaleurs de l'été···· 87
秋分【しゅうぶん・shuubun】autumn solstice ／ équinoxe d'automne················ 90
十月【じゅうがつ・jugatsu】october ／ octobre················ 92
秋の朝【あきのあさ・akinoasa】autumn morning ／ matin d'automne················ 96
秋の昼【あきのひる・akinohiru】autumn noon ／ après-midi d'automne············ 100
秋の暮【あきのくれ・akinokure】autumn dusk ／ nuit tombante de l'automne·· 101
秋の夜【あきのよ・akinoyo】autumn night ／ soirée d'automne················ 106
夜長【よなが・yonaga】long night ／ longue nuit d'automne················ 109
秋澄む【あきすむ・akisumu】fresh air of autumn ／ fraicheur de l'automne ····· 112
冷やか【ひややか・hiyayaka】autumn chill ／ fraîcheur d'automne················ 114

爽やか【さわやか・sawayaka】fresh air of autumn/ fraîcheur d'automne 117

秋麗【あきうらら・akiurara】beautiful autumn / belle journée d'automne 120

秋深し【あきふかし・akifukashi】deep autumn / automne profond 123

行く秋【いくあき・ikuaki】passing of autumn / fin de l'automne 126

晩秋【ばんしゅう・banshu】late autumn / fin d'automne 127

秋惜しむ【あきおしむ・akioshimu】autumnal regret / regrets d'automne 128

天文（てんもん・tenmon）astronomy ／ astronomie

秋の日【あきのひ・akinohi】bright autumn day / soleil d'automne 130

秋晴【あきばれ・akibare】nice fall day / belle journée d'automne 134

秋の色【あきのいろ・akinoiro】autumn scene / paysage d'automne 135

秋の声【あきのこえ・akinokoe】autumn voice / voix d'automne 137

秋の空【あきのそら・akinosora】autumn sky / ciel d'automne 141

空高し【そらたかし・soratakashi】high sky of autumn / ciel haut d'automne 146

秋の雲【あきのくも・akinokumo】autumn clouds / nuages d'automne 148

鰯雲【いわしぐも・iwashigumo】cirrocumulus / nuages moutonnés 151

月【つき・tsuki】moon / lune 152

上り月【のぼりつき・noboritsuki】

　first moon quarter / premier quartier de lune 156

降り月【くだりつき・kudaritsuki】

　last moon quarter / dernier quartier de lune 159

三日月【みかづき・mikazuki】crescent moon / lune croissante 161

半月【はんげつ・hangetsu】half moon / demi lune 165

名月【めいげつ・meigetsu】moon / lune 166

無月【むげつ・mugetsu】night without the moon / nuit sans lune 177

雨月【うげつ・ugetsu】rainy moon / lune de pluie 182

有明月【ありあけづき・ariakezuki】morning moon / lune du matin 184

秋の星【あきのほし・akinohoshi】autumn star / étoile d'automne ········· 186

カシオペア【かしおぺあ・kashiopea】Cassiopeia / Cassiopée ········· 188

星月夜【ほしづきよ・hoshizukiyo】starry night / ciel étoilé ········· 191

天の川【あまのがわ・amanogawa】milky way / voie lactée ········· 195

流れ星【ながれぼし・nagareboshi】shooting star / étoile filante ········· 199

秋風【あきかぜ・akikaze】autumn wind / vent d'automne ········· 205

秋の嵐【あきのあらし・akinoarashi】antumn storm / orages d automne ········· 212

台風【たいふう・taifu】typhoon / typhon ········· 215

秋の雨【あきのあめ・akinoame】autumn rain / pluie d'automne ········· 219

秋時雨【あきしぐれ・akishigure】

    light autumn rain / pluie légère d'automne ········· 226

稲妻【いなづま・inazuma】lightning / éclair ········· 227

秋の虹【あきのにじ・akinoniji】autumn rainbow / arc-en-ciel d'automne ········· 231

秋夕焼【あきゆうやけ・akiyuyake】

    autumn sunset / coucher de soleil d'automne ········· 233

霧【きり・kiri】fog / brume ········· 237

露【つゆ・tsuyu】dew / rosée ········· 248

地理 (ちり・chiri) geography / geographie

秋の山【あきのやま・akinoyama】autumn mountain / montagne d'automne ·· 254

刈田【かりた・karita】harvested ricefield / rizière moissonnée ········· 257

秋の浜【あきのはま・akinohama】autumn shore / plage d'automne ········· 258

水澄む【みずすむ・mizusumu】clarity of water / eau claire ········· 260

秋の川【あきのかわ・akinokawa】autumn river / rivière d'automne ········· 260

秋の湖【あきのうみ・akinoumi】autumn lake / lac d'automne ········· 262

秋の海【あきのうみ・akinoumi】autumn sea / mer d'automne ········· 263

秋の潮【あきのしお・akinoshio】autumn tides / marées d'automne ········· 265

生活 (せいかつ・seikatsu) life / vie

七夕【たなばた・tanabata】the Star Festival / festival des étoiles ········· 268

新酒【しんしゅ・shinshu】new sake / saké nouveau ········· 270

新米【しんまい・shimmai】new rice / nouveau riz ········· 273

案山子【かがし・kagashi】scarecrow / épouvantail ········· 275

温め酒【ぬくめざけ・nukumezake】warm sake / saké chaud ········· 279

村芝居【むらしばい・murashibai】village theater / théâtre villageois ········· 280

秋思【しゅうし・shushi】autumn sadness / tristesse d'automne ········· 283

行事 (ぎょうじ・gyoji) event / ceremonie

聖人祭【せいじんさい・seijinsai】all saints / la Toussaint ········· 290

子規忌【しきき・shikiki】
Shiki's memorial / anniversaire de la mort de Shiki ········· 292

動物 (どうぶつ・dobutsu) animals / animaux

鹿【しか・shika】deer / cerf ········· 296

猪【いのしし・inoshishi】wild boar / sanglier ········· 298

雉【きじ・kiji】pheasant / faisan ········· 299

渡鳥【わたりどり・wataridori】migratory birds / oiseaux migrateurs ········· 299

小鳥【ことり・kotori】bird coming / les oiseaux de retour ········· 305

燕帰る【つばめかえる・tsubamekaeru】
swallow comming away / retour d'hirondelle ········· 306

栗鼠【りす・risu】squirrel / écureuil ········· 310

鵙【もず・mozu】bull-headed shrike / pie-grieche ········· 311

鶫【つぐみ・tsugumi】thrush / merle ········· 312

椋鳥【むくどり・mukudori】white-cheeked starling / etourneau ········· 313

鵲【かささぎ・kasasagi】magpie / pie ········· 314

鶉【うずら・uzura】quail / caille ··· 316

啄木鳥【きつつき・kitsutsuki】woodpecker / pivert ··· 317

雁【かり・kari】wild goose / oie sauvage ··· 318

鷹渡る【たかわたる・takawataru】crossing hawk / vol d'un faucon ··· 321

鱸【すずき・suzuki】sea bass / loup ··· 323

秋鯖【あきさば・akisaba】mackerel / maquereau ··· 324

鰯【いわし・iwashi】sardine / sardine ··· 324

鮭【さけ・sake】salmon / saumon ··· 327

秋の蝶【あきのちょう・akinocho】autumn butterfly / papillon d'automne ··· 328

秋の蛇【あきのへび・akinohebi】autumn snake / serpent d'automne ··· 331

蜻蛉【とんぼう・tombo】dragonfly / libellule ··· 334

赤蜻蛉【あかとんぼ・akatombo】red dragonfly / libellule rouge ··· 337

蟋蟀【こおろぎ・korogi】cricket / grillon ··· 339

鈴虫【すずむし・suzumushi】bell cricket,grillon / le chant Evoque un grelot ··· 342

蟷螂【かまきり・kamakiri】praying mantis / mante ··· 343

植物（しょくぶつ・shokubutsu）plant ／ plante

秋薔薇【あきそうび・akisobi】autumn rose / rose d'automne ··· 346

金木犀【きんもくせい・kimmokusei】fragrant olive tree / olivier odorant ··· 350

木槿【むくげ・mukuge】rose of sharon / rose chamallow ··· 352

芙蓉【ふよう・fuyo】confererate rose / cotton rose mallow ··· 355

桃【もも・momo】peach / peche ··· 356

梨【なし・nashi】pear / poirier ··· 358

柿【かき・kaki】Japanese persimmon / plaquemine kaki ··· 359

熟柿【じゅくし・jukushi】ripe persimmons ··· 361

林檎【りんご・ringo】apple / pomme ··· 362

葡萄【ぶどう・budo】grapes / raisin ··· 365

栗【くり・kuri】chestnut / marron, chataignier……369

柘榴【ざくろ・zakuro】pomegranate / grenades……372

無花果【いちじく・ichijiku】figue / figuier……375

胡桃【くるみ・kurumi】walnut, walnut tree / noix, noyer……376

青蜜柑【あおみかん・aomikan】
　green mandarin / mandarin vert / green orange / orange vert……378

オリーブの実【おりーぶのみ・oribunomi】green olive / olive verte……379

檸檬【れもん・remon】lemon, citron / citronnier……380

紅葉【もみじ・momiji】
　autumn leaves, fall lovage, maple / feuilles de l'érable rouge……382

黄葉【こうよう・koyo】leaves turn yellow / feuilles jaunes……389

黄落【こうらく・koraku】yellowing and falling of broadleaf trees……391

楓【かえで・kaede】maple / l'érable……392

桐一葉【きりひとは・kirihitoha】one paulownia leaf……392

銀杏散る【いちょうちる・ichochiru】
　falling ginkgo leaves / la chute des feuilles de ginkgo……393

銀杏【いちょう・icho】yellow autumn ginkgo / ginkgo jaune d'automne……394

銀杏【ぎんなん・ginnan】ginkgo nut / noix de ginkgo……396

蔦【つた・tsuta】ivy / lierre……396

カンナ【かんな・kanna】canna……399

蘭【らん・ran】oriental orchids / orchidées……400

ダリア【だりあ・daria】dahlia……401

朝顔【あさがお・asagao】morning glory / volubilis……402

コスモス【こすもす・kosumosu】cosmos / cosmos……404

草の花【くさのはな・kusanohana】grass flower……407

鬼灯【ほおずき・hozuki】thud of apples……408

菊【きく・kiku】chrysanthemum / chrysantheme……408

敗荷【やれはす・yarehasu】fading lotus / lotus fané ……… 414
南瓜【かぼちゃ・kabocha】pumpkin / citrouilles ……… 416
秋茄子【あきなす・akinasu】autumn eggplant / aubergine d'automne ……… 418
落穂【おちぼ・ochibo】gleaning / glanage ……… 418
芒【すすき・susuki】Japanese pampas grass / herbes des pampas ……… 419
桔梗【ききょう・kikyo】Japanese bellflower / campanule ……… 421
竜胆【りんどう・rindo】gentian / gentian ……… 423
茸【きのこ・kinoko】mushroom / champignon ……… 425

解説　鈴木比佐雄 ……… 430
あとがき　向瀬美音　〈Afterword〉……… 448
Postface ……… 452

私が考える俳句とは

ナディン　レオン/Nadine Léon
フランス/France

　私の俳句との冒険は、2017年に息子からのプレゼントとして、イタリア語の本「Poesie Zen」(Lucien StrykとTakhashi Ikemoto著、Newton Compton Editori出版)を受け取ったときに始まりました。それを読んで、私の書き方が変わりました。

　俳句は伝統とモダニズムが融合した日本の美学であり、その基本原則の3つは象徴性、節制、空虚である。具体的で、地味で、単純で、日常的で、自発的なものすべてを好むことによって、暗黙のうちに感情を伝え、雰囲気を描くのが作者の技術である。この繊細な芸術は、物事のはかなさを感じさせたり（もののあわれ）、はかなさや不完全さに美を感じさせたり（わびさび）、神秘的で不可解なものに美を感じさせたり（幽玄）、繊細さを感じさせたり（しおり）、ユーモアに軽妙さを感じさせたり（かるみ）することができる。俳句では、安定と進化という相反する2つの原理が共存している。安定は季語の使い方にあり、進化は作者のものの見方にある。

　しかし、ルールについて語るよりも、精神について語ったほうがいいと思う。とはいえ、俳句は高度に体系化されたジャンルである。制約は恣意的なものではなく、俳句の起源そのものにその存在を負っている。実際、禅の精神からすれば、俳句は先験的に精神から距離を置き、視覚、聴覚、触覚、味覚、嗅覚のいずれであれ、感覚的知覚に焦点を当てるべきである。しかし、俳句は概

念を直接的に示すことはしないが、具体的なイメージを用いてシンボルを伝え、それを第二の読解レベルで概念化することができる。

　俳句の始祖とされる芭蕉は遍歴の詩人であり、禅への関心が俳句に精神的な刻印を与えた。禅は、全体との一体化を達成するために、自然への単純な帰属意識への入り口として身体を使う修行に基づいている。俳句では、これは小宇宙と大宇宙の対立に通じ、無限を前にした小ささの感覚と共感のつながりを示唆している。表面的には、俳句は二元性の形を提示している。というのも、小宇宙と大宇宙、はかないものと不変のもの、人間と自然、近いものと遠いもの、さらには集団と個人といった対立は、実際には同じ全体の一部であり、不可分であり、相互に関連しているからである。

　原則として、俳句には季節や集団的な出来事を示す季語が含まれる。季語は、繰り返されるサイクルに組み込まれた時間の流れを表し、第二の表現は、今この瞬間に経験した個人的な出来事に関連している。このように、俳句は儚いものと自然の循環性、宇宙の動きとの関連、あるいは共有の出来事や祝祭と向き合っている。一般的に言えば、俳句は絶え間ない変化（不易流行）に対して不変であることを表現している。

　俳句は未完成の詩であり、読み手によってその完成度を見いだすものだと言われてきた。言葉にならないものこそ、解釈空間が生まれる場所なのだ。俳句が簡潔でなければならないのはこのためであり、読者の反応を誘発するのに必要なぎりぎりのイメージを提供し、描写したり述べたりするのではなく、示唆したり喚起したりするためである。成功する俳句とは、語られることのない空間の中で力強く自らを現し、読者の魂を揺さぶることができるものであり、その目的は読者の中にある種の共鳴を生み出すこと

である。感覚や感情を呼び起こしたり、驚きや不思議のレベルへと導いたりすることができ、心の流れを一瞬止めて読者の内なる沈黙を引き出すことができる。個人的には、このような驚きの効果に惹かれ、言葉を超越するような形で表現したいと思う。俳句は、2つの異なる表現に切れ、切れ字を挟む「取り合わせ」スタイルで構成され、各句は論理的な言説の糸を断ち切り、心の裂け目を開いて「間」を挿入する。「間」は沈黙の空間である。読者に受容性を開き、言葉の響きを定着させる間を示す。間とは、繋がりながら分離する一過性の空白であり、宙吊りの時間における通過の場である。

　もともと俳句の主な目的のひとつは、読者を非心理的な次元に導くことだった。その削ぎ落とされた言葉によって、俳句は物事の本質を把握し、静寂を貫く助けとなる。俳句はそのシンプルさにおいて、私たちを喜ばせ、私たちを取り巻く他のすべてのものを打ち消すような小さな無を通して、私たちを自然とのつながりへと導いてくれる。全体によって打ち消されるのはエゴではなく、両者の分離が解消されるのだ。

　この種の詩には、表現されないもの、時には表現できないものへの扉を開く才能がある。それがこの詩の本質の一部なのだ。わずかな言葉で、理性的なものを超えて、直感と暗示の領域へと私たちを誘う。それでいて、現実とその実験に深く根ざしている。個人的には、俳句は瞑想に近いと思う。スピリチュアルな開放に必要な空虚さが生まれるのは、内なる沈黙の中であり、それは私にとって、宇宙全体を循環し、私たちの内と周囲の万物の間につながりを生み出す宇宙エネルギーを受容することにほかならない。

フランスにおける俳句事情とは？

　俳句は、17世紀に芭蕉によって俳句の文脈から切り離されて生

まれた日本の短詩である。その2世紀後、子規が俳句と改名した。俳句は、連歌の冒頭の一節であり、短歌の連なりであった。日本が西洋化した後、二つの文化は互いに影響を受け合った。俳句は19世紀に西洋に伝わり、多くの詩人によって取り入れられた。俳句は、ソーシャルネットワーク上での交流によって促進され、今日に至るまで非常に流行している。何よりも、俳句は無常の詩と見なされている。このような特徴にもかかわらず、俳句は時の試練に耐え、現代詩へと進化してきた。俳人たちはしばしば集まり、句作ワークショップを開いている。俳壇には、俳人同士が切磋琢磨する句会もある。パリで開催される句会は特に人気がある。

　一般的に、フランスの俳句は、子規が提唱した季語や5・7・5のリズムのような、任意となった特定のルールから解放されている。俳句の特徴は、「まこと」、自発性、信憑性、そして通常最終行にある驚きの効果である。「私」は一人称で行動や感情を表現するのに使われる。しかし、共感の効果によって、何よりも「普遍的な私」になる。

　これまでのところ、俳句が長く続いているのは、俳句が伝える重要なメッセージによるものだと考えている。私の知る限り、この短詩は自然との再接続への誘いである。

　俳句は私たちに、心に固執し続けるのではなく、五感で世界に耳を傾け、時空との関係を再構築することを学ぶよう求めているのだ。

Qu'est-ce que le haïku selon moi
Nadine Léon

Mon aventure avec le haïku a commencé en 2017 lorsque j'ai reçu, en cadeau de mon fils, un ouvrage en italien : Poesie Zen, de Lucien Stryk et Takhashi Ikemoto, édition Newton Compton Editori… cette lecture a changé ma façon d'écrire.

Le haïku correspond au sens de l'esthétisme japonais qui conjugue la tradition avec le modernisme. Trois des principes fondamentaux sont le symbole, la sobriété et le vide. L'habileté de l'auteur est de transmettre implicitement une émotion et de peindre une atmosphère en privilégiant tout ce qui est concret, sobre, simple, quotidien, spontané. À travers l'évocation, cet art subtil peut exprimer le sentiment de la fugacité des choses (mono no aware), saisir la beauté dans la fragilité et l'imperfection (wabi sabi) ou dans ce qui il y a de mystérieux et d'impénétrable (yugen), ou encore suggérer la délicatesse (shiori) ou bien une certaine légèreté à travers l'humour (karumi).

Dans le haïku, les deux principes opposés de stabilité et d'évolution coexistent. La stabilité se retrouve notamment dans l'utilisation du kigo et l'évolution dans la façon de l'auteur de percevoir les choses.

Mais plus que de parler de règles, je crois qu'il est préférable de parler d'esprit. Le haïku n'en reste pas moins un genre très codifié. Les contraintes, loin d'être arbitraires, doivent leur existence aux origines même du haïku. En effet, pour son esprit zen, le haïku devrait a priori s'éloigner du mental et s'inscrire dans la perception sensorielle, visuelle, auditive, tactile, gustative ou olfactive. Mais si le haïku n'expose pas de concepts directement, il utilise par contre des images concrètes porteuses de symbole qui, dans un second niveau de lecture, peuvent relever du domaine du conceptuel.

Bashô, considéré le maître à l'origine du haïku, était un poète itinérant et son intérêt pour le zen donna une empreinte spirituelle au haïku. Le zen repose sur une pratique qui utilise la porte du corps comme passage pour arriver à la conscience de notre simple appartenance à la nature, afin de réaliser l'union avec le tout. Dans le haïku cela se traduit par une confrontation entre le microcosme et le macrocosme qui suggère un sentiment de petitesse face à l'infini et de connexion d'empathie. Le haïku présente à priori une forme de dualité. Toutefois dans sa totalité, le haïku devient l'expression de la non-dualité, car les oppositions microcosme/macrocosme, éphémère/immuable, humain/nature, proche /lointain et même collectif/individuel sont en réalité partie d'un même tout, indivisibles et en interrelation.

En règle générale, le haïku contient un kigo pour indiquer la saison ou des événements collectifs. Le kigo représente le flux du temps inséré dans la répétition des cycles, alors que la deuxième expression reporte un fait personnel vécu dans l'instant présent. Le haïku met ainsi en confrontation l'éphémère face à la cyclicité de la nature liée aux mouvements cosmiques ou bien face à des évènements communs ou des festivités. En ligne générale il exprime l'immuabilité en rapport au changement continu (fueki ryukō).

On dit que le haïku est un poème inachevé et qu'il trouve sa complétude grâce au lecteur, le caractère suggestif des mots offrant une multitude d'interprétations possibles. Le non-dit est le lieu où s'élabore l'espace interprétatif. C'est le motif pour lequel le haïku doit être succin et offrir les images à peine nécessaires pour déclencher une réaction chez le lecteur, pour suggérer ou évoquer, au lieu de décrire ou énoncer. Un haïku réussi est celui capable de se révéler avec force dans l'espace du non-dit, faisant vibrer l'âme de celui qui lit, son but étant de générer une certaine résonance chez le lecteur. Il peut évoquer des sensations ou des sentiments ou bien nous porter à un niveau tel de stupeur, d'émerveillement, capable d'arrêter momentanément le flux du mental et de susciter le silence intérieur du lecteur. Personnellement c'est cet effet de stupeur, de saisissement qui m'attire et que j'aime produire à travers une sorte de dépassement des mots. Dans les compositions construites selon le toriawase, avec deux expressions distinctes entrecoupées d'une césure, kireji, chaque haïku rompt le fil logique du discours pour ouvrir une brèche dans le mental où s'insinue le ma. Le ma est un espace de silence. Il marque une pause qui ouvre à la réceptivité et laisse le temps à la résonance des mots de s'installer chez le lecteur, un peu comme le temps de pause entre l'inspiration et l'expiration. Le ma est un vide transitoire qui sépare tout en reliant, un lieu de passage au temps suspendu.

À l'origine l'un des objectifs principaux du haïku est donc de porter le lecteur dans la dimension du non-mental. Dans son langage dépouillé il nous aide à cueillir l'essence des choses et à pénétrer le silence. Dans sa simplicité il nous fait entrer en connexion avec la nature, à travers un petit rien qui nous ravit et annule tout ce qui nous entoure. Ce n'est pas l'ego qui s'annule devant le tout, mais c'est la séparation entre les deux qui se dissout.

Ce genre de poème a dans sa genèse le don d'ouvrir une porte à l'inexprimé, quelque fois à l'inexprimable. Cela fait partie de son essence même. Rien qu'avec quelques mots il nous conduit au-delà du rationnel, dans le domaine de l'intuition et du suggéré. Et pourtant il reste profondément ancré dans le réel et dans son expérimentation. Personnellement je trouve que le haïku est très proche de la méditation. C'est dans le silence intérieur que peut se produire le vide nécessaire à l'ouverture spirituelle, qui n'est autre pour moi que la réceptivité à l'énergie cosmique circulant dans tout l'univers et créant un lien entre toutes choses, en nous et autour de nous.

Quelle est la situation du haïku en France?
Le haïku est un poème bref japonais né au 17e siècle du pinceau de Bashô, à partir d'un détachement du hokku de son contexte et que Shiki a rebaptisé deux siècles plus tard haïku. Le hokku constituait la strophe d'ouverture du renga, une suite de tankas composés en collectif. Après l'occidentalisation du Japon nos deux cultures ont connu une influence réciproque. En effet, arrivé en Occident au 19e siècle et réadapté, le haïku a conquis de nombreux poètes. Il est resté très en vogue jusqu'à nos jours, facilité par les échanges sur les réseaux sociaux. Le haïku est surtout vu comme un poème de l'impermanence. Malgré cette caractéristique il a su résister au passage des siècles et s'est évolué jusqu'à devenir de la poésie contemporaine, certains se sont urbanisés, d'autres ont abordé des thèmes engagés. Des groupes de poètes se donnent souvent rendez-vous pour des ateliers d'écriture. Dans le cadre du haïku sont également organisés des kukaï, compétitions cordiales entre hajins. En particulier, le kukaï qui se déroule à Paris est très participé.
En général, les haïkus français se sont affranchis de certaines règles qui sont devenues facultatives, comme le kigo ou le rythme 5/7/5

prôné par Shiki, tout en maintenant avec rigueur le non-dit. Leur signe particulier est le makoto, spontanéité et authenticité, ainsi que l'effet surprise, la plupart du temps situé dans la ligne finale. Le « je » pour exprimer une action ou un ressenti en première personne peut être utilisé. Toutefois, par l'effet de l'empathie, il devient, plus qu'autre chose, un « je universel ».

Jusqu'à présent je crois que la longévité du haïku est due au message important qu'il transmet. En ce qui me concerne, ce poème bref est une invite à renouer avec la nature.
Le haïku demande de ne pas rester fixés dans le mental, mais d'apprendre à écouter le monde avec nos sens et de redimensionner notre rapport avec l'espace-temps.

私にとって俳句とは

デニス　カンバラウ/Dennys Cambarau

イタリア/Italy

　母が私にくれた1冊の本が、私の人生を大きく変えることになるとはまだ知らなかった。それは1997年、私が法学部の若い大学生だった頃のことだ。日本の豊かな文化や伝統を愛し、憧れ続けてきた私が、今、手にしているのは、私にとってかけがえのないもの、つまり、イメージや感情の凝縮であり、私が住みたいと思っていた遠い場所への光だった。しかし、俳句とは何だろう？俳句のルーツが江戸時代（1603-1867）にあることは周知の通りだが、その起源は連歌や短歌など、それ以前の詩の形式にまで遡ることができる。

「芭蕉」こと松尾宗房金作（1644-1694）は、このジャンルを文芸の域にまで高めた人物であり、この詩的ジャンルを「俳句」と呼ぶようになったのは、より新しい正岡子規（1867-1902）である。他の権威ある作家たちも、同じ問いを自らに投げかけ、ある者は比喩を用い、またある者は単純な考察を、私の考えでは、常にある西洋の伝統に従って、高揚感をもって、ある種の尊大さをもって、驚くような方法でそれを行ってきたと言わなければならない。俳句は、たった3行の詩でありながら、それに値しない。この詩のジャンルは、できるだけ簡潔であるべきで、多くを語らず、多くを暗示するものであるべきだとよく言われる。空白、間、増幅し示唆する言葉にならないもの。

　俳句を特徴づける要素は4つある。5・7・5の形式、季語、つまり時系列的な連想を与える季語、切れ字、そして最後に、非常に

重要な取り合わせである。日本で生まれ、日本の文化が色濃く反映されたこのタイプの俳句は、すでに述べたように、その美しさと（見かけの）単純さゆえに、世界中に急速に広まった。5/7/5に関しては、実際、次のことがわかる。

　例えば、英語やイタリア語など、ラテン文字で表記されるアルファベットと、音韻の種類によって、絵文字で表記される日本語とはまったく異なる。秋の代表的な季語である「月」を例にとると、日本語の「月」は1つの絵文字「月」でできているが、英語では「moon」（1音節）、イタリア語では「luna」（2音節）である。

　そのため、音節の辻褄が合わず、ある言語から別の言語へ、厳密な音節計算から「逸脱」することなく同じ詩的思想を翻訳することは、時には不可能ではないにせよ、困難であると理解されている。このため、西洋の伝統では、日本の俳句の典型的な構造を維持しつつも、修正を加えたり、ある種の弾力性を保持したりするような措置が取られてきた。私が話しているイタリア語では、5/7/5の構造を維持することが決定されたが、単純な正書法による計算か、長い時間をかけて蓄積された規則と構造を持つ計量詩の計算か、どちらかを選択できるようにした。

　しかし、問題はこれだけにとどまらない。というのも、今見てきたように、季節の参照にもこのような問題が生じるからだ。「虹」、「夏の雨」、「モンスーン」などついてはどうだろうか。

　ある種の動物や昆虫はその土地固有のものであり、ある種の大気現象は必ずしも春に特別に降る雨の結果とは限らず、モンスーンの季節は地球上の他の場所、たとえばインドだけに関係し、他の場所には関係しない。このような理由から、ここでも、時間だけでなく、詠まれる空間も考慮した小さなバリエーションが採用されることになり、地球上のさまざまな場所で独自の方式が採用

されることになったのである。しかし、「切れ」については、このようなことはないようだ。

　一方、切れ字の場合は、構文論的な意味での切れは、一方の言語であろうと他方の言語であろうと、ポーズによって確保することができるので、あまり問題はないように思われる。イタリア語では、他の言語と同様、句読点、たとえばコンマ、フルストップ、感嘆符、コロン、クエスチョンマークが使われる（ダッシュも使われる）。日本語では、や、かななどの助詞を使って表現される。言い換えれば、俳句という構成は、それにもかかわらず形式を超越している。繰り返しになるが、「取り合わせ」は、世界中のどの言語でも、誰にとっても同じである。

　これは「一物全体」の場合であり、文字どおり「単一の概念、単一のイメージ、単一の要素」という意味である。具体的に言えば、「取り合わせ」は「切れ」と密接に結びついている。「取り合わせ」があることで、2つの半球や正方形のイメージの間に意味的な逆転が生まれるのである。

　前述したように、「取り合わせ」には2つのタイプがある。「取り合わせ」とは、詠み込まれたイメージと詠み込まれたイメージが調和し、互いに支え合っている場合の「取り合わせ」と、2つの半球のイメージが対照的である場合の「二物衝撃」である。俳句とはこういうものだ。この短い句は、シンプルでありながら複雑な文化の蒸留であり、私にとって万物の統合を昇華させる詩である。俳句は、詩の形式で語るのではなく、その実質で語るからだ。簡潔さ、語られていないが含蓄のあるもの、それは孔雀の尾のように扇状に広がる。俳句は、詩は、人生であり、人間の魂はそれに浸っている。しかし、ここで私はひとつ付け加えたい。俳句はしばしば明示的な比喩を用いず、暗示的な比喩しか用いないが、見る人の目も違えば、観察される庭も違う。

よく知られているように、様々な種類のものがある、「イタリア風」、「イギリス風」、「フランス風」もある。つまり、観察する主体、認識する行為だけが違うのではなく、対象も違うということだ。これこそが人生を美しくするものである。宇宙の多様性は、しかし、異なるものにも詩にも同じ種を持っている。

(1)「俳句は月を指す指である」──R.H.ブライス、「俳句は宇宙を映す一滴の露である」──三島由紀夫、「良い俳句は静かな池に投げ込まれた石のようなものである」──ドナルド・キーン「俳句は3行の小さな宇宙である」──ジャック・ケルアック。

(2)「間」は日本文化における基本的な概念であり、大雑把に訳せば「空白」、「間」、「沈黙」である。しかし、その意味は単純な語彙的定義をはるかに超えている。それは一種の肥沃な空白、可能性を秘めた中断を表し、それによって要素は呼吸し、互いに関係し合うことができる。

(3) 俳句、特に古典俳句には季語が必要である。俳句には季語が必要で、『歳時記』には良い句を作るために必要な季語がすべて掲載されている。

Cosa è per me lo haiku

Dennys Cambarau

È passato molto tempo da quando mia madre mi regalò un libro del quale ancora non sapevo che avrebbe cambiato per sempre la mia vita: una piccola, semplice e bella raccolta di poesie haiku. Era il lontano 1997, quando cioè fui un giovane studente universitario in Giurisprudenza. Ricordo che per me fu amore a prima vista: io che da sempre ho amato e ammirato il Giappone per la sua ricca cultura e tradizione, ora tenevo tra le mani quell'oggetto per me decisamente prezioso: un condensato di immagini ed emozioni, uno spiraglio verso quel luogo lontano in cui avrei voluto vivere. Ma cosa è uno haiku? Tutti noi sappiamo che lo haiku trova le sue radici nel periodo Edo del Giappone (1603-1867), sebbene le sue origini si facciano risalire a certe forme di poesia precedenti, come la renga e la tanka, e, oltremodo, sappiamo pure che il poeta (haijin) Matsuo Munefusa Kinsaku, in arte "Bashō" (1644-1694) è colui che ha elevato tale genere a forma d'arte letteraria, mentre è al più recente Masaoka "Shiki" (1867-1902) che dobbiamo tale nome per questo genere poetico. Altri autorevoli autori , è bene dirlo, si sono posti la stessa domanda, e lo hanno fatto in modo sorprendente, chi usando delle metafore e

---

1 "Un haiku è un dito che punta alla luna." - R. H. Blyth; "L'haiku è una goccia di rugiada che riflette l'universo." - Yukio Mishima; "Un buon haiku è come un sasso gettato in uno stagno silenzioso; le sue increspature si espandono all'infinito." - Donald Keene; "Un haiku è un piccolo universo in tre versi." - Jack Kerouac.

2 Il "Ma" (間) è un concetto fondamentale nella cultura giapponese che si traduce approssimativamente come "spazio vuoto", "pausa", "intervallo" o "silenzio". Tuttavia, il suo significato va ben oltre la semplice definizione lessicale. Rappresenta una sorta di vuoto fertile, un'interruzione carica di potenzialità, che permette agli elementi di respirare e di entrare in relazione tra loro.

chi trascrivendo delle semplici riflessioni, sempre e comunque, a parer mio, secondo una certa tradizione occidentale, in modo esuberante e con un certo senso di ampollosità. E lo haiku, componimento di appena tre versi, non merita questo, anzi… Spesso si afferma che tale genere poetico debba essere il più sintetico possibile, dicendo sì poco, ma sottintendendo molto: che cioè si debba aprire a "ventaglio", e per farlo si avvale di un concetto cardine, che è quello del "MA" : il vuoto, la pausa, il non detto che amplifica e suggestiona. Quattro sono gli elementi che caratterizzano lo haiku: la forma del 5/7/5; il kigo , ovvero una parola della stagione di riferimento che gli dà una collocazione temporale; il kireji, ovvero "carattere che taglia"; e, infine, il toriawase, importantissimo, che può essere di due tipi (torihayasi e nibutsu shōgeki). Nato in Giappone, e della cultura giapponese fortemente intriso, come è stato accennato, questo tipo di componimento, per la sua bellezza e la sua (apparente) semplicità, ha trovato rapida diffusione in tutto il mondo, ora recependo, altre volte rifiutando, la sua struttura. Per quanto riguarda il 5/7/5, vediamo che infatti, per alcune incongruità e peculiarità tra una lingua e l'altra, spesso la sillabazione non viene rispettata: si pensi, per esempio al fatto che le altre lingue, per esempio inglese o quella italiana (quella che parlo io, per intenderci), per il loro alfabeto in caratteri latini, ma anche per il tipo di fonetica, sono ben diverse da quella giapponese caratterizzata dai pittogrammi. Prendiamo un kigo tipico dell'autunno per specificare il concetto, come per esempio "luna", che in giapponese è costituita da un solo pittogramma od "on", 月

---

3 Ovvero, letteralmente, "parola della stagione". Lo haiku, soprattutto classico, per essere tale, ha bisogno di un riferimento stagionale. Esistono antologie, i Saijiki, che contengono, appunto, tutte le parole necessarie per scrivere dei buoni componimenti.

(tsuki), mentre in inglese è moon (una sillaba) e in italiano luna (luna, due sillabe)… Si capisce quindi che la sillabazione non torna, rendendo difficile, se non a volte impossibile, tradurre lo stesso pensiero poetico da una lingua all'altra se non "sforando" dalla rigida computazione sillabica. Per questo motivo, nella tradizione occidentale si sono prese delle misure che tendessero sì a preservare la struttura tipica dell'haiku giapponese, ma apportando delle modifiche o garantendo una certa elasticità. Nella lingua che parlo io, come detto, quella italiana, si è deciso di mantenere tale struttura del 5/7/5, dando però la possibilità di poter scegliere tra la semplice computazione ortografica o quella della poesia metrica, con le sue regole e la sua struttura sedimentatesi nel tempo, permettendo così una maggiore, come detto, elasticità nei componimenti. Ma i problemi non finiscono qui, perché, come vediamo adesso, questi si presentano anche per alcuni riferimenti stagionali: non sempre sono gli stessi, e non sempre sono così lineari. Ritornando all'esempio del kigo "luna", ben sappiamo che questa, visibile ovunque, sia la stessa per tutti i popoli della terra, ma che dire di altri lemmi, come per esempio quello di "arcobaleno", "pioggia estiva", "monsoni", etc? Certe specie di animali o insetti, poi, sono indigene, legate cioè al loro territorio; certi fenomeni atmosferici non sempre sono frutto delle piogge che cadono specificamente in primavera, mentre la stagione dei monsoni, riguarda solo ed esclusivamente altri luoghi della terra, come l'India, e non altri. È soprattutto per questo motivo che anche qui si è deciso di adottare delle piccole variazioni che tendessero a considerare non solo il tempo, ma anche lo spazio in cui il componimento è scritto, portando in questo modo diversi luoghi della terra ad adottare un proprio Saijiki. Sul kireji, invece, non sembrano esserci troppi problemi, visto che la cesura in senso sintattico, sia in una lingua che nell'altra, possono essere garantiti da una pausa. Se in italiano, così come in altre lingue, vengono usati i segni di interpunzione, quali la virgola",", il punto".", il punto esclamativo"!" i due punti":" e il punto interrogativo"?" (ma anche il semplice trattino "-", in giapponese, invece, viene resa usando particelle agglutinanti, come YA, KANA, etc… Come dire, un componimento, quello dello haiku, che trascende comunque la forma, tanto da essere sostanza, come vedremo adesso nel parlare e trattare del Toriawase. Il toriawase, è bene ribadirlo, è per tutti uguale, in tutte le lingue del mondo, sebbene anche qui ci siano peculiarità dovute talvolta all'assenza del kireji nei componimenti: è il caso dell'ichibutsujitate, che letteralmente significa "fatto di una sola cosa": un unico concetto, un'unica immagine, un solo elemento. Nello specifico possiamo dire che il toriawase è strettamente legato al kireji: è infatti in sua presenza che possiamo avere un ribaltamento semantico tra i due emistichi o quadretti di immagini che si vengono a creare. In questo modo, un emistichio, detto emistichio superiore, avrà una immagine, e l'altro emistichio, detto emistichio inferiore, ne avrà un'altra… Come accennato, esistono due tipi di toriawase: il torihayasi, quando le immagini create e presenti nel componimento sono armoniose e si sostengono a vicenda; il nibutsu shōgeki, quando invece le immagini dei due emistichi entrano in contrasto tra di loro. Ecco, dunque, nella forma, ciò che è uno haiku… ma per me? Possiamo ora, giunti in questo luogo, dare una risposta… Questo breve componimento, questo semplice e al contempo complesso distillato di cultura è una poesia che per me sublima la sintesi del Tutto. Ogni cosa può esser detta, ma anche intesa, con uno haiku, ogni cosa… Perché lo haiku non parla con la forma dei versi, ma con la sua sostanza: la brevità, il non detto ma sottinteso, che, come la coda di un pavone, si apre a ventaglio. Lo haiku, la poesia, è vita e tanto ne è intrisa l'anima dell'Uomo. Vorrei qui comunque, aggiungere un dettaglio. Sebbene spesso lo haiku non si avvalga delle metafore esplicite, ma solo implicite, vorrei dire e affermare che diversi sono gli occhi di chi guarda, e diversi sono i giardini che vengono osservati: se esiste un giardino "giapponese" (che, come è noto sono di molti tipi), ne esiste anche uno anche "all'italiana", o "all'inglese", o" alla francese"... Questo per dire che non è solo il soggetto che osserva, nell'atto di percepire, a essere differente, ma anche l'oggetto. È questo che rende così bella la vita: la diversità appunto cosmica, che però ha lo stesso seme, sia nelle diverse cose che in poesia: Sta allo haijin capire questo: essere, prima di sembrare, imitando la vita nell'arte o l'arte nella vita. Grazie!

俳句の概要

ポール・カルス/Paul Callus
マルタ/Malta

　俳句は日本を代表する短詩のひとつである。日本の伝統的な詩である和歌の影響を受けており、17世紀に生まれたと言われている。1670年代、松尾芭蕉（現在では日本で最も有名な俳人とされている）が日本各地を旅したおかげで、この詩の形式は人々にとってより身近なものになった。日本の作家、正岡子規が現在の俳句の形式を確立したのは19世紀になってからである。

　伝統的な俳句は主に自然や季節からインスピレーションを得ているため、俳句を作るときには季語を使う。季語は、歳時記と呼ばれる一種の暦辞典に載っている。
　季語は五十音順ではなく、季節ごとに、時候、地理、天文、行事、動植物、人間生活などに分類されている。重要なのは、歳時記には春夏秋冬と正月の5つの季節が含まれていることである。

　伝統的な俳句に必要なもう一つの条件は、「切れ字」である。これは、2つの独立したアイデアやイメージを並置したり、間を作ったりするために使われる。日本語の俳句では、切れ字は1音節または2音節（か、かな、けり、らむ、し、つ、や）で構成される。英語では「切れ字」に相当するものはなく、コロン（：）、長いダッシュ（—）、省略記号（...）が使われる。

　日本人は俳句を、「音（モーラ）」と呼ばれる17の音韻単位か

らなる直線で書く。「短い音節」には1つのモーラがあるが、「長い音節」にはそれ以上のモーラがある。（個人的には、日本の俳句に音節があるとは言わない。）日本語の俳句は5-7-5音の単位に分けることができる。

英語に翻訳される場合、日本の俳句はしばしば3行で表現される。これは、英語で書かれた俳句は3行で書かなければならないという意味ではない。また、伝統的な日本の俳句を模倣するために、5-7-5の音節数に従わなければならないというのも誤解である。デイヴィッド・スタインドル＝ラストはこう言っている。「俳句の3行を5音節、7音節、5音節にすることは、日本の原句に表面的に合わせることにすぎない。重要なのは精神である。」

では、5-7-5の形式を使うことは間違っているのだろうか？　俳句の流れ、自発性、伝達性を妨げない限り、間違いなくそうである。

今岡恵子氏はこう言っている……「俳句の外形にこだわりすぎるあまり、その本質を見失うことがある」。

このトピックは、主に英語の俳句を扱っているが、フランス語、イタリア語、ドイツ語、マルタ語など、他の言語にも当てはまることを指摘してもよいだろう。

現在、多くの俳人・俳人が、自制心に縛られることなく自己を表現しようと努力していると思う。それは3行俳句のほかに、1行俳句（簡潔明瞭な表現を基本とする単句）、一筆書き俳句（1枚の絵に1句を添えたもの）、とりあわせ俳句（一見無関係な2つの題材を調和させる俳句）、そして円環俳句や一字俳句など、より大胆な「自由形式」俳句など、さまざまな俳句の形式に現れてい

る。多くの場合、キーワードは「簡潔さ」である。
［俳句の他のジャンル、たとえば川柳、俳文、俳画、俳諧についても言及することを忘れてはならない。］

　最後に、多作な作家マイケル・ディラン・ウェルチからの俳句作家へのアドバイスを紹介しよう。「季節を意識し、五感で感じるものを意識する。自分の感覚を客観的に書く。客観と主観の使い分けができるようになるのが好ましい。描写と推論の違いを学び、読者に推論をさせないようにし、その代わりに、読者に、あなたが提示する注意深く並置された客観的描写から、アイデアやつながりを推論させる。このように、自分の五感を通して得た感覚を頼りに、並置のテクニックを使えば、あなたの俳句は素晴らしいものになる。」

2024年12月

Haiku at a Glance

Paul Callus

Haiku is one of the most popular Japanese short poetry forms. It is said to have been influenced by Waka traditional Japanese poetry, and originated in the 17th-century. This poetry form became more accessible to the people in the 1670s thanks to Matsuo Basho (nowadays regarded as Japan's most famous poet) during his travels round Japan. It was not until the 19th century that Japanese writer Masaoka Shiki established haiku in its current format.

Traditional Haiku are mainly inspired by nature and the seasons, therefore when writing a haiku one makes use of a kigo (a seasonal word). Seasonal words can be found in a type of calendar-dictionary called a saijiki.

These kigo are not listed alphabetically, but by seasons, and are divided into categories which include celestial and terrestrial phenomena, weather, events, plants, animals, and human life. It is important to know that saijiki contain 5 seasons which are spring, summer, autumn, winter, and the New Year.

Another requirement in traditional haiku is the kireji which means a 'cutting word', also known as a caesura. It is used to juxtapose 2 independent ideas or images, or to create a pause. In Japanese haiku a kireji consists of 1 or 2 sound syllables (ka, kana, keri, ramu, shi, tsu, ya). In English there is no direct equivalent to kireji, instead we use a colon (:), a long dash (–) or an ellipsis (…).

The Japanese write haiku in a straight line consisting of 17 phonetic units called morae (or on). A 'short syllable' has one mora, but a 'long syllable' has more. (Personally, I would not say that Japanese haiku have syllables; 'mora counts' makes more sense.) A Japanese haiku can be broken into 5-7-5 sound units.

When translated into English, Japanese haiku are often presented in a three-line format. This does not mean that haiku written in English have to be written in 3 lines. It is also a misunderstanding to say that one has to follow a 5-7-5 syllable count in order to mimic traditional Japanese haiku. David Steindl-Rast had this to say: "To make the three lines of a haiku 5, 7, and 5 syllables long is a merely superficial conformity to the Japanese original. What counts is the spirit."

So, is it wrong to use a 5-7-5 format? Definitely not, as long as it does not hinder the flow, spontaneity, and delivery of the haiku, but it should not be the 'ultimate aim'.
Keiko Imaoka said that… "By concerning ourselves too much with the outward form of haiku, we can lose sight of its essence."
May I point out that this topic, although mainly dealing with English haiku, can also apply to other languages, such as French, Italian, German, Maltese, etc.

I believe that nowadays, many haikuists/haijin are striving to express themselves without the fetters of restraint. This manifests itself in the various formations that are in use apart from the 3-line haiku: the 1-line haiku (monoku - based on brevity and clarity in expression) and (ichibutsujitate containing a single image with a run-on sentence); the 2-line haiku that thrives on the use of toriawase (where two seemingly unrelated subjects are paired in a harmonious manner); and other 'free-form' haiku that are more daring, such as circular haiku and one-word haiku. In many instances the keyword is 'brevity'.

[I must not forget to mention other genres of haiku such as senryu, haibun, haiga and shahai.]

Finally, here is some advice to writers of haiku from prolific author Michael Dylan Welch who says: "When you write your haiku, focus on perceptions and images. Be aware of the seasons and what you perceive through your five senses. Write about your perceptions objectively. Strive to master the understanding of what is objective and subjective in what you write. Learn the difference between description and inference, so your poem can avoid doing any inferring for the reader; instead, let the reader infer ideas and connections from the carefully juxtaposed objective descriptions you present. With this focus, relying on the perceptions you receive through your five senses, and using the technique of juxtaposition, your haiku can be excellent."

December, 2024

俳句の道　愛

タンポポ・アニス/Tanpopo Anis
インドネシア/Indonesia

　趣味の料理、華道、写真に加えて、応用数学、音楽、茶道などを学んできました。俳句の世界に入ったとき、趣味で学んできたことが俳句と関連し、共鳴していることに驚き、俳句の道に興味を持つようになりました。

　俳句に興味を持ったのは2005年、祖父の親友であった故福岡良男先生（元東北大学医学部名誉教授）から鷹羽狩行著『俳句を味わう』をいただいたことがきっかけでした。この本は、聖母病院に入院していたときの私の良き伴侶でした。痛みをギフトに変えるという視点に転換したターニングポイントでした。俳句は非常に繊細な芸術であり、不完全な中に美を見出し、儚い中に強さを見出すことを教えてくれました。そう、俳句の「精神」のひとつである「わび・さび」をここで知ったのです。

　俳句は、17音の漢字を1行に書くという非常に短い形式であり、また、5-7-5のパターンで3行に下方向に配置したり、長短（または短長）の概念で2行に配置したりして、外国語に変換することもできます。添えられた季語は、五感でとらえた今この瞬間が、その情景が展開する季節を意味します。

　俳句では、季語だけでなく、切れ字や切れ（中略）も重要な役割を果たします。切れ字も切れも、読者に想像や解釈の余地を与えるために、一瞬の休止や中断を設けるものです。

　俳句の世界がどれほどユニークであることか。人間の五感を捉えた結果を、わずか数語で表現します。もちろん、これは容易な

ことではないですが、不可能なことでもありません。「自制」、より正確に言えば、何を表現すべきか、何を表現すべきでないかを決める規律があれば、すべて達成できます。これは、ピタゴラスの言葉が俳句の要件に非常に適していることを思い出させます。「多くの言葉で少しを語るのではなく、少しの言葉で多くを語りなさい。」

芭蕉、蕪村、一茶、子規など、自然からインスピレーションを得た古典俳句を読むことで、自分がいる場所の季節の移り変わりを感じ取る感覚を磨くことができるようになりました。俳人（俳人4人）は自然と一体となっているだけでなく、読者である私も、彼らが俳句を詠んだ自然の中へと冒険に出かけるのです。まるで私の魂が溶け込んでいくかのようです。

また、日本の著名な俳人の現代俳句もいくつか読みました。例えば、

有馬朗人（Arima Akito）の
手袋を落し自分の記憶までも
手袋を落として、自分の記憶まで失ってしまった

金子兜太（Kaneko Tota）の
暗黒や関東平野に火事一つ
暗闇の中
関東平野に火事が一つ

長谷川櫂（Kai Hasegawa）の
魂の銀となるまで冷し酒
大空はきのふの虹を記憶せず

黛まどか（Madoka Mayuzumi）の

別な人を見てゐる彼のサングラス
　現代俳句を読み、学ぶことは、私の心を豊かにしてくれます。俳句の真髄である自然に近づくだけでなく、人間にも近づくことができます。私は、人間の感情を理解し、共感し、現代の世の中の喧騒の中で起こっていることに共感することを学びました。人間は、抱えている問題も含めて、宇宙の一部ではないでしょうか？

　古典俳句も現代俳句もどちらも同じように楽しいと思います。俳句は、楽しめて、心に響いて、多くのことを教えてくれる本質を得られるものであれば、私は好きです。俳句は料理に似ていると思います。俳句の主題やトピックは材料のようなもので、俳句の作者（作者）はシェフのようなものです。俳句（および料理）の成功は、俳句の作者（およびシェフ）が目の前の材料をどのように組み合わせるかによって決まります。バランスの取れた構成と適切な調理法（執筆テクニック）が、興味深く良い俳句（および美味しい料理）を生み出すのです。
　2018年に91歳で亡くなった伝説のフランス料理界の巨匠ポール・ボキューズの言葉が思い出されます。「クラシックでもモダンでも、料理は一つだけだ…美味しい料理だ」（原文はフランス語）クラシックでもモダンでも、料理は一つだけだ…美味しい料理だ。
　ポール・ボキューズの言葉に触発され、私は「現代俳句と古典俳句の分類があるが、私の魂にはたった一つの俳句がある。それは、私の魂を満足させる良い俳句だ」と思いました。
　俳句は日本で生まれましたが、宇宙への畏敬を強調するというその独特な特徴は普遍的なものです。俳句は世界中に広がり、各地の地理や文化に適応しながら発展しましたが、日本国外での俳

句の発展は、その「母国」である日本の俳句（17音の音数）のような俳句のジャンルを完全に同化させるには至っていません。

外国の詩人による国際俳句を楽しむことで、彼らの作品に込められた地域の知恵について多くを学びました。四季のない熱帯の国々の俳人も、自分の住む土地の自然や風習に合わせた俳句を詠むことを学んでいます。なぜなら、日本の歳時記にある季語のすべてを外国の俳人に適切に適用できるわけではないからです。

俳句の柔軟性と、文化（宗教、風習）や季節を越えて世界に浸透する力は、俳句を世界遺産（無形文化遺産）に指定するにふさわしいものです。この崇高な願いが叶うことを願っています。

俳句が現代でも人気を保ち、時代に即したものとなるためには、俳句の「魂」のひとつである侘び寂びを基盤としつつ、現代的なテーマや象徴を取り入れた「新鮮で意味深い」俳句をいかに書くかが、現代の俳人にとっての課題であると思います。

「インドネシア語の俳句」と「俳句の中のインドネシア」の概観

インドネシアで俳句が知られるようになったのは、1939年にアミル・ハムザ（1911-1946）が著した『東方の香り（SETANGGI TIMUR）』という本がきっかけでした。この本には、古典中国詩の翻訳、松尾芭蕉の俳句の翻訳、そして古典アラビア詩のいくつかの翻訳が含まれていました。

俳句の世界では、欧米での俳句の発展と比較すると、インドネシアはまだ歴史が浅いかもしれません。2014年からインドネシアではFacebook上の俳句コミュニティが現れ始めました。その一つが、クルニアワン・ジュナエディ氏（インドネシアの首都ジャカルタ在住のシニアジャーナリスト）が創設した「ニュー・ハイ

ク・インドネシア」というグループで、私は2015年から現在まで、ガーデンコンセプトを持つニュー・ハイク・インドネシア（NHI）の管理を任されています。NHIのメンバーは、さまざまな民族で構成されており、地域言語も全く異なります（インドネシアには718もの地域言語があります！）。NHIの日常的な活動では、国語であるインドネシア語を使用しています。その発展に伴い、一部のメンバーは地域言語（母語）で俳句を書いてみようとし始め、管理者は他のメンバーが意味を理解できるように、インドネシア語の翻訳を提供するように求めています。

　メンバーの希望に応えるため、「地域言語俳句」の特別コラムを設けました。また、管理を容易にするため、管理者も異なる母国語を持つ民族で構成されています。

　2023年初頭、ニュー・ハイク・インドネシア（NHI）のメンバーで小中学校の教師として働く数名が、生徒たちに俳句を紹介しました。生徒たちはインドネシア語で俳句を書く練習にとても熱心に取り組みました。ジャワ島やスマトラ島の複数の小学校から俳句の指導依頼がありました。しかし、距離や時間の制約により、小学校の先生方が生徒たちに俳句を教える際に、Zoomを活用することにしました。NHIには、俳句を通じて自然や環境を尊重し、感謝し、大切にすることを生徒たちに教える小学校の先生たちのための特別な俳句コミュニティもあります。

2024年12月30日

THE HAIKU PATH I LOVE
Tanpopo Anis

In addition to pursuing my hobbies of cooking, flower arranging, and photography, I studied applied mathematics, music, and the tea ceremony. When I entered the world of haiku, I was surprised to find that the things I was studying as a hobby actually correlated and resonated with haiku, and that's what sparked my interest in the path of haiku.

I became interested in haiku in 2005 when I received a book called "Haiku wo ajiwau" (俳句を味わう) written by Takaha Shugyō (鷹羽狩行), from my grandfather's close friend, the late doctor Fukuoka Yoshio, the Professor Emeritus of Tohoku University School of Medicine, in 2005 . This book became my companion when I was hospitalized at Seibo Hospital. It was a turning point that changed my perspective on pain into a gift. Haiku is a very delicate art, and it taught me to see beauty in imperfection and strength in fragility. Yes, it was here that I came to know wabi-sabi, one of the "spirits" of haiku.

Haiku with its very short form, only 17 onji written in one line (for Japanese haiku) and also can be converted into foreign languages with a 5-7-5 pattern arranged downwards into three lines, or arranged in two lines with a long and short concept (or a short and long concept), holds its own depth of meaning if we break it down. The accompanying KIGO connects the writer with nature where the present moment captured by their five sensory senses marks a season in which the scene takes place.

In haiku, not only seasonal words but also kireji and kire (caesura) play an important role. both of kireji and kire create a momentary pause or interruption for giving an opportunity to the readers to imagine and interpret it.

How unique the world of haiku is. Expressing the results of capturing the five senses of human body in just a few words. Of course, this is not easy, but it is not impossible. It can all be achieved with "self-control", or more precisely, the discipline to decide what should and should not be expressed. This reminds me of the words of Pythagoras, which I think are very relevant to the requirements of haiku: "Do not say little with many words, but much with few." (多くの言葉で少しを語るのではなく、少しの言葉で多くを語りなさい)

Reading the classic haiku poems inspired by nature, such as those by Basho, Buson, Issa, and Shiki, has taught me to train my senses to respond to the changing seasons of the place I am in. Not only are the writers (4 haijins) at one with nature, but I am as the reader also taken on an adventure to the nature where they wrote their haiku. And it's as if my soul melts into it.

I also read some modern haiku by famous Japanese poets, such as:

Akito Arima (有馬朗人)

手袋を落し自分の記憶までも

I dropped my gloves and even lost my memories

Tōta Kaneko (金子兜太)

暗黒や関東平野に火事一つ

darkness

there is a single fire on the Kanto Plain

Kai Hasegawa (長谷川櫂)
魂の銀となるまで冷し酒
chilled sake
until the soul becomes silver

大空はきのふの虹を記憶せず
the sky does not remember yesterday's rainbow

Madoka Mayuzumi (黛まどか)
別な人　見てゐる彼の　サングラス
his sunglasses looking at someone else

Reading and studying modern haiku enriches my mind. It not only brings me closer to nature, which is the heart of haiku, but also to human beings. I learn to understand human feelings, sympathize and empathize with what is happening in the hustle and bustle of the world these days. Aren't humans with all their problems also part of the universe?

I think both classical and modern haiku are equally enjoyable. I like haiku as long as I can enjoy it, touch my soul, and get the essence that can teach me a lot. I think haiku is like cooking. The subject or topic of a haiku is like the ingredients, and the haiku poet (author) is like the chef. The success of a haiku (and cooking) depends on how the haiku poet (and chef) combines the ingredients in front of them. A well-balanced composition and proper cooking method (writing technique) will produce an interesting and good haiku (and delicious cooking).

It reminds me of a line written by Paul Bocuse, the legendary French culinary master who passed away in 2018 at the age of 91: "Classique ou moderne, il n'y a qu'une seule cuisine...La Bonne".(古典的でも現代的でも、料理は一つだけ‥‥それは美味しい料理)   Whether classic or modern, there is only one cuisine...good cuisine.

Inspired by the words of Paul Bocuse, I thought, "There is the classification of modern haiku and classical haiku, but to my soul there is only ONE HAIKU: that is a GOOD HAIKU that satisfies my soul."

Haiku originated in Japan, but its unique characteristic of emphasizing reverence for the universe is universal. Haiku has spread around the world and developed while adapting to local geographies and cultures, although its development outside of Japan has not completely assimilated the genre of haiku like its "mother" (the 17 onji in Japanese haiku).

Enjoying the international haiku written by foreign poets has taught me a lot about the local wisdom they bring to their work. Even poets from tropical countries without four seasons learn to adapt their haiku to the nature and customs of the place they live, because not all of the seasonal words in the Japanese saijiki can be properly applied to foreign poets.

The flexibility of haiku and its power to permeate the world beyond culture (religion, customs) and seasons make it truly worthy of being designated a World Heritage (Intangible Cultural Heritage). I hope this noble wish will come true.

I think the challenge for haiku poets today is : how to write "fresh and meaningful" haiku that incorporate modern themes and symbols while still being based on wabi-sabi as one of the "soul" of haiku, in order that haiku can remain popular and relevant in the modern age.

A Glimpse of "Haiku in Indonesian" and "Indonesia in Haiku"

Haiku first became known in Indonesia through a book called SETANGGI TIMUR (The Fragrance of the East) written by Amir Hamzah (1911-1946) in 1939. The book included translations of classical Chinese poetry, translations of Matsuo Basho's haiku, and some translations of classical Arabic poetry.

In the world of haiku, Indonesia may still be too young when compared to the development of haiku in Europe and America. Haiku communities on Facebook began to emerge in Indonesia since 2014, one of which is the group "New Haiku Indonesia" founded by Kurniawan Junaedhie (a senior Indonesian journalist domiciled in Jakarta, the capital of Indonesia) and then asked me to manage New Haiku Indonesia (NHI) which has a garden concept, since 2015 until now. NHI members consist of various ethnic groups with completely different regional languages (718 regional languages in Indonesia!). In NHI's daily activities, we use the national language : Indonesian. In its development, some members began to try to write haiku in regional languages (their mother tongue) and the administrators requires them to provide translations in Indonesian so that other members can understand the meaning.

To accommodate the wishes of members, we have a special column for "regional language haiku". Administrators also consist of ethnic groups with different mother tongues, with the aim of making it easier to manage it.

In early 2023, several members of New Haiku Indonesia (NHI) who work as elementary and junior high school teachers introduced haiku to their students. The students were very enthusiastic about practicing writing haiku in Indonesian. We received requests from several elementary schools in Java and Sumatra to introduce haiku. However, due to distance and time constraints, we decided to use Zoom to help elementary school teachers teach haiku to their students. NHI also has a special haiku community for elementary school teachers who are active in educating their students to respect, appreciate, and care about nature and the environment through haiku.

2024.12.30

アラブの舞台における俳句

モハメド・ベンファレス/Mohammed Benfares

モロッコ/Morocco

俳人、翻訳家、「俳句世界（H W）」誌およびウェブサイト・グループ・ディレクター、モロッコ

アラブ世界における俳句についてのこの短い記事では、以下に焦点を当てる。

1. 簡単な歴史的概要
2. 現地の俳句
3. 秋の俳句

1. 歴史的概観

俳句は、簡潔さ、詩的な新しさを愛する多くの人々を誘惑する。そのため、俳句は国際的な慣行となり、翻訳、研究、解説を通じて俳句を同化させようとする努力に支えられ、協会やクラブを作り、国内および国際的な会合を開催している。俳句を「アラビア語」、「チュニジア語」、「エジプト語」、「アルジェリア語」、「サウジアラビア語」、「シリア語」などと呼び、俳句を「国語化」しようとする者さえいる。

また、「俳句は日本人にしかできない」と主張する人もいる。しかし、海外における俳句の実践は、俳句というジャンルの十分な同化を意味するとは言い難く、むしろ新しくて魅力的な詩質を持つジャンルを受け入れ、味わおうとする試みであることに変わりはない。アラブの地における俳句の統合は、俳句の名前を変えたり歪めたりすることによってジャンルの首を捻ることではなく、

俳句自身の基盤や表現的、構造的、詩的、美的特性を歪めることでもなく、その土地の自然や文化的要素を挿入し、具体的な物事の現実を歪める余計な要素や比喩のない言語を採用することによってなされるべきであることは言うまでもない。

さらに、我々には比喩的でおしゃべりな言葉を使いたがる傾向はあるものの、今日の主流は、具体的な情景、簡潔さ、単純な言葉という俳句の基本的なルールを守ることにある。

俳句がアラブの地に到着したのは、西洋に上陸してから約1世紀後のことで、英語とフランス語からの翻訳、そして日本の偉大な俳人の作品を翻訳したシリアのモハマド・ウダイマーによる日本語からの直接翻訳のおかげである。アラブのいくつかのグループやクラブが、俳句の普及に努めている。

そして、古典、近代、現代俳句の普及に特化したウェブサイトを5ヶ国語で立ち上げた。(https://www.haikuworld24.com/)

俳人の数は日々増え続けており、俳句集やアンソロジーの出版、Facebookのグループの急増によって、このジャンルは活況を呈している。古典・現代を問わず、積極的に活動する詩人もいる。アラブ世界にはアラビア語、フランス語、スペイン語、英語で作品を書く70人ほどの俳人がおり、モロッコには30人ほどの俳人（男女）がいる。しかし、読者の数は常に増え続けている。

2. 地元の俳句

ローカル俳句とは、その土地の社会文化、言語、自然の要素を取り入れたアラビア語の俳句を意味する：

アイッサ・アバルカン／モロッコ
椰子の葉は雫を垂らす通り雨（美音訳）

アミナ・ハティミ／モロッコ

囀やオリーブの葉に摘んだお茶（美音訳）

ファテン・アンワル／パレスチナ
日暮時月の近くにミモレット（美音訳）

マリカ・エル・ブジディ／モロッコ
熱波来る白きターバンの老人（美音訳）

Khadija Wannas／モロッコ
アネモネの色褪せたる村の結婚式（美音訳）

サメ・デルイチ／モロッコ
井戸の側のバケツに雨の落ちにけり（美音訳）

ムイナ・アル・アチャリ／モロッコ
チュルギや柳の下の老いた猫（美音訳）

チャナズ・ユセフ／シリア
唐突に秋風来るアフリーヌ（美音訳）

3. 秋の俳句
アラビア語圏の俳人は季節の季語を使って俳句を作る。次の表は季語（秋）を使った例である：
ザヤ・ヨウクハンナ／オーストラリア
秋の風羊飼ひの笛の音よ（美音訳）

ハヤト・アーメド／シリア
葉の飛翔海の彼方に日の落ちる（美音訳）

ハルバ・アル・ホサリ／シリア
葬式や秋の木の葉はついてゆき（美音訳）

モハメド・ベンファレス／モロッコ
秋の海漁師の籠に水のせせらぎ（美音訳）

ファイザ・ウアタチ／チュニジア
初時雨殻の下には蝸牛（美音訳）

チャーラ・ブディバ／アルジェリア
道端や枝葉は静かに落ちてゆき（美音訳）

ジャマール・モハメド／シリア
秋の暮船一匹の魚と戻る（美音訳）

オルファ・クチュク・ブハディダ／チュニジア
秋の夜やベッドの横に過去の色（美音訳）

4. 結論として
　アラブの文学シーンにおける俳句は、活発かつ進化している。外国語を話す人々は、交流の影響や世界的なグループやアンソロジーへの参加から、このジャンルを迅速に統合できる。しかし、特に国による俳句の公式承認、活動助成金の付与、教育カリキュラムへの俳句の導入など、まだ多くの課題が残されている。
　加えて、外国、特に日本との協力は、俳句へのアクセスと同化を促進し、日本におけるこの分野のアラビア語作品への認識を高めることができるだろう。

Le Haiku sur la Scène Arabe
Mohammed Benfares

Par : Mohammed Benfares -Maroc
Haijin, traducteur et directeur du groupe, Revue et Site Haiku World (H W)

Dans cet article succinct traitant du haiku dans le monde arabe, nous mettrons l'accent sur :
1. Bref aperçu historique
2. Haiku local
3. Haïku d'automne

1. Aperçu historique

Le haïku présente une tentation pour de nombreux amoureux de la concision, brièveté et nouveauté poétique. C'est pourquoi le haïku est devenu une pratique internationale soutenue par des efforts visant son assimilation par les traductions, études et commentaires en créant associations et clubs et en organisant des rencontres nationales et internationales. Il y en a même qui sont allés jusqu'à « la nationalisation » en parlant du haïku « arabe », « tunisien », « égyptien » « algérien » saoudien, « syrien » ...

Par ailleurs, certains prétendent que le haïku ne peut être que japonais. Il n'en demeure pas moins que sa pratique à l'étranger ne signifie guère une assimilation suffisante du genre, mais une tentative de réception et de dégustation d'un genre à la poéticité à la fois nouvelle et attrayante. Il va de soi que l'intégration du haïku sur le sol arabe ne doit passer par tordre le cou du genre en changeant ou déformant son nom ou fausser ses fondements propres et ses caractéristiques expressives, structurelles, poétiques et esthétiques, mais par l'insertion d'éléments locaux naturels ou culturels en adoptant une langue épurée des superflus et des métaphores déformant la réalité des choses concrètes.

Par ailleurs, le penchant dominant aujourd'hui - et malgré un certain empressement et une tendance d'usage d'une langue métaphorique et bavarde- vise à préserver les règles de base du haïku : scène concrète, concision, brièveté, et langage simple.

Le haïku s'est posé tardivement sur la terre arabe, un siècle environ après son atterrissage en Occident, et ce grâce à la traduction de l'anglais et du français puis directement du japonais par le syrien Mohamad Oudaimah qui a traduit les œuvres des grands maitres haïku du Japon. Plusieurs groupes et clubs arabes œuvrent pour diffuser le genre. Parmi eux, le groupe que j'administre depuis 2017:

Le nombre de haijins ne cesse d'augmenter chaque jour et le genre est en plein essor par la publication des recueils, anthologies et la prolifération des groupes Facebook. Certains poètes (classiques et modernes) se sont convertis en haijins très actifs. Le monde arabe compte quelques 70 haijins dont une trentaine (hommes et femmes) au Maroc écrivant en : arabe, français, espagnol et anglais. Mais le nombre des lecteurs progresse incessamment.

2. Haiku local

On entend par Haiku Local, le haiku arabophone intégrant des éléments socio-culturels, linguistiques et naturels sur place :

Haijin	Haiku	haijin	Haiku
Aissa Abarkan/ Maroc	averse- la feuille du palmier dégouline en vacillant	Amina Hatimi/ Maroc	pépiements - sur les feuilles d'olivier siffle le thé des cueilleuses
Faten Anwar/ Palestine	la nuit le minaret en seul à proximité de la lune	Malika El Bouzidi / Maroc	canicule- un turban blanc couvre la tête du vieillard
Khadija Wannas/ Maroc	mariage de village- sous les sabots se fanent les anémones!	Sameh Derouich/ Maroc	bord du puits le seau accueille la pluie
Mouina Al Achari/ Maroc	chergui sous le saule s'étire un vieux chat	Chahnaz Youssef/ Syrie	automne un vent soudain déracine le vieux olivier d'Afrine (en Syrie)

3. Haiku d'automne

Les haijins arabophones composent les haikus avec kigos saisonniers. Dans le tableau suivant des exemples avec le kigo (Automne):

Haijin	Haiku	haijin	Haiku
Zaya Youkhanna/ Australia	le vent d'automne s'harmonisant à la flûte du berger	Hayat Ahmed / Syrie	feuille volante- derrière l'océan tombe le soleil
Harba Al-Hosari - Syrie	procession les feuilles accompagnent le cercueil	Mohammed Benfares/ Maroc	mer d'automne dans le panier du pêcheur murmure l'eau
Faiza Ouachtati/ Tunisie	première pluie sous la coquille s'étire un escargot	Chahra Boudiba/ Algérie	bords de chemin les feuilles tombent en silence
Jamal Mohamed/ Syrie	coucher automnal- avec un seul poisson revient la barque	Olfa Kchouk Bouhadida/ Tunisie	nuit d'automne ~ au chevet de mon lit les couleurs du passé

4. En guise de conclusion :

Le haiku sur la scène littéraire arabe est en mode actif et évolutif. Ceux qui parlent des langues étrangères sont les plus aptes à intégrer vite le genre vu l'impact des échanges et les participations aux groupes et anthologies universels. Toutefois il reste beaucoup à faire notamment dans la reconnaissance officielle par les autorités du haiku en octroyant des subventions aux activités et en introduisant le genre dans le curriculum de l'éducation.

Par ailleurs, la collaboration avec les parties étrangères, notamment japonaises est à même de faciliter l'accès et l'assimilation du haiku et de faire connaître la production arabophone en la matière au Japon.

時候

(じこう)

(jiko)

season

saison

立秋 【りっしゅう・risshu】
the first day of fall / premier jour de l'automne

One of the 24 solar terms. It is one of the four seasonal milestones (Risshun, Rikka, Risshu, and Ritto). Autumn is from this day to the day before Ritto. It falls around August 7 in the new calendar. It is actually the hottest time of the year, but it is also the time when the sound of the wind in the morning and evening suddenly reminds us of autumn.

立秋や南瓜スープを嬰が食み

pumpkin soup — a baby tastes the first autumn

タンポポ　アニス/Tanpopo Anis
（インドネシア/Indonesia）

立秋や陽は涼しさを編んでるやう

premier jour d'automne — le soleil semble tissé de fraicheur

ローザ　マリア　ディ　サルバトーレ/Rosa Maria Di Salvatore
（イタリア/Italy）

幼子の目に映る月秋に入る

first day of autumn — the moon is beautiful tonight for the little boy

primo giorno d'autunno — è bella la luna stasera per il ragazzino

デニス　カンバロウ/Dennys Cambarau
（イタリア/Italy）

立秋や故郷にゆく夜行バス　　　　　　　　亜仁寿（自訳）

the first day of autumn — night bus to my hometown

タンポポ　アニス/Tanpopo Anis
（インドネシア/Indonesia）

波立てるコーヒーカップ秋立つ日
> premier jour de l'automne — l'´orage dans une tasse pénurie de café
>> アメルラディヒビ　ベント　チャディ/AmelLadhibi Bent Chadly
>>> (チュニジア/Tunisia)

立秋や葉擦れの音のかさかさと
> on the first day of autumn — the crunching of leaves
> nel primo giorno d'autunno — lo scrocchio delle foglie
>> アンジェラ　ジオルダーノ/Angela Giordano
>>> (イタリア/Italy)

立秋や葉つぱの覆ひたる地面
> the first day of autumn — leaves begin to cover the ground
>> スカディ/Sukadi(インドネシア/Indonesia)

秋に入る木陰の色の変はらずに
> sunlit trees — the color of shade the same in autumn
>> バリー　レビン/Barrie Levine(米国/United States)

新しき色の展開秋に入る
> autumn — the unfolding of new colours
>> キム　オルムタック　ゴメス/Kim Olmtak Gomes
>>> (オランダ/Holland)

華やかさ見せる木立や今朝の秋
> the trees show their flamboyance — autumnal pride
>> キム　オルムタック　ゴメス/Kim Olmtak Gomes
>>> (オランダ/Holland)

秋来る暖色のもの目について

> here is autumn — all the warm colors at a glance
> ecco l'autunno — tutti i caldi colori in uno sguardo
>
> アンジェラ　ジオルダーノ/Angela Giordano
> （イタリア/Italy）

立秋やインクの匂ふ新聞紙

> first day of autumn — the smell of newspaper ink flowing in the wind
>
> タンポポ　アニス/Tanpopo Anis（インドネシア/Indonesia）

立秋や彩葉をはさむ日記帳

> beginnng of autumn — a colourful leave sticks in my diary
>
> マフィズディン　チュードハリー/Mafizuddin Chowdhury
> （インド/India）

立秋や机に海の絵葉書を

> the first day of fall — on my desktop seaside postcard
>
> アンナ　イリナ/Ana Irina（ルーマニア/Romania）

立秋や空にはためく紅白旗　　　　　　　　亜仁寿（自訳）
　〈インドネシア独立79年〉

> beginning of autumn — the red and white flag fluttering in the sky　　　　　〈79 years of Indonesian independence〉
>
> タンポポ　アニス/Tanpopo Anis（インドネシア/Indonesia）

風冷えて落ち葉の渦に秋来たる

> vent glacé — dans un tourbillon de feuilles arrive l'automne
>
> パトリック　ソンプル/Patrick Somprou
> （フランス/France）

肩に落つ髪の数本秋に入る

> qualche capello caduto sulle spalle — e' già autunno
> a few hairs fallen on the shoulders — it's already autumn
>
> マリア　パテルリーニ/Maria Paterlini
> （イタリア/Italy）

畑に鷗撒くトラクター今朝の秋

> premier jour d'automne dans le champs un tracteur sème des mouettes
>
> ジェラール　ドユモン/Gérard Dumon
> （フランス/France）

雨洗ふ夏の埃や秋立つ日

> premier jour d'automne — la pluie lave la poussière d'été
>
> イザベル　カルバロ　テール/Isabelle Carvalho Teles
> （フランス/France）

約束のグレーの霧雨秋来る

> premier jour de l'automne — pluie fine et grisaille au rendez-vous
>
> パトリック　ソンプル/Patrick Somprou
> （フランス/France）

我と影橋を渡りて秋立つ日

> traversant le pont moi et mon ombre — premier jour d'automne
>
> エレナ　ズアイン/Elena Zouain（ルーマニア/Romania）

立秋や夕方響く鐘の音

> premier jour d'automne — les cloches sonnent pour les vêpres
>
> アンヌ-マリー　ジュベール-ガヤール/Anne-Marie Joubert-Gaillard
> （フランス/France）

秋立つ日カレンダーのみ知つている

> premier jour d'automne — seul le calendrier est au courant
> アンヌ-マリー　ジュベール-ガヤール/Anne-Marie Joubert-Gaillard
> （フランス/France）

立秋や光の器なる山湖

> first day of fall — mountain lake as vessel of light
> 中野千秋/Chiaki Nakano（日本/Japan）

引き出しの旅券取り出す今朝の秋

> premier jour d'automne — envie de sortir les passeports du tiroir
> 向瀬美音/Mine Mukose（日本/Japan）

秋初め【あきはじめ・akihajime】
beginning of autumn / début de l'automne

It is the beginning of autumn. The time when you can feel a slight hint of autumn even though the heat is still severe.

秋初め細き樹々には金の塊

> automne — arbres aux silhouettes graciles pépites dorées
> トゥーン　チャベ/Tounès Thabet
> （チュニジア/Tunisia）

遠くより秋と列車の近づきぬ

> treno lontano — s'avvicina l'autunno poco per volta
> デニス　カンバロウ/Dennys Cambarau
> （イタリア/Italy）

貝殻に海の怒涛を聞きて秋
> autumn — the roar of the sea in the shells
> autunno — il fragore del mare nelle conchiglie
>> アンジェラ　ジオルダーノ/Angela Giordano(イタリア/Italy)

秋めきて色合ひ変わる服の色
> autumn in the air — the colors of my clothing changing
>> バリー　レビン/Barrie Levine(米国/United States)

秋めきて蒼白になる移民の顔
> retour d'automne — les visages pâles des immigrés
>> ソニア　ベン　アマール/Sonia Ben Ammar(チュニジア/Tunisia)

まだ熱のこもつてをりぬ初秋の葉
> lingering heat — early fall of summer leaves
>> キム　オルムタック　ゴメス/Kim Olmtak Gomes(オランダ/Holland)

秋めきてプラタナスの葉揺らす風
> il vento spoglia i rami del platano — giunge l'autunno
>> マリア　パテルリーニ/Maria Paterlini(イタリア/Italy)

秋めきて枝葉見知らぬ道へ行く
> une à une les feuilles des arbres vers un chemin inconnu — automne
>> フテン　フルチ/Feten Fourti(チュニジア/Tunisia)

秋初め髪に見つける初白髪
> ma première mèche de cheveux blancs au vent — début de l'automne
>> ソニア　ベン　アマール/Sonia Ben Ammar(チュニジア/Tunisia)

髪に風樹皮の香乗せて秋来る
> capelli al vento ― con l'odore di resina torna l'autunno
>> ローザ　マリア　ディ　サルバトーレ/Rosa Maria Di Salvatore
>>> (イタリア/Italy)

秋初めミントの枝葉香りたる
> début d'automne ― sans pluie l'odeur forte des feuilles de menthe
>> ラルビ　リミ/Larbi Limi(モロッコ/Morocco)

風の鍵盤秋の悲しき音となる
> du clavier du vent ― un air d automne un peu triste t évoque
>> フテン　フルチ/Feten Fourti(チュニジア/Tunisia)

ガラス窓叩く雨粒秋の音
> la pluie tape sur la vitre ― mélodie d'automne
>> ソニア　ベン　アマール/Sonia Ben Ammar(チュニジア/Tunisia)

輝ける秋よ花嫁頬染めて
> autumn glow ― the blushing face of the bride
>> ポール　カルス/Paul Callus(マルタ/Malta)

黄金の秋に溶けゆく広葉樹
> forêt de feuillus ― sa silhouette disparaît dans les ors de l'automne
>> イザベル　カルバロ　テール/Isabelle Carvalho Teles(フランス/France)

水面には秋の輝く湖畔かな
> bord du lac ― dans l'eau les reflets de l'automne
>> イザベル　カルバロ　テール/Isabelle Carvalho Teles
>>> (フランス/France)

わが皮膚の薄さや秋の訪れて
> automne — une fine épaisseur sur ma peau
> autumn — a thin layer on my skin
>> アンヌ　デアルベルト/Anne Dealbert（フランス/France）

秋初めポーチで雨のコンサート
> début d'automne — le concert de la pluie dans la véranda
>> フランソワーズ　モリス/Francoise Maurice（フランス/France）

祖母の目に悲しみ浮かぶ秋初め
> early autumn — in grandmother's eyes a veil of sadness
> inizio autunno — negli occhi di nonna un velo di tristezza
>> アンジェラ　ジオルダーノ/Angela Giordano（イタリア/Italy）

山頂の色づき秋のラプソディ
> a burst of colours on the mountain peak — autumn rhapsody
>> バーバラ　オルムタック/Barbara Olmtak（オランダ/Holland）

君の肌は蜂蜜のやう甘き秋
> douceur d'automne — son regard sur le miel de sa peau.
>> カリン　コシュト/Karine Cocheteux（フランス/France）

秋やさし最後の薔薇の散る園庭
> mite autunno — sola in un giardino l'ultima rosa
>> アルベルタ　カテリナ　マトリ/Alberta Caterina Mattoli（イタリア/Italy）

隣家より秋の料理のハーブの香
> my neighbour's autumn cooking — the wind carries italian herbs
>> キム　オルムタック　ゴメス/Kim Olmtak Gomes
>> （オランダ/Holland）

晴れ渡る青空秋の木々のため
> clear skies — backdrop of blue for trees in autumn
>> バリー　レビン/Barrie Levine（米国/United States）

サフランの雌蕊摘みたる金の秋
> l'or d'automne — bientôt la cueillette des pistils de safran
>> イメルダ　セン/Imelda Senn（スイス/Switzerland）

アラビアのハープよ秋の囁きよ
> murmures d'automne — quelques notes d'une harpe arabe
>> アメルラディヒビ　ベント　チャディ/AmelLadhibi Bent Chadly
>> （チュニジア/Tunisia）

秋絢爛赤一色の田園よ
> rosse emozioni — sussurri d'autunno nella campagna
>> パトリチア　カバローネ/Patrizia Cavallone（イタリア/Italy）

秋絢爛風はパジャマを乾かせり
> automne — les pyjamas sèchent dans le vent
>> マルセル　ペルチエ/Marcel Peltier（フランス/France）

一度だけ風になりたき秋であり
> autumn — i want to be the wind just once
>> ザンザミ　イスマイル/Zamzami Ismail
>> （インドネシア/Indonesia）

足元に森の囁く秋の音
> bruissements d'automne — la forêt chuchote sous mes pas
>> イザベル　カルバロ　テール/Isabelle Carvalho Teles
>> （フランス/France）

パレットに季節陳列今は秋

> étalage de saisons ― cette palette colorée de l'automne
>
> アメルラディヒビ　ベント　チャディ/AmelLadhibi Bent Chadly
>
> (チュニジア/Tunisia)

情熱はまだ燃えてをり秋赤し

> rosso autunno ― la passione assopita di nuovo ardente
>
> アルベルタ　カテリナ　マトリ/Alberta Caterina Mattoli(イタリア/Italy)

葉擦れなる秋の寂しき音のする

> freamăt de frunziș ― cântecul toamnei melancolic
>
> rustle of leafage ― the melancholy song of autumn
>
> ガブリル　バル/Gavril Bâle(ルーマニア/Romania)

一陣の風が硝子を砕く秋

> crepe d'autunno ― un pugno di vento frantuma il vetro
>
> リトリア　ガンドルフィ/Littoria Gandolfi(イタリア/Italy)

秋初め二羽の雀のゐるベンチ

> début de l'automne ― deux moineaux se rejoignent sur le banc du parc
>
> エレナ　ズアイン/Elena Zouain(ルーマニア/Romania)

秋初めマルメロの葉は風に舞ふ

> automne ― les feuilles du cognassier dansent pour le vent
>
> スアド　ハジリ/Hajri(チュニジア/Tunisia)

埃つぽき床を踏みたる秋初め

> bientôt l'automne ― je marche sur le sol poudreux
>
> エリック　デスピエール/Eric Despierre(フランス/Ftance)

砂粒の指間に流る秋初め
> début d'automne — le sable file entre mes doigts
>> シュピー　モイサン/Choupie Moysan（フランス/France）

粉を引く歯車響く野辺の秋
> campo autunnale — il suono di una vecchia ruota di mulino
> autumn field — the sound of an old mill-wheel
>> ダニエラ　ミッソ/Daniela Misso（イタリア/Italy）

葉の渦に秋の匂ひの立ちにけり
> the scent of autumn — a swirl of leaves beneath the trees
>> キム　オルムタック　ゴメス/Kim Olmtak Gomes
>> （オランダ/Holland）

かんばせを吹きゆく風や秋初め
> beginning of autumn — the harsh wind blows on my face
>> ナッキー　クリスティジーノ/Nuky Kristijno
>> （インドネシア/Indonesia）

秋初め梵鐘の音に葉の飛翔
> automne — les feuilles voltigent au son du carillon
>> エブリン　ベラール/Evelyne Belard（ベルギー/Begium）

秋の葉のひとひら生と死を舞ひぬ
> automne — danse de la feuille la mort et la vie
>> トゥーン　チャベ/Tounès Thabet（チュニジア/Tunisia）

壊れたる鏡に皺や秋初め
> début d'automne — sur le miroir brisé première ride
>> アブダラ　ハジイ/Abdallah Ḥajji（モロッコ/Morocco）

秋の秘密風がすべてを撒き散らす

> autumn secrets — the wind disperses everything
>
> ファトマ　ゾラ　ハビス/Fatma Zohra Habis
>
> (チュニジア/Tunisia)

秋の庭雨は降つたり止んだりす

> la pioggia che cade e non cade — giardino d'autunno
>
> ナザレナ　ランピーニ/Nazarena R.(イタリア/Italy)

収穫や国力として秋の土　　　　　　　　　　　亜仁寿（自訳）

> the harvest — autumn soil for the strength of the country
>
> タンポポ　アニス/Tanpopo Anis(インドネシア/Indonesia)

新学期秋の匂ひの中にあり

> the beginning of the school year — the smell of autumn
> početak školske godine — miris jeseni
>
> ズデンカ　ムリナー/Zdenka Mlinar(クロアチア/Croatia)

黄色き葉拾ひて秋は手の中に

> pick up fallen yellow leaves — autumn in my hand
> nhặt lá vàng rơi — mùa thu trong tay tôi
>
> ディン　ニュエン/Dinh Nguyen(ベトナム/Vietnam)

金の葉の紙吹雪輝ける秋

> glory of autumn — confetti of golden leaves
>
> キム　オルムタック　ゴメス/Kim Olmtak Gomes(オランダ/Holland)

青といふ青を極めて秋の空

> the intensity of brilliant blue — an autumn sky
>
> ポール　カルス/Paul Callus(マルタ/Malta)

秋の静寂(しじま)葉群に落つる雨の音
　silenzio autunnale — il ticchettio della pioggia sopra le foglie
　　　　　　　ガブリエラ　デ　マシ/Gabriella De Masi(イタリア/Italy)

秋めくや遠のいてゆく鳥の声
　the birdsong ever more distant — signs of autumn
　il canto degli uccelli sempre più lontano — segnali d'autunno
　　　　　　　アンジェラ　ジオルダーノ/Angela Giordano(イタリア/Italy)

金色の炎よ秋の地平線
　autumn horizon — draped in golden flames
　　　　　　　キム　オルムタック　ゴメス/Kim Olmtak Gomes
　　　　　　　　　　　　　　　　　　　(オランダ/Holland)

秋初めしじまの声のまた揺れる
　nuovo autunno — la voce del silenzio ancora vibra
　　　　　　　ミケーレ　ポチエロ/Michele Pochiero(イタリア/Italy)

秋初め君の頬つぺにある笑窪
　autunno — ancora le fossette nelle guance
　　　　　　　ガブリエラ　デ　マシ/Gabriella De Masi(イタリア/Italy)

針の音編み目のごとく秋描く
　cliquetis d'aiguilles — maille après maille elle écrit l'automne
　　　　　　　ジェラール　デユモン/Gérard Dumon(フランス/France)

空つぽのベンチに秋が座してゐる
　an empty bench autumn sits quietly on it
　prazna klop nanjo tiho seda jesen
　　　　　　　ディミトリー　シュクルク/Dimitrij Škrk(スロベニア/Slovenia)

秋の七草香り漂ふ句を集め

> seven flowers of autumn ― I concoct a fragrant haiku
>
> キム　オルムタック　ゴメス/Kim Olmtak Gomes（オランダ/Holland）

秋進み夜はだんだん長くなる

> arrière saison ― inlassablement la nuit grignote le jour
>
> ジェラール　マレシャル/Gerard Marechal
>
> （フランス/France）

はからずも秋の西風ページ捲る

> sans que je le veuille une page se tourne ― vent d'ouest d'automne
>
> ナディン　レオン/Nadine Léon（フランス/France）

瓦礫の下の我が影薄き秋進む

> l'automne ― sous la ruine mon ombre est incertaine
>
> ジェラール　マレシャル/Gerard Marechal
>
> （フランス/France）

秋初め水平線に燕の飛翔

> inizio autunno ― ponte tra mare e cielo rondini in volo
>
> パトリチア　センシ/Patrizia Cenci（フランス/France）

たなびく雲秋を押す出す日の光

> ciel de traîne chaque rayon de soleil repousse l'automne
>
> フランソワーズ　ヴォルポエ/Françoise Volpoet
>
> （フランス/France）

秋来るスカートのへり長くして

> un altro autunno ― un po' più lungo l'orlo della gonna
>
> アンナ　リモンディ/Anna Rimondi（イタリア/Italy）

秋初め柱時計は夜数え
> passager de l'automne — la vieille horloge compte les nuits
>
> エリック　デスピエール/Eric Despierre
>
> (フランス/France)

秋初め雨は悲しみ注ぎ込む
> début d'automne — la pluie instille sa tristesse
>
> パトリック　ソンプル/Patrick Somprou(フランス/France)

平原の木々の奏づる秋の歌
> vast plains of quiet trees render their lonely songs — I hear autumn hum
>
> ラシュミ　モハパトラ/Rashmi Mohapatra(インド/India)

しみじみと朝の珈琲薫る秋
> tasting autumnal fulfillment — the aroma of morning coffee
>
> キム　オルムタック　ゴメス/Kim Olmtak Gomes(オランダ/Holland)

秋の欠片濡れた枝葉は絵画のやう
> morceau d'automne — le feuillage mouillé semble peint
>
> エリック　デスピエール/Eric Despierre(フランス/France)

秋初めいと美しき海と空
> début d'automne — mer et ciel de toute beauté
>
> ナジハ　フェダウイ/Naziha Feddaoui
>
> (アルジェリア/Algeria)

草原の秋の花の間に死んだ蝶
> fleur d'automne dans l'herbe verte — je cueille un papillon mort
>
> ナディン　レオン/Nadine Léon(フランス/France)

秋の葉や虚しく空に舞ひ上がり
> feuille d'automne ― atteindre le ciel en vain
>
> イザベル　ラマン/Isa Lamant（フランス/France）

ポケットに古き切符や秋の枝葉
> feuilles d'automne ― dans ma poche un vieux ticket de train
>
> リミ　ラルビ/Limi Larbi（モロッコ/Morocco）

夜のしじま秋は軋む枝葉より来
> au silence de la nuit ― craquement des feuilles rappelle l'automne
>
> レリア　ベン/Leila Ben（チュニジア/Tunisia）

悲しき秋戦場の子は天使へと
> un triste autunno ― nelle zone di guerra bimbi con le ali
>
> クルッチ　ヴィットリア/Colucci Vittoria（イタリア/Italy）

ガザの秋少女の瞼永遠(とわ)に閉づ
> autunno a Gaza ― la bimba copre gli occhi la bimba copre gli occhi
>
> ガブリエラ　デ　マシ/Gabriella De Masi
> （イタリア/Italy）

秋来る扉の前に風は待ち
> automne ― l'attente du vent au seuil des portes
>
> リミ　ラルビ/Limi Larbi（モロッコ/Morocco）

耕作地石の触れ合ふ秋の音
> sons d'automne ― au champs labouré le foisonnement des pierres
>
> リミ　ラルビ/Limi Larbi（モロッコ/Morocco）

輝く秋数多の色で編むカンバス
> automne — tresse aux multiples couleurs toile lumineuse
>
> トウーン　チャベ/Tounès Thabet(チュニジア/Tunisia)

輝く秋目を惹きつける真紅の実
> le regard attiré par les baies vermillon — l'automne brille
>
> アルベルタ　カテリナ　マトリ/Alberta Caterina Mattoli(イタリア/Italy)

黄ばんだ写真秋色彩で語りたる
> foto ingiallite — l'autunno si racconta con i colori
>
> ローザ　マリア　ディ　サルバトーレ/Rosa Maria Di Salvatore
>
> (イタリア/Italy)

秋の悪夢影に目覚める我の影
> cauchemar d'automne —se réveillant dans l'ombre mon ombre
>
> ジェラール　マレシャル/Gerard Marechal
>
> (フランス/France)

秋来る森の香りを深呼吸
> respiro piano i profumi del bosco — un altro autunno
>
> ローザ　マリア　ディ　サルバトーレ/Rosa Maria Di Salvatore
>
> (イタリア/Italy)

朗報を持ちて故郷へ秋初め
> beginning of autumn — good news that you will be back home
>
> ディア　ヌクスマ/Dyah Nkusuma(インドネシア/Indonesia)

秋やさし金の息吹に舞ふ蜻蛉
> douceur de l'automne où la libellule bleue danse au souffle doré
>
> ジョワ　デウ　ビーブル/Joie de Vivre(フランス/France)

秋の色旅する南から北へ
> du sud au nord — voyage dans les nuances de l'automne
>
>> マルチン デユレ/Martine Duret（フランス/France）

秋の匂ひ分刻みにて夜の更ける
> autumn scent — minute by minute the night in the making
>
>> プロビール　グプタ/Probir Gupta（インド/India）

煌めく秋光の粒と笑む瞳
> automne — chatoyant coulent des pèpites de lumière coulent des pèpites de lumière
>
>> フテン　フルチ/Feten Fourti（チュニジア/Tunisia）

秋の歌葉の囁きと詩人の歩
> șoaptele frunzelor — sub pașii poetului doar o romanță
> the whispers of leaves — under poet's footsteps the song of autumn
>
>> ダニエラ　トピルセーン/Daniela Topîrcean
>>（ルーマニア/Romania）

秋の扉コートのポケットに俳句
> porte d'automne — dans la poche du manteau le premier poème
>
>> アブダラ　ハジイ/Abdallah Hajji（モロッコ/Morocco）

風立ちて秋の匂ひのやつて来る
> with the wind comes a scent of autumn
> col vento arriva il profumo dell'autunno
>
>> アンジェラ　ジオルダーノ/Angela Giordano
>>（イタリア/Italy）

どこまでもここが真ん中秋の航

   all the way we are in the middle autumn cruise

中野千秋/Chiaki Nakano(日本/Japan)

好きだけど恋とは言へず秋初め

   I like you but not in love with you — beginning of autumn

中野千秋/Chiaki Nakano(日本/Japan)

中庭や秋の足音そこはかと

   la cour — le bruit des pas d'automne légèrement résonne

向瀬美音/Mine Mukose(日本/Japan)

果てしなき雲の広がり秋告げる

   une étendue infinie de nuages — l'automne

向瀬美音/Mine Mukose(日本/Japan)

まづ雲の形変へたる秋はじめ

   l'automne commence — les nuages changent de forme

向瀬美音/Mine Mukose(日本/Japan)

九月【くがつ・kugatsu】
september / septembre

This is the month to love the moon more than anything else. Although the mornings and evenings are cool, the lingering summer heat is still intense. After the equinoxes, autumn deepens and we can hear the sound of insects at night. On the other hand, this is the month of typhoons, which bring damage to many parts of Japan.

九月来る世界はすでに限界に
> début septembre — le monde est à bout de ses forces
>> オルファ　クチュク　ブハディダ/Olfa Kchouk Bouhadida
>>> (チュニジア/Tunisia)

やはらかき九月寒さは言葉より
> mite settembre — viene dalle parole il grande freddo
>> アナ　リモンディ/Anna Rimond(イタリア/Italy)

九月来る閉めたる扉そして過去
> premier de septembre — fermant la porte de la maison et à mon passé
>> アンヌ-マリー　ジュベール-ガヤール/Anne-Marie Joubert-Gaillard
>>> (フランス/France)

九月来て鳥の巣空となりにけり
> settembre — sotto le grondaie i nidi abbandonati
>> ガブリエル　デ　マシ/Gabriella De Masi
>>> (イタリア/Italy)

九月来る霧の中より雨の音
> september — the sound of rain inside the fog
> settembre — il suono della pioggia dentro la nebbia
>> アンジェラ　ジオルダーノ/Angela Giordano
>>> (イタリア/Italy)

思ひ出は九月の波にさらはれぬ
> septembre — la mer emporte des souvenirs avec une vague
> cerul de toamnă — dincolo de norii grei toate culorile
>> マリン　ラダ/Marin Rada(ルーマニア/Romania)

欠伸して渇きの残る九月かな
> september — thirsty cracks of summer do not stop yawning
> rujan — žedne pukotine ljeta ne prestaju zijevati
>> ズデンカ　ムリナー/Zdenka Mlinar（クロアチア/Croatia）

九月の夜曇つた窓に雨叩く
> notte di settembre — batte la pioggia sui vetri appannati
>> マリオ　デ　サンティス/Mario. De Santis（イタリア/Italy）

色褪せし新鮮な風九月来る
> torna settembre — l'aria più chiara e cruda sfuma i colori
>> マリア　パテルリーニ/Maria Paterlini（イタリア/Italy）

身のうちの闇は語らず九月の夜
> sera di settembre — il silenzio del buio dietro i miei passi
>> マリオ　デ　サンティス/Mario. De Santis（イタリア/Italy）

九月の陽黒麦の花輝けり
> soleil de septembre — la brillance des fleurs de blé noir
>> フランソワーズ　デニウ-ルリエーブル/Françoise Deniaud-Lelièvre
>> （フランス/France）

九月来る豪雨しやがれた声を持ち
> septembre — le bruit rauque de l'eau torrentielle
>> ソニア　ベン　アマール/Sonia Ben Ammar
>> （チュニジア/Tunisia）

褐色のパレット九月半ばなり
> mi-septembre — l'automne prépare sa palette fauve
>> ラシダ　ジェルビ/Rachida Jerbi（チュニジア/Tunisia）

君眠る墓地に九月の花が咲く
> al cimitero — i fiori settembrini che ti piacevano
>
> アグネーゼ　ジアロンゴ/Agnese Giallongo（イタリア/Italy）

美しき九月よ君が生まれたる
> september — my most beautiful month you were born
>
> アグネーゼ　ジアロンゴ/Agnese Giallongo（イタリア/Italy）

髪の毛に赤き葉の乗る九月かな
> septembre — une feuille rouge sur ses cheveux
>
> シルビー　テロラズ/Sylvie Theraulaz（フランス/France）

九月の風俳句で世界一周す
> vent de septembre — à travers vos haïkus je fais le tour du monde
>
> スアド　ハジリ/Souad Hajri（チュニジア/Tunisia）

君の目の中に空ある九月来る
> september — just a piece of sky inside your eyes
> i settembrini — solo un pezzo di cielo
>
> アンジェラ　ジオルダーノ/Angela Giordano（イタリア/Italy）

ひとひらの葉の風に舞ふ秋の囁き
> chuchotis d'automne — une feuille s'envole dans le vent
>
> エレナ　ズアイン/Elena Zouain（ルーマニア/Romania）

静かなる雨窓伝ふ九月の朝
> la pluie silencieuse dégouline à la fenêtre matin de septembre
>
> フランソワーズ　デニオ-ルリエーブル/Françoise Deniaud-Lelièvre（フランス/Ftance）

貝殻の中の波音九月の浜

settembre al mare — il rumore delle onde nella conchiglia

テレサ　アルジオラ/Teresa Argiolas（イタリア/Italy）

九月の夜肩にショールと風の歌

soir de septembre — sur mes épaules une écharpe de laine le chant du vent

トゥーン　チャベ/Tounès Thabet

（チュニジア/Tunisia）

木々の葉に透ける九月の光かな

lumière de septembre presque transparentes — les feuilles des arbres

アメルラディヒビ　ベント　チャディ/AmelLadhibi Bent Chadly

（チュニジア/Tunisia）

九月の浜鷗の遊ぶ蒼き空

plage de septembre dans le bleu du ciel — le jeu des mouettes

イザベル　カルバロ　テール/Isabelle Carvalho Teles

（フランス/France）

九月の午後狩人の追ふ森の住民

doux après-midi de septembre — les habitants du bois traqués par les chasseurs.

ジャニン　シャルメトン/Jeanine Chalmeton

（フランス/France）

小さき黄の果実九月の贈り物

autunno piccole bacche gialle dono di settembre

イバナ/Ivana（イタリア/Italy）

良き風に顔を撫でられ九月尽

> end of September — the caresses on the face of the mild climate
> fine settembre — le carezze sul viso del clima mite
>
> アンジェラ　ジオルダーノ/Angela Giordano
> （イタリア/Italy）

九月尽濡れた匂ひの通りかな

> end of September — wet smell along the avenue
> fine settembre — odore di bagnato lungo il viale
>
> パトリチア　カバローネ/Patrizia Cavallone
> （イタリア/Italy）

水色のリボンほどきて九月来る

> untie the light blue ribbon — September is coming
>
> 中野千秋/Chiaki Nakano（日本/Japan）

校庭に並ぶ学童九月来る

> les enfants s'alignent dans le cour — Septembre
>
> 向瀬美音/Mine Mukose（日本/Japan）

残暑【ざんしょ・zansho】
the late summer heat / dernières chaleurs de l'été

The heat after the first day of autumn. Usually, hot days continue through the end of August. After it cools down once, the heat sometimes returns.

詰みチェスの逃げれぬやうな残暑かな

> lingering heat — like a checkmate in chess with no way out
>
> タンポポ　アニス/Tanpopo Anis（インドネシア/Indonesia）

駅地下のカレーの匂ふ残暑かな　　　　　　　　　亜仁寿（自訳）
> lingering heat — the smell of curry in the basement of the station
>
> タンポポ　アニス/Tanpopo Anis（インドネシア/Indonesia）

天蓋より黄色き光さす残暑
> late summer heat — yellow flashes from the canopies
>
> キム　オルムタック　ゴメス/Kim Olmtak Gomes
>
> （オランダ/Holland）

太陽は赤き絹なる残暑かな
> dernière chaleur de l'été — soleil de soie rouge
>
> カリーヌ　コシュト/Karine Cocheteux
>
> （フランス/France）

髪を結ひバレエ教室秋暑し
> late summer heat — neat buns of girls in ballet class
>
> ナッキー　クリスティジーノ/Nuky Kristijno
>
> （インドネシア/Indonesia）

秋暑し空を響かすドラムの音
> late summer heat — the percussionist's drum rolls echo in the sky
>
> ポール　カルス/Paul Callus（マルタ/Malta）

残暑なり辛きもの食べ赤き顔
> lingering heat—red face after eating spicy food
>
> エル　ハミド/El Hamied（インドネシア/Indonesia）

秋暑しまださよならの手を振らず
> late summer heat — not waving yet goodbye
>
> アナ　イリナ/Ana Irina（ルーマニア/Romania）

秋暑し帽子の下の髪濡れて

> late summer heat — my wet hair under the cap
>
> ナッキー　クリスティジーノ/Nuky Kristijno
>
> (インドネシア/Indonesia)

空気にも薔薇の中にも残暑かな

> ancora estate nell'aria e nelle rose — petali in terra
> still summer in the air and in the roses — petals on the ground
>
> マリア　パテルリーニ/Maria Paterlini(イタリア/Italy)

雷を落とすゼウスや秋暑し

> late summer heat — Zeus sends thunderbolts out of the blue
>
> ポール　カルス/Paul Callus(マルタ/Malta)

もう一杯麦茶が欲しき残暑かな　　　　　亜仁寿（自訳）

> I want one more cup of barley tea — the late summer heat
>
> タンポポ　アニス/Tampopo(インドネシア/Indonesia)

映画館出て残暑の衰へず

> leaving the cinema — the late summer heat continues
>
> 中野千秋/Chiaki Nakano(日本/Japan)

やはらかに髪結上ぐる残暑かな

> wear softly my hair up — late summer heart
> coiffer mollement mon chignon — fin de l'ete
>
> 向瀬美音/Mine Mukose(日本/Japan)

目覚めより錠剤五粒秋暑し

> migraine au réveil — dernière chaleurs de l'été
>
> 向瀬美音/Mine Mukose(日本/Japan)

混沌は混沌を呼び秋暑し

| chaos sur chaos — dernière chaleurs de l'été

            向瀬美音/Mine Mukose（日本/Japan）

> **秋分**【しゅうぶん・shuubun】
>
> **autumn solstice / équinoxe d'automne**
>
> One of the 24 solar terms. The day when the longitude of the sun reaches 180 degrees. It is in the middle of the eighth month of the lunar calendar, 15 days after the White Dew, and roughly falls on the 22nd or 23rd day of the 9th month. The length of day and night are the same, and from this point on, night gradually becomes longer, and the "long autumn nights" begin here

家系図をネットで調べたる秋分

| équinoxe d'automne — cherchant ma généalogie sur internet

    フランソワーズ　マリー　チュイリエ/FrançoiseMarie Thuillier

                （フランス/France）

秋分や雁は空の色を変へて

| les oies sauvages rompent la platitude du ciel — équinoxe d'automne

           ラシダ　ジェルビ/Rachida Jerbi

               （チュニジア/Tunisia）

秋分や山小屋の窓閉められて

| équinoxe d'automne — les volets fermés des chalets hors saison

           イメルダ　セン/Imelda Senn

              （スイス/Switzerland）

レンズ豆のスープ準備する秋分

équinoxe d'automne — préparer la soupe aux lentilles

アメルラディヒビ　ベント　チャディ/AmelLadhibi Bent Chadly
(チュニジア/Tunisia)

秋分や昼間と夜の同じ波長

équinoxe d'automne — jour et nuit sur la même longueur d'onde

カディジャ　エル　ブルカディ/Khadija El Bourkadi(モロッコ/Morocco)

秋分や決勝チーム同じスコア

équinoxe d'automne — même score pour les deux finalistes

カディジャ　エル　ブルカディ/Khadija El Bourkadi
(モロッコ/Morocco)

秋分や墓前の花を摘んでをり

autumn equinox — picking flowers for the grave

キム　オルムタック　ゴメス/Kim Olmtak Gomes(オランダ/Holland)

秋分や三つ編みに白黒のリボン

équinoxe d'automne — sur ses deux tresses un ruban en noir et blanc

スアド　ハジリ/Souad Hajri(チュニジア/Tunisia)

秋分や日の半分は星の下

équinoxe d'automne — la moitié du jour sous les étoiles

マルレーヌ　アレクサ/Marlene Alexa(フランス/France)

秋分や光と影のハーモニー

autumn equinox — light and dark in harmony

キム　オルムタック　ゴメス/Kim Olmtak Gomes(オランダ/Holland)

秋分や朝食の長きコーヒー

> giorno di equinozio — un caffè lungo a colazione
>
> ガブリエラ　デ　マシ/Gabriella De Masi
> （イタリア/Italy）

秋分や赤き髪してサロン出て

> autumnal equinox — she exits the salon with auburn hair
>
> ポール　カルス/Paul Callus（マルタ/Maila）

秋分やこのごろ加速する時間

> autumnal equinox — time accelerated these days
>
> 中野千秋/Chiaki Nakano（日本/Japan）

秋分や二種の地酒を味はひぬ

> équinoxe d'automne — déguster deux types de saké local
>
> 向瀬美音/Mine Mukose（日本/Japan）

十月【じゅうがつ・jugatsu】
october / octobre

It is a pleasant month, neither hot nor cold. The weather is changeable, but when it is sunny, the air is clear and pleasant. Autumn leaf peeping and athletic meets are popular in this month.

やはらかき十月詩には幸せを

> douceur d'octobre — habillés de bonheur mes poèmes
>
> アメルラディヒビ　ベント　チャディ/AmelLadhibi Bent Chadly
> （チュニジア/Tunisia）

十月の空に燕のバレエかな
> deux d'octobre — dans le ciel un ballet d'hirondelles
>> フランソワーズ　デニウ-ルリエーブル/Françoise Deniaud-Lelièvre
>>> （フランス/France）

水凍り木々震へたる十月来
> octobre — les arbres s'agitent et l'eau souffre de froid
>> スアド　ハジリ/Souad Hajri（チュニジア/Tunisia）

十月や笛吹く古きティーポット
> douceur d'octobre — la vieille théière siffle à nouveau
> october mildness — the old teapot whistles again
>> イザベル　ラマン-ムニエ/Isabelle Lamant-Meunier（フランス/France）

喜びと紅茶の香混ざる十月
> douceur d'octobre — mêlée au parfum du thé la joie de mes amis
>> イザベル　ラマン-ムニエ/Isabelle Lamant-Meunier（フランス/France）

十月の空に広がる鳥の群れ
> ciel d'octobre — en essaims les oiseaux se répandent
>> カメル　メスレム/Kamel Meslem（アルジェリア/Algeria）

十月や雲を貫く城の塔
> ciel d'octobre — les tours du château transpercent les nuages gris
> october sky — the castle towers pierce the grey clouds
>> イザベル　ラマン-ムニエ/Isabelle Lamant-Meunier（フランス/France）

十月やフェンネルの香を飛ばす風
> matin d'octobre — l'odeur du fenouil vole avec le vent
>> フランソワーズ　モリス/Francoise Maurice（フランス/France）

十月の甘き空気と苦き珈琲
> caffè amaro — così dolce l'aria d'ottobre
>> ガブリエラ　デ　マシ/Gabriella De Masi
>>> （イタリア/Italy）

十月の朝椋鳥のコンサート
> matin d'octobre — sur les fils le concert des sansonnets
>> フランソワーズ　デニウ-ルリエーブル/Françoise Deniaud-Lelièvre
>>> （フランス/France）

朝風や十月に出る旬のもの
> brise matinale — octobre offrant ses primeurs
>> フテン　フルチ/feten fourti（チュニジア/Tunisia）

十月末大地すつかり乾きたる
> la terre sèche du parterre aux soleils — derniers jours d'octobre
>> フランソワーズ　デニウ-ルリエーブル/Françoise Deniaud-Lelièvre
>>> （フランス/France）

愛の余韻儚き十月の雨よ
> pioggia d'ottobre — gli amori passeggeri lasciano il segno
> october rain — fleeting loves leaves sign
>> クリスティーナ　プルビレンティ/Cristina Pulvirenti
>>> （イタリア/Italy）

十月末夜霧の中に魔女の国
> veil of fog on the last night of october — the kingdom of witches
> veo magle u zadnjoj listopadskoj noći — carstvo vještica
>> ズデンカ　ムリナー/Zdenka Mlinar
>>> （クロアチア/Croatia）

十月の夜空一つの星のため

> nuit d'octobre — tout le ciel pour une seule étoile
>
> スアド　ハジリ/Souad Hajri（チュニジア/Tunisia）

我が髪に赤き輝き十月来

> octobre—des reflets roux dans mes cheveux
>
> キャロリン　コッペ/Caroline Coppé（ベルギー/Belgium）

池の歌に風の色あり十月の落暉

> crépuscule d'octobre — les couleurs du vent dans le chant de l'étang
>
> エレナ　ズアイン/Elena Zouain（ルーマニア/Romania）

十月や凍る影にはつか光

> octobre avec l'ombre glacee un peu de lumiere
>
> マルレヌ　アレクサ/Marlene Alexa（フランス/France）

十月の色を憂鬱なカンバスに

> pe şevaletul melancoliei — pânze cu tuşe de octombrie
> on the easel of melancholy — canvases with october touches
>
> ミハエラ　ポデウット　レニュタ/Mihaela Poduţ Ienuţaş
>
> （ルーマニア/Romania）

さまざまな色彩十月の空よ

> teintes variables — le ciel s'amuse en octobre
>
> マルセル　ペルティエ/Marcel Peltier（フランス/France）

十月やピンクリボンの月の来て

> listopad — mjesec ružičaste vrpce
>
> ズデンカ　ムリナー/Zdenka Mlinar（クロアチア/Croatia）

十月の日差しが枝に混ざりゆく

> giallo d'ottobre — il sole si confonde dentro le fronde
> october yellow — the sun blends into the branches
>
> マリア　パテルリーニ/Maria Paterlini（イタリア/Italy）

十月の雨甘やかに匂ふ土

> sweet smell of the soil—rainy october
>
> ナッキー　クリスティジーノ/Nuky Kristijno（インドネシア/Indonesia）

十月の空の青さよブーケトス

> bouquet toss — the blueness of october sky
>
> 中野千秋/Chiaki Nakano（日本/Japan）

十月や土まみれなるスニーカー

> sneaker souillés de terre — octobre
>
> 向瀬美音/Mine Mukose（日本/Japan）

秋の朝【あきのあさ・akinoasa】
autumn morning / matin d'automne

After Risshu (the first day of autumn), mornings and evenings become brisk and refreshing, even though the lingering summer heat is still intense. Morning in autumn gives us a strong impression of the time of year. From mid-autumn to late autumn, there are many mornings that feel chilly.

空の色解き放つ鳥秋の夜明け

> aube d'automne — débouche de couleurs au ciel une nuée d'oiseaux
>
> カメル　メスレム/Kamel Meslem（アルジェリア/Algeria）

雨粒と祈り流るる秋の夜明け

> aube automnale — coule la voix du muezzin avec les gouttes de pluie
>
> アメルラディヒビ　ベント　チャディ/AmelLadhibi Bent Chadly
>
> （チュニジア/Tunisia）

秋暁や山道進む確かな歩

> aube d'automne — sur le chemin de la montagne je prouve mes pas
>
> アブダラ　ハジイ/Abdallah Hajji（モロッコ/Morocco）

秋の朝窓いつぱいに広ぐ空

> dimineți de toamnă — cerul umple fereastra
> autumn mornings — the sky fills the window
>
> ミレラ　ブライレーン/Mirela Brailean
>
> （ルーマニア/Romania）

音もなく羽落ちて来る秋の朝

> autumn morning — a bird feather fell without a sound
>
> エル　ハミド/El Hamied（インドネシア/Indonesia）

コーヒーと俳句のありて秋の朝

> autumn morning — coffee and haiku
>
> キム　オルムタック　ゴメス/Kim Olmtak Gomes
>
> （オランダ/Holland）

黄金の日差しや秋の朝が来て

> the golden sun radiates — autumn morning has come
>
> スカディ　ソノカリヨ/Sukadi Sonokaryo
>
> （インドネシア/Indonesia）

中庭の箒の音や秋の朝

> autumn's morning — sound of broom sweeping the courtyard
> ナッキー　クリスティジーノ/Nuky Kristijno（インドネシア/Indonesia）

秋の朝音無き風に葉の散りて

> matin d'automne — au silence du vent les feuilles au sol
> カメル　メスレム/Kamel Meslem（アルジェリア/Algeria）

秋の朝雨粒大地目覚ませり

> matin d'automne — goutte à goutte la pluie réveille l'odeur de la terre
> スアド　ハジリ/Souad Hajri（チュニジア/Tunisia）

菊茶淹れしじまを待てる秋の朝

> autumn morning — chrysanthemum tea and waiting silence
> buổi sáng mùa thu — trà hoa cúc và khoảng lặng đợi chờ
> ディン　ヌグエン/Dinh Nguyen（ベトナム/Vietnam）

秋の朝夜の静寂(しじま)をはらふ烏

> les corneilles chassent les silences de la nuit — matin d'automne
> ナディン　レオン/Nadine Léon（フランス/France）

絶え間なくロビンの鳴いて秋の朝

> autumn morning — passionately delivered a robin's song
> ポール　カルス/Paul Callus（マルタ/Malta）

花びらは本に挟まれ秋の朝

> autumn morning — on the book page rose petals fall asleep
> buổi sáng mùa thu — trên trang sách cánh hoa hồng ngủ quên
> ディン　ヌグエン/Dinh Nguyen（ベトナム/Vietnam）

秋暁や静けき海に揺れる鷗

> aube d'automne — les mouettes se balancent sur la mer calme
>
> カルメン　バシキリ/Carmen Baschieri
>
> (イタリア/Italy)

秋暁やしじまを破る鳥の声

> autumn sunrise — a songbird's melody breaks the morning hush
>
> ポール　カルス/Paul Callu(マルタ/Malta)

秋の朝樹々に風の優しき息

> matin d'automne — tout doux le chuchotement du vent dans les arbres
>
> スアド　ハジリ/Souad Hajri(チュニジア/Tunisia)

カップより湯気の踊れる秋の朝

> dancing figure in the steam from the cups — autumn morning
>
> プロビール　ギュプタ/Probir Gupta
>
> (インド/India)

秋暁や丘に解けてゆく光

> autumn dawn — a glow unfurls across the hills
>
> ポール　カルス/Paul Callus(マルタ/Malta)

水差しの何かささやく秋の朝

> autumn morning — mumbling something jug
>
> 中野千秋/Chiaki Nakano(日本/Japan)

美容液うすく重ねる秋の朝

> mettre légèrement du sérum — matin d'automne
>
> 向瀬美音/Mine Mukose(日本/Japan)

秋の昼【あきのひる・akinohiru】
autumn noon / après-midi d'automne

It is the time of day when the air is clear and the autumnal atmosphere is deepening. The shadows of the trees and the sun's rays also show the unique colors of autumn.

秋の午後黄を分かち合ふ蝶と菊
> autumn afternoon — butterflies and chrysanthemums share yellow
> chiều mùa thu — bướm và hoa cúc chia nhau sắc vàng
> ディン　ヌグエン/Dinh Nguyen（ベトナム/Vietnam）

秋の昼眠気を誘ふ風が吹く
> autumn evening — feeling drowsy by the breezy wind
> ナッキー　クリスティジーノ/Nuky Kristijno（インドネシア/Indonesia）

秋の午後川の水面に光の埃
> après-midi d'automne — sur le bleu de la rivière poussière de lumière
> スアド　ハジリ/Souad Hajri（チュニジア/Tunisia）

秋の午後葉擦れの音のするばかり
> autumn afternoon — only the sound of leaves carried by wind
> chiều mùa thu — chỉ có tiếng lá được gió cuốn đi
> ディン　ヌグエン/Dinh Nguyen（ベトナム/Vietnam）

ゆつたりとポーチに座る秋の午後
> autumn afternoon — sitting on the porch in mellow mood
> ポール　カルス/Paul Callus（マルタ/Malta）

教会の塔いくつある秋の昼

> how many church towers — autumn noon
>
> 中野千秋/Chiaki Nakano（日本/Japan）

繰り返しバイエルの曲秋の昼

> morceaux de Beyer répétés — après-midi d'automne
>
> 向瀬美音/Mine Mukose（日本/Japan）

友禅を畳んでをりぬ秋の昼

> plier mes kimonos soigneusement — après-midi d'automne
>
> 向瀬美音/Mine Mukose（日本／Japan）

秋の暮【あきのくれ・akinokure】
autumn dusk / nuit tombante de l'automne

It can mean either the dusk of an autumn day or the end of the season of autumn. The two meanings have been used since ancient times, and in many cases the two meanings resonate with each other. The word has been sung since ancient times, and has come to symbolize the "areness of things" and "loneliness". It has become a seasonal word that symbolizes "the beauty of things" and "loneliness".

秋の暮屋根打つ雨のタンバリン

> autumn evening — the sound of rain a tambourine on the roofs
> sera autunnale — il suono della pioggia un tamburello sui tetti
>
> アンジェラ　ジオルダーノ/Angela Giordano（イタリア/Italy）

秋の暮風にざわめく枝葉あり

> autumn evening — rustling of leaves in the wind
>
> ポール　カルス/Paul Callus（マルタ/Malta）

秋の暮祖母は幼なに本を読む

> sera d'autunno — la nonna legge storie al suo piccino
> autumn evening — grandmother reads stories to her little one
>
> カルメン　バシキリ/Carmen Baschieri（イタリア／Italy）

秋の暮最後の鴨が地平線

> autumn twilight — the last duck on the edge of the horizon
> crepuscolo autunnale — l'ultima anatra sul filo dell'orizzonte
>
> アンジェラ　ジオルダーノ/Angela Giordano
> （イタリア／Italy）

秋の暮小銭数えるホームレス

> homeless man counting coins — autumn evening
>
> タンポポ　アニス/Tanpopo Anis（インドネシア／Indonesia）

鉄条網に雀の番秋の暮

> autumn evening — a pair of sparrows on a barbed-wire fence
>
> タンポポ　アニス/Tanpopo Anis（インドネシア／Indonesia）

枯菊と祖父の骨壷秋の暮

> withered chrysanthemum near the grandpa's urn — autumn evening
>
> イシ　ヘルヤント/Isni Heryanto
> （インドネシア／Indonesia）

ゆつくりと歩を進めたる秋の暮

> cammino piano — troppo lungo questo tramonto
>
> ローザ　マリア　ディ　サルバトーレ/Rosa Maria Di Salvatore
> （イタリア／Italy）

各階にスープの匂ふ秋の暮

> soir d'automne — une autre odeur de soupe à chaque étage
> autumn evening — an another smell of soup on each floor
>
> イザベル　ラマン-ムニエ/Isabelle Lamant-Meunier
> （フランス/France）

秋の暮角度を変へる木々の影

> autumn evening — shadow of the tree changes its angle
>
> マフィズディン　チュードハリー/Mafizuddin Chowdhury（インド/India）

古き村にちさき出来事秋の暮

> sera d'autunno — piccoli eventi fluiscono nel borgo antico
> autumn evening — tiny events flow in the ancient village
>
> クリスティーナ　プルビエンティ/Cristina Pulvirenti（イタリア/Italy）

サクソフォンその音が呼ぶ秋の暮

> saxophone — its sound makes the autumn sunset darker
>
> タンポポ　アニス/Tanpopo Anis（インドネシア/Indonesia）

秋の暮毛布掛けやる祖母の膝

> autumn evening — I put a blanket over grandma's legs
>
> キム　オルムタック　ゴメス/Kim Olmtak Gomes（オランダ/Holland）

秋の暮暖炉のそばの薪の山

> autumn evening — I gaze at the woodpile near the hearth
>
> キム　オルムタック　ゴメス/Kim Olmtak Gomes（オランダ/Holland）

雷の色持つ鐘や秋の暮

> sera d'autunno — la campana ha il colore del temporale
>
> ガブリエラ　デ　マシ/Gabriella De Masi（イタリア/Italy）

振り向いて母に手を振る秋の暮　　　　　　　　亜仁寿（自訳）
> I turn around and wave one hand to mother — autumn evening
>
> 　　　　　　　　タンポポ　アニス/Tanpopo Anis（インドネシア/Indonesia）

葉の渦に忍び寄りたる秋の暮
> leaves slowly swirling — sluggishness of late autumn creeps in
>
> 　　　　　　　　キム　オルムタック　ゴメス/Kim Olmtak Gomes
>
> 　　　　　　　　　　　　　　　　　　（オランダ/Holland）

秋の暮真つ赤に染まる地平線
> autumn sunset — blazing red horizon
>
> 　　　　　　　　ナッキー　クリスティジーノ/Nuky Kristijno
>
> 　　　　　　　　　　　　　　　　　　（インドネシア/Indonesia）

梟が夢を引き裂く秋の暮
> amurg de toamnă — cântecul cucuvelei sfâșie un vis
> autumn twilight — the song of the owl tear apart a dream
>
> 　　　　　　　　ダニエラ　トピルセーン/Daniela Topîrcean
>
> 　　　　　　　　　　　　　　　　　　（ルーマニア/Romania）

秋の暮髪に新たに白きもの
> autumn twilight — new silver strands inside the hair
> crepuscolo d'autunno — nuovi fili argentati dentro i capelli
>
> 　　　　　　　　アンジェラ　ジオルダーノ/Angela Giordano
>
> 　　　　　　　　　　　　　　　　　　（イタリア/Italy）

秋の暮烏の声の不気味さよ
> autumn dusk — cawing songs predict eerie darkness
>
> 　　　　　　　　キム　オルムタック　ゴメス/Kim Olmtak Gomes
>
> 　　　　　　　　　　　　　　　　　　（オランダ/Holland）

秋の暮ダンス教室長引きて
> autumn evening — dancing class lasts longer
>
> ナッキー　クリスティジーノ/Nuky Kristijno
>
> (インドネシア/Indonesia)

秋の暮祖母は幼き日を語り
> sera d'autunno — la nonna che racconta la sua infanzia
>
> アンジェラ　ジオルダーノ/Angela Giordano
>
> (イタリア/Italy)

子の暮し親の暮しや秋の暮
> son's life our life — autumn evening
>
> 中野千秋/Chiaki Nakano(日本/Japan)

秋の暮一番楽な人は君
> autumn dusk — most comfortable with you
>
> 中野千秋/Chiaki Nakano(日本/Japan)

白き帆船沖合をゆく秋の暮
> voiliers blancs au large — nuit tombante de l'automne
>
> 向瀬美音/Mine Mukose(日本/Japan)

何処より梵鐘の音や秋の暮
> son de cloche d'on ne sait où — soir d'automne
>
> 向瀬美音/Mine Mukose(日本/Japan)

「月光」を奏でてみたき秋の暮
> envie de jouer 'clair de lune' — soir d'automne
>
> 向瀬美音/Mine Mukose(日本/Japan)

秋の夜【あきのよ・akinoyo】
autumn night / soirée d'automne

The nights are getting longer and longer, and there is a sense of quiet. Outside, the moon is rising and insects are singing. On such nights, I can concentrate on various tasks such as studying.

秋の夜や同じ方向見る夫婦

un vieux couple regardant dans la même direction — soir d automne

フテン　フルチ/feten fourti(チュニジア/Tunisia)

秋の夜やしじまに思想黄ばみたる

sere d'autunno — i pensieri ingialliti dentro i silenzi

マリア　ビアンカ/Maria Bianca(イタリア/Italy)

秋の夜やひゆうひゆう笛を鳴らす風

sera d'autunno — nel canneto il suono flautato del vento

ガブリエラ　デ　マシ/Gabriella De Masi

(イタリア/Italy)

秋の夜やドアには青きリボン掛け

sera d'autunno — sul portone un fiocco azzurro

ガブリエラ　デ　マシ/Gabriella De Masi

(イタリア/Italy)

祭壇に黄色き花を秋の夜

soir d'automne — des fleurs jaunes sur l'autel

ベルナデット クエン/Bernadette Couenne

(フランス/Ftance)

秋の夜や筆を取る間の雨の音
> nuit d'automne — pendant que j'écris la pluie tombe
>
> カメル　メスレム/Kamel Meslem
>
> （アルジェリア/Algeria）

赤ワイングラス一杯秋の夜
> autumn evening — drink a glass of red wine
>
> ナニ　マリアニ/Nani Mariani（オーストラリア/Austealia）

秋の夜やシルクのショール肩にかけ
> sera d'autunno — sulle spalle lo scialle di seta
>
> ガブリエラ　デ　マシ/Gabriella De Masi
>
> （イタリア/Italy）

月映すにはたづみ踏む秋の夜
> notte d'autunno — in una pozzanghera calpesto la luna
>
> ビットリア　コルッチ/Vittoria Colucci（イタリア/Italy）

秋の夜や砂漠の月に魅了され
> nuit d'automne — dans le désert la lune me séduit
>
> カメル　メスレム/Kamel Meslem（アルジェリア/Algeria）

秋の夜や孤独は星を傷つける
> autumn night — loneliness hurts the stars
> notte autunnale — solitudine ferisce le stelle
>
> アニコ　パップ/Anikó Papp（ハンガリー/Hungary）

胡桃割りして過ごしたる秋の夜
> soirée d'automne — sur le casse-noix la patine du temps
>
> エレナ　ズアイン/Elena Zouain（ルーマニア/Romania）

秋の夜や空の怒りか潮の渦
> nuit d'automne — déferlement de la marée colère du ciel
>
> トゥーン　チャベ/Tounès Thabet
>
> （チュニジア/Tunisia）

秋の夜や川の水面に青き月
> nuit d'automne — flotte sur la surface de la rivière la lune bleue
>
> スアド　ハジリ/Souad Hajri（チュニジア/Tunisia）

秋の夜や恋人長き黒髪を
> nuit d'automne — l'amie a de longs cheveux noirs
>
> カメル　メスレム/Kamel Meslem（アルジェリア/Algeria）

秋の夜や夢にすがりて風のままに
> nuit d'automne — je vogue au gré du vent accrochée à mes rêves
>
> スアド　ハジリ/Souad Hajri（チュニジア/Tunisia）

秋の夜徐々に減りたるチェスの駒
> autumn night — chess pieces that gradually decrease
>
> エル　ハミド/El Hamied（インドネシア/Indonesia）

秋の夜や夢への道を作る風
> notte d'autunno — il brusio del vento fa strada ai sogni
> autumn night — the buzz of the wind makes way for dreams
>
> マリア　パテルリーニ/Maria Paterlini（イタリア/Italy）

秋の夜を照らす提灯輝けり
> automne —lanterne éclairant la nuit lumière en mille reflets
>
> トゥーン　チャベ/Tounès Thabet
>
> （チュニジア/Tunisia）

秋の夜や波の轟音にしじまと平和
> sara d'autunno — pace e silenzio nel fragore dell'onda
>
> フランチェスコ　パラディノ/Francisco Palladino
> (イタリア/Italy)

秋の夜のzoom句会に猫の声
> cat's voice at zoom kukai — autumn night
>
> 中野千秋/Chiaki Nakano(日本/Japan)

金色のショパンの響き秋の宵
> soir d'automne — le son doré de chopin
>
> 向瀬美音/Mine Mukose(日本/Japan)

夜長【よなが・yonaga】
long night / longue nuit d'automne

It refers to the long autumn nights. After the autumnal equinox, the nights become longer than the days, and the long nights become more comfortable. The lingering summer heat is gone, and people are more motivated to work and read at night. This seasonal word corresponds to "hinayoi" in spring.

長き夜を持て余したる不眠症
> long night — a struggle with insomnia
>
> ポール　カルス/Paul Callus(マルタ/Malta)

雲の下彷徨ふ記憶長き夜
> longue nuit d'automne — sous les nuages ma mémoire erre
>
> カメル　メスレム/Kamel Meslem
> (アルジェリア/Algeria)

サイレンの途切れ途切れに長き夜
> long night — the intermittent sound of a siren
> lunga notte — il suono int ermittente di una sirena
>> アンジェラ　ジオルダーノ/Angela Giordano
>> （イタリア/Italy）

長き夜や結論のなき話合ひ
> long night — the debating's not resulted decision yet
>> アリアニ　ユハナ/Ariani Yuhana
>> （インドネシア/Indonesia）

風の囁き磯波歌ふ長き夜
> murmure du vent — à la longueur de nuit le ressac chante
>> カメル　メスレム/Kamel Meslem
>> （アルジェリア/Algeria）

賑やかにポーカーをして長き夜
> long night — noisy chat in poker game
>> ナッキー　クリスティジーノ/Nuky Kristijno
>> （インドネシア/Indonesia）

長き夜や月は燕の巣の近く
> longue nuit — près du nid d'hirondelles la lune
>> キャロル　デイウゼイド/Carole Dieuzeide
>> （フランス/France）

長き夜や煙草の煙まだ残り
> long night — the smoke from my cigarette is still billowing
>> エル　ハミド/El Hamied（インドネシア/Indonesia）

長き夜の分娩室に千羽鶴　　　　　　　　　亜仁寿（自訳）
> long light — the smoke from my cigarette is still billowing
>
> 　　　　　　　　　　　　タンポポ　アニス/Tanpopo Anis
> 　　　　　　　　　　　　　　　　　　（インドネシア/Indonesia）

長き夜や素早く並べたるカード
> long night — busy fingers arranging cards
>
> 　　　　　　　エル　ハミド/El Hamied（インドネシア/Indonesia）

長き夜や本を心の友として
> long nights of autumn — books keep me company
>
> 　　　　　　　　　　ポール　カルス/Paul Callus（マルタ/Malta）

長き夜や壁にランプの影差して
> lunga notte — ombra dell'abat-jour sul muro
> long night — shadow of the bedside lamp on the wall
>
> 　　　　　　　　　ダニエラ　ミッソ/Daniela Misso（イタリア/Italy）

長き夜の古き映画のノイズかな
> long night — noise and flickering old movie
>
> 　　　　　　　　　　　　中野千秋/Chiaki Nakano（日本/Japan）

長き夜や「枕草子」ひもときぬ
> longue nuit — au début de 'Makuranosoushi'
>
> 　　　　　　　　　　　向瀬美音/Mine Mukose（日本/Japan）

秋澄む【あきすむ・akisumu】
fresh air of autumn / fraicheur de l'automne

> The clear autumn air. During this time of year, the dry, cool air over the continent flows in, making the air far and wide clear. Not only what we see, but also the sounds of things seem to be clearer and more resonant.

歩み入る君の温もり秋気澄む

fresh air of autumn — he steps into the warmth of her heart
ポール　カルス/Paul Callus（マルタ/Malta）

秋気澄むちこりの花の青きこと

cielo chiaro d'autunno — l'azzurrità dei fiori di cicoria
autumn sky — the blueness of chicory flowers
カルメン　バシキリ/Carmen Baschieri
（イタリア/Italy）

秋気澄む肺を労るごとくかな

giving my lungs a treat — fresh air of autumn
ポール　カルス/Paul Callus（マルタ/Malta）

轟音を立てる小川や秋気澄む

roaring stream — clear autumn air
ruscello ruggente aria limpida autunnale.
アニコ　パップ/Anikó Papp（ハンガリー/Hungry）

秋気澄む軽きショールを肩に乗せ

fresh air of autumn — a light shawl over my shoulders
ローザ　マリア　ディ　サルバトーレ/Rosa Maria Di Salvatore
（イタリア/Italy）

静けさが肺の奥まで秋澄めり
  l'air est nettoyé — le calme se respire à grands poumons
  the air is cleared — the calm is breathed deep into my lungs
        マリー クレール　ブルゴ/marie-claire burgos
                （フランス/France）

秋澄めり葉の渦巻きを犬が追ひ
  fresh air of autumn — dogs chasing swirling leaves
        キム　オルムタック　ゴメス/Kim Olmtak Gomes（オランダ/Holland）

秋澄めり深呼吸などしてをりぬ
  the fresh air of autumn — breathe deeply
        ポール　カルス/Paul Callus（マルタ/Malta）

一列に並ぶカヤック秋澄めり
  kayaks parked in a single row — clear autumn
        ナッキー　クリスティジーノ/Nuky Kristijno（インドネシア/Indonesia）

秋澄めり葉のなき枝の鳥の黙
  fresco d'autunno — il silenzio degli uccelli sui rami vuoti
  fresh autumn — il silenzio degli uccelli sui rami vuoti
        マリア　パテルリーニ/Maria Paterlini（イタリア/Italy）

秋澄めりマティスの赤も青も好き
  fresh air of autumn — l like red of Matisse also blue
        中野千秋/Chiaki Nakano（日本/Japan）

みはるかす伊豆の島々秋澄めり
  à perte de vue les îles d'Izu — fraicheur de l'automne
        向瀬美音/Mine Mukose（日本/Japan）

秋気澄むトランペットのよく響き

> l'air d'automne clair — la trompette résonne bien
>
> 向瀬美音/Mine Mukose（日本/Japan）

秋気澄むときをり届く鵙の声

> l'air d'automne clair — de temps en temps les crie de pie-grieche
>
> 向瀬美音/Mine Mukose（日本/Japan）

冷やか【ひややか・hiyayaka】
autumn chill / fraîcheur d'automne

As autumn comes to an end and winter approaches, we sometimes feel the coolness of the air and objects that touch our skin. This feeling on the skin is cool. It is also referred to people's mannerisms and attitudes. On the other hand, the seasonal word for winter, "cold," refers to the feeling of the entire body.

秋寒や咳にニワトコシロップを

> verrà il freddo — sciroppo di sambuco contro la tosse
>
> ステファニア　アンドレオニ/Stefania Andreoni
> （イタリア/Italy）

秋寒しショールを肩に乗せ散歩

> autumn chill — my first evening walk wearing a shawl
>
> バリー　レビン/Barrie Levine（米国/United States）

秋冷のランプの灯る通りかな

> un viale illuminato da lampioni — freddo autunno
>
> a lamp lit avenue — cold autumn
>
> ダニエラ　ミッソ/Daniela Misso（イタリア/Italy）

秋冷やベンチで毛布分け合つて

> cold air of autumn — we share a blanket on the bench
>
> ポール　カルス/Paul Callus（マルタ/Malta）

秋寒しかつての愛を思ふ人

> brise froide d'automne — le vieillard se remémore ses aventures amoureuses
>
> ミュドハー　アリラキ/Mudher Aliraqi（イラク/Itaq）

秋寒し父のポンチョを着せられて

> dad put on daddy's poncho for me — cold autumn
>
> イシ　ヘルヤント/Isni Heryanto（インドネシア/Indonesia）

秋寒し子ども等と待つ雨の駅

> long wait with my children on the train platform — cold autumn rain
>
> バリー　レビン/Barrie Levine（米国/United States）

秋寒し孤独な墓へ祈る時

> autunno freddo — una preghiera per una tomba solitaria
>
> アグネーゼ　ジアロンゴ/Agnese Giallongo（イタリア/Italy）

一セント硬貨に伸ばす手寒き秋

> cold autumn — her trembling hand out streching for a dime
>
> ナッキー　クリスティジーノ/Nuky Kristijno（インドネシア/Indonesia）

冷まじや親族間で議論して

> colder air — the heated discussions with relatives
>
> aria più fredda — le accese discussion con i parenti
>
> アンジェラ　ジオルダーノ/Angela Giordano（イタリア/Italy）

小さき歩で訪れる秋朝の涼
> fraîcheur matinale—l'automne à petits pas
>> フランソワーズ　モリス/Francoise Maurice
>>> (フランス/France)

秋冷やミトンの中にゐる子猫
> cold autumn day — kitten sleeping in my mitten
>> キム　オルムタック　ゴメス/Kim Olmtak Gomes(オランダ/Holland)

秋涼し木々の葉つぱで遊ぶ風
> fraîcheur d'automne —le vent joue avec les feuilles des arbres
>> アメル　ラドヒビ　ベント　チャディー/Amel Ladhibi Bent Chadly
>>> (チュニジア/Tunisia)

村人は薪を運びて秋寒し
> colder autumn — villagers push firewood carts
>> キム　オルムタック　ゴメス/Kim Olmtak Gomes
>>> (オランダ/Holland)

冷ややかやわが分身の水の上
> autumn chill — my alter ego on the surface of water
>> 中野千秋/Chiaki Nakano(日本/Japan)

秋寒し教室にある人体図
> fraîcheur d'automne — l'écorché dans la salle de classe
>> 向瀬美音/Mine Mukose(日本/Japan)

うつしよは地獄絵のごとそぞろ寒
> froideur — le monde comme une image de l'enfer
>> 向瀬美音/Mine Mukose(日本/Japan)

冷やかや遺産相続長引きて

> froideur — succession bien prolongée
>
> 向瀬美音/Mine Mukose（日本/Japan）

爽やか【さわやか・sawayaka】
fresh air of autumn/ fraîcheur d'automne

The word "refreshing" originally meant a light, dry autumn breeze. Next, it came to mean the feeling of being enveloped by the wind, and furthermore, it came to mean the pleasant feeling of autumn.

新涼や木の葉も震へ出す頃か

> fraîcheur d'automne — bientôt les feuilles tremblent
>
> ソニア　ベン　アマール/Sonia Ben Ammar（チュニジア/Tunisia）

爽やかやシナモンスティック味見して

> fresco tonificante — gustando un bastoncino di cannella
> fresh crisp brisk — tasting a cinnamon stick
>
> ダニエラ　ミッソ/Daniela Misso（イタリア/Italy）

爽やかな風に帽子をさらはれぬ

> fresh air of autumn — my hat flies away in a sudden breeze
>
> バリー　レビン/Barrie Levine（米国/United States）

爽やかや君の秘密の手紙持ち

> fraîcheur d'automne — ta lettre dissimulée dans ma poche
>
> リミ　ラルビ/Limi Larbi（モロッコ/Morocco）

爽やかやダルメシアンと朝の森
> morning walk with dalmatian in the urban forest — crispy brisk
>
>> イシ　ヘルヤント/Isni Heryanto
>>
>>> （インドネシア/Indonesia）

爽やかや風の調べの新しく
> a fresh start — the winds of change sing a new key
>
>> ポエトリー　プロン/poetry prone

新涼やうなじに君の息かかり
> fraîcheur d'automne—ton souffle sur ma nuque
>
>> ベルナデット　クエン/Bernadette Couenne
>>
>>> （フランス/France）

新涼や旅行チケット引き出しに
> fraîcheur d'automne — dans le tiroir il y a encore un billet valable pour le voyage
>
>> アブダラ　ハジイ/Abdallah Hajji
>>
>>> （モロッコ/Morocco）

爽やかや単身赴任の自己紹介　　　　　　　亜仁寿（自訳）
> fresh crisp brisk — self-introduction of tanshin funin
>
>> タンポポ　アニス/Tanpopo Anis
>>
>>> （インドネシア/Indonesia）

爽やかや窓を大きく美容室
> fresh air of autumn — beauty salon with large window
>
>> 中野千秋/Chiaki Nakano（日本/Japan）

新涼や心のしこり癒す風
> fraîcheur d'automne- — le vent apaise le cœur
>
> 向瀬美音/Mine Mukose(日本/Japan)

まとめ髪放ちてみたる涼新た
> fraîcheur d'automne — dénoue mes cheveux noirs
>
> 向瀬美音/Mine Mukose(日本/Japan)

新涼や異国の首都に一人立ち
> fraîcheur d'automne — seule dans la capitale étrangère
>
> 向瀬美音/Mine Mukose(日本/Japan)

爽籟に応ふるごとく椰子揺れる
> fraîcheur d'automne — les cocotiers se balancent
>
> 向瀬美音/Mine Mukose(日本/Japan)

秋気澄む少女の奏づバイオリン
> fraîcheur d'automne — une fille joue du violon
>
> 向瀬美音/Mine Mukose(日本/Japan)

爽やかやペン先すいすい進む朝
> fraîcheur — la plume glisse bien
>
> 向瀬美音/Mine Mukose(日本/Japan)

秋麗【あきうらら・akiurara】
beautiful autumn / belle journée d'automne

A sunny autumn day. A beautiful, shining, and enchanting day in spring.

秋麗や君の気分の変はる色
> beautiful autumn — the colours of her changing moods
>> ポール　カルス/Paul Callus（マルタ/Malta）

秋うらら地球のコート金色に
> manto d'autunno — si veste la terra con spruzzi d'oro
>> シルビア　ビストッチ/Silvia Bistocchi（イタリア/Italy）

真つ白な雲の旅路や秋麗
> autunno — sul viaggio degli uccelli nuvole bianche
>> アンナ　リモンディ/Anna Rimondi（イタリア/Italy）

蜘蛛の巣は手紙の代はり秋うらら
> une belle journée d'automne — aujourd'hui pas de lettres juste une araignée
>> イメルダ　セン/Imelda Senn（スイス/Switzerland）

秋麗や光はきつと天使なる
> luci d'autunno — forse è soltanto un angelo
>> ジオンバナ　ジオイア/Giovanna Gioia（イタリア/Italy）

川底に転がる小石秋うらら
> ciottoli sul fondo del fiume — bella giornata autunnale
> pebbles at the bottom of the river — nice fall day
>> ダニエラ　ミッソ/Daniela Misso（イタリア/Italy）

日の中に伸びをする猫秋麗

> nice fall day ― a cat stretching in the sun
>
> ダニエラ　ミッソ/Daniela Misso（イタリア/Italy）

牧場の羊の平和秋うらら

> aria d'autunno ― il tranquillo brucare delle pecore
>
> アルベルタ　カテリナ　マトリ/Alberta Caterina Mattoli（イタリア/Italy）

秋麗ゆつくり沈む水面の葉

> beautiful autumn ― floating leaves slowly sink into ponds
>
> アリアニ　ユハン/Ariani Yuhan（インドネシア/Indonesia）

秋うらら日差しの中をドライブし

> driving into the sunset ― beautiful autumn
>
> クリスティーナ　チン/Christina Chin（マレーシア/Malaysia）

秋うらら隠れ家のごと山のカフェ

> bright autumn day ― a very beautiful hidden cafe surrounded by mountains
>
> スカディ　ソノカヨ/Sukadi Sonokaryo
>
> （インドネシア/Indonesia）

羽広げたる白鳥よ秋麗

> belle journée d'automne ― le cygne blanc déploie ses ailes
>
> ベルナデット　クエン/Bernadette Couenne
>
> （フランス/France）

秋麗葉つぱの渦の多様性

> beautiful autumn ― leaves swirl in a dance of diversity
>
> キム　オルムタック　ゴメス/Kim Olmtak Gomes（オランダ/Holland）

歩と落葉を数えてみたり秋うらら

> belle journée d'automne — compter les pas et les feuilles qui tombent
>
> エレナ　ズアイン/Elena Zouain（ルーマニア/Romania）

秋うらら嘴ぶつける二羽の鳥

> beautiful autumn — a pair of birds clashing beaks
>
> エル　ハミド/El Hamied（インドネシア/Indonesia）

秋麗や羊の放牧静かなる

> aria d'autunno — il tranquillo brucare delle pecore.
>
> アルベルタ　カテリナ　マトリ/Alberta Caterina Mattoli（イタリア/Italy）

秋うらら番の雁が湖をゆく

> beautiful autumn — a pair of geese crossing the colorful lake
>
> タンポポ　アニス/Tanpopo Anis
>
> （インドネシア/Indonesia）

秋麗ビルを浮かべて濠の水

> beautiful autumn — buildings float on the moat water
>
> 中野千秋/Chiaki Nakano（日本/Japan）

秋麗や屋根さ緑の迎賓館

> belle journée d'automne — le toit vert de la state guest house
>
> 向瀬美音/Mine Mukose（日本/Japan）

忙しなき子等の婚姻秋うらら

> belle journée d'automne-mariages successifs des enfants
>
> 向瀬美音/Mine Mukose（日本/Japan）

秋麗や采女の袖に明日香風

向瀬美音/Mine Mukose（日本/Japan）

秋麗やうまさけ三輪の巫女の舞

向瀬美音/Mine Mukose（日本/Japan）

> ### 秋深し【あきふかし・akifukashi】
> **deep autumn / automne profond**
>
> It refers to the deepening of autumn, or late autumn (October), when loneliness is in the air, but it is also probably a psychological term.

無関心な人々の影秋深し

profondo autunno — persone indifferenti diventano ombre
deep autumn — indifferent people becomes shadows

クリスティーナ　プルビレンティ/Cristina Pulvirenti
（イタリア/Italy）

黄昏の古き小径や秋深し

passi di vecchio nel tramonto autunnale — fino al cancello

アンナ　リモンディ/Anna Rimondi（イタリア/Italy）

秋深し祖父の時計が音鳴らし

profondo autunno — rintocchi dell'orologio a pendolo
deep autumn — strokes of the grandfather clock

ダニエラ　ミッソ/Daniela Misso（イタリア/Italy）

秋深し瞳の奥のノスタルジー

> automne profond — la nostalgie au fond des yeux
>
> オルファ　クチュク　ブハディダ/Olfa Kchouk Bouhadida
> (チュニジア/Tunisia)

秋深し古きピアノに母おらず

> deep autumn — the old piano without mom's fingers
>
> タンポポ　アニス/Tanpopo Anis(インドネシア/Indonesia)

秋深し眠りに入りゆく大地

> late autumn — grass withers and the land goes dormant
>
> キム　オルムタック　ゴメス/Kim Olmtak Gomes
> (オランダ/Holland)

道化師の悲しき笑顔秋深し　　　　　　　　　　亜仁寿（自訳）

> the clown's sad smile — deep autumn
>
> タンポポ　アニス/Tanpopo Anis(インドネシア/Indonesia)

秋深し祖父の視線の虚ろなる

> deep autumn — a grandfather's blank gaze
>
> エル　ハミド/El Hamied(インドネシア/Indonesia)

秋深し影に濃くなる太陽のしみ

> macchie di luce — sempre più in penombra questo autunno
>
> アントニオ　ジラルディ/Antonio Girardi(イタリア/Italy)

ヴィオロンの弦の壊れて秋深し

> deep autumn — my violin string has broken
>
> タンポポ　アニス/Tanpopo Anis(インドネシア/Indonesia)

秋深し君は黒髪解き放ち

> deep autumn — unraveling the night in your black hair
>
> ジョノ　ファドリ/Jono Fadli（インドネシア/Indonesia）

秋深し薔薇の光に重さあり

> toamnă profundă — greutatea luminii pe trandafiri
> automne profond — le poids de la lumière sur les roses
>
> マリン　ラダ/Marin Rada（ルーマニア/Romania）

秋深しや君の唇いよよ濃く

> deep autumn — the crimson colour of your lips
>
> ナッキー　クリスティジーノ/Nuky Kristijno（インドネシア/Indonesia）

秋深し珈琲店の赤いドア

> deep autumn — red door of coffee shop
>
> 中野千秋/Chiaki Nakano（日本/Japan）

遠ざかる列車の汽笛秋深し

> le train siffle au loin — automne profond
>
> 向瀬美音/Mine Mukose（日本/Japan）

指揮棒の先に黙あり秋深し

> automne profond — silence à la baguette de chef d'orchestre
>
> 向瀬美音/Mine Mukose（日本/Japan）

行く秋【いくあき・ikuaki】
passing of autumn / fin de l'automne

The passing of autumn. The transition from autumn to winter. Unlike "going spring," this seasonal term is filled with a sense of desolation and expresses a deep regret for the passing of autumn. The word "going" is used to describe the passing of the seasons, as if one were a traveler, but it refers only to spring and autumn, and not to "going summer" or "going winter".

行く秋の珈琲店のドアチャイム
> passing of autumn — door chime of coffee shop
>
> 中野千秋/Chiaki Nakano（日本/Japan）

行く秋や住所録また一つ消し
> fin de l'automne — j'efface un carnet d'adresses
>
> 向瀬美音/Mine Mukose（日本/Japan）

行く秋やときをり届く波の音
> fin de l'automne — de temps en temps bruit des vagues
>
> 向瀬美音/Mine Mukose（日本/Japan）

行く秋や美しきもの全て連れ
> fin d'automne — il apporte tout ce qui est beau
>
> 向瀬美音/Mine Mukose（日本/Japan）

晩秋 【ばんしゅう・banshu】
late autumn / fin d'automne

Autumn is divided into early autumn, mid-autumn, and late autumn. As autumn deepens, there is a sense of loneliness as winter approaches.

晩秋やますます強く風の音

> late autumn — sound of the wind gets stronger
>
> ナッキー　クリスティジーノ/Nuky Kristijno
> （インドネシア/Indonesia）

晩秋や祖父の時計の音のする

> autunno inoltrato — rintocchi dell'orologio a pendolo
> late autumn — strokes of the grandfather clock
>
> ダニエラ　ミッソ/Daniela Misso（イタリア/Italy）

晩秋や本の隙間に猫の声

> late autumn — cat's voice between books
>
> 中野千秋/Chiaki Nakano（日本/Japan）

ヴィオロンはハ短調なり末の秋

> morceau de violon en do mineur — fin de l'automne
>
> 向瀬美音/Mine Mukose（日本/Japan）

秋惜しむ【あきおしむ・akioshimu】
autumnal regret / regrets d'automne

Autumn is the season word for regretting the passing of autumn. It is a more subjective term than "autumn is going". It has been considered from ancient times as a poetic sentiment relative to "regretting the passing of spring.

日本語の読めぬメニューや秋惜しむ　　　　　　　亜仁寿（自訳）
| autumnal regret — unreadable japanese dishes menu
| 　　　　　　　タンポポ　アニス/Tanpopo Anis（インドネシア/Indonesia）

秋惜しむ本に挟める黄色き葉
| remaining autumn — in my book a yellow leaf
| mùa thu còn lại — trong cuốn sách của tôi một chiếc lá vàng
| 　　　　　　　ディン　ヌグエン/Dinh Nguyen（ベトナム/Vietnam）

歩む道一期一会や秋惜しむ　　　　　　　亜仁寿（自訳）
| the path I walk once in the lifetime—autumn regret
| 　　　　　　　タンポポ　アニス/Tanpopo Anis（インドネシア/Indonesia）

秋惜しむ首を傾げてテディベア
| regret the end of autumn — teddy bear tilting its head
| 　　　　　　　中野千秋/Chiaki Nakano（日本/Japan）

Kigo Gallery-1

鰯雲/cirrocumulus …p151（鰯雲と富士山・山梨県精進湖）

月/moon …p153（名月と月見団子と芒）

天の川/milky way …p195（上高地の天の川・長野県）

霧/fog …p237（霧の白川郷・岐阜県）

天(てんもん)文

(tenmon)
astronomy
astronomie

秋の日【あきのひ・akinohi】
bright autumn day / soleil d'automne

It is the light of an autumn day, an autumn day. The autumn sun brings lingering summer heat, but it gradually freshens up, and in late fall, the sun's rays visibly fade. The autumn day gradually becomes shorter after the autumnal equinox, and by the time winter approaches, the days all go down at once, as they say.

ゴンドラで愛の告白秋日和

> bright autumn day — love declaration on the gondola
>
> タンポポ　アニス/Tanpopo Anis（インドネシア/Indonesia）

廃屋に形見いくつか秋日差す

> deserted cabin — autumn sun illuminates the mementos
>
> キム　オルムタック　ゴメス/Kim Olmtak Gomes（オランダ/Holland）

秋の日や蝶はその影踊らせて

> lumière d'automne — dans la cour un papillon fait danser son ombre
>
> ナディン　レオン/Nadine Léon（フランス/France）

をちこちに子らの自転車秋日差す

> autumn sun — scattered with children's bikes
>
> ナニ　マリアニ/Nani Mariani（オーストラリア/Australia）

秋日和孤独な馬のゐる浜辺

> autumn sun — lonely horse ride on a lonely beach
>
> ナッキー　クリスティジーノ/Nuky Kristijno（インドネシア/Indonesia）

秋の日のしじまに滑り込みにけり

> soleil d'automne — je me faufile en silence
>
> エリック　デスピエール/Eric Despierre（フランス/France）

秋の日や嬰児(みどりご)の泣く乳母車

> autumn sun — the baby cries in her strollers
>
> ナッキー　クリスティジーノ/Nuky Kristijno
>
> （インドネシア/Indonesia）

秋の日や風のみ変へる空の青

> soare de toamnă — doar vântul schimbă culoarea albastră
>
> soleil d'automne — seul le vent change de couleur bleu
>
> マリン　ラダ/Marin Rada（ルーマニア/Romania）

玄関に眠る猫ゐる秋日和

> shy autumn sun — on the doorstep my cat's sunbathing
>
> アドニス　シザー/Adoni Cizar（パレスティナ/the Palestine）

秋の日や桑の初めの黄色き葉

> rayon d'automne — la première feuille jaune du mûrier
>
> アブダラ　ハジイ/Abdallah Hajji（モロッコ/Morocco）

秋日さす罅あるフロントガラスかな

> early autumn sun — reflections on a cracked windshield
>
> ジェリー　ブラビ/Gerry Bravi（カナダ/Canada）

傾けた細きカップに秋日差す

> in the slender cup between the chin and shoulder rests the autumn sun
>
> プロビール　ギュプタ/Probir Gupta（インド/India）

穀物の畑に黄色く秋日差す
  the yellow sun in autumn — wheat fields
    キム　オルムタック　ゴメス/Kim Olmtak Gomes（オランダ/Holland）

秋の日や君の乾いたくちびるに
  soif d'automne — le soleil de midi sur tes lèvres séchées
    リミ　ラルビ/Limi Larbi（モロッコ/Morocco）

秋の日や旧家に声の戻りたる
  sole d'autunno — tornano le voci nella vecchia casa
    ミレラ　エステル　ペノンヌ　マシ/Mirella Ester Pennone Masi
    （イタリア/Italy）

秋の日や月桂樹の葉に土香り
  soleil d'automne — feuille à feuille le laurier-sauce parfume le sol
    フランソワーズ　デニオ-ルリエーブル/Françoise Deniaud-Lelièvre
    （フランス/France）

秋の日や窓の水滴消えてゆき
  soleil d'automne — la buée s'efface sur la fenêtre
    エレナ　ズアイン/Elena Zouain（ルーマニア/Romani）

秋の日や故郷の道に古き歌
  soleil d'automne — sur le chemin du village natal une vieille chanson
    アブダラ　ハジイ/Abdallah Hajji（モロッコ/Morocco）

雌ライオン首の後ろに受く秋日
  back of her neck autumn sun on locks of hair the lioness
    プロビール　ギュプタ/Probir Gupta（インド/India）

秋光や空を捕へる水溜り

> lumière utomnale — des flaques éblouissantes des flaques éblouissantes
>
> ナディン　レオン/Nadine Léon（フランス/France）

メランコリー覆ひ尽くして秋日差す

> tiepido autunno — un raggio di sole copre la malinconia
> warm autumn — a ray of sunshine covers the melancholy
>
> マリア　パテルリーニ/Maria Paterlini（イタリア/Italy）

秋の日やちさき雀は影見つけ

> lumière d automne — le petit moineau découvre le côté ombre
>
> ラシダ　ジェルビ/Rachida Jerbi（チュニジア/Tunisia）

秋の日や波の輝きクリスタル

> sole d'autunno — con schegge di cristallo l'onda risplende
>
> ジナ　ボナセーラ/Gina Bonasera（イタリア/Italy）

煌めきてグラスの水に秋日差す

> a glass of water — twinkling autumn sunshine
>
> タンポポ　アニス/Tanpopo Anis
> （インドネシア/Indonesia）

水底のジオラマ世界秋日和

> diorama world on the bottom of the water — ninc fall day
>
> 中野千秋/Chiaki Nakano（日本/Japan）

秋の日の山のかたちに島がある

> bright autumn day — island in the shape of mountain
>
> 中野千秋/Chiaki Nakano（日本/Japan）

四世代集ふ秋日やお食ひ初め

les jours d'automne quatre générations se réunissent — premier repas du bébé

向瀬美音/Mine Mukose（日本/Japan）

> **秋晴**【あきばれ・akibare】
> nice fall day / belle journée d'automne
>
> Clear autumn weather. It is the same thing as "autumn weather," but the word "autumn weather" has a slightly stronger sound than "autumn weather.

秋晴や果実に蜂の群がりて

belle journée d'automne — guêpes aux fruits mûres

ラシダ　ジェルビ/Rachida Jerbi（チュニジア/Tunisia）

君の目の深さに迷ひ秋の晴

autumn clearing — i get lost in the depths of your eyes
schiarita autunnale — mi perdo nel profondo dei tuoi occhi

アンジェラ　ジオルダーノ/Angela Giordano（イタリア/Italy）

秋晴や木立の描く万華鏡

nice fall day — the trees a kaleidoscopic painting

キム　オルムタック　ゴメス/Kim Olmtak Gomes（オランダ/Holland）

出航の準備整ふ秋の晴

bright autumn day — she is ready to sail

ナッキー　クリスティジーノ/Nuky Kristijno

（インドネシア/Indonesia）

放射線療法初日秋の晴

> on this bright day — the first radiotherapy session
> in questo giorno luminoso — la prima seduta di radioterapia
>> アンジェラ　ジオルダーノ/Angela Giordano（イタリア/Italy）

秋晴や後回しする家のこと

> putting off house chores — nice fall day
>> クリスティーナ　チン/Christina Chin（マレーシア/Malaysia）

秋晴や舳先に丸い水平線

> nice fall day — rounded horizon in front of bow
>> 中野千秋/Chiaki Nakano（日本/Japan）

秋の色【あきのいろ・akinoiro】
autumn scene / paysage d'automne

Autumnal colors. Specifically, it refers to the colors of golden rice paddies and mountains tinted with autumn leaves.

秋の色のろ羊歯の上跳ねてをり

> couleurs d'automne — bondissant des fougères le jeune chevreuil
>> イザベル　カルバロ　テール/Isabelle Carvalho Teles（フランス/France）

白き筆湿らせてより秋の色

> moistening his brush white turns into an autumn scene
>> キム　オルムタック　ゴメス/Kim Olmtak Gomes（オランダ/Holland）

秋の色孤独の去つてゆきにけり

> loneliness gone gazing at those autumn colors
>> ナッキー　クリスティジーノ/Nuky Kristijno（インドネシア/Indonesia）

秋の色泉の側に座る平和
> couleurs d'automne — assis près de la source me voici en paix
>
> ジェラール　ドユモン/Gérard Dumon（フランス/France）

街角に目を和ませて秋の色
> autumn colors — every corner of the city warms my eyes
>
> エル　ハミド/El Hamied（インドネシア/Indonesia）

鉱床に秋色をした瑪瑙かな
> autumn colours — mines for precious agate
>
> ザヤ　ヨウクハンナ/Zaya youkhanna
>
> （オーストラリア/Australia）

薄つすらと微笑む空は秋の色
> tenui sorrisi — malinconico autunno nel mio cielo
> faint smiles — melancholic autumn in my sky
>
> マリア　パテルリーニ/Maria Paterlini（イタリア/Italy）

みづうみや瑠璃色といふ秋の色
> autumn scene — the lake of lapis lazuli color
>
> 中野千秋/Chiaki Nakano（日本/Japan）

白き船統べ完璧な秋の色
> ajouter un bateau blanc — couleur d'automne parfaite
>
> 向瀬美音/Mine Mukose（日本/Japan）

ゆくりかにまほろば大和秋の色
>
> 向瀬美音/Mine Mukose（日本/Japan）

秋の声 【あきのこえ・akinokoe】
autumn voice / voix d'automne

The sound of a quiet noise. It does not necessarily mean the sound of nature, such as the wind or a murmuring stream, nor does it mean the sound of people making noises.

秋の声踏まれて匂ふ森の道

> tthe trodden path of forest scent — autumn voice
>
> クリスティーナ　チン/Christina Chin（マレーシア/Malaysia）

秋の声遠くで誰か伐採す

> voix d'automne — au loin quelqu'un coupe du bois
>
> ラシダ　ジェルビ/Rachida Jerbi（チュニジア/Tunisia）

秋の声風に葉擦れの音のして

> autumn whispers — rustling leaves in the wind
>
> ダニエラ　ロディ/Daniela Rodi（フィンランド/Finland）

森に東風赤くなりたる秋の声

> voix d'automne — le rugissement du vent d'est sur la forêt
>
> マリン　ラダ/Marin Rada（ルーマニア/Romania）

祖父の部屋の止まつたラジオ秋の声

> radio without signal in grandpa's room — autumn voice
>
> イシ　ヘルヤント/Isni Heryanto（インドネシア/Indonesia）

秋の声窓に静かに葉の落ちる

> autumn voice — leaves fall silently past my window
>
> タンポポ　アニス/Tanpopo Anis（インドネシア/Indonesia）

葦畑よく聞こえたる秋の声
> champ de roseaux — très audible la voix d'automne
>> アブダラ　ハジイ/Abdallah Hajji（モロッコ/Morocco）

秋の声きこりの笑ひ森満たす
> voix d'automne — éclats de rires des bûcherons emplissant la forêt
>> カディジャ　エル　ブルカディ/Khadija El Bourkadi（モロッコ/Morocco）

廃屋より葦のざわめき秋の声
> voix d'automne — dans la maison abandonnée le bruissement des roseaux
>> アブダラ　ハジイ/Abdallah Hajji（モロッコ/Morocco）

秋の声足元の葉の軋みたる
> voice of autumn — the crunching of leaves under my feet
>> ポール　カルス/Paul Callus（マルタ/Malta）

秋の声色づく木々の溜息よ
> voix d'automne — le soupir des feuilles jaunes
>> アブダラ　ハジイ/Abdallah Hajji（モロッコ/Morocco）

秋の声かりがね空を暗くせり
> voix d'automne — les canards sauvages obscurcissent le ciel
>> ラシダ　ジェルビ/Rachida Jerbi（チュニジア/Tunisia）

秋の声赤と黄色の葉が踊る
> echoes of autumn — the red and yellow leaves dance in the wind
> echi d'autunno — le foglie rosse e gialle danzano al vento
>> アンジェラ　ジオルダーノ/Angela Giordano（イタリア/Italy）

瞑想の呼吸の深く秋の声
> autumn voice — deep breathe in meditation
>
> タンポポ　アニス/Tanpopo Anis（インドネシア/Indonesia）

秋の声響きてよりの憂鬱かな
> with the echoes of autumn in the heart the dull melancholy
> con gli echi d'autunno nel cuore la cupa malinconia
>
> アンジェラ　ジオルダーノ/Angela Giordano（イタリア/Italy）

ばたばたと鳩の羽ばたき秋の声　　　　　　　亜仁寿（自訳）
> flapping pigeons' wings — autumn voice
>
> タンポポ　アニス/Tanpopo Anis（インドネシア/Indonesia）

唐松と樅に羽音や秋の声
> suoni d'autunno — tra i larici e gli abeti voli chiassosi
> sounds of autumn — among the larches and fir trees noisy flights
>
> パトリチア　カバローネ/Patrizia Cavallone（イタリア/Italy）

秋の声雨樋を打つ雨の音
> voce d'autunno — ticchettio della pioggia sulla grondaia
> autumn voice — tinkling of rain on the gutter
>
> ダニエラ　ミッソ/Daniela Misso（イタリア/Italy）

楓の葉赤く染めたる秋の声
> le foglie d'acero tinte di rosso — voce d'autunno
>
> リタ　モア/Rita Moar（イタリア/Italy）

ゆつくりとなりゆく歩調秋の声
> autumn voice — the quick urban footsteps slowing down
>
> キム　オルムタック　ゴメス/Kim Olmtak Gomes（オランダ/Holland）

学祭を応援したる秋の声　　　　　　　　　　　　亜仁寿（自訳）
　autumn voice — cheering for campus festival
　　　　　　　　　　　　　　　タンポポ　アニス/Tanpopo Anis
　　　　　　　　　　　　　　　　　　　　（インドネシア/Indonesia）

ひつそりと葉つぱの中を秋の声
　solitudine — la voce dell'autunno vibra tra foglie
　solitude — the autumn voice vibrates between leaves
　　　　　　　　　クリスティーナ　プルビレンティ/Cristina Pulvirenti
　　　　　　　　　　　　　　　　　　　　（イタリア/Italy）

恍惚の月のソナタよ秋の声
　moonlight sonata — rapturous autumnal voice
　　　　　　　　　　　キム　オルムタック　ゴメス/Kim Olmtak Gomes
　　　　　　　　　　　　　　　　　　　　（オランダ/Holland）

木々を抜け風の囁く秋の声
　cool wind whispers low through the branches of the trees — autumn's silent song
　　　　　　　　　　　　　　　エウジェン/Eugene（ロシア/Russia）

みづうみに掛かる浮橋秋の声
　floating bridge over the lake — autumn voice
　　　　　　　　　　　　　　　中野千秋/Chiaki Nakano（日本/Japan）

湯浴みして聴き分けてゐる秋の声
　baignade — distinguer la voix d'automne
　　　　　　　　　　　　　　　向瀬美音/Mine Mukose（日本/Japan）

秋の空【あきのそら・akinosora】
autumn sky / ciel d'automne

A clear sky. In autumn, we often experience rain, but later, the sky clears up and becomes refreshing when a migratory high-pressure system from the continent covers the area.

秋の空色彩全て含まれて

> ciel d'automne — il voit de toutes les couleurs
>
> オルファ　クチュク　ブハディダ/Olfa Kchouk Bouhadida
>
> (チュニジア/Tunisia)

鳥はもう歌はなくなり秋の空

> ciel d'automne — l'oiseau ne chante plus
>
> アブダラ　ハジイ/Abdallah Hajji(モロッコ/Morocco)

秋の空メランコリーな色をして

> autumn sky — the colours of melancholy
>
> ポール　カルス/Paul Callus(マルタ/Malta)

秋の空アガパンテスの枯れにけり

> ciel d'automne — les agapanthes presque toutes fanées
>
> フランソワーズ　デニウ-ルリエーブル/Françoise Deniaud-Lelièvre
>
> (フランス/France)

秋空や落暉に赤くなる心

> ciel d'automne — sous le soleil couchant mon esprit rougit
>
> カメル　メスレム/Kamel Meslem
>
> (アルジェリア/Algeria)

秋空や猫は腹見せ砂の上
> hot gravel ― cat's tummy turning to the autumn sky
>> キム　オルムタック　ゴメス/Kim Olmtak Gomes
>>> (オランダ/Holland)

木々の葉の隙間に迫る秋の空
> cracks in the trees' foliage ― autumn sky creeping through
>> キム　オルムタック　ゴメス/Kim Olmtak Gomes
>>> (オランダ/Holland)

同じ目より笑みと涙や秋の空
> rires et larmes dans le même œil ― ciel d automne
>> フテン　フルチ/Feten Fourti(チュニジア/Tunisia)

遠くより鳥の啼き声秋の空
> ciel d'automne ― le chant des oiseaux s'entend de loin
>> カメル　メスレム/Kamel Meslem(アルジェリア/Algeria)

白鷺の数を数へて秋の空
> counting white herons in flight ― autumn sky
>> クリスティーナ　チン/Christina Chin
>>> (マレーシア/Malaysia)

秋の空馬の毛並みは陽に映えて
> cielo d'autunno ― li manto del cavallo lucente al sole
>> アルベルタ　カテリナ　マトリ/Alberta Caterina Mattoli(イタリア/Italy)

秋空や飛行機雲の付けた傷
> scie bianche ― graffi nel cielo terso d'autunno
>> ガブリエラ　デ　マシ/Gabriella De Masi(イタリア/Italy)

秋空の青さの中に広き海
> blue sky in autumn — an expanse of sea
>> キム　オルムタック　ゴメス/Kim Olmtak Gomes（オランダ/Holland）

窓いっぱい広がる秋の朝の空
> dimineți de toamnă — cerul umple fereastra
> autumn mornings — the sky fills the window
>> ミレラ　ブライレーン/Mirela Brailean（ルーマニア/Romania）

秋空や日を目覚めませる雁の声
> autumn sky — wild geese sing the sun awake
>> マリリン　アッシュボッフ/Marilyn Ashbaugh（米国/United States）

秋空の下に生命溢れたり
> ancora sotto — l'alto cielo d'autunno sempre più vita
> still under the high autumn — more and more life
>> クリスティーナ　プルビレンティ/Cristina Pulvirenti（イタリア/Italy）

秋空や凧は浜辺に見捨てられ
> ciel d'automne — un cerf-volant abandonné sur la plage
>> エレナ　ズアイン/Elena Zouain（ルーマニア/Romania）

秋空や川に沿つて羽ばたきの音(ね)
> ciel d'automne — battement d'ailes le long du ruisseau
>> エレナ　ズアイン/Elena Zouain（ルーマニア/Romania）

秋空やその青色の果てしなく
> ciel d'automne — le bleu cède sa place difficilement
>> オルファ　クチュク　ブハディタ/Olfa Kchouk Bouhadida
>> （チュニジア/Tunisia）

秋空やチャペルに響く「アヴェマリア」　　　　亜仁寿（自訳）
| autumn sky — Ave Maria reverberating in the chapel
　　　　　　　　タンポポ　アニス／Tanpopo Anis（インドネシア／Indonesia）

届いたよニュースニーカー秋の空　　　　　　　亜仁寿（自訳）
| the new sneakers have arrived — autumn sky
　　　　　　　　タンポポ　アニス／Tanpopo Anis（インドネシア／Indonesia）

秋空や葉は渦巻きて風と舞ふ
| ciel d'automne doux — les feuilles en tourbillon, dansent avec le vent
　　　　　　　　　　　　　　エウジェン／Eugene（ロシア／Russia）

秋空をさ迷ふ雲は絵を描く
| sous le ciel d'automne — les nuages vagabonds peignent des tableaux
　　　　　　　　　　　　　　エウジェン／Eugene（ロシア／Russia）

土砂降りのあとの晴れ間や秋の空
| autumn weather — after the downpour the reemerging sun
　　　　　　　　　　　ポール　カルス／Paul Callus（マルタ／Malta）

足揃え飛ぶ水溜り秋の空
| mon saut à pieds joints fait éclater le ciel d'automne dans la flaque d'eau
　　　　　　　　　　ナディン　レオン／Nadine Léon（フランス／France）

秋空やすでに疲れたやうな木々
| against the autumn sky — trees already show barrenness of winter
　　　　　キム　オルムタック　ゴメス／Kim Olmtak Gomes（オランダ／Holland）

桃色に暮れる秋空脈早し
> sunset in autumn sky ― pulse quickens
>> プロビール　ギュプタ/Probir Gupta（インド/India）

秋空にまだ灰色のひとところ
> autumn sky ― there are still remnants of gray
>> エル　ハミド/El Hamied（インドネシア/Indonesia）

無限なる愛のごとくに秋の空
> autumn sky ― her unlimited love
>> ザヤ　ヨウクハンナ/Zaya youkhanna
>> （オーストラリア/Australia）

海よりも青の深くて秋の空
> bluer than the sea ― autumn sky
>> クリスティーナ　チン/Christina Chin
>> （マレーシア/Malaysia）

もうつばめ飛ぶことのなき秋の空
> non vola più la rondine nel cielo ― vuoto d'autunno
> no longer flies the swallow in the sky ― emptiness of autumn
>> マリア　パテルルリーニ/Maria Paterlini
>> （イタリア/Italy）

雲間より奈落のごとし秋の空
> the abyss between cloud ― autumn sky
>> 中野千秋/Chiaki Nakano（日本/Japan）

空高し【そらたかし・soratakashi】
high sky of autumn / ciel haut d'automne

In autumn, the atmosphere becomes clearer and the sky seems higher. This is "autumn high," but "sky high" is more common

雲にある青き斑点秋高し

> high sky of autumn — blue-patched clouds
>
> ポール　カルス/Paul Callus（マルタ/Malta）

空高し北極に吾も加はりぬ

> ciel haut d'automne—au pôle nord je te rejoins
>
> アメル　ラヒビ　ベント　チャディ/Amel Ladhibi Bent Chadly
>
> （チュニジア/Tunisia）

空高し女の欲はきりがなく

> the quest of women breaking the glass ceiling — high sky of autumn
>
> バーバラ　オルムタック/Barbara Olmtak
>
> （オランダ/Holland）

秋高し青き瞳の新生児

> high sky of autumn — blue eyes of the newborn baby
>
> マフィズディン　チュードハリ/Mafizuddin Chowdhury
>
> （インド/India）

秋高し気分を癒す一人旅

> igh sky of autumn — solo trip for relaxation
>
> タンポポ　アニス/Tanpopo Anis
>
> （インドネシア/Indonesia）

富士山へ伸びる国道空高し　　　　　　　　　　　　亜仁寿（自訳）

| national highway leading to Mount Fuji — high sky of autumn

タンポポ　アニス/Tanpopo Anis
（インドネシア/Indonesia）

空高し空の重さが山の上

| si avverte il peso — alto cielo d'autunno sulla montagna
| the weight is felt — high autumn sky on the mountain

クリスティーナ　プルビエンティ/Cristina Pulvirenti
（イタリア/Italy）

心てふ無限の器秋高し

| heart is a vessel of infinite capacity — high autumn sky

中野千秋/Chiaki Nakano（日本/Japan）

白波の寄する海岸秋高し

| flots écumeux au rivage — ciel haut d'automne

向瀬美音/Mine Mukose（日本/Japan）

隠し事なくなる齢秋高し

| l'âge sans secret — ciel haut d'automne

向瀬美音/Mine Mukose（日本/Japan）

秋の雲【あきのくも・akinokumo】
autumn clouds / nuages d'automne

Autumn clouds float in and out of the clear azure sky. Scaly clouds, cirro-cumulus clouds, and other white autumn clouds are clear and impressive.

秋の雲空は神秘のメランコリー
| nuages d'automne — la mélancolie inexpliquée du ciel
リミ　ラルビ/Limi Larbi（モロッコ/Morocco）

秋の雲大地は水を切望す
| blancs et légers les — la terre avide d'eau
ラシダ　ジェルビ/Rachida Jerbi（チュニジア/Tunisia）

秋の雲空つぽの巣に震へる葉
| nubi d'autunno — nei nidi ormai vuoti tremano foglie
ジーナ　ボナセーラ/Gina Bonasera（イタリア/Italy）

秋の雲逆光に肌輝きぬ
| autumn clouds — against the light the glow of your skin
| nubi autunnali — in controluce il chiarore della tua pelle
アンジェラ　ジオルダーノ/Angela Giordano（イタリア/Italy）

秋の雲ブロンドの髪伸びにけり
| nuages d'automne — ses cheveux blonds repoussent
ベルナデット　クエン/Bernadette Couenne（フランス/France）

秋の雲日々忙しく変化して
| autumn clouds — the continuous changes of this fast life
ポール　カルス/Paul Callus（マルタ/Malta）

秋の雲まだ浮かびたるわが野望

> autumn clouds — my desire is still floating
>
> エル　ハミド/El Hamied（インドネシア/Indonesia）

秋の空馬のたてがみ手にうねる

> ciel d'automne — ondulation de la crinière du cheval sur la main
>
> エレナ　ズアイン/Elena Zouain（ルーマニア/Romania）

眺めれば遠のいてゆく秋の雲

> nube d'autunno — se la guardo più a lungo si allontana
> autumn cloud — if I look at it longer it recedes
>
> パオラ　トレビッセン/Paola Trevisson（イタリア/Italy）

秋の雲ポプに決めたるグレーヘア

> autumn clouds — the new bob style of her gray hair
>
> ナッキー　クリスティジーノ/Nuky Kristijno（インドネシア/Indonesia）

秋の雲思考は風を追ひかける

> autumn clouds — thoughts chase the wind
> nubi autunnali — i pensieri inseguono il vento
>
> アンジェラ　ジオルダーノ/Angela Giordano（イタリア/Italy）

秋の雲夜明の端を撫でてゆく

> the autumn clouds part stroking the edges of dawn light tears through the dark
>
> ラシュミ　モハパトラ/Rashmi Mohapatra（インド/India）

当てもなくかくも気ままな秋の雲

> autumn clouds drifting aimlessly — light tears through the dark
>
> キム　オルムタック　ゴメス/Kim Olmtak Gomes（オランダ/Holland）

秋の雲最初の風に俳句乗せ

> nuages d'automne — j'offre un haiku au premier vent qui passe
>
> ナディン　レオン/Nadine Léon（フランス/France）

秋の雲父の戦の怪我痛む

> nubi d'autunno — al papà duole la ferita di guerra
>
> ガブリエル　デ　マシ/Gabriella De Masi（イタリア/Italy）

秋の雲古き枝なる父の杖

> profilo d'autunno — si cercano e si trovano due nuvole
>
> ジオバンナ　ジオイア/Giovanna Gioia（イタリア/Italy）

秋の雲振り子時計の止まりたる

> the pendulum clock isn't working—autumn clouds
>
> クリスティーナ　チン/Christina Chin
> （マレーシア/Malaysia）

彗星の控へめになる秋の雲

> nuages d'automne —la comète se fait discrète
>
> フランソワーズ　デニオ-ルリエーブル/Françoise Deniaud-Lelièvre
> （フランス/France）

秋の雲白黒写真の祖父の顔

> autumn clouds — black and white grandfather portrait
>
> ザヤ　ヨウクハンナ/Zaya youkhanna
> （オーストラリア/Australia）

不死鳥やドラゴンもゐて秋の雲

> take the form of phoenix and dragon autumn cloud
>
> 中野千秋/Chiaki Nakano（日本/Japan）

鰯雲【いわしぐも・iwashigumo】
cirrocumulus / nuages moutonnés

Clouds that spread across the sky like a school of sardines. They are also called scaly clouds because they resemble fish scales. It is said that when this cloud is seen, a school of sardines arrives.

鰯雲追ひかけ合つてゐる小波

| cirrocumulus — small waves chasing each other to the beach
| ザンザミ　イスマイル/Zamzami Ismail（インドネシア/Indonesia）

鰯雲平らに見える空であり

| the sky is flat in my eyes — cirrocumulus
| ナニ　マリアニ/Nani Mariani（オーストラリア/Australia）

この部屋も空も覆ひて鰯雲

| in una stanza e in cielo i cirrocumuli peso opprimente
| in a room and in the sky cirrocumulus oppressive weight
| クリスティーナ　プルビエンティ/Cristina Pulvirenti
| （イタリア/Italy）

水に溶くテンペラ絵の具鰯雲

| cirri — un po' di tempera nell'acqua
| cirrus clouds — a bit of tempera paint in the water
| ダニエラ　ミッソ/Daniela Misso（イタリア/Italy）

鰯雲揺れながらゆくわがボート

| cirrocumulus — my bumpy boat ride
| ナッキー　クリスティジーノ/Nuky Kristijno
| （インドネシア/Indonesia）

鰯雲歯医者の椅子に口開けて
> cirrocumulus — mouth wide open in the dentist's chair
>> 中野千秋/Chiaki Nakano(日本/Japan)

鰯雲金色に染め落暉かな
> nuages moutonnés — rayons dorés du soleil couchant
>> 向瀬美音/Mine Mukose(日本/Japan)

老いてなほ何を求めて鰯雲
> nuages moutonnés — que cherchez-vous dans votre vieillesse
>> 向瀬美音/Mine Mukose(日本/Japan)

鰯雲水色の空欲しいまま
> nuages moutonnés — bénéficier d'un ciel bleu
>> 向瀬美音/Mine Mukose(日本/Japan)

月【つき・tsuki】
moon / lune

It is the autumn moon. Together with flowers in spring and snow in winter, it represents the four seasons of Japan. The reason why the word "moon" refers to the autumn moon is because the sky is clear and the moon shines bright and large during the autumn and winter seasons.

忘却の穴に潜り込みたる月
> par les trouées se faufile la lune se faufile— la lune
>> マルレナ　アレクサ/Marlena Alexa
>> (フランス/France)

葉の落ちるところに花と月明り
> where the leaf just fell — flowers and moonlight
> nơi chiếc lá vừa rơi — hoa và ánh trăng
>> ディン　ニュグエン/Dinh Nguyen（ベトナム/Vietnam）

梟の悲しき歌よ月の下
> autumn moon — the owl murmurs a sad song
>> ナッキー　クリスティジーノ/Nuky Kristijno（インドネシア/Indonesia）

月の出や山に戻れる羽の音　　　　　　　　　　　亜仁寿（自訳）
> moonrise — the sound of feathers returning to the mountain
>> タンポポ　アニス/Tanpopo Anis（インドネシア/Indonesia）

道の辺や月の登りを待つ老人
> un vieil homme se dépêche d'atteindre — la lune au bout du chemin
>> アブダラ　ハジイ/Abdallah Hajji（モロッコ/Morocco）

夜の松香りの上に月明かり
> pinède au soir — au-dessus des parfums la lune.
>> マルレーヌ　アレクサ/Marlene Alexa（フランス/France）

ブルームーンカフェに流れるモダンジャズ
> blue moon — modern jazz flowing in the café
>> タンポポ　アニス/Tanpopo Anis（インドネシア/Indonesia）

月光にじつとしてゐる猫がをり
> notte: m'affaccio immobile nel chiar di luna un gatto...
> night — I look out motionless in the moonlight a cat...
>> マウリチオ　ブランカレオーニ/Maurizio Brancaleoni（イタリア/Italy）

スーパーブルームーン飛行機の着陸始まりぬ
| super lune bleue — le commencement de l'atterrissage
オルファ　クチュク　ブハディダ/Olfa Kchouk Bouhadida
（チュニジア/Tunisia）

老松の傷に差したる月明り
| the stillness of moonlight — on the scar of old pine tree
| sự tĩnh lặng của ánh trăng — of old pine tree của cây thông già
ディン　ヌグエン/Dinh Nguyen（ベトナム/Vietnam）

夜をゆく良き距離保ちわれと月
| me and the moon walking through the night walking through the night
タンポポ　アニス/Tanpopo Anis
（インドネシア/Indonesia）

月光の照らす小径をどこまでも
| wandering miles and miles — walking through the night
プロビール　ギュプタ/Probir Gupta（インド/India）

満月や息を呑むほど美しき
| full moon — her beauty looks breathtaking
ザヤ　ヨウクハンナ/Zaya youkhanna
（オーストラリア/Australia）

葉群撫で月踊らせる風の吹く
| feuillage brassé — le vent fait danser la lune
フランソワーズ　デニオ-ルリエーブル/Françoise Deniaud-Lelièvre
（フランス/France）

囁く枝に引つかかりたる秋の月
> automne ― l'arbre murmure à la lune accrochée aux branches
>
> トゥーン　チャベ/Tounès Thabet
>
> (チュニジア/Tunisia)

月光や波の泡なるカタルシス
> waves lashing the moonlit beach foams of catharsis
>
> プロビール　ギュプタ/Probir Gupta(インド/India)

裸木や月の明かりで眠れない
> albero spoglio ― mi toglie il sonno la luce della luna
>
> アンナ　リモンディ/Anna Rimondi(イタリア/Italy)

窓辺の灯誰もゐぬ道に秋の月
> finestre illuminate ― per le strade deserte luna d'autunno
>
> ナザレナ　ランピニ/Nazarena Rampini
>
> (イタリア/Italy)

秋の月海に映れる一つの顔
> un solo volto che si specchia sul mare ― luna d'autunno
>
> デニス　カンバロウ/Dennys Cambarau
>
> (イタリア/Italy)

月光を頼りにしたる家路かな
> forgotten flashlight finding my way home borrowing moonlight
>
> ジェリー　ブラビ/Gerry Bravi(カナダ/Canada)

月の船金星と同じ波に乗る
> barque lunaire ― sur les mêmes ondes Vénus
>
> シュピー　モイサン/Choupie Moysan(フランス/France)

月登る猫の瞳の緑めく
> moon rise — the cat's eyes a new shade of green
>> ジェリー　ブラビ/Gerry Bravi
>>> (カナダ/Canada)

満月や指で大切な人描き
> la luna piena — con il dito disegno l'indefinibile
>> アントニオ　ジラルディ/Antonio Girardi
>>> (イタリア/Italy)

満月やまひまひの這ふ道光り
> striscia la lumaca — illumina una scia la luna piena
>> アントニオ　ジラルディ/Antonio Girardi(イタリア/Italy)

月の出を待つ間に少し酔ひにけり
> get drunk a little — while waiting moonrise
>> 中野千秋/Chiaki Nakano(日本/Japan)

名月を迎へてよりの予約席
> celebrating the harvest moon reserved seat
>> 中野千秋/Chiaki Nakano(日本/Japan)

上り月【のぼりつき・noboritsuki】
first moon quarter / premier quartier de lune

The moon gradually waxes from the first day of the lunar calendar to the fifteenth night of the lunar calendar. It expresses the feeling of love for the moon as it expands from a crescent moon to a half moon on the upper sine, and then to a beautiful full moon.

上り月対極したる白と黒
> first moon quarter — two sides always opposite black and white
>> ザンザミ　イスマイル/Zamzami Ismail
>>> (インドネシア/Indonesia)

ベニチアの木陰運河に上り月
> Venezia ombrosa — primo quarto di luna sul canal grande
>> アナ　リモンディ/Anna Rimondi(イタリア/Italy)

上り月選択のため小休止
> first quarter moon — I pause to consider my options
>> ポール　カルス/Paul Callus(マルタ/Malta)

上り月波に揺らるるカヌーあり
> first moon quarter — light blue canoe up and down as wave moves
>> アリアニ　ユハナ/Ariani Yuhana
>>> (インドネシア/Indonesia)

星々は嬰の周りに上り月
> quarter moon — all the stars near the babies
>> アグネーゼ　ジアロンゴ/Agnese Giallongo
>>> (イタリア/Italy)

上り月神の秘密の数多あり
> first moon quarters — so much God's secret ahead
>> アリアニ　ユハナ/Ariani Yuhana(インドネシア/Indonesia)

新しき計画立てる上り月
> first moon quarter — planning for new project
>> アリアニ　ユハナ/Ariani Yuhana(インドネシア/Indonesia)

上り月子等のための野外シネマ
> primo quarto di luna — un cinema all'aperto per bambini
> first moon quarter — an open air cinema for children
>> ダニエラ　ミッソ/Daniela Misso（イタリア/Italy）

波に乗り踊る魂上り月
> lune gibbeuse croissante — l'âme danse sur les vagues
> waxing gibbous moon — the soul dances on the waves
>> ミュールバッハ　アキツ/F.Mühlebach akitsu（フランス/France）

アンテナの上の雉鳩上り月
> a step away from the waxing moon —turtle dove on the antenna
> a un passo dalla luna crescente: tortora sull'antenna
>> マウリチオ　ブランカレオーニ/Maurizio Brancaleoni（イタリア/Italy）

再会の約束をして上り月
> first moon quarter — their promise for reunion
>> ナッキー　クリスティジーノ/Nuky Kristijno（インドネシア/Indonesia）

砂浜の最後の散歩上り月
> dernière promenade sur la plage — premier quartier de lune
>> エレナ　ズアイン/Elena Zouain（ルーマニア/Romania）

人生に保つ秘密や上り月
> first quarter moon — that part of her life which she keeps secret
>> ポール　カルス/Paul Callus（マルタ/Malta）

上り月昔の歌をデュエットで
> first moon quarter — duet of old songs
>> 中野千秋/Chiaki Nakano（日本/Japan）

降り月 【くだりつき・kudaritsuki】
last moon quarter / dernier quartier de lune

The moon gradually wanes from the full moon on the night of the 15th to the half-moon on the last sine. The moon rises later and later, and the moon can be seen until dawn, but it also causes a certain loneliness.

恋人へパンを切りたる下り月

> last moon quarter — slice of bread for lover
> ザンザミ　イスマイル/Zamzami Ismail（インドネシア/Indonesia）

降り月柊越しに煌めけり

> lune gibbeuse d aôut — à travers le houx elle vole en éclats
> フランソワーズ　ガブリエル/Françoise Gabriel
> （ベルギー/Belgium）

降り月一陣の風雲払う

> gusts of wind sweep the chimney smoke — last moon quarter
> クリスティーナ　チン/Christina Chin（マレーシア/Malaysia）

降り月わたしはいつも不安定

> luna calante — sono sempre instabile sotto il suo influsso
> alling moon — I am always unstable under its influence
> クリスティーナ　プルビレンティ/Cristina Pulvirenti
> （イタリア/Italy）

小窓より鷗鳴きたる降り月

> dernier quartier de lune — le cri des goélands derrière les vasistas
> フランソワーズ　モリス/Françoise Maurice
> （フランス/France）

降り月心重くて笑へない
> luna calante — si fa più greve il cuore senza sorrisi
> falling moon — the heart becomes heavier without smiles
>
> カルメン　バシキリ/Carmen Baschieri
>
> （イタリア/Italy）

降り月いつものやうに振り出しへ
> last moon quarter — return to the beginning regularly
>
> アリアニ　ユハニ/Ariani Yuhana
>
> （インドネシア/Indonesia）

降り月ミシン踏む音静かなり
> last quarter moon — the sound of sewing machine has quieted
>
> タンポポ　アニス/Tanpopo Anis
>
> （インドネシア/Indonesia）

梟と孤独を分かつ下り月
> last moon quarter—the owl'murmur share my loneliness
>
> ナッキー　クリスティジーノ/Nuky Kristijno
>
> （インドネシア/Indonesia）

完璧でないが完成下り月
> last moon quarter — completed although not perfect
>
> エル　ハミド/El Hamied（インドネシア/Indonesia）

下り月別れの言葉切り出せず
> last moon quarter — can't bring myself to say goodbye
>
> 中野千秋/Chiaki Nakano（日本/Japan）

三日月 【みかづき・mikazuki】
crescent moon / lune croissante

The third day of the eighth lunar month. It is also called the "brow moon" because it is as thin as a drawn eyebrow. It shines faintly in the western sky in the evening and soon sets.

三日月や気持ち変はらぬままですか

> crescent moon — do you still love me?
>
> クリスティーナ　チン/Christina Chin（マレーシア/Malaysia）

三日月や歩み短くなりし祖父

> grandfather's steps are shortened — crescent moon
> si accorciano i passi del nonno — luna crescente
>
> アンジェラ　ジオルダーノ/Angela Giordano（イタリア/Italy）

三日月やわが魂の一部分

> part of a whole my soul — crescent moon
>
> ザンザミ　イスマイル/Zamzami Ismail
>
> （インドネシア/Indonesia）

三日月や日ごと短くなる余生

> life gets shorter day by day — crescent moon
> la vita si accorcia giorno per giorno — luna crescente
>
> アンジェラ　ジオルダーノ/Angela Giordano（イタリア/Italy）

子守歌のごとき讃美歌三日の月

> cradle-hymn in silence sounds — crescent moon
>
> バーバラ　オルムタック/Barbara Olmtak
>
> （オランダ/Holland）

三日月や私の変はらない部分
　　luna crescente — la parte migliore di me immutabile
　　　　　　　　アンジェラ　ジオルダーノ/Angela Giordano（イタリア/Italy）

三日月や水平線に人の影
　　lune croissante — les ombres des gens à l'horizon
　　　　　　　　エウジェニア　パラシブ/Eugénia Paraschiv（ルーマニア/Romania）

三日月やおしやべり夜を乱さぬやう
　　croissant de lune — pour ne pas troubler la nuit nos chuchotis
　　　　　　　　ナディン　レオン/Nadine Léon（フランス/France）

三日月やジャスミンの香の古き家
　　crescent moon — jasmine scent in old house
　　　　　　　　アユング　ヘルマワン/Ayung Hermawan（インドネシア/Indonesia）

三日月や叶わぬ夢の客として
　　luna crescente — sono ospite del sogno che mai si avvera
　　crescent moon — I am guest of the dream that never comes true
　　　　　　　　クリスティーナ　プルビレンティ/Cristina Pulvirenti（イタリア/Italy）

三日月や孤独の重き日暮時
　　luna crescente — grava la solitudine al crepuscolo
　　crescent moon — solitude weighs at twilight
　　　　　　　　クリスティーナ　プルビレンティ/Cristina Pulvirenti（イタリア/Italy）

三日月や入り組む枝の間に光り
　　luna crescente — nella trama dei rami brillio di occhi
　　crescent moon — eyes shine in the weave of the branches
　　　　　　　　パトリチア　カバローネ/Patrizia Cavallone（イタリア/Italy）

言の葉の満たせぬ空虚三日の月
> falce di luna — quel vuoto incolmabile con le parole
>
> ミケーレ　ポチエロ/Michele Pochiero（イタリア/Italy）

三日月や白き銀河に浮かびをり
> voie lactée — sur la traînée blanche prend place le croissant
>
> スアド　ハジリ/Souad Hajri（チュニジア/Tunisia）

空に逃げ光る三日月美しき
> échappant au ciel — la beauté scintillante du croissant de lune
>
> フテン　フルチ/feten.fourti（チュニジア/Tunisia）

三日月や天地の間に白き蝶
> croissant de lune — un papillon blanc flotte entre ciel et terre
>
> スアド　ハジリ/Souad Hajri（チュニジア/Tunisia）

三日月やシャッター越しにパン屋の香
> croissant de lune — dès l'aube l'odeur du fournil derrière les volets clos
>
> crescent moon — at dawn the smell of the bakery behind the closed shutters
>
> イザベル　ラマン-ムニエ/Isabelle Lamant-Meunier（フランス/France）

三日月や鎌より君の手の匂ひ
> smell of your hands from the sickle — crescent moon
>
> プロビール　ギュプタ/Probir Gupta（インド/India）

三日月や水平線に消える船
> autumn crescent moon — a ship sailing towards the horizon
>
> バーバラ　オルムタック/Barbara Olmtak（オランダ/Holland）

三日月や転換点にある地球
> crescent moon — mother earth at its tipping point
>
> バーバラ　オルムタック/Barbara Olmtak(オランダ/Holland)

三日月や人生にある浮き沈み
> crescent moon — life is full with ups and downs
>
> キム　オルムタック　ゴメス/Kim Olmtak Gomes(オランダ/Holland)

三日月が漁船を連れて湾静か
> quiet bay — crescent moon accompanies fishing boat
>
> ザンザミ　ユクハンナ/Zaya youkhanna
>
> (オーストラリア/Australia)

ゆつたりと祖母のゆり椅子三日の月
> autumn crescent moon — the gentle back and forth of grandma's rocking chair
>
> バーバラ　オルムタック/Barbara Olmtak(オランダ/Holland)

三日月や水夫が一人海をゆき
> lone sailor navigating night's ocean — crescent moon
>
> バーバラ　オルムタック/Barbara Olmtak(オランダ/Holland)

三日月の光りに開けるブラインド
> shimmering crescent in the darkening sky— you open the blinds
>
> プロビール　ギュプタ/Probir Gupta(インド/India)

礼拝を知らせるモスク三日の月
> crescent moon — call for prayer from nearby mosque
>
> ナッキー　クリスティジーノ/Nuky Kristijno
>
> (インドネシア/Indonesia)

三日月や空を見守るピラミッド

automne le croissant vogue sur les nuages — la pyramide veillant le ciel

トゥーン　チャベ/Tounès Thabet

(チュニジア/Tunisia)

三日月や引き潮のごと我が心

lune croissante — à marée basse la mer et mon moral

アンヌ-マリー　ジュベール-ガヤール/Anne-Marie Joubert-Gaillard

(フランス/France)

三日月を浮かべてよりの山湖かな

crescent moon — floating on the mountain lake

中野千秋/Chiaki Nakano(日本/Japan)

半月【はんげつ・hangetsu】
half moon / demi lune

A word used to describe the middle of autumn. It refers to the half-moon, which looks like a bow with a string stretched across it.
The bow-shaped moon on the evening of the 7th or 8th day of the 8th month of the lunar calendar is a bright upper-half moon,
 while the bow-shaped moon at midnight on the 22nd or 23rd day of the 8th month of the lunar calendar is a bright lower-half moon

---

半月や蜘蛛はまあるく巣を網みて

demie lune — l'araignée tisse sa toile en cercles

イメルダ　セン/Imelda Senn

(スイス/Switzerland)

半月や農夫は鎌を研いでをり

> half moon — a farmer hones his sickle
>
> ポール　カルス/Paul Callus（マルタ/Malta）

半月や睫毛1本君の頬に

> demie lune — un cil sur ta joue
>
> イザベル　カルバロー　テール/Isabelle Carvalho Teles（フランス/France）

半月や絵本のなかは舞踏会

> half moon — in a picture book a ball
>
> 中野千秋/Chiaki Nakano（日本/Japan）

名月【めいげつ・meigetsu】
moon / lune

It is the moon on the fifteenth day of the eighth lunar month. The moon is so big that you can almost reach it if you stretch out your hand to touch it, as Issa said in his haiku, "Is it a child crying out for the moon? Dumplings, chestnuts, and sweet potatoes are placed on three sides of the moon, and thin ears are arranged to honor the moon.

孤独なり秋満月に負けぬべし

> solitude — ne décrois pas ô pleine lune d'automne
>
> ミュドハー　アリラキ/Mudher Aliraqi
>
> （イラク/Iraq）

落としたるコインを探し背なに月

> moon on her back bent — she is in search of her coin
>
> クリスティーナ　チン/Christina Chin
>
> （マレーシア/Malaysia）

月光の湖(うみ)静まりて恋に落つ
> innamorati — il lago accarezzato dalla luna
>
> ステファニア　アンドレオニ/Stefania Andreoni
> （イタリア/Italy）

満月や大樹の奥に金の時間
> derrière le grand arbre — se cache l'heure dorée se cache l'heure dorée
>
> アメルラディヒビ　ベント　チャディ/AmelLadhibi Bent Chadly
> （チュニジア/Tunisia）

海に差す垂直の影月今宵
> full moon — vertical shadow beam in the calm sea
>
> タンポポ　アニス/Tanpopo Anis
> （インドネシア/Indonesia）

満月や遠くより梟の歌
> nuit de pleine lune — il tempo che ci resta è così poco
>
> フランソワーズ　デニウ-ルリエーブル/Françoise Deniaud-Lelièvre
> （フランス/France）

ポケットに真珠の欠片月の夜
> dans ma poche un coquillage nacré — souvenir d'une promenade au clair de lune
>
> リュシー　ソレイユ/Lucie Soleil（フランス/France）

満月や双子向ひ合ふ胎盤
> pleine lune — face à face les jumeaux dans le placenta
>
> オルファ　クチュク　ブハディダ/Olfa Kchouk Bouhadida
> （チュニジア/Tunisia）

月明り命の芽吹く輪を描いて

> splende la luna — tra i nudi germogli il cerchio della vita
> the moon is shining — the circle of life sprouts among the naked
>
> リットリア　ガンダルフィ/Littoria Gandolfi（イタリア/Italy）

金の目の黒猫眠る木に満月

> pleine lune dans les arbres — dans mes bras un chat noir aux yeux d'or s'endort
>
> フランソワーズ　マリー　チュイリエ/FrançoiseMarie Thuillier
> （フランス/France）

秋の月終の枝葉にあるしじま

> luna d'autunno — il silenzio delle ultime foglie
> fiori di fiume — scrivo aspettando il tramonto
>
> ジオバンナ　ジオイア/Giovanna Gioia（イタリア/Italy）

老人の見つめる微光良夜なる

> full moon — old man staring at the crack of light
>
> アユング　ヘルマワン/Ayung Hermawan
> （インドネシア/Indonesia）

静謐な湖に漁師のゐる月夜

> splende la luna — e nel silente lago un pescatore
>
> アンジェラ　ジオルダーノ/Angela Giordano
> （イタリア/Italy）

満月や荒海の船速度上げ

> full moon — ships at highest speed on swelling sea
>
> スニタ　パラヲン/Sunita U D Palawon
> （インドネシア/Indonesia）

月光や孤独の壁を超えるほど
> luna d'autunno — la luce oltre il muro della solitudine
> lune d'automne — la lumière au-delà du mur de la solitud
>> ミケーレ　ポチエロ/Michele Pochiero（イタリア/Italy）

万物へ水彩のごと月明り
> acquerello — un tenue velo di luna copre ogni cosa
> watercolour — a faint veil of moon covers everything
>> クリスティーナ　プルビレンティ/Cristina Pulvirenti
>> （イタリア/Italy）

満月の河原に立てば物悲し
> ferma sul fiume — sa di malinconia la luna piena
>> ジオバンナ　ジオイア/Giovanna Gioia（イタリア/Italy）

水たまりに映る月光噛む鴉
> pioggia di settembre — nella pozzanghera il corvo becca la luna
>> ガブリエラ　デ　マシ/Gabriella De Masi（イタリア/Italy）

満月や犬は遠吠へのち静か
> un cane randagio abbaia alla luna piena — essa resta muta
>> マリオ　デ　サンティス/Mario De Santis（イタリア/Italy）

秋の月浜に一匹亀のゐて
> luna d'autunno — sulla spiaggia giace una tartaruga
>> ガブリエラ　デ　マシ/Gabriella De Masi（イタリア/Italy）

満月や糸の先には蜘蛛のゐて
> admirer la lune — une araignée au bout du fil
>> イメルダ　セン/Imelda Senn（スイス/Switerland）

満月や最後のパズル埋めてをり
> pleine lune de septembre — le dernier morceau du puzzle posé
>> ラシダ　ジェルビ/Rachida Jerbi（チュニジア/Tunisia）

名月や収穫したる畑のもの
> bringing in the crops from the fields — full september moon
>> クリスティーナ　チン/Christina Chin（マレーシア/Malaysia）

雲隠れ我が心中に刺さる棘
> luna velata — quella spina conficcata nell'anima
> veiled moon — that thorn stuck in the soul
>> カルメン　バシキリ/Carmen Baschieri（イタリア/Italy）

煌々と月に見られてゐる逢瀬
> la luna è qui per spiare — il nostro incontro
> without secrets — moon is here to spy our meeting
>> クリスティーナ　プルビレンティ/Cristina Pulvirenti（イタリア/Italy）

名月やテラスに草の香り嗅ぎ
> luna piena di metà settembre — profumo di erba in veranda
> full moon of mid-september — grass fragrance in the veranda
>> ダニエラ　ミッソ/Daniela Misso（イタリア/Italy）

月光や星空に震へる心
> notte di luna — sotto un cielo stellato un cuore vibra
>> マリオ　デ　サンティス/Mario De Santis（イタリア/Italy）

満月や犬は行つたり来たりして
> luna piena di settembre — il cane corre avanti e indietro
>> ガブリエル　デ　マシ/Gabriella De Masi（イタリア/Italy）

巡礼の影長くして月明り
> long shadow of a pilgrim — moon
>
>   ダニエラ　ミッソ/Daniela Misso（イタリア/Italy）

ぼんやりと雲のベールに銀の月
> her subtle presence — clouds veil a sliver of moon
>
>   ポール　カルス/Paul Callus（マルタ/Malta）

静かな夜月に休息賜りぬ
> calme nuit — sous la lune je trouve mon repos
>
>   カメル　メスレム/Kamel Meslem（アルジェリア/Algeria）

月今宵小さな宴温かし
> full moon of mid-September — small warm reunion
>
>   アリアニ　ユハナ/Ariani Yuhana
>
>   （インドネシア/Indonesia）

素晴らしき名月犬は遠吠へす
> soir une pleine lune resplendissante — un chien n'arrête pas d'aboyer
>
>   ピイ　ダニエル/Py Daniel（フランス/France）

消えてゆく水面の月を舐める猫
> rippling pond — cat licking the fading moonlight
>
>   アユング　ヘルマワン/Ayung Hermawan
>
>   （インドネシア/Indonesia）

満月やそばかすの君可愛くて
> full moon of September — I gaze at her freckled face
>
>   ポール　カルス/Paul Callus（マルタ/Malta）

抱擁や山頂照らす月明り
> autumn evenings — mountain peak and moon in a hug
>
> レフィカ　デディック/Refika Dedić
>
> （ボスニア　ヘルチェゴビナ/Bosnia and Herzegovina）

秋の葉や月夜のベッド柔らかき
> foglie d'autunno — nelle notti di luna soffici letti
>
> リットリア　ガンダルフィ/Littoria Gandolfi
>
> （イタリア/Italy）

満月や泣くのは稚児か木兎か
> nuit de pleine lune — c'est un bébé qui pleure ou bien un hiboux
>
> イメルダ　セン/Imelda Senn（スイス/Switzerland）

名月や形を変える池の波
> moon — small waves over the pond change the shape
>
> アリアニ　ユハナ/Ariani Yuhana
>
> （インドネシア/Indonesia）

望の月あなたと今宵初キスを
> full moon — the first time you kissed me
>
> ナニ　マリアニ/Nani Mariani（オーストラリア/Australia）

満月や出産予定あと一日（ひとひ）
> pleine lune — encore un jour avant l'accouchement
>
> スアド　ハジリ/Souad Hajri（チュニジア/Tunsia）

十五夜や白きドレスに淡き光
> quinzième lune — blanche satiné dans sa robe flambant
>
> カメル　メスレム/Kamel Meslem（アルジェリア/Algeria）

桑震へ川面に映る月白し

> frisson du mûrier — le blanc de la lune dans la rivière
>
> キャロル　デイウゼイド/Carole Dieuzeide
>
> （フランス/France）

月光に消えゆく影の空虚感

> pouring silence into the valley — autumn moon
>
> バリー　レビン/Barrie Levine（米国/United States）

秋の月薔薇に冷たき風の吹く

> luna d'autunno — il vento freddo sulle rose
>
> ガブリエル　デ　マシ/Gabriella De Masi
>
> （イタリア/Italy）

満月の光に溶けてゆく悲嘆

> luna piena — si scioglie la tristezza nella tua luce
>
> カルメン　バシキリ/Carmen Baschieri（イタリア/Italy）

丘の上の廃車の窓に望の月

> the window of the broken old car on the hill — full moon
>
> イシ　ヘルヤント/Isni Heryanto（インドネシア/Indonesia）

中秋の月まろやかになるワイン

> harvest moon — wine is getting fatter
>
> ザンザミ　イスマイル/Zamzami Ismail
>
> （インドネシア/Indonesia）

風は雲弾ませてゐる秋の月

> stanotte il vento fa galoppar le nubi — luna snebbiata
>
> アンナ　リモンディ/Anna Rimondi（イタリア/Italy）

トンネルの暗さの果ての月明り
  poteci umbroase la capătul tunelului singură luna
  shady paths at the end of the tunnel only the moon
                    ダニエラ　トピルセーン/Daniela Topircean
                                        (ルーマニア/Romania)

月出て半分解る君のこと
  moon — I might know half of you
                    イワン　セティアワン/Iwan Setiawan(インドネシア/Indonesia)

荒海や強風月も動かして
  mare grosso — questo libeccio sposta anche la luna
                    ガブリエル　デ　マシ/Gabriella De Masi(イタリア/Italy)

秋の月同じ孤独を噛みしめて
  autumn moon — sharing the same feeling of loneliness
                    ナッキー　クリスティジーノ/Nuky Kristijno
                                        (インドネシア/Indonesia)

月昇る孤独な心灯しつつ
  rising moon — the illumination of a lonely heart
                    ポール　カルス/Paul Callus(マルタ/Malta)

光輪や月は冷き化粧して
  halo brumeux — lune maquillée de froidure
                    リュシー　ソレイユ/Lucie Soleil(フランス/France)

秋の月窓辺で風の軋みたる
  lune d'automne — sur ma fenêtre le vent gémit
                    アブダラ　ハジイ/Abdallah Hajji(モロッコ/Morocco)

秋の月輝いてゐる湖面かな
> autumn moon — the lighted surface of the lake glitters
>> ナッキー　クリスティジーノ/Nuky Kristijno（インドネシア/Indonesia）

屋根のアンテナ満月刺すごとし
> quasi trafitta delle antenne sui tetti la luna piena
> almost pierced by antennas on the roofs the full moon
>> マウリチオ　ブランカレオーニ/Maurizio Brancaleoni（イタリア/Italy）

月上る魂浮かぶ暗き湾
> la luna piena sale dal golfo oscuro tra ombra e anima
> full moon rises from obscure gulf between shadow and soul
>> クリスティーナ　プルビエンティ/Cristina Pulvirenti（イタリア/Italy）

夕暮れや月の雫の音したり
> pénombre — le son des gouttes couleur de lune
>> キャロル　ディウゼイド/Carole Dieuzeide（フランス/France）

月の道我と交はる猫の影
> simplement la lune dans l'allée l'ombre d'un chat croise la mienne
>> ナディン　レオン/Nadine Léon（フランス/France）

月運ぶヒトコブラクダゐる砂丘
> sur la dune — un dromadaire porte la lune
>> アブダラ　ハジイ/Abdallah Hajji（モロッコ/Morocco）

耳元に何か囁くブルームーン
> blue moon — a quiet whisper in my ear
>> エル　ハミド/El Hamied（インドネシア/Indonesia）

満月に手を広げたる木の天辺
| cima degli alberi — le braccia tese verso la luna piena

リタ　モアール/Rita Moar（イタリア/Italy）

月光や空まで伸びる糸杉よ
| chiaro di luna quasi sfiorano il cielo alti cipressi

アルベルタ　カテリナ　マトリ/Alberta Caterina Mattoli（イタリア/Italy）

秋の月クローゼットに雷雨の香
| luna d'autunno — nei panni stesi odore di temporale

ガブリエル　デ　マシ/Gabriella De Masi

（イタリア/Italy）

白き詩を纏ふ妖精月明り
| luna de toamnă — îmbrăcată-n versuri albe Fata Morgana
| autumn moon — dressed in white verses the Morgana Girl

ダニエラ　トピルセーン/Daniela Topîrcean

（ルーマニア/Romania）

月の出を待つ間に少し酔ひにけり
| get drunk a little while waiting moonrise

中野千秋/Chiaki Nakano（日本/Japan）

名月を迎へてよりの予約席
| celebrating the harvest moon — reserved seat

中野千秋/Chiaki Nakano（日本/Japan）

果てしなき潮の満ち引き月今宵
| le flux et le reflux infinis — lune d'automne

向瀬美音/Mine Mukose（日本/Japan）

砂浜に残る足跡月今宵

> ses pas sur le sable — lune d'automne
>
> 向瀬美音/Mine Mukose（日本/Japan）

名月やハープを滑る白き指

> lune de la mi-automne — doigt blanc glisse sur la harpe
>
> 向瀬美音/Mine Mukose（日本/Japan）

月光や柄滑らかな銀の匙

> clair de lune — cuiller d'argent au motif lisse
>
> 向瀬美音/Mine Mukose（日本/Japan）

無月【むげつ・mugetsu】

night without the moon / nuit sans lune

On the night of the famous moon on the 15th day of the 8th lunar month, the sky is cloudy and the moon is hidden. It is unfortunate that the long-awaited moon is hidden from view, but it is also a tasteful scene. Depending on the thickness and movement of the clouds, the moon's light leaking through the clouds is also a nice touch.

離れゐて信頼し合ふ無月かな

> night moonless — trust each other even though far apart
>
> エル　ハミド/El Hamied（インドネシア/Indonesia）

産卵の海亀が来る無月の夜

> sea turtles return to lay eggs — night without the moon
>
> クリスティーナ　チン/Christina Chin
>
> （マレーシア/Malaysia）

君を恋ふ思ひの募る無月かな
> night without the moon — I'm missing you
>
> リナ　ダルサ/Rina Darsa（インドネシア/Indonesia）

山村に灯りのともる無月かな
> moonless night — the lights of a village on the mountain
>
> ダニエラ　ミッソ/Daniela Misso（イタリア/Italy）

人生の後も道あり無月の夜
> the road continues at the end of life's journey — night without the moon
>
> バーバラ　オルムタック/Barbara Olmtak（オランダ/Holland）

月見草匂ひてよりの無月かな
> moonless night — the smell of evening primrose flowers
> noć bez mjesečine — miris cvjetova noćurka
>
> ズデンカ　ムリナー/Zdenka Mlinar（クロアチア/Croatia）

言の葉に幸せもらふ無月かな
> night without the moon — his words make me happy
>
> ローザマリア　ディ　サルバトーレ/Rosa Maria Di Salvatore（イタリア/Italy）

梟の黄色き瞳無月の夜
> notte senza luna — gli occhi gialli dell'assiolo
>
> ガブリエル　デ　マシ/Gabriella De Masi（イタリア/Italy）

無月の夜綱渡りする我が心
> moonless night — with the wind blowing my heart is erratic
>
> ナニ　マリアニ/Nani Mariani（オーストラリア/Australia）

無月なり北極星に向かひたる
> nuit sans lune — l'étoile polaire et moi.
>> シュピー　モイサン/Choupie Moysan（フランス/France）

無月の夜肌と肌とを寄せ合へり
> nuit sans lune — peau-à-peau
>> エウジェニア　パラシブ/EugéniaParaschiv（ルーマニア/Romania）

ゆくらかに闇になりたる無月かな
> notte senza luna — lentamente mi abituo al buio
>> ガブリエル　デ　マシ/Gabriella De Masi（イタリア/Italy）

無月なり君の心にある光
> nuit sans lune — la lumière dans ton coeur
>> エウジェニア　パラシブ/EugéniaParaschiv
>> （ルーマニア/Romania）

苛まれ罪悪感の無月かな
> moonless night — that guilt haunts me
>> ザンザミ　イスマイル/Zamzami Ismai（インドネシア/Indonesia）

無月の夜裸体を隠す長き髪
> night without moon — your naked body enshrouded in the long hair
>> ミレラ　ブライレーン/Mirela Brailean（ルーマニア/Romania）

無月の夜屋敷の前で吠える犬
> night without the moon — barking dog in front of tall fenced house
>> アリアナ　ユハナ/Ariani Yuhana（インドネシア/Indonesia）

曖昧なメッセージ受く無月かな
> il reçoit un vague message — nuit sans lune
>> アブダラ　ハジイ/Abdallah Hajji（モロッコ/Morocco）

恋人は今は何処に無月の夜
> night without the moon — where has my lover gone
>> ポール　カルス/Paul Callus（マルタ/Malta）

触れたくて触れられたくて無月の夜
> another night without the moon — I hunger for her touch
>> ポール　カルス/Paul Callus（マルタ/Malta）

屋根の上に猫の影ある無月かな
> notte senza luna — silhouette di un gatto sul tetto
> moonless night — silhouette of a cat on the roof
>> ダニエラ　ミッソ/Daniela Misso（イタリア/Italy）

難民のテント満杯なる無月
> stuffy refugee tents — night without the moon
>> タンポポ　アニス/Tanpopo Anis（インドネシア/Indonesia）

無月の夜漁師は櫂を隠したり
> nuit sans lune — sur la plage le pêcheur cache les rames de son barque
>> アブダラ　ハジイ/Abdallah Hajji（モロッコ/Morocco）

無月の夜君の指に濡れた砂糖
> nuit sans lune — du sucre humide sur tes doigts
>> エリック　デスピエール/Eric Despierre
>> （フランス/France）

梟のいびき聞こえる無月かな
> night without the moon — owl snores
>
> ナッキー　クリスティジーノ/Nuky Kristijno
>
> (インドネシア/Indonesia)

恋人と別れたばかりなる無月
> just broke up with my boyfriend — a night without moon
>
> ナニ　マリアニ/Nani Mariani (オーストラリア/Australia)

波音の高まるごとく無月かな
> night without moon — sound of the wave seems louder
>
> ナッキー　クリスティジーノ/Nuky Kristijno
>
> (インドネシア/Indonesia)

手品師の手より偽札出て無月
> night without the moon — counterfeit money from the magician's hand
>
> 中野千秋/Chiaki Nakano (日本/Japan)

矛先の相手分からぬ無月かな
> sans connaître pointe d'une lance — nuit sans lune
>
> 向瀬美音/Mine Mukose (日本/Japan)

手のひらに涙の重さ無月の夜
> nuit sans lune — dans la paume le poids des larmes
>
> 向瀬美音/Mine Mukose (日本/Japan)

今生の遺灰の軽さ無月なり
> légèreté des cendres d'une vie — nuit sans lune
>
> 向瀬美音/Mine Mukose (日本/Japan)

雨月 【うげつ・ugetsu】
rainy moon / lune de pluie

> The Mid-Autumn Moon cannot be seen because of rain. There is a feeling of regret for not being able to see the beautiful moon.

雨の月モスクで夜の祈りせり

> rainy month — it's time to night pray at the mosque
>
> ザンザミ　イスマイル/Zamzami Ismail
> （インドネシア/Indonesia）

雨月なり新婦の真珠光りたる

> lune de pluie — les perles brillent autour du cou de la mariée
>
> アメルラディヒビ　ベント　チャディ/AmelLadhibi Bent Chadly
> （チュニジア/Tunisia）

雨月なり故郷の村へ帰りたる

> lune de pluie — mon retour au village natal
>
> アブダラ　ハジイ/Abdallah Hajji（モロッコ/Morocco）

海水が陸へ押し寄す雨月かな

> rainy moon — sea water streams into the land
>
> アリアナ　ユハナ/Ariani Yuhana（インドネシア/Indonesia）

寂しさに雫渦巻く雨月かな

> the water dripping on the roof curls up in your loneliness — rainy moon
>
> ザンザミ　イスマイル/Zamzami Ismail
> （インドネシア/Indonesia）

聖人像に後光の差せる雨月かな
> rainy moon — a halo around the image of a saint
>> ザヤ　ヨウクハンナ/Zaya youkhanna（オーストラリア/Australia）

老農夫の乾いた視線雨月の夜
> rainy moon — the dry eyes of the old farmer
> luna piovosa — gli occhi secchi del vecchio contadin
>> アンジェラ　ジオルダーノ/Angela Giordano（イタリア/Italy）

洋服に嵐の匂ひ雨月の夜
> luna piovosa — nei panni stesi l'odore del temporale
>> ガブリエラ　デ　マシ/Gabriella De Masi（イタリア/Italy）

生家去る新婦の顔よ雨月の夜
> visage de la mariée quittant maison parentale — lune de pluie
>> カディジャ　エル　ブルカディ/Khadija El Bourkadi
>> （チュニジア/Tunisia）

渓谷に光る石ある雨月かな
> lune de pluie — au bord de la vallée les pierres brillantes
>> アブダラ　ハジイ/Abdallah Hajji（モロッコ/Morocco）

われの名はナニ・マリアニよ雨の月
> rainy moon — my name is Nani Mariani
>> ナニ　マリアニ/Nani Mariani（オーストラリア/Australia）

顔覆ふヴェールのごとき雨月かな
> rainy moon — a girl hides her face in a white veil
>> マリリン　アッシュボフ/Marilyn Ashbaugh
>> （米国/United States）

身の飾り外してよりの雨月かな

> remove the decoration from body and mind — rainy moon
>
> 中野千秋/Chiaki Nakano(日本/Japan)

ぬばたまの黒髪の艶雨月なる

> le lustre des cheveux noirs — lune de pluie
>
> 向瀬美音/Mine Mukose(日本/Japan)

有明月【ありあけづき・ariakezuki】
morning moon / lune du matin

The moon remains in the sky even at dawn. In ancient times, the poem was written in the style of a traveler leaving in the morning, stepping on the shadow of the moon in Ariake.

有明の月トンネルの向こう側

> at the end of the woody tunnel — a bright morning moon
>
> クリスティーナ　チン/Christina Chin
>
> (マレーシア/Malaysia)

有明の月こつそりと朝帰り

> morning moon — she sneaks home after a night out
>
> ポール　カルス/Paul Callus(マルタ/Malta)

大声で雄鶏鳴いて朝の月

> morning moon — rooster singing out loud
>
> ナッキー　クリスティジーノ/Nuky Kristijno
>
> (インドネシア/Indonesia)

降りてゆく寺の階段朝の月
> morning moon — down the stairs of the head monk's temple
>
> イシ　ヘルヤント/Isni Heryanto
>
> (インドネシア/Indonesia)

朝の月村の灯りのまだ残る
> luna mattutina — le luci del villaggio ancora accese
> morning moon — the village lights still lit
>
> ダニエラ　ミッソ/Daniela Misso(イタリア/Italy)

現実と夢の出会ひて朝の月
> morning moon — meeting between dreams and reality
>
> エル　ハミド/El Hamied(インドネシア/Indonesia)

船室に有明月を迎へけり
> cabin window — inviting morning moon
>
> 中野千秋/Chiaki Nakano(日本/Japan)

業平の沓の音なり朝の月
> la lune du matin — le bruit des socques de bois de Kotohira
>
> 向瀬美音/Mine Mukose(日本/Japan)

秋の星 【あきのほし・akinohoshi】
autumn star / étoile d'automne

The stars can be seen all year round, but the stars in autumn, when the atmosphere is clearer, have a special feeling, and this term is intended to express that feeling. The Big Dipper, including Cygnus and the anchor star (Cassiopeia), is called the "Autumn Big Dipper.

満潮に溢るる川よ秋の星

> high tide floods the river — autumn star
>
> クリスティーナ　チン/Christina Chin
>
> (マレーシア/Malaysia)

秋の星笑顔の下にある孤独

> autumn star — she hides her loneliness behind a smile
>
> ポール　カルス/Paul Callus (マルタ/Malta)

秋の星水平線に港の灯

> étoile d'automne — les éclats du phare à l'horizon
>
> フランソワーズ　デニウ-ルリエーブル/Françoise Deniaud-Lelièvre
>
> (フランス/France)

王冠の輝いてゐる星月夜

> šešir na glavi prosjaka — kraljici u čast
> the splendor of the royal crown — starry sky
>
> ズデンカ　ムリナー/Zdenka Mlinar (クロアチア/Croatia)

秋の星アニスの香るハーブティー

> sweet aroma of stars anise herb tea — my autumn stars
>
> タンポポ　アニス/Tanpopo Anis (インドネシア/Indonesia)

君の声一瞬で消え秋の星

> stelle d'autunno — in un attimo scompare la sua voce
>
> ジオバンナ　ジオイア/Giovanna Gioia(イタリア/Italy)

秋の星暖炉に杜松の弾ける音

> étoiles d'automne — dans la cheminée le crépitement du genévrier
>
> アブダラ　ハジイ/Abdallah Hajji(モロッコ/Morocco)

君のチュチュ薔薇色なりて秋の星

> étoile d'automne — son tutu de couleur rose
>
> アメルラディヒビ　ベント　チャディ/AmelLadhibi Bent Chadly
>
> (チュニジア/Tunisia)

秋の星笑みに隠された言の葉

> étoile d'automne — dans son sourire les mots cachés
>
> エレナ　ズアイン/Elena Zouain(ルーマニア/Romania)

秋の星子等は数へること学ぶ

> with the autumn stars a child learns to count
>
> con le stelle autunnali un bimbo impara a contare
>
> アンジェラ　ジオルダーノ/Angela Giordano(イタリア/Italy)

亡き友を探してをりぬ秋の星

> autumn stars — quest for the deceased friend
>
> プロビール　ギュプタ/Probir Gupta(インド/India)

寝る前に短編ひとつ秋の星

> reading a short story before sleeping — autumn star
>
> 中野千秋/Chiaki Nakano(日本/Japan)

カシオペア 【かしおぺあ・kashiopea】
Cassiopeia / Cassiopée

The Japanese name for the constellation Cassiopeia. The five stars are arranged in the shape of a W, and this is likened to the anchor of a boat. It is also called "Yamagata-boshi" (mountain-shaped star) because of the shape of the five stars. It is opposite the Big Dipper, which is opposite the North Star.

泣きながら空港でハグカシオペア

> Cassiopeia — I come to cry and hug at airport
>
> タンポポ　アニス/Tanpopo Anis
> （インドネシア/Indonesia）

カシオペア空の一等席にあり

> Cassiopeia — her presence always attracts attention
>
> ナニ　マリアニ/Nani Mariani
> （オーストラリア/Australia）

カシオペア金の糸空刺繡せり

> le ciel brodé de fils d'or — Cassiopée reine
>
> ラチダ　ジェルビ/Rachida Jerbi（チュニジア/Tunisia）

寝れぬ夜カシオペアのみ共にする

> notte insonne — mia unica compagna Cassiopea
>
> アンナ　リモンディ/Anna Rimondi（イタリア/Italy）

カシオペア君の心の闇深し

> Cassiopea — il lato oscuro del tuo carattere
>
> アンジェラ　ジオルダーノ/Angela Giordano
> （イタリア/Italy）

カシオペア宇宙は全て星座なり
> Cassiopea — nell'universo di tutte le costellazioni
>> アグネーゼ　ジアロンゴ/Agnese Giallongo
>>> (イタリア/Italy)

慈悲深き女王陛下カシオペア
> Cassiopeia — queen policy about humanity
>> アリアナ　ユハナ/Ariani Yuhana
>>> (インドネシア/Indonesia)

君待てば海辺に光るカシオペア
> Cassiopea — by the sea waiting for your arrival
>> ナニ　マリアニ/Nani Mariani(オーストラリア/Australia)

カシオペア口に出せずに悔いてをり
> Cassiopeia — I regret not having spoken words
>> タンポポ　アニス/Tanpopo anis(インドネシア/Indonesia)

黄金の軌跡描けるカシオペア
> fil d'or de l'écriture — Cassiopée dessine dans le ciel sa course
>> アンヌ-マリー　ジュベール-ガヤール/Anne-Marie Joubert-Gaillard
>>> (フランス/France)

カシオペア空しき恋の鏡かな
> Cassiopeia — a vain affair with the mirror
>> ポール　カルス/Paul Callus(マルタ/Malta)

カシオペア仄に下界照らしたり
> Cassiopeia — gleaming down in the lower world boundary
>> タンポポ　アニス/Tanpopo anis(インドネシア/Indonesia)

林間に囁く光カシオペア
> Cassiopeia — its light whispering through the trees
>> キム　オルムタック　ゴメス/Kim Olmtak Gomes
>>> （オランダ/Holland）

カシオペア割れた鏡を捨て去つて
> Cassiopeia — she discards the cracked mirror
>> ポール　カルス/Paul Callus（マルタ/Malta）

カシオペア手を振つている小さき手
> Cassiopeia—the tiny hand waved
>> エル　ハミド/El Hamied（インドネシア/Indonesia）

カシオペア長旅終えた漁師たち
> Cassiopée—les pêcheurs reviennent d'un long voyage
>> アブダラ　ハジイ/Abdallah Hajji
>>> （モロッコ/Morocco）

カシオペア馬は野原を駆け回る
> horses gallop the vast flat plains—Cassiopeia
>> クリスティーナ　チン/Christina Chin
>>> （マレーシア/Malaysia）

山塊の息吹の上のカシオペア
> Cassiopeia — breathing of black mountain mass
>> 中野千秋/Chiaki Nakano（日本/Japan）

さざなみの奏でる輪舞カシオペア
> Cassiopée — une danse circulaire par ondulations
>> 向瀬美音/Mine Mukose（日本/Japan）

君の目に言葉溢れてカシオペア

> Cassiopée — les mots transparaissent dans tes yeux
>
> 向瀬美音/Mine Mukose(日本/Japan)

櫂を持つ空の航行カシオペア

> bateau à rames dans le ciel — Cassiopée
>
> 向瀬美音/Mine Mukose(日本/Japan)

星々のしじまに燃ゆるカシオペア

> les étoiles s'embrasent dans le silence — Cassiopée
>
> 向瀬美音/Mine Mukose(日本/Japan)

星月夜【ほしづきよ・hoshizukiyo】
starry night / ciel étoilé

It is a night sky with no moon and only starlight. It is a starry sky as bright as the moon.

未だ待つ最終列車星月夜

> starry night — I'm still waiting for the last train
>
> ザンザミ イスマイル/Zamzami Ismail(インドネシア/Indonesia)

星月夜菩提樹咲けるこの静寂

> notte stellata — serenata sommessa tra i tigli in fiore
>
> アンナ リモンディ/Anna Rimondi(イタリア/Italy)

星月夜芥子に光の粒の落ち

> notte stellata — granelli di luce su papaveri di grano
>
> パトリチア カバロネ/Patrizia Cavallone(イタリア/Italy)

星月夜遠くに青の震へたる
> notte stellata — in lontananza tremano azzurri gli astri
>> アンナ　リモンディ/Anna Rimondi（イタリア/Italy）

星月夜遠くに愛を語る声
> notte stellata — una voce lontana parla d'amore
>> アンナ　リモンディ/Anna Rimondi（イタリア/Italy）

白き薔薇のトンネルの下星月夜
> sous la tonnelle de roses blanches — le ciel étoilé
>> ベルナデット　クエン/Bernadette Couenne
>>> （フランス/France）

星月夜しなのき静かにセレナーデ
> notte stellata — serenata sommessa tra i tigli in fiore
>> アンナ　リモンディ/Anna Rimondi（イタリア/Italy）

星月夜独立記念のセレモニー
> starry night — independence day celebration parties
>> アリアナ　ユハナ/Ariani Yuhana（インドネシア/Indonesia）

星月夜両橋に血族関係
> ciel étoilé — d'un bout à l'autre parenté-
>> エウジェニア　パラシブ/Eugénia Paraschiv
>>> （ルーマニア/Romania）

狼の遠吠へ響く星月夜
> ciel étoilé — sur la colline les yeux des loups vers la lune
>> アブダラ　ハジイ/Abdallah Hajji
>>> （モロッコ/Morocco）

星月夜ピアノの音が風の中
> starry night — the tinkling piano flowing in the wind
>
> タンポポ　アニス/Tanpopo Anis(インドネシア/Indonesia)

星月夜飽きることなくベランダに
> starry night — never tired of sitting on the veranda
>
> ナニ　マリアニ/Nani Mariani(オーストラリア/Australia)

さよならはなかなか言へず星月夜
> starry night — hard to say goodbye
>
> ナニ　マリアニ/Nani Mariani(オーストラリア/Australia)

夢破れ涙乾かす星月夜
> notte stellata — asciugo le lacrime dei sogni infranti
>
> starry night — I dry the tears of broken dreams
>
> クリスティーナ　プルビレンティ/Cristina Pulvirenti(イタリア/Italy)

青の上に白き飛沫や星月夜
> una spruzzata di candeggina sul blu — cielo stellato
>
> a splash of bleach on blue — starry sky
>
> ダニエラ　ミッソ/Daniela Misso(イタリア/Italy)

星月夜足跡はもう消えている
> cielo stellate le orme calcate già invisibili
>
> footprints already invisible — trodded footprints already invisible
>
> クリスティーナ　プルビレンティ/Cristina Pulvirenti(イタリア/Italy)

星月夜チャールズ王が戴冠す
> stary night — King Charles coronation
>
> アリアナ　ユハナ/Ariani Yuhana(インドネシア/Indonesia)

透明な夜に魅せられて星月夜

> clarté de nuit — étoiles et lune autour d'elle fascinées
>
> カメル　メスレム/Kamel Meslem（アルジェリア/Algeria）

水槽の魚は眠れず星月夜

> nuit des étoiles — poisson d'aquarium sans sommeil
>
> アブダラ　ハジイ/Abdallah Hajji（モロッコ/Morocco）

星月夜静かな水に未草

> une nuit aux rayons d'étoiles — le lotus sur l'eau couché
>
> カメル　メスレム/Kamel meslem（アルジェリア/Algera）

星月夜難民テントに灯る蠟燭

> ciel étoilé—dans chaque tente de réfugiés une bougie
>
> アブダラ　ハジイ/Abdallah Hajji（モロッコ/Morocco）

人生の西への旅や星月夜　　　　　　　　　　亜仁寿（自訳）

> starry night — a life's journey to the west
>
> タンポポ　アニス/Tanpopo Anis（インドネシア/Indonesi）

笑ひ声絶えないキャンプ星月夜

> starry night endless laughter at the camp — endless laughter at the camp
>
> ナッキー　クリスティジーノ/Nuky Kristijno
>
> （インドネシア/Indonesia）

ロザリオを抱へて眠る星月夜

> starry night — holding the rosary in her peaceful sleep
>
> タンポポ　アニス/Tanpopo Anis
>
> （インドネシア/Indonesia）

星月夜願ひを描くわれの指

> ciel étoilé — mes doigts dessinent mes vœux
>
> starry sky — my fingers draw my wishes
>
> ミュールバッハ　アキツ/F.Mühlebach akitsu（フランス/France）

どの夢が叶ふだらうか星月夜

> starry night — which dream should I make come true first
>
> エル　ハミド/El Hamied（インドネシア/Indonesia）

星月夜銀の小皿の角砂糖

> starry night — sugar cubes on a small silver plate
>
> 中野千秋/Chiaki Nakano（日本/Japan）

天の川【あまのがわ・amanogawa】
milky way / voie lactée

Numerous stars lying in a band in the clear night sky in early autumn. Because it looks like a river, it is also called a "galaxy" or "Ginhan". It is the river that separates Orihime and Hikoboshi in the Tanabata legend, and the two are allowed to cross it once a year on the night of the seventh day of the seventh lunar month to meet.

金星を指差す孫や天の川

> Galaxy — grand child appoints east sky saying that's venus
>
> キム　オルムタック　ゴメス/Kim Olmtak Gomes（オランダ/Holland）

空つぽの漁網が海に天の川

> at sea under the milky way — empty fishnets
>
> ザンザミ　イスマイル/Zamzami Ismail
>
> （インドネシア/Indonesia）

天の川手を繋ぎ合ふ家路なり
> milky way — holding hands on the way home
>
> ダニエラ　ミッソ/Daniela Misso（イタリア/Italy）

千の眼に希望のありて天の川
> milky way — a great meaning of the thousand eyes hope
>
> ジョノ　ファドリ/Jono Fadli（インドネシア/Indonesia）

天の川乳房含ませ星見上ぐ
> voie lactée du bébé au sein — maman les yeux dans les étoiles
>
> シュピー　モイサン/Chupie Moysan（フランス/France）

波の音通り抜けたる天の川
> passed through the sound of waves — milky way
>
> ザンザミ　イスマイル/Zamzami Ismail
>
> （インドネシア/Indonesia）

望遠鏡覗く子どもや天の川
> milky way — grand son holds telescop toward sky
>
> アリアナ　ユハナ/Ariani Yuhana
>
> （インドネシア/Indonesia）

天の川遠距離恋愛保つこつ
> milky way — how to survive a long-distance relationship
>
> タンポポ　アニス/Tanpopo Anis
>
> （インドネシア/Indonesia）

天の川空の深さは如何ばかり
> sonder la profondeur du ciel — voie lactée
>
> ラシダ　ジェルビ/Rachida Jerbi（チュニジア/Tunisia）

山頂に寺院の光天の川
> voie lactée — lumières du temple au sommet de la montagne
>> アブダラ　ハジイ/Abdallah Hajji（モロッコ/Morocco）

暗き目の自信に満つる天の川
> voie lactée — ses yeux sombres s'illuminent de fierté
>> カディジャ　エル　ブルカディ/Khadija El Bourkadi
>> （モロッコ/Morocco）

天の川神のみが知るわが寿命
> milky way — only God knows my age limit
>> タンポポ　アニス/Tanpopo Anis（インドネシア/Indonesia）

天の川知識の道をひたむきに
> voie lactée — la route du savoir en toute confiance
>> カディジャ　エル　ブルカディ/Khadija El Bourkadi
>> （モロッコ/Morocco）

天の川鳥と飛行機交差せり
> sur la voie lactée — avion et oiseau se croisent
>> スアド　ハジリ/Souad Hajri（チュニジア/Tunisia）

天の川言ひ残すこと何も無く
> milky way — I have nothing left to say
>> イワン　セティワン/Iwan Setiawan（インドネシア/Indonesia）

銀漢や君はあまりに偉大なる
> there are not enough words to express his greatness — galaxy
>> ザンザミ　イスマイル/Zamzami Ismail
>> （インドネシア/Indonesia）

我が旅のまだ続きたる天の川　　　　　　　　亜仁寿（自訳）
> milky way — my journey still continues
>> タンポポ　アニス/Tanpopo Anis（インドネシア/Idonesia）

天の川難民の波を横切りて
> voie lactée — traversée d'un flot de réfugiés
>> ベルナデット　クエン/Bernadette Couenne
>> （フランス/France）

天の川蒼きインクに夢溶けて
> voie lactée — dans mon encre bleue mon rêve se dissout
>> アブダラ　ハジイ/Abdallah Hajji（モロッコ/Morocco）

海の音横切る船跡天の川
> sillage du bateau à travers les bruits de la mer — voie lactée
>> エレナ　ズアイン/Elena Zouain（ルーマニア/Romania）

赤ワイン君と乾杯天の川　　　　　　　　　　亜仁寿（自訳）
> red wine — toast with you beneath the milky way
>> タンポポ　アニス/Tanpopo Anis（インドネシア/Indonesia）

君の目の輝いてをり天の川
> milky way — I can only see the sparkle in your eyes
>> ナッキー　クリスティジーノ/Nuky Kristijno
>> （インドネシア/Indonesia）

天の川母のネックレスのごと光る
> via latte — la collana di perle di mia madre
> voie lactée — le collier de perle de ma mére
>> フランチェスコ　パラディノ/Francisco Palladino（イタリア/Italy）

薔薇の香の届くだらうか天の川

> reds rose for my love — does the scent reach beyond the milky way
>
> キム　オルムタック　ゴメス/Kim Olmtak Gomes
>
> (オランダ/Holland)

天の川煙のやうに過去未来

> milky way — past and future drift like smoke
>
> 中野千秋/Chiaki Nakano(日本/Japan)

流れ星 【ながれぼし・nagareboshi】
shooting star / étoile filante

The light emitted by cosmic dust entering the atmosphere and emitting light due to frictional heat. On plateaus without artificial light, stars flow one after another as if falling.

流れ星海に悲しき刹那かな

> a moments of sadness in the sea — shooting star
>
> タンポポ　アニス/Tanpopo Anis(インドネシア/Idonesia)

流星や先祖の国を探しつつ

> shooting star — searching for my ancestors' shores
>
> キム　オルムタック　ゴメス/Kim Olmtak Gomes
>
> (オランダ/Holland)

それぞれの人に意味あり流れ星

> each person gives their own meaning — shooting star...
>
> ジョーノ　ファドリ/Jono Fadli(インドネシア/Idonesia)

喜びと悲哀の間流れ星

> shooting star — I am between joy and sorrow in the light
>
> ジョーノ　ファドリ/Jono Fadli（インドネシア/Idonesia）

一粒の涙こぼれて流れ星

> shooting star — a tear slipping down
>
> ダニエラ　ミッソ/Daniela Misso（イタリア/Italy）

流れ星目にたつぷりと焼き付けて

> stelle cadenti — scrutare il cielo fino a stancarsi gli occhi
>
> ガブリエラ　デ　マシ/Gabriella De Masi（イタリア/Italy）

流星や戦火の煙避けながら

> shooting stars — escape of the clouds of war smoke
> zvijezde padalice — bijeg ratnih oblaka dim
>
> ズデンカ　ムリナー/Zdenka Mlinar（クロアチア/Croatia）

願ひ事叶へてくれぬ流れ星

> stelle cadenti e nemmeno un desiderio — scoraggiamento
>
> マリア　ビアンカ/Maria Bianca（イタリア/Italy）

流れ星去年と同じ願ひごと

> cade una stella — lo stesso desiderio dell'anno scorso
> a star falls — the same desire of last year
>
> ニコレッタ　イグナッティ/Nicoletta Ignatti
>
> （イタリア/Italy）

流星や娘の夢想始まりぬ

> stella cadente — i sogni ad occhi aperti di un ragazza
>
> アンナ　リモンディ/Anna Rimondi（イタリア/Italy）

流星やその声深きより出でて
> étoile filante — cette voix émanant des profondeurs
>> モハメド　ベンファレス/Mohammed Benfares（モロッコ/Morocco）

流れ星空に一行祈り文
> shooting star — a line of prayer through the sky
>> ザンザミ　イスマイル/Zamzami Ismael（インドネシア/Indonesia）

流星や拍手の中のバレリーナ
> étoile filante — la ballerine quitte l'opéra sous une salve d'applaudissements
>> カディジャ　エル　ブルカディ/Khadija El Bourkadi
>> （モロッコ/Morocco）

流星や母と娘は同じ刺青
> étoile filante — mère et fille le même tatouage
>> ナタシャ　カール　ベスソノフ/Natacha Karl Bezsonoff
>> （フランス/France）

流星や愛の始まりその終わり
> stella cadente — dove inizia e finisce un desiderio
>> アントニオ　ジラルディ/Antonio Girardi（イタリア/Italy）

流星や息だけで言ふ願ひごと
> shooting star — whisper my wish in a breath...
>> ミレラ　ブライレーン/Mirela Brailean（ルーマニア/Romania）

流れ星水平線で溶けにけり
> étoile filante — au passage elle fond à l'horizon
>> アブデラク　アタラ/Abdelhak Attalah（アルジェリア/Algeria）

運命は神へ戻りて流れ星
> shooting star — another fate returns to its creator
>
> ザンザミ　イスマイル/Zamzami Ismail（インドネシア/Indonesia）

果しなき秘めた熱情流れ星
> stella cadente — la passione nascosta che non ha fine
> shooting star — hidden passion without end
>
> クリスティーナ　プルビレンティ/Cristina Pulvirenti
> （イタリア/Italy）

流星や名も無き花を輝かせ
> stelle cadenti a illuminare fiori senza nome
>
> リディア　マンドラチア/Lidia Mandracchia（イタリア/Italy）

流星や願ひは天高く飛翔
> stelle cadenti — un desiderio vola lassù nel cielo
>
> ローザ　マリア　ディ　サルバトーレ/Rosa Maria Di Salvatore
> （イタリア/Italy）

流星や消えることなき旅ごころ
> stella cadente — desiderio d'altrove inesaudito
>
> リタ　モアール/Rita Moar（イタリア/Italy）

流星や全ての願ひ空に散り
> stelle cadenti — tutti i desideri sparsi nel cielo
>
> アグネーゼ　ジオロンゴ/Agnese Giallongo（イタリア/Italy）

流れ星未完の句集の題名に
> étoile filante — le titre de mon recueil inachevé
>
> アブダラ　ハジイ/Abdallah Hajji（モロッコ/Moroco）

流星や心に満ちてゆく希望
> stelle cadenti — infonde una speranza e ubriaca i cuori
> shooting stars — it instills hope and intoxicates hearts
>> パトリチア　カバローネ/Patrizia Cavallone（イタリア/Italy）

流れ星地球を通過する塵よ
> pluie d'étoiles filantes — poussière de passage sur terre
>> エレン　ズアイン/Elena Zouain（ルーマニア/Romania）

流星や思ひがけずに願ひごと
> shooting star — an extra bonus wish when least expected
>> ポール　カルス/Paul Callus（マルタ/Malta）

流星や煌めいてゐるイヤリング
> shooting star — dazzling sparkling earrings of diamonds
>> ナッキー　クリスティジーノ/Nuky Kristijno（インドネシア/Indonesia）

流星の祝福持ちて鎮火して
> the blessing of the shooting stars — a extinguished fire
> blagoslov zvijezda padalica — ugašena vatra
>> ズデンカ　ムリナー/Zdenka Mlinar（クロアチア/Croatia）

涙して眺めてをりぬ流れ星
> meteor shower — a tears in their eyes
> kiša meteora — suze u njihovim očima
>> ズデンカ　ムリナー/Zdenka Mlinar（クロアチア/Croatia）

流星やパリは聖火を手渡して
> shooting star — Paris hands over the olympic torch
>> キム　オルムタック　ゴメス/Kim Olmtak Gomes（オランダ/Holland）

流星や伝記に書かぬ言葉あり
| shooting star — word limit for biography
アンナ　イリナ/Ana Irina（ルーマニア/Romania）

水中の魚(うを)のやうなる流れ星
| comme un poisson dans l'eau — l'étoile filante
ベルナデット　クエン/Bernadette Couenne
（フランス/Ftance）

初めての子にキスの雨流れ星
| shooting star—shower of kisses to her first born child
ナッキー　クリスティジーノ/Nuky Kristijno
（インドネシア/Indonesia）

我が旅や一期一会の流れ星　　　　　　　　　　亜仁寿（自訳）
| my journey — no day is exactly the same, just as shooting star
タンポポ　アニス/Tanpopo Anis（インドネシア/Indonesia）

主の祈り静かに捧げ流れ星
| lord's prayer in silent worship — shooting star
バーバラ　オルムタック/Barbara Olmtak（オランダ/Holland）

流れ星無痛で赤子生まれたり
| étoile filante — sans douleurs la naissance du bébé
オルファ　クチュク　ブハディダ/Olfa Kchouk Bouhadida
（チュニジア/Tunisia）

寝転べは波音ばかり流れ星
| lie down with you only sound of waves— shooting stars
中野千秋/Chiaki Nakano（日本/Japan）

半世紀ぶりの横顔星流る

> ton profil après un demi-siècle — étoile filante

向瀬美音/Mine Mukose（日本/Japan）

秋風【あきかぜ・akikaze】
autumn wind / vent d'automne

The wind that blows in autumn. The autumn breeze that blows around the time of the first day of autumn is the wind that signals the arrival of autumn. In early autumn, the wind blows with lingering summer heat, gradually becoming fresher, and in late autumn, it blows with cool air. The wind is also called "golden wind" because autumn corresponds to the "Golden Element" in the Five Elements theory, and "white wind" because the color of autumn corresponds to white.

秋の囁き葉になり風に舞ひたくて

> Ah devenir feuille pour m'envoler dans le vent — chuchotis d'automne

ナディン　レオン/Nadine Léon（フランス/France）

秋風や枝奏でたるバイオリン

> vent d'automne — une branche se frotte contre une branche violon de nature

オルファ クチュク　ブハディダ/Olfa Kchouk Bouhadida（チュニジア/Tunisia）

秋風や種の生命飛んでゆき

> autumn wind — seeds fly to a new life
> jesenski vjetar — sjemenke lete u novi život

ズデンカ　ムリナー/Zdenka Mlinar（クロアチア/Croatia）

枕辺に思考の嵐秋の風
> autumn wind — a whirlwind of thoughts above the pillow
> vento autunnale — un vortice di pensieri sopra il cuscino
>> アンジェラ　ジオルダーノ/Angela Giordano（イタリア/Italy）

淡き月糸杉の間に秋の風
> vent d'automne — entre deux cyprès la lune pâle
>> アブダラ　ハジイ/Abdallah Hajji（モロッコ/Morocco）

秋風を梢にとどめノスタルジー
> brise automnale — sur les arbres un peu de nostalgie
>> アメルラディヒビ　ベント　チャデイ/AmelLadhibi Bent Chadly
>> （チュニジア/Tunisia）

ハープの音色なき風が広げたる
> soffio d'autunno — si diffonde nell'aria un suono d'arpa
>> マリア　パテルリーニ/Maria Paterlini（イタリア/Italy）

秋風や歩幅の中に浮く枝葉
> autumn wind — between steps of floating leaves
>> ザンザミ　イスマイル/Zamzami Ismail
>> （インドネシア/Indonesia）

秋風や渦を巻きたる我が思ひ
> vents forts d'automne — un tourbillon dans ma tête
>> シュピー　モイサン/Choupie Moysan（フランス/France）

秋風や夢のかけらは葉の舞に
> vento d'autunno — briciole d'un sogno in una danza di foglie
>> リットリア　ガンドルフィ/Littoria Gandolfi（イタリア/Italia）

秋風や枝葉の踊る薄明り

vent d'automne — l'ultime ballet des jeunes feuilles dans la lumière pâle

autumn wind — the final ballet of young leaves in the pale light

イザベル　ラマン　ムニエ/sabelle Lamant Meunier
（フランス/France）

秋風や畑に雀群れをなし

vento d'autunno — stormi di passeri sui campi

ガブリエル　デ　マシ/Gabriella De Masi（イタリア/Italy）

秋風や幸せほんの束の間に

vent d'automne — quelques instants de bonheur

アメルラディヒビ　ベント　チャディ/AmelLadhibi Bent Chadly
（チュニジア/Tunisia）

指先にハープ秋風流れけり　　　　　　　　　亜仁寿（自訳）

a harp — autumn wind flowing from fingertips

タンポポ　アニス/Tanpopo Anis
（インドネシア/Indonesia）

浜辺には年寄ばかり秋の風

on the beach are elderly people — winds of autumn

na plaži su osobe starije životne dobi — vjetrovi jeseni

ズデンカ　ムリナー/Zdenka Mlinar（クロアチア/Croatia）

山間を囁くやうに秋の風

voce d'autunno — il sibilo del vento tra i monti

autumn voice — the whistling of wind in the mountains

ダニエラ　ミッソ/Daniela Misso（イタリア/Italy）

秋風に逆巻く波や座礁船
> the wave curls in the autumn wind — the boats aground
> s'arriccia l'onda nel vento d'autunno — le barche in secca
>> アンジェラ　ジオルダーノ/Angela Giordano（イタリア/Italy）

秋風や肌と心に染み込んで
> penetra nella pelle e dentro il cuore — vento d'autunno
> penetrates the skin and into the heart — autumn wind
>> アンナ　リモンディ/Anna Rimondi（イタリア/Italy）

秋風や祖母の呼吸の苦しげに
> with the autumn wind the grandmother's labored breathing
> col vento d'autunno il respiro affannoso della nonna
>> アンジェラ　ジオルダーノ/Angela Giordano（イタリア/Italia）

秋風や色とりどりに葉は舞ひて
> autumn wind — colorful leaves in a dance colorful leaves in a dance
> vento d'autunno — foglie variopinte in una danza
> vent d'automne — feuilles colorées dans une danse
>> パトリチア　カバローネ/Patrizia Cavallone（イタリア/Italy）

秋風や火薬の匂ふぬいぐるみ
> autumn wind — stuffed toy with the smell of gunpowder
>> タンポポ　アニス/Tanpopo Anis（インドネシア/Indonesia）

秋風や葉がかさかさと鳴る戸口
> vento autunnale — fruscio di foglie alla mia porta
> autumn wind — rustling of leaves at my doorway
>> ダニエラ　ミッソ/Daniela Misso（イタリア/Italy）

魂と枝葉が震へ秋の風

> leaves in the autumn wind — my soul trembles
> foglie nel vento d'autunno — la mia anima trema
>
> アンジェラ　ジオルダーノ/Angela Giordano
> （イタリア/Italy）

追へばより遠のくものや秋の風

> autumn wind — the more you chase, the more it gets away
>
> エル　ハミド/El Hamied（インドネシア/Indonesia）

最後のキス秋風の中に甘き林檎

> ultimo bacio nel vento autunnale mele dolci
>
> ナザレナ　ランピニ/Nazarena Rampini
> （イタリア/Italy）

野の花に母の匂ひの秋の風

> autumn wind caressing wildflowers — the scent of mother's lullaby
> gió mùa thu vuốt ve hoa dại — thơm lời mẹ ru
>
> ディン　ニュグエン/Dinh Nguyen（ベトナム/Vietnam）

服を脱ぐ道の木々なり秋の風

> vent d'automne — sur mon chemin les arbres se déshabillent
>
> カメル　メスレム/Kamel Meslem
> （アルジェリア/Algeria）

秋風や雲へ泡へと鷗飛び

> vent d'automne — tantôt sur l'écume tantôt dans le nuage la mouette
>
> ラシダ　ジェルビ/Rachida Jerbi（チュニジア/Tunisia）

秋風にかくも儚き葉つぱかな
> fragili foglie — il vento autunnale non da' sollievo
> fragile leaves — the autumn wind gives no relief
>> マリア　パテルリーニ/Maria Paterlini（イタリア/Italy）

フルートに愁ひ奏でる秋の風
> solitude — dans sa flûte il verse tout son spleen vent d'automne
>> スアド　ハジリ/Souad Hajri（チュニジア/Tunisia）

島の鐘秋風に鳴り郷愁の波
> carillon des îles tintant dans le vent d'automne — vague nostalgie
>> フランソワーズ　バルポエ/Françoise Volpoet
>> （フランス/France）

秋風や木々に別れを囁く葉
> vent automnal — les feuilles murmurent leurs adieux aux arbres
>> スアド　ハジリ/Souad Hajri（チュニジア/Tunisia）

空つぽの草を抜けゆく秋の風
> crisp autumn wind — empty glass
>> プロビール　ギュプタ/Probir Gupta（インド/India）

秋風や最後のひと葉落ちてゆき
> autumn wind bellows at the leaves — a last one trickles down
>> キム　オルムタック　ゴメス/Kim Olmtak Gomes
>> （オランダ/Holland）

古き記憶の根を盗みたる秋の風
> vecchie radici — i ricordi rubati al vento d'autunno
>> アントニオ　ジラルディ/Antonio Girardi（イタリア/Italy）

紙飛行機茂みに消えて秋の風
> autumn wind — a paper airplane disappears behind the bushes
>
> タンポポ　アニス/Tanpopo Anis（インドネシア/Indonesia）

雑草に金色撒ける秋の風
> l'herbe folle et verte parsemée d'or de l'automne — rafales de vent
>
> ミシェル　ベルトラン/Michel Berthelin（フランス/France）

秋の風葉群光と影の中
> vento d'autunno — sciame di foglie al vento tra luce e ombra
>
> シモネッタ　パンコッテイ/Simonetta Pancotti（イタリア/Italy）

秋風や千の葉群に夕陽消え
> vento d'autunno — il tramonto si perde tra mille foglie
>
> ナザレナ　ランピニ/Nazarena Rampini（イタリア/Italy）

秋風や数回鳴きて消える鶴
> juste quelques cris — déjà les grues disparaissent au vent de l'automne
>
> ジョワ　デウ　ビーブル/Joie de Vivre（フランス/France）

秋風や雲も枝葉も川の上
> autumn breeze — clouds and leaves flow on the river
> brezza d'autunno — sul fiume scorrono nuvole e foglie
>
> アンジェラ　ジオルダーノ/Angela Giordano（イタリア/Italy）

秋風やもう葉の落ちた大通り
> vento d'autunno — le foglie già caduche lungo il viale
>
> ミレラ　エステル　ペノンヌ　マシ/Mirella Ester Pennone Masi
> （イタリア/Italy）

秋風や祖母の写真を愛撫して
> brezza d'autunno — sulla foto di nonna una carezza
>
> ダニエラ　ミッソ/Daniela Misso（イタリア/Italy）

秋風や淋しきものは瓶の口
> autumn wind — the loneliest is mouth of bottle
>
> 中野千秋/Chiaki Nakano（日本/Japan）

感性の錆落とすべく秋の風
> enlever la rouille des sens — vent d'automne
>
> 向瀬美音/Mine Mukose（日本/Japan）

短調の和音続きて秋の風
> accord mineur continu — vent d'automne
>
> 向瀬美音/Mine Mukose（日本/Japan）

秋の嵐【あきのあらし・akinoarashi】
antomn storm / orages d automne

A storm that blows in autumn with the passage of a front. However, it is not as strong as a typhoon.

初嵐娘は腕に隠れたり
> orages d automne — ma fille se cache dans mes bras
>
> フテン　フルチ/feten.fourti（チュニジア/Tunisia）

初嵐木の葉混乱したりけり
> orage en vue — les feuilles désorientées les feuilles désorientées
>
> ゾラ　ナブリ　タベ/Zohra nabli tabet（チュニジア/Tunisia）

難民の祖国の地図を濡らす嵐

> oage — dans la poche du réfugié la carte de sa patrie se mouille
>
> アブダラ　ハジイ/Abdallah Hajji
>
> (モロッコ/Morocco)

雨に葉に秋の嵐の予兆あり

> tempête automnale — pluie et feuilles glougloutent vers les avaloirs
>
> スアド　ハジリ/Souad Hajri(チュニジア/Tunisia)

初嵐我が憂鬱を吹き飛ばし

> la mareggiata — lascio andare questa malinconia
>
> アンジェラ　ジオルダーノ/Angela Giordano
>
> (イタリア/Italy)

嵐の夜空のベンチと街路灯と

> un temporale — sulle panchine vuote illuminate dai lampioni
>
> マリオ　デ　サンティス/Mario De Santis
>
> (イタリア/Italy)

花びらの狂つたダンス嵐来る

> pétales envolées — la tempête prend le soin de rythmer leur danse affolée
>
> ナジェ　ボクリ/Najet Bokri(チュニジア/Tunisia)

嵐の夜ゆつくり警報ベルの鳴る

> slowly goes out a bell sound — autumn vespers
> lento si spegne un suono di campana — vespro autunnale
>
> アンジェラ　ジオルダーノ/Angela Giordano
>
> (イタリア/Italy)

嵐過ぎ真青な湖に戻りけり

> typhoon passed — sky blue reflected on the lake that returns to calm
>
> 　　　　　　　タンポポ　アニス/Tanpopo Anis（インドネシア/Indonesia）

嵐来る鷗は羽で知らせたる

> présageant la tempête — les mouettes font signe aux pêcheurs
>
> 　　　　　　　　　　ゾラ　ナブリ　タベ/Zohra nabli tabet
>
> 　　　　　　　　　　　　　　　　　　（チュニジア/Tunisia）

人生のどんでん返し嵐の夜

> soir d'orage — un coup de théâtre dans ma vie.
>
> 　　　　　　　ナタシャ　カール　ベズソノフ/Natacha Karl Bezsonoff
>
> 　　　　　　　　　　　　　　　　　　（フランス/France）

初嵐音の重さの変わりたる

> orages d'automne — le poids changeant du bruit
>
> 　　　　　　　エレナ　ズアイン/Elena Zouain（ルーマニア/Romania）

初嵐ショールの中に砂の粒

> tempête — dans mon châle les grains de sable
>
> 　　　　　　　アブダラ　ハジイ/Abdallah Hajji（モロッコ/Morocco）

砂嵐砂丘のオアシス消えにけり

> tempête de sable — entre les dunes je perds l'oasis
>
> 　　　　　　　アブダラ　ハジイ/Abdallah Hajji（モロッコ/Morocco）

初嵐かんばせに受く水飛沫

> autumn storm water splash on my face
>
> 　　　　　　　中野千秋/Chiaki Nakano（日本/Japan）

まどろみの中まで秋の嵐かな

> autumn storm — coming even into slumber
>
> 中野千秋/Chiaki Nakano（日本/Japan）

初嵐日本列島縦長し

> tempête — îles japonaises longuement étirées
>
> 向瀬美音/Mine Mukose（日本/Japan）

台風【たいふう・taifu】
typhoon / typhon

A tropical cyclone that forms in the North Atlantic or the South China Sea and has maximum wind speeds of 17 meters per second or higher. It often strikes Japan around the time of the harvest season, causing severe damage.

台風や家を巻き込む円錐形

> typhoon — grey giant cone shaped turns around sweeping houses
>
> ザンザミ　イスマイル/Zamzami Ismail
>
> （インドネシア/Indonesia）

台風や重き旅にて着く葉書

> typhoon — postcard heavy travel
>
> ザンザミ　イスマイル/Zamzami Ismail
>
> （インドネシア/Indonesia）

台風や時間を無駄にしない祖父

> typhoon — the grandfather resists the neglect of time
>
> tifone — il nonno resiste all'incuria del tempo
>
> アンジェラ　ジオルダーノ/Angela Giordano（イタリア/Italy）

地平線跨ぎ台風去つてゆく
> calm the heart — a typhoon across the horizon
> pacato il cuore — un tifone attraverso l'orizzonte
>> アンジェラ　ジオルダーノ/Angela Giordano（イタリア/Italy）

野分来て灯りの消えた墓の上
> tifone — sulle tombe i lumini spenti
>> ガブリエラ　デ　マシ/Gabriella De Masi（イタリア/Italy）

台風や丘にテントの避難民
> typhon — sur la colline les tentes des affligés
>> アブダラ　ハジイ/Abdallah Hajji（モロッコ/Morocco）

台風や政治討論続きたる
> typhoon — politicians debate stage
>> アリアニ　ユハナ/Ariani Yuhana（インドネシア/Indonesia）

台風や母なる自然怒りたる
> typhoon — the anger of mother's nature
>> マリア　ブライレーン/Mirela Brailean
>> （ルーマニア/Romania）

台風や移民は旅を続けたる
> typhon — les émigrés clandestins continuent leur traversée
>> オルファ　クチュク　ブハディタ/Olfa Kchouk Bouhadida
>> （チュニジア/Tunisia）

自然界の怒り爆発台風来
> typhoon — nature vents her anger from ocean to ocean
>> ポール　カルス/Paul Callus（マルタ/Malta）

玄関に枝葉の山や台風来

> tifone — mucchi di foglie sulla soglia di casa
>
> ガブリエラ　デ　マシ/Gabriella De Masi（イタリア/Italy）

家庭内暴力のあと台風過

> typhoon — the devastation of domestic abuse
>
> ポール　カルス/Paul Callus（マルタ/Malta）

古き詩を読む地下倉庫台風来

> typhoon — locked in the cellar reading old poems
> typhon — enfermé à la cave à lire d'anciens poèmes
>
> ジャン　ユーグ　シュイ/Jean-Hughes Chuix
> （フランス/France）

オリーブは影を抱きしめ台風来

> tempête d'automne — l'olivier embrassant son ombre
>
> アブダラ　ハジイ/Abdallah Hajji（モロッコ/Morocco）

息苦しほどの静寂野分去る

> stifling — the silence after a cold autumn storm
>
> クリスティーナ　チン/Christina Chin
> （マレーシア/Malaysia）

台風や本の中身は整然と

> typhoon — the writing in the book is still neatly arranged
>
> エル　ハミド/El Hamied（インドネシア/Indonesia）

台風の去つた青空鳥の群

> the typhoon has passed — flock of birds flying in the blue sky
>
> タンポポ　アニス/Tanpopo Anis（インドネシア/Indonesia）

台風過鳥はしじまを聞いてをり
> fin de l'orage — les oiseaux se taisent pour écouter le silence
>
> イザベル　カルバロ　テール/Isabelle Carvalho Teles
> （フランス/France）

台風や抱きついてくる見知らぬ子
> typhoon — an unknown child hugged me
>
> エル　ハミド/El Hamied（インドネシア/Indonesia）

台風が新しき砂丘作る浜
> typhon — nouvelles dunes sur la côte déserte
>
> エレナ　ズアイン/Elena Zouain
> （ルーマニア/Romania）

猫の眼の金色めきて大嵐
> un peu plus d'or — dans les yeux du chat
> big storm — a little more gold in the cat's eyes
>
> イザベル　ラマン/Isa Lamant（フランス/France）

まどろみの中まで秋の嵐かな
> autumn storm coming even into my slumber
>
> 中野千秋/Chiaki Nakano（日本/Japan）

台風の渦をほどいてみたきかな
> typhoon — I want to untangle its vortex
>
> 中野千秋/Chiaki Nakano（日本/Japan）

そこはかと野分の予兆眠る猫
> au premier signe de typhon — le chat dort sans pressentiment
>
> 向瀬美音/Mine Mukose（日本/Japan）

台風過素知らぬ空のすきとほる

> fin de l'orage — le ciel innocent est si bleu
>
> 向瀬美音/Mine Mukose(日本/Japan)

秋の雨【あきのあめ・akinoame】
autumn rain / pluie d'automne

Rainfall in autumn. There are various types of rainfall, including heat-relieving rain in early autumn, strong and heavy rain brought by typhoons, and cold rain in late autumn, but the long autumn rainfall caused by autumn rain fronts is the most impressive. Compared to the spring rain, the autumn long rain has a sad atmosphere

秋雨や村のスープは田舎風

> autumn rain — scent of broth in the village
>
> pioggia autunnale — profumo di brodo nel paese
>
> ダニエラ ミッソ/Daniela Misso(イタリア/Italy)

秋の雨大地の匂ひ立ちにけり

> première pluie d'automne — dans l'air l'odeur de la terre
>
> スアド ハジリ/Souad Hajri(チュニジア/Tunisia)

秋の雨シンバル響く幕開けか

> un bruit de timbales — le rideau bouge — pluie d'automne
>
> フランソワーズ チュイリエ/Thuillier Françoise
> (フランス/France)

秋雨や君の手帳に筆滑り

> pluie d'automne — ma plume glisse dans ton carnet
>
> カリン コシュト/Karine Cocheteux(フランス/France)

秋雨や言葉残さず消える君
> elle disparaît sans laisser un mot — pluie d'automne
>> アブデラヒム　ベンサイド/Abderrahim Bensaïd
>>> (モロッコ/Morocco)

秋雨や艶を増したる鳩の羽
> pluie d'automne — la tourterelle lisse ses plumes
>> フランソワーズ　デニオ-ルリエーブル/Françoise Deniaud-Lelièvre
>>> (フランス/France)

樹々はみな天に感謝す秋の雨
> pluie d'automne — les arbres remercient le ciel
>> ベルナデット　クエン/Bernadette Couenne(フランス/France)

秋雨や褐色の葉の絨毯に
> pluies d'automne — un tapis de feuilles rousses
>> イザベル　カルバロ　テール/Isabelle Carvalho Teles
>>> (フランス/France)

秋雨や翡翠翼を広げたる
> pluie d'automne — le martin-pêcheur déploie ses ailes
>> イメルダ　セン/Imelda Senn(スイス/Switzerland)

秋雨に流されて気の澄み渡る
> si rinfresca e purifica l'aria — pioggia autunnale
>> アンジェラ　ジオルダーノ/Angela Giordano(イタリア/Italy)

秋雨を裸で浴びる荒野かな
> autumn rain — wilderness nude bath
>> ザンザミ　イスマイル/Zamzami Ismail(インドネシア/Indonesia)

秋雨の庭新しくなりにけり
> pluie d'automne — renouveau du jardin
>> アンヌ-マリー　ジュベール-ガヤール／Anne-Marie Joubert-Gaillard
>>> （フランス／France）

秋雨や何かの伝言なのかしら
> pluie d'automne — messagères
>> エウジニア　パラシブ／Eugénia Paraschiv
>>> （ルーマニア／Romania）

大仏の顔に斑点秋の雨
> spots of the great Buddha statue's face — autumn rain
>> タンポポ　アニス／Tanpopo Anis（インドネシア／Indonesia）

秋雨や猫背伸びして欠伸して
> pluie d'automne — à la fenêtre un chat s'étire et l'autre bâille
>> ナディン　レオン／Nadine Léon（フランス／France）

秋雨や冷えた空気に誘はれて
> pioggia autunnale — mi porta verso casa l'aria di sempre
>> アントニア　ジラルディ／Antonio Girardi（イタリア／Italy）

カクテルに飾るパラソル秋の雨
> pioggia d'autunno — un ombrellino sul cocktail alla frutta
>> ガブリエラ　デ　マシ／Gabriella De Masi
>>> （イタリア／Italy）

秋雨や飲み込む大地喜びて
> pluie automnale — le coeur de la terre se réjouit
>> スアド　ハジリ／Souad Hajri（チュニジア／Tunisia）

遊び場の急に静かに秋の雨
> autumn rain — sudden silence of the playground
>
> バリー　レビン/Barrie Levine（米国/United States）

新聞に包んだ卵秋の雨
> pioggia autunnale — in un vecchio giornale le uova fresche
>
> ガブリエラ　デ　マシ/Gabriella De Masi（イタリア/Italy）

曇天より雫浮く葉や秋の雨
> pluie — sur les feuilles des gouttes de ciel gris
>
> ナディン　レオン/Nadine Léon（フランス/France）

葉についた太陽洗ふ秋の雨
> washing sunlight off the leaves — autumn rain
>
> バリー　レビン/Barrie Levine（米国/United States）

秋雨の中に震へる馬車の音
> shiverings sound of the horse carts in the autumn rain
>
> ザンザミ　イスマイル/Zamzami Ismail
>
> （インドネシア/Indonesia）

秋雨や地面を探る祖父の杖
> autumn rain — grandfather's stick probes the ground
> pioggia autunnale — il bastone del nonno sonda il terreno
>
> アンジェラ　ジオルダーノ/Angela Giordano（イタリア/Italy）

金銀に輝く枝葉秋の雨
> pluie d'automne — les feuilles d'or auréolées d'argent
>
> フランソワーズ　デニオ-ルリエーブル/Françoise Deniaud-Lelièvre
>
> （フランス/France）

秋雨や通りに彩を溢れさす
> autumn rain — flooding the street with color
>> マリリン　アッシュボフ/Marilyn Ashbaugh
>>> (米国/United States)

秋雨や何処も同じ寂寥感
> poggia notturna — in tutti i posti desolazione
>> アグネーゼ　ジオロンゴ/Agnese Giallongo(イタリア/Italy)

秋雨や収穫の時期告げる鐘
> autumn rain — the bells of the sky herald the time of harvest
>> ザヤ　ヨウクハンナ/Zaya Youkhanna
>>> (オーストラリア/Australia)

秋雨や紙に詩歌をしたためて
> retour des pluies — sur un papier les mots d'une poésie
>> シルビー　テロラズ/Sylvie Theraulaz(フランス/France)

秋雨や家に染み込む静寂なり
> pioggia d'autunno — un silenzio assorto entra in casa
>> アンジェラ　バルディ/Angela Baldi(イタリア/Italy)

秋の雨音符の跳る古き池
> autumn rain — musical notes falling into the old pond
>> タンポポ　アニス/Tanpopo Anis(インドネシア/Indonesia)

秋の雨わが手の中に空集め
> autumn rain — gathering in my hands a little bit of sky
>> ローザ　マリア　ディ　サルバトーレ/Rosa Maria Di Salvatore
>>> (イタリア/Italy)

秋雨や優しくなれる緑と花
> pluie généreuse d'automne — la verdure et les fleurs plus tendres
>
> アメルラディヒビ　ベント　チャディ/AmelLadhibi Bent Chadly
>
> （チュニジア/Tunisia）

秋の雨亀の甲羅に跳ね上がる
> autumns rain — dancing on turtle's carapace
>
> ラシュミ　モハパトラ/Rashmi Mohapatra（インド/India）

秋雨やリュックの底に金の砂
> pioggia d'autunno — in fondo allo zaino sabbia doratav
>
> ナザレナ　ランピニ/Nazarena Rampini
>
> （イタリア/Iraly）

秋雨や金の枝葉は光増し
> première pluie — les feuilles d'or plus éclatantes
>
> マルレヌ　アレクサ/Marlene Alexa
>
> （フランス/France）

秋雨や猫は隠れて箱の中
> autumn rain — a cat takes shelter inside a box
>
> デニス　カンバロウ/Dennys Cambarau（イタリア/Iraly）

秋の雨濡れたタイルの匂ひかな
> autumn rain — the smell in the house of wet tiles
>
> エル　ハミド/El Hamied（インドネシア/Indonesia）

秋雨や石丸くする川の音
> pluie d'automne — le bruit de la rivière arrondit les galets
>
> エレナ　ズアイン/Elena Zouain（ルーマニア/Romania）

秋雨や小道に錆びた葉重なり
> pluie d'automne — les feuilles rousses damassent le sentier
>
> マルレヌ　アレクサ/Marlene Alexa
>
> （フランス/France）

秋雨や雨傘の上にスタッカート
> pluie automnale — son staccato continu sur mon parapluie
>
> フランソワーズ　ボルポエ/Françoise Volpoet
>
> （フランス/France）

蜘蛛の巣はダイヤちりばめ秋の雨
> toile d'araignée sertie de diamantines — automne pluvieux
>
> スアド　ハジリ/Souad Hajri
>
> （チュニジア/Tunisia）

秋雨や行方なき葉が隅に寄り
> autumn afternoon rain — homeless leaf fly into small corner
> mưa chiều mùa thu — chiếc lá vô gia cư bay vào góc nhỏ
>
> ディン　ニュグエン/Dinh Nguyen
>
> （ベトナム/Vietnam）

珈琲が終はれば別れ秋の雨
> autumn rain — we part ways when coffee is done
>
> 中野千秋/Chiaki Nakano（日本/Japan）

秋時雨【あきしぐれ・akishigure】
light autumn rain / pluie légère d'automne

> It refers to the rain that falls at the end of autumn, but soon stops, leaving a somewhat wistful feeling. It has been used since the Kokinshu. Shigure means winter.

ラジオより静かな曲や秋時雨
> light autumn rain — calm music plays on the radio
>
> ポール　カルス/Paul Callus（マルタ/Malta）

秋時雨長きバカンス終わる日に
> le prime piogge — dopo la lunga estate si torna a casa
>
> マリア　パテルリーニ/Maria Paterlini（イタリア/Italy）

甘やかな虚無を囁き秋時雨
> light autumn rain — whispers of sweet nothings
>
> ポール　カルス/Paul Callus（マルタ/Malta）

ドビュッシー静かに流れ秋時雨
> light autumn rain — calming music by Debussy
>
> ポール　カルス/Paul Callus（マルタ/Malta）

テーブルの蠟燭消えて秋時雨　　　　　　　　　　亜仁寿（自訳）
> the candle on the table going out — drizzle in late autumn
>
> タンポポ　アニス/Tanpopo Anis（インドネシア/Indonesia）

赤煉瓦倉庫濡らして秋時雨
> autumn light rain — wetting the red brick warehouse
>
> 中野千秋/Chiaki Nakano（日本/Japan）

詩のための言の葉いくつ秋時雨

> pluie légère d'automne — combien des mots pour le poème
>
> 向瀬美音/Mine Mukose（日本/Japan）

秋時雨高層ビルの灯の潤む

> pluie légère d'automne-immeuble — tour se mouille de lumière
>
> 向瀬美音/Mine Mukose（日本/Japan）

稲妻【いなづま・inazuma】
lightning / éclair

A flash of lightning that seems to crack the sky. While the loud thunder is a summer term, lightning is an autumn term because it was believed to produce rice.

稲妻や空に広がる縞模様

> le temps d'un éclair — zébrures dans le ciel
>
> ベルナデット　クエン/Bernadette Couenne
>
> （フランス/France）

稲光り骨の髄まで怖れけり

> lightning bolt — fear creeps into the bones
>
> レフィカ　デディック/Refika Dedić
>
> （ボスニア　ヘルチェ　ゴビナ/Bosnia and Herzegovina）

稲光り空びりびりに引き裂いて

> lightning bolt — rips the sky to pieces
>
> レフィカ　デディック/Refika Dedić
>
> （ボスニア　ヘルチェ　ゴビナ/Bosnia and Herzegovina）

稲光り夜空は裂けてしまひけり
> éclairs dans la nuit — le ciel se déchire en tonnant
> lightning in the night — the sky is torn apart by thunder
>
> キュディレロ　プルム/Cudillero Plume
>
> （フランス/France）

命日や詩人天から稲光り
> heavenly lightninges on the poet's nameday — St. Elijah the Thunderbolt
> nenapisani filmski scenarij — pjesnikovo siromaštvo
>
> ズデンカ　ムリナー/Zdenka Mlinar（クロアチア/Croatia）

眠る虎起こすべからずはたた神
> don't wake the sleeping tiger — thunder boom
>
> ザンザミ　イスマイル/Zamzami Ismail
>
> （インドネシア/Indonesia）

焼畑に広がる土地や稲光り
> lightning — expansing lands by firing forests
>
> アリアナ　ユハナ/Ariani Yuhana（インドネシア/Indonesia）

君の目に恐怖の過ぎる稲光
> lightning — for a split second fear in her eyes
>
> ポール　カルス/Paul Callus（マルタ/Malta）

稲妻を激しく反射する海よ
> scarica un fulmine — sullo specchio del mare occhi impetuosi
> lightning discharges on the mirror of sea — impetuous eyes
>
> クリスティーナ　プルビレンティ/Cristina Pulvirenti
>
> （イタリア/Italy）

秋の雷人形撫でてゐたりけり

> tuoni d'autunno — accarezzo la mia bambola
>
> ジオバンナ　ジオイア/Giovanna Gioia（イタリア/Italy）

稲光夢見続けてゐたりけり

> eclair — celà ne m'empêche pas de rêver
>
> カディジャ　エル　ブルカディ/Khadija El Bourkadi
>
> （モロッコ/Morocco）

稲光女王崩御のニュースあり

> lighting — queen death news
>
> アリアナ　ユハナ/Ariani Yuhana
>
> （インドネシア/Indonesia）

雷鳴や心臓の拍けたたまし

> tonnerre et éclair — le rythme cardiaque est assourdissant
>
> パトリチア　カバローネ/Patrizia Cavallone（イタリア/Italy）

雷鳴や一瞬家の揺れるごと

> the thunder that follows a lightning — my house shakes
>
> クリスティーナ　チン/Christina Chin
>
> （マレーシア/Malaysia）

稲妻や露の攻撃はまだ続き

> lightning — russian won't stop attacking Ukraine
>
> アリアナ　ユハナ/Ariani Yuhana（インドネシア/Indonesia）

稲光真夜中のドア叩く音

> lightning — in the middle of the night sharp knocks on the door
>
> ポール　カルス/Paul Callus（マルタ/Malta）

雷鳴や関節軋む音のして
> tonnerre d'automne — le craquement des articulations
>> アブダラ　ハジイ/Abdallah Hajji（モロッコ/Morocco）

ギャロップや稲妻だんだん近づきて
> chevaux au galop — les éclairs d'orage de plus en plus proches
>> イザベル　カルバロ　テール/Isabelle Carvalho Teles
>> （フランス/France）

音までを数える母よ稲光
> lightning — mother counts the interval between flash and sound
>> ポール　カルス/Paul Callus（マルタ/Malta）

稲光あたふたとする水牛よ
> lightning — buffalo lost control
>> ザンザミ　イスマイル/Zamzami Ismail
>> （インドネシア/Indonesia）

雷の波空の腑に深き怒り
> vagues de tonnerre — des entrailles du ciel une immense colère
>> イザベル　カルバロ　テール/Isabelle Carvalho Teles
>> （フランス/France）

その度にドラムの響く稲光
> lightning — drum rolls after each flash
>> ポール　カルス/Paul Callus（マルタ/Malta）

稲妻や跡形もなく割れる空
> lightning — the sky cracked without a trace
>> エル　ハミド/El Hamied（インドネシア/Indonesia）

稲妻や俳句の神が降りてくる

> lightning — descent muse of haiku
>
> 中野千秋/Chiaki Nakano（日本/Japan）

秋の虹【あきのにじ・akinoniji】

autumn rainbow / arc-en-ciel d'automne

A rainbow in autumn. While summer rainbows clearly hang in the sky, autumn rainbows are often pale in color and disappear quickly.

秋の虹世界の町をつなぐやう

> arc-en-ciel d'automne — reliant toutes les villes du monde
>
> オルファ　クチュク　ブハディダ/Olfa Kchouk Bouhadid
>
> （チュニジア/Tunisia）

大地へのプロムナードや秋の虹

> arc en ciel d'automne — vers de terre en promenade
>
> エウジェニア　パラシブ/Eugénia Paraschiv
>
> （ルーマニア/Romania）

ゆつくりと時に寄り添ふ秋の虹

> autumn rainbow — accompanying the streak of time slowly and slowly
>
> ナニ　マリアニ/Mani Mariani
>
> （オーストラリア/Australia）

秋の虹未来にきつといいことが

> arcobaleno d'autunno — i colori d'un futuro migliore
>
> シルビア　ビストッチ/Silvia Bistocchi（イタリア/Iyaly）

秋の虹子はカラフルなものを描き
> autumn rainbow — children draw various colours objects..
>
> アリアナ　ユハナ/Ariani Yuhana（インドネシア/Indonesia）

君の不在心配したり秋の虹
> il s'inquiète de son absence — arc-en-ciel d'automne
>
> アブデラヒム　ベンサイド/Abderrahim Bensaïd
>
> （モロッコ/Morocco）

天と地に艶やかな橋秋の虹
> a colorful bridge between heaven and earth — autumn rainbow
> un ponte colorato tra cielo e terra — arcobaleno d'autunno
>
> アンジェラ　ジオルダーノ/Angela Giordano（イタリア/Italy）

秋の虹澄んだ湖面に映りたり
> reflections on the crystal clear lake — autumn rainbow
>
> クリスティーナ　チン/Christina Chin（マレーシア/Malaysia）

ロンドンは涙と薔薇や秋の虹
> arcobaleno — sull'autunno di Londra lacrime e rose
>
> シルビア　ビストッチ/Silvia Bistocchi（イタリア/Italy）

女王の帽子鮮やか秋の虹
> arc-en-ciel d'automne — indélébiles les couleurs des chapeaux de la reine
>
> ジャニン　シャルメトン/Jeanine Chalmeton（フランス/France）

押し花を本の間に秋の虹
> arcobaleno autunnale — fiori secchi tra le pagine di un libro
>
> ダニエラ　ミッソ/Daniela Misso（イタリア/Italy）

秋の虹老いても褪せぬ希望あり

> autumn rainbow — hope does not fade with old age
>
> ポール　カルス/Paul Callus（マルタ/Malta）

秋の虹君の笑顔に釘付けに

> autumn rainbow — I was stunned by her beautiful smile
>
> スカディ　ソノカヨ/Sukadi Sonokaryo（インドネシア/Indonesia）

友情の色合ひをして秋の虹

> autumn rainbow — the colours of friendship
>
> キム　オルムタック　ゴメス/Kim Olmtak Gomes（オランダ/Holland）

秋の虹ひとつは君の好きな色

> autumn rainbow—one of which is still your favorite color
>
> エル　ハミド/El Hamied（インドネシア/Indonesia）

秋の虹追ひかけてゐるハイウエイ

> autumn rainbow chasing all the way — highway
>
> 中野千秋/Chiaki Nakano（日本/Japan）

秋夕焼【あきゆうやけ・akiyuyake】
autumn sunset/ coucher de soleil d'automne

However, the word "sunset" is a summer term. Unlike the intense color and heat of summer sunsets, autumn sunsets are somewhat lonely.

秋夕焼果物の影の甘く濃く

> crepuscolo autunnale — danzano le ombre sui frutti maturi
>
> シルビア　ビストッチ/Silvia Bistocchi（イタリア/Italy）

秋夕焼や綿飴いちごの味のして
> zucchero filato — il tramonto sa di fragola
>
> ジオバンナ　ジオイア/Giovanna Gioia（イタリア/Italy）

秋夕焼無限に広ぐ夕日なり
> coucher de soleil d'automne — le crépuscule s'étend à l'infini
>
> ソニア　ベン　アマール/Sonia Ben Ammar
>
> （チュニジア/Tunisia）

秋夕焼混ざりたる色連なりぬ
> tramonto — i colori mescolati nel canale
>
> ステファニア　アンドレオニ/Stefania Andreoni
>
> （イタリア/Italy）

壮大な海に灯台秋夕焼
> rosso tramonto — il faro gia' acceso sul mare immenso
>
> アルベルタ　カテリナ　マトリ/Alberta Caterina Mattoli（イタリア/Italy）

紫の秋の夕焼け陽は湖に
> il cielo viola — sul lago al crepuscolo luci riflesse
>
> アルベルタ　カテリナ　マトリ/Alberta Caterina Mattoli（イタリア/Italy）

秋夕焼どこから出づるメランコリー
> couchant d'automne — je ne sais quoi de tendrement mélancolique dans le coeur
>
> フテン　フルチ/feten.fourti（チュニジア/Tunisia）

秋夕焼虚しさの影消えにけり
> al crepuscolo — le ombre scompaiono nel mio vuoto
>
> マリオ　デ　サンティス/Mario De Santis（イタリア/Italy）

港には九月の秋の夕焼よ
> promeneurs de septembre — déjà le crépuscule baigne le port
>
> ジャニン　シャルメトン/Jeanine Chalmeton（フランス/France）

夕焼けに赤く染まれるアルジェの村
> couleur du village — au crépuscule il vire au rouge
>
> アタラ　アブデラティフ/Attalah Abdellatif（アルジェリア/Algeria）

秋夕焼思ひ出とみに蘇る
> pensées — dans les rayons du crépuscule un souvenir
>
> カメル　メスレム/Kamel Meslem（アルジェリア/Algeria）

秋夕焼和らぐ光空に浮く
> declin du jour d'automne — une lumière tamisée baigne au ciel
>
> カメル　メスレム/Kamel Meslem（アルジェリア/Algeria）

紅き光樹々を染めたる秋夕焼
> une lumire rouge teinte les arbres — tombée du jour d'automne
>
> カメル　メスレム/Kamel Meslem（アルジェリア/Algeria）

秋夕焼薔薇色の雲かフラミンゴ
> sur le ciel crépusculaire — un nuage rose ou un flamant flamboyant
>
> アメルラディヒビ　ベント　チャディ/AmelLadhibi Bent Chadly
>
> （チュニジア/Tunisia）

空満たす赤と金色秋夕焼
> autumn sunset — from bright red to golden hues filling the sky
>
> ナッキー　クリスティジーノ/Nuky Kristijno
>
> （インドネシア/Indonesia）

樫の葉を舐めてゐるごと秋夕焼

> tongue of sunlight licking the leaves of the oak_ autumn sunset
>
> プロビール　ギュプタ/Probir Gupta（インド/Indoa）

丘さへもさよならと言ひ秋夕焼

> utumn sunset — hills too saying sayonara
>
> プロビール　ギュプタ/Probir Gupta（インド/Indoa）

秋夕焼メランコリーな葦の歌

> couchant d'automne — le chant mélancolique des roseaux
>
> エレナ　ズアイン/Elena Zouain
>
> （ルーマニア/Romania）

秋夕焼赤く眩しき地平線

> autumn sunset — dazzling red sky at the edge of horizon
>
> ナッキー　クリスティジーノ/Nuky Kristijno
>
> （インドネシア/Indonesia）

秋夕焼け畑の中に祖父独り　　　　　　　　　　亜仁寿（自訳）

> autumn sunset — grandfather alone in the field
>
> タンポポ　アニス/Tanpopo Anis
>
> （インドネシア/Indonesia）

今生の影を並べて秋夕焼

> the shadows stand side — by side autumn sunset
>
> 中野千秋/Chiaki Nakano（日本/Japan）

伴天連の殉教はるか秋夕焼

> au loin le martyre chrétien — couchant d'automne
>
> 向瀬美音/Mine Mukose（日本/Japan）

刻々と墨絵のごとく秋夕焼

> de plus en plus comme lavis — couchant d'automne
>
> 向瀬美音/Mine Mukose（日本/Japan）

包まるる黄金の渦秋夕焼

> enveloppé par un tourbillon dore — couchant d'automne
>
> 向瀬美音/Mine Mukose（日本/Japan）

霧【きり・kiri】
fog / brume

A phenomenon that occurs in autumn when fine particles of water form in the air like white smoke. The same phenomenon occurs not only in autumn but also in spring, and is called haze (a seasonal term for spring). In contrast to "haze," which flutters in the distance, "mist" is cool and lingers in the air.

朝霧やパン一切れにベリージャム

> brume matinale — une tartine à la gelée de mûre
>
> フランソワーズ　デニオ-ルリエーブル/Françoise Deniaud-Lelièvre
>
> （フランス/France）

パレットに日の出と秋の霧の色

> palette du peintre — couleur brume d'automne au soleil levant
>
> イザベル　カルバーロ　テール/Isabelle Carvalho Teles
>
> （フランス/France）

夕霧や山の麓に翁ゐて

> foggy twilight — old man at the foot of the hill
>
> アユング　ヘルマワン/Ayung Hermawan（インドネシア/Indonesia）

朝霧や残月そして港に船
> la luna indugia tra nebbie mattutine — la barca in porto
>
> アンナ　リモンディ/Anna Rimondi（イタリア/Italy）

夢破れ伝説の城は霧の中
> rêves effilochés — la brume habille le château de légendes
>
> ジャニン　シャルメトン/Jeanine Chalmeton
>
> （フランス/France）

夕間暮川面に霧の立ち込める
> nebbia al tramonto — i contorni del fiume si uniscono
>
> ジオバンナ　ジオイア/Giovanna Gioia（イタリア/Italy）

霧立ちて人の形の消えにけり
> the outlines of the people have vanished — autumn fog
> svaniti i contorni delle persone — nebbia d'autunno
>
> アンジェラ　ジオルダーノ/Angela Giordano
>
> （イタリア/Italy）

霧襖背中に震へありにけり
> echarpe brumeuse — frissons sur l'échine
>
> リュシー　ソレイユ/Lucie Soleil（フランス/France）

喪の月や影はぼんやり霧の中
> mourning moon — blurry shadows in the mist
>
> クリスティーナ　チン/Christina Chin（マレーシア/Malaysia）

平原の農村隠す秋の霧
> brouillard d'automne — dans la plaine le village agricole caché
>
> カメル　メスレム/Kamel Meslem（アルジェリア/Algeria）

山霧や日の出冠のごときに
> una corona di nebbia sui monti — alba d'autunno
>
> シルビア　ビストッチ/Silvia Bistocchi(イタリア/Italy)

秋霧や鷗も迷子になる広さ
> foschia d'autunno — un gabbiano si perde nell'immenso
>
> ガブリエラ　デ　マシ/Gabriella De Masi(イタリア/Italy)

街灯の明かりに霧は消えゆけり
> lampadaire allumé — le brouillard se dissipe
>
> リュシー　ソレイユ/Lucie Soleil(フランス/France)

韻文にわれを忘れて霧の夜
> seguo la rima — e me stessa dimentico sera nebbiosa
> I follow the rhyme and forget myself — misty evening
>
> クリスティーナ　プルビエンティ/Cristina Pulvirenti
> (イタリア/Italy)

朝霧やシーツに隠れたる体
> ceața din zori — trupul iubitei ascuns sub voalul de in
> the dawn mist — the lover's body hidden under the linen veil
>
> ダニエラ　トピシーン/Daniela Topîrcean(ルーマニア/Romania)

霧の帯海へたなびき君を待つ
> la nebbia è un obi disteso sopra il mare — sera d'attesa
>
> アンナ　リモンディ/Anna Rimondi(イタリア/Italy)

山霧や真珠色なるベルベット
> brume au loin sur la montagne — blanc nacré des nuages veloutés
>
> リュシー　ソレイユ/Lucie Soleilu(フランス/France)

薄霧や丘は稜線重ねつつ
> light fog — behind that hill are layers of other hills
>
> ザンザミ　イスマイル/Zamzami Ismail
>
> (インドネシア/Indonesia)

薄霧や二羽の白鳥湖の上
> thin fog — a pair of swans flapping on the surface of the lake
>
> ザンザミ　イスマイル/Zamzami Ismail
>
> (インドネシア/Indonesia)

秋の霧潤ふ肌の輝きて
> foschia autunnale — la luminosità della tua pelle liscia
>
> アンジェラ　ジオルダーノ/Angela Giordano（イタリア/Italy）

霧の絵に音もなく孤独の欠片
> foggy — a painting of fragments of silence in solitude
>
> ナニ　マリアニ/Nani Mariani（オーストラリア/Australia）

霧の朝クロワッサンを温めぬ
> nebbia al mattino — il profumo di brioches calde
> morning fog — the scent of hot croissants
>
> ダニエラ　ミッソ/Daniela Misso（イタリア/Italy）

薄霧や木々は浮かんで空中に
> low mist — a tree floats in mid-air
>
> ポール　カルス/Paul callus（マルタ/Malta）

姿なき鶫の声や霧深し
> foothills — dusky thrush sound clear in the fog
>
> タンポポ　アニス/Tanpopo Anis（インドネシア/Indonesia）

黒き鳥の嘴黄色霧の中
> dense haze — the yellow beak of a blackbird on the branch
> densa foschia — l becco giallo di un merlo sul ramo
>> アンジェラ　ジオルダーノ/Angela Giordan（イタリア/Italy）

秋の霧湖に光を散りばめて
> nebbia autunnale — sulle creste del lago quel po' di luce
> autumn mist — on the crests of lake that little bit of light
>> クリスティーナ　プルビエンティ/Cristina Pulvirenti（イタリア/Italy）

バーチャルな友達ばかり秋の霧
> all'apparenza amici virtuali — nebbia d'autunno
>> ジオバンナ　ジオイア/Giovanna Gioia（イタリア/Italy）

朝霧や街と思考を覆ひたる
> un velo sulla citta' ed i pensieri — aube brumeuse
>> アルベルタ　カテリナ　マトリ/Alberta Caterina Mattoli（イタリア/Italy）

霧立ちて祖母の思ひ出色褪せぬ
> the memory of the grandmother still brilliant — autumn mist
> la memoria della nonna ancora brillante — bruma d'autunno
>> アンジェラ　ジオルダーノ/Angela Giordano（イタリア/Italy）

灯台へ続ける霧の深き道
> strada di nebbia — uno sciame di fari segna la via
>> シルビア　ビストッチ/Silvia Bistocchi（イタリア/Italy）

子は森に踏み込んで行く濃霧の日
> l'enfant en forêt — frimas de l'automne
>> エウジェニア　パラシブ/EugéniaParaschiv（ルーマニア/Romania）

朝靄や林檎の落つる鈍き音
> misty morning — the falling apples' muffled sound
>> ジャック　ミショネ/Jacques Michonnet（フランス/France）

君の目の青さに欠ける岸の霧
> quai des brumes — dans ses yeux le bleu qui manque
>> シュピー　モイサン/Choupie Moysan（フランス/France）

霧の湖さざめく波の微光粒
> nebbia autunnale sulle creste del lago quel po' di luce
> autumn mist — on the crests of lake that little bit of light
>> クリスティーナ　プルビエンティ/Cristina Pulvirenti
>> （イタリア/Italy）

引潮や静かに消えてゆく海霧
> low tide — the silent retreat of sea fog
>> クリスティーナ　チン/Christina Chin（マレーシア/Malysia）

秋の霧悲しみ響く四十雀
> brume d'automne — le chant d'une mésange teinté de chagrin
>> フランソワーズ　モリス/Francoise Maurice（フランス/France）

柔らかき雰囲気村に秋の霧
> ambiance ouatée — premières brumes automnales sur le village
>> ブリジット　モンルブー/Brigitte Monloubou（フランス/France）

霧深し愛されること疑はず
> thickened fog — I still delude myself she will love me
>> マウリチオ　ブランカレオーニ/Maurizio Brancaleoni
>> （イタリア/Italy）

霧深し君の心は戻らない
> nebbia addensata: mi illudo ancora che mi vorrà bene
> thickened fog — I still delude myself she will love me
>> マウリチオ　ブランカレオーニ/Maurizio Brancaleoni
>>> (イタリア/Italy)

朝霧やゆつくり進む老人の歩
> brouillard de l'aube — d'un pas lent un vieil homme chemine
>> カメル　メスレム/Kamel Meslem(アルジェリア/Algeria)

老人が網を広げる霧の中
> autumn fog — the old man spread the net
>> エル　ハミド/El Hamied(インドネシア/Indonesia)

霧襖光を渇望してやまぬ
> automne châle de brume — l'âme avide de lumière
>> トウーン　チャベ/Tounès Thabet(チュニジア/Tunisia)

朝霧や沼を渡れる雁の声
> matin brumeux — les voix des oies sauvages traversent les marais
>> エレナ　ズアイン/Elena Zouain(ルーマニア/Romania)

霧深しページ憂鬱満たしたる
> brume d'automne — un ennui remplit la page
>> エレナ　ズアイン/Elena Zouain(ルーマニア/Romania)

霧深ししなのき長袖着てゐるやう
> maniche lunghe sulle foglie del tiglio un velo di nebbia.
>> ナザレナ　ランピニ/Nazarena Rampini
>>> (イタリア/Italy)

過去のドア開いて閉じて霧の中
> adrift in the fog — doors of the past opening and closing
>
> ジェリー　ブラヴィ/Gerry Bravi(カナダ/Canada)

朝霧や母が最後の息をして
> early morning mist — my mother's last breath on the bed
>
> タンポポ　アニス/Tanpopo Anis
>
> (インドネシア/Indonesia)

憂鬱や静寂の後ろに霧の立ち
> spleen — derrière ce silence la brume se lève
>
> カメル　メスレム/Kamel Meslem(アルジェリア/Algeria)

静けさや霧は色彩覆ひたる
> nebbia d'autunno — nei colori velati silenzio
>
> フロリンダ/Florinda(イタリア/Italy)

霧のかけら鷺の声空独り占め
> lambeaux de brume d'un cri le héron cendré s'approprie le ciel
>
> ナディン　レオン/Nadine Léon(フランス/France)

霧雨の線路の上のかたつむり
> rain drizzle on the train track — snail crawls
>
> ザヤ　ヨウクハンナ/Zaya youkhanna
>
> (オーストラリア/Australia)

忘れられた城の現れる霧の森
> derrière la forêt apparaît dans la brume un château oublié
>
> アグネス　ボーマル/Agnes Beaumale
>
> (フランス/France)

夕霧や家々の灯の琥珀色
> nebbia di sera — una luce ambrata dentro le case
> evening fog — inside the houses amber light
>> ダニエラ　ミッソ/Daniela Misso（イタリア/Italy）

霧雨や猫毛繕ひゆつくりと
> brouillasse — mon chat prolonge sa toilette
>> パトリック　ソンプル/Patrick Somprou（フランス/France）

秋霧や木々の葉つぱはもうなくて
> brume d'automne — d'un souffle la feuille n'est plus de l'arbre
>> ナディン　レオン/Madine Léon（フランス/France）

秋の霧葦は未だに生き生きと
> nebbia d'autunno — il canneto brulica ancora di vita
>> ミレラ　エステル　ペノンヌ　マシ/Mirella Ester Pennone Masi
>> （イタリア/Italy）

霧雨の降る日や祖母のドライアイ
> drizzle — grandma's dry eyes
> acquerugiola — gli occhi secchi della nonna
>> アンジェラ　ジオルダーノ/Angela Giordano（イタリア/Italy）

霧深し足音だけの歩道橋
> epais brouillard — juste le bruit des pas sur la passerelle
>> パトリック　ソンプル/Patrick Somprou（フランス/France）

朝霧やシュールな静謐な風景
> alba nebbiosa — surreale scenario di tranquillita
>> アルベルタ　カテリナ　マトリ/Alberta Caterina Mattoli（イタリア/Italy）

甲高き声あげ鷲が霧をゆく
> screeching sound — an eagle flies through the mist
>
> エル　ハミド/El Hamied（インドネシア/Indonesia）

霧立ちて漁師は銀の川に触れ
> ceața de toamnă — luntrașul atinge râul argintiu
> autumn mist — the fisherman touches the silver river
>
> ダニエラ　トピセーン/Daniela Topîrcean
> （ルーマニア/Romania）

朝霧や胡桃の木だけある窓辺
> brouillard du matin — seul le noyer à ma fenêtre
>
> ジャニン　シャルメトン/Jeanine Chalmeton
> （フランス/France）

霧の湖月に向かつて魚が跳ね
> mists rise from the lake reflections of autumn light fish leap for the moon
>
> ラシュミ　モハパトラ/Rashmi Mohapatra（インド/India）

霧晴れて全容見せて富士の山
> the fog clears — mount Fuji in its immensity
>
> キム　オルムタック　ゴメス/Kim olmtak Gomes
> （オランダ/Holland）

霧の窓開けて葉つぱの水の粒
> premier brouillard — fenêtre ouverte, les feuilles perlent
> first fog — open window, beads of water on the leaves
>
> ミュールバッハ　アキツ/F.Mühlebach akitsu
> （フランス/France）

秋の日の夜明けはすでに霧かかり
> nebbia nel sole alba d'autumo
> brouillard daus le soleil lever de soleil d'automne
>
> フランチェスコ　パラディノ/Francisco Palladino
> （イタリア/Italy）

石と玉の間に昔の冬の霧の匂ひ
> tra marmi e pietre un profumo antico nebbia d'autunno
>
> フランチェスコ　パラディノ/Francisco Palladino
> （イタリア/Italy）

朝霧や淡海にかかる長き橋
> brume matinale — grand pont au-dessus du lac 'Biwako'
>
> 向瀬美音/Mine Mukose（日本/Japan）

薄霧や伊豆大島の遙かなる
> brouillard léger — lointaine 'Izuooshima'
>
> 向瀬美音/Mine Mukose（日本/Japan）

山霧やまほろば大和沈めたる
>
> 向瀬美音/Mine Mukose（日本/Japan）

露【つゆ・tsuyu】
dew / rosée

A ball of water tied to a blade of grass or other plant. Dew occurs throughout the year, but is most common in autumn, so the word dew simply means autumn. Since dew disappears quickly, it is also a symbol of transience.

子等飛べば芝生の露も飛びにけり

> un bimbo salta — schizza fresca rugiada tra l'erba fitta
>
> ミケーレ　ポチエロ/Michele Pochiero
>
> (イタリア/Italy)

露と嵐交はるるちさき朝（あした）かな

> petit matin — la rosée épouse la pluie d'orage...
>
> アンヌ-マリー　ジュベール-ガヤール/Anne-Marie Joubert-Gaillard
>
> (フランス/France)

露雫母の最後の言葉とも

> dew drops — last message from my mom
>
> ザンザミ　イスマイル/Zamzami Ismail (インドネシア/Indonesia)

蛇口には一筋の水秋の露

> rosée d'automne — un filet d'eau s'écoule du robinet
>
> ベルナデット　クエン/Bernadette Couenne
>
> (フランス/France)

秋の露小さき雛の軽き布団

> léger duvet du petit poussin — rosée d'automne
>
> ベルナデット　クエン/Bernadette Couenne
>
> (フランス/France)

朝露や睡蓮の湖静かなる
> morning dew — calm peace rests on the water lily lake
>> クリスティーナ　チン/Christina Chin（マレーシア/Malaysia）

小休止枝葉の上に露雫
> short break — dew drops on leaves
>> ザンザミ　イスマイル/Zamzami Ismail（インドネシア／Indonesia）

秋の露水浴びのいと楽しくて
> rosée d'automne — le plaisir de baignade
>> エウジェニア　パラシブ/EugéniaParaschiv（ルーマニア/Romania）

秋の露赤子に含む乳のごと
> rosée d'automne — la première goutte de colostrum pour le nouveau-né
>> オルファ　クチュク　ブハディダ/Olfa Kchouk Bouhadida
>> （チュニジア/Tunisia）

秋の露生命誕生瑞々し
> rosée d'automne — l'instant de notre naissance
>> エウジェニア　パラシブ/EugéniaParaschiv（ルーマニア/Romania）

金色の枝葉に露の朝日かな
> foglie dorate — la prima luce brilla sulla rugiada
> golden leaves — first light shines on dew
>> クリスティーナ　プルビエンティ/Cristina Pulvirenti（イタリア/Italy）

露雫落ちて大地の濡れにけり
> outtelettes de rosée — enfin mouillée la nature
>> ゾラ　ナブリ　タベ/Zohra nabli tabet（チュニジア/Tunisia）

露雫裸足で歩く修行僧
> autumn dew — the bare feet of a ascetic
>> ミルセア　モルドバン/Mircea Moldovan
>>> (ルーマニア/Romania)

夜明け待つ薔薇の花弁に露雫
> wait for dawn — dew droplets on rose petals
>> ザンザミ　イスマイル/Zamzami Ismail
>>> (インドネシア/Indonesia)

朝露や静かな羽の蝶のゐて
> nell'aurora di rugiada — su ali silenziose una farfalla
> in the dewy dawn — on silent wings a butterfly
>> パトリチア　カバローネ/Patrizia Cavallone(イタリア/Italy)

露しづく墓前の花に宿りたる
> drops of dew — on your flowers from your grave
>> アグネーゼ　ジアロンゴ/Agnes Giallongo(イタリア/Italy)

露雫涙を溜めている瞳
> dewdrops — tears swell in her eyes
>> ポール　カルス/Paul Callus(マルタ/Malta)

皺くちやの葉に染み込んで露雫
> drops of dews rubbing ointment on the wrinkled leaves
>> プロビール　ギュプタ/Probir Gupta(インド/India)

朝露や夜明けに平野喉癒し
> rugiada all'alba — si disseta il prato prima del giorno
>> リタ　モアール/Rita Moar(イタリア/Italy)

万華鏡の世界となりぬ露葎

> un caleidoscopio di colori — campo rugiadoso
> a kaleidoscope of colours — dewy field

ダニエラ　ミッソ/Daniela Misso（イタリア/Italy）

露雫裸足になつて歩きたし

> rosée — j'aimerais marcher pieds-nus
> dew — I would like to walk barefoot

ミュールバッハ　アキツ/F.Mühlebach akitsu
（フランス/France）

朝露や君の唇濡したる

> nuage de rosée — la fraicheur mouille tes lèvres

エリック　デスピエール/Eric Despierre
（フランス/France）

あかときや光まみれの草と露

> soleil levant — le champ d'herbe et de rosée trempées de lumière.

ナディン　レオン/Nadine Léon（フランス/France）

道沿ひの葉の煌めきて露雫

> rugiada — le foglie brillano lungo il sentiero
> dew — leaves shimmer along the path

ダニエラ　ミッソ/Daniela Misso（イタリア/Italy）

初キス薔薇の露雫

> dew drops on roses — first kiss
> giọt sương trên hoa hồng — nụ hôn đầu tiên

ディン　ニュグエン/Dinh Nguyen
（ベトナム/Vietnam）

光の真珠薔薇の上には露雫

> perle di luce — le gocce di rugiada sopra le rose
>
> ローザマリア　ディサルバトーレ/Rosa Maria Di Salvatore
> 　　　　　　　　　　　　　　　　　　　　　　（イタリア/Italy）

曲線で出来てる宇宙露の玉

> dew drop — the universe made of curves
>
> 中野千秋/Chiaki Nakano（日本/Japan）

地 (ちり) 理

(chiri)
geography
geographie

秋の山 【あきのやま・akinoyama】
autumn mountain / montagne d'automne

The mountains stand out clearly in the clear air. The lush green mountain, which retains the vestiges of summer, changes to a mountain of fruitfulness, and is eventually colored with autumn leaves in late fall. The mountain is also a popular destination for hikers, mushroom pickers, and autumn leaf peepers.

物言はぬ秋の山々愛すべき

> I likè this silence — autumn mountain
>
> ザンザミ　イスマイル/Zamzami Ismail
>
> (インドネシア/Indonesia)

旧友と無言で歩く秋の山

> montagna d'autunno — tranquille passeggiate con una vecchia amica
>
> automn mountain — quiet walks with an old friend
>
> カルメン　バシキリ/Carmen Baschieri (イタリア/Italy)

秋の山谷間に寺のありにけり

> autumn mountain temple — descending on the valley stillness
>
> キム　オルムタック　ゴメス/Kim Olmtak Gomes (オランダ/Holland)

秋の山谷へ下れる牛の群

> autumn mountains — cows go down to the valleys
>
> ポール　カルス/Paul Callus (マルタ/Malta)

ハイカーは草の中なり秋の山

> in glasses of a mountain biker — autumn mountain
>
> イシ　ヘルヤント/Isni Heryanto (インドネシア/Indonesia)

秋の山驢馬の鳴き声不意を打つ

> montagna autunnale — il raglio di un asino inaspettato
>
> ミケーレ　ポチエロ/Michele Pochiero（イタリア/Italy）

秋の山栗の香纏ふ褐色の風

> le vent fauve a le parfum de chataignes — montagne d'automne
>
> ラシダ　ジェルビ/Rachida Jerbi（チュニジア/Tunisia）

秋の山琥珀色めく夕明り

> montagna d'autunno — la luce ambrata della sera
>
> autumn mountain — the amber light of the evening
>
> ダニエラ　ミッソ/Daniela Misso（イタリア/Italy）

秋の山ヨガ上昇の姿勢なり

> montagne d'automne — des postures de yoga en élévation
>
> ベルナデット　クエン/Bernadette Couenne
>
> （フランス/France）

秋の山慎ましく服脱ぎにけり

> montagne d'autunno — i fianchi sempre più spogli
>
> シルビア　ビストッチ/Silvia Bistocchi（イタリア/Italy）

我が村より日は登りたり秋の山

> montagne d'automne — le soleil se lève de mon village
>
> アブダラ　ハジイ/Abdallah Hajji（モロッコ/Morocco）

秋の山羊の匂ひのシェパードと

> autumn mountain — shepherds withe the smell of sheep
>
> エウジェニア　パラシブ/Eugénia Paraschiv
>
> （ルーマニア/Romania）

秋の山極彩色の帽子なり
　　chapeau multicolore — ellle peint les montagnes d'automne
　　　　　　　　　　シュピー　モイサン/Choupie Moysan（フランス/France）

金色のタッチで変はる秋の山
　　montagnes d'automne — une touche dorée change la peinture
　　　　　　　　　　オルファ　クチュク　ブハディダ/Olfa Kchouk Bouhadida
　　　　　　　　　　　　　　　　　　　　　　　　（チュニジア/Tunisia）

消えゆける光を追ひて秋の山
　　follow its fading light — autumn mountain
　　　　　　　　　　クリスティーナ　チン/Christina Chin（マレーシア/Malaysia）

坂道や朝日を受けて秋の山
　　the ride up hill — autumn mountain looks stunning at sunrise
　　　　　　　　　　ナッキー　クリスティジーノ/Nuky Kristijno（インドネシア/Indonesia）

秋の山静かに聳え風の中
　　monte d'autunno — il silenzio nel vento lassù in cima
　　autumn mountain — silence in the wind up there
　　　　　　　　　　クリスティーナ　プルビエンティ/Cristina Pulvirenti
　　　　　　　　　　　　　　　　　　　　　　　　（イタリア/Italy）

秋の山君のこだまを探したる
　　montage d'automne — je quête l'écho qu'elle me renvoie.
　　　　　　　　　　イスマーヘン　カーン/Ismahen Khan（チュニジア/Tunisia）

秋の山の枝葉は川を黄くす
　　foglie d'autunno della montagna all pianura un fume giallo
　　　　　　　　　　フランチェスコ　パラディノ/Francisco Palladino（イタリア/Italy）

しばらくは入日を溢す秋の山

> flooding the sunset for a while — autumn mountain
>
> 中野千秋/Chiaki Nakano（日本/Japan）

いただきは雲の匂ひよ秋の山

> l'odeur du nuage au sommet — montagne d'automne
>
> 向瀬美音/Mine Mukose（日本/Japan）

> ### 刈田【かりた・karita】
> **harvested ricefield / rizière moissonnée**
>
> Rice field after harvesting. Rice is dried and bags of rice husks are packed between the rice paddies. It is a relaxing view of the countryside after the harvest.

刈田にて脱穀といふ解脱かな

> threshing in harvested rice fields — moments of revelation
>
> ポール　カルス/Paul Callus（マルタ/Malta）

人去りて鳥動き出す刈田かな

> harvested rice field — when workers leave birds move in
>
> ポール　カルス/Paul Callus（マルタ/Malta）

籾仕舞う刈田の小屋となりにけり

> harvested ricefield — farmers reserve dry paddy in small wood hut
>
> アリアナ　ユハナ/Ariani Yuhana
>
> （インドネシア/Indonesia）

日没に仕事納める刈田かな

harvested rice field — the workers follow the setting sun

ポール カルス/Paul Callus（マルタ/Malta）

女達は赤子を背負ふ刈田かな

harvested rice field — vilage woman holds her baby on her back

アリアナ　ユハナ/Ariani Yuhana

（インドネシア/Indonesia）

飛びかかる茶色い飛蝗ゐる刈田

harvested ricefield — brown grasshopper attack

アリアナ　ユハナ/Ariani Yuhana

（インドネシア/Indonesia）

山脈は屏風のごとし刈田道

mountains like a folding screen — harvested rice field road

中野千秋/Chiaki Nakano（日本/Japan）

すいすいと銀輪滑る刈田道

velo glisse comme un poisson dans la risière moissonnée

向瀬美音/Mine Mukose（日本/Japan）

秋の浜【あきのはま・akinohama】
autumn shore / plage d'automne

A deserted beach after summer. It often gets rough due to typhoons and other factors, and has a somewhat desolate atmosphere.

足跡に俳句の生まれ秋の浜

> one haiku born from footprints — autumn shore
>
> タンポポ　アニス/Tanpopo Anis
>
> （インドネシア/Indonesia）

枝先に激しき風や秋の浜

> spiaggia d'autunno — vento impetuoso sul bordo del ramo
>
> フランチェスコ　パラディノ/Francisco Palladino
>
> （イタリア/Italy）

秋の浜鉛兵隊見守る砂の城

> plage d'automne — un soldat de plomb surveille le château de sable
>
> ラシダ　ジェルビ/Rachida Jerbi
>
> （チュニジア/Tunisia）

秋の海岸辺の漁師糸投げる

> mare autunnale — in riva un pescatore lancia la lenza
>
> テレサ　アルジオラ/Teresa Argiolas
>
> （イタリア/Italy）

秋の浜悲しみの波落ち着けり

> autumn beach — high waves of grief finally find calm
>
> キム　オルムタック　ゴメス/Kim Olmtak Gomes
>
> （オランダ/Holland）

秋の浜鷗水平線示す

> plage en automne — une seule mouette me montre l'horizon de la mer
>
> リミ　ラルビ/Limi Larbi（モロッコ/Morocco）

> **水澄む**【みずすむ・mizusumu】
> **clarity of water / eau claire**
>
> The clarity of water in autumn. Because the atmosphere is clearer in autumn, the flow of water also feels clearer

水澄めり君の波形と吾の波形

clarity of water — your waveform my waveform

中野千秋/Chiaki Nakano（日本/Japan）

松園のかそけき素描水澄めり

向瀬美音/Mine Mukose（日本/Japan）

> **秋の川**【あきのかわ・akinokawa】
> **automn river / rivière d'automne**
>
> The river reflects sardine clouds and dragonflies flit about the water's edge. In autumn, the air is cooler and the water is clearer. Children playing on the riverbank are not as active as in the summer.

秋の川水と星々共に旅

râul de toamnă — călătorind împreună apa și stelele

rivière d'automne — voyager ensemble l'eau et les étoiles

マリン　ラダ/Marin Rada
（ルーマニア/Romania）

秋の川樫の葉ときをり雲隠し

rivière d'automne — feuilles de chêne cachent les nuages de temps en temps

エレナ　ズアイン/Elena Zouain

(ルーマニア/Romania)

歩みつつ忘るる悩み秋の川

fiume d'autunno — camminando dimentico tutti gli affannia
autumn river — walking I forget all troubles

クリスティーナ　プルビエンティ/Cristina Pulvirenti

(イタリア/Italy)

表面の石の反りたる秋の川

autumn river — the stone bounced off the surface

エル ハミド/El Hamied (インドネシア/Indonesia)

葉が落ちて浮き沈みして秋の川

autumn river — leaves fall and float

キム　オルムタック　ゴメス/Kim Olmtak Gomes

(オランダ/Holland)

海岸で砂に吸はれて秋の川

absorbed into the sand at seashore — autumn river

中野千秋/Chiaki Nakano (日本/Japan)

秋の川底ひの小石月宿す

galets d'automne au fond de la rivière — la lumière de la lune

向瀬美音/Mine Mukose (日本/Japan)

秋の湖【あきのうみ・akinoumi】
autumn lake / lac d'automne

The surrounding mountains are brightly colored and the lake reflects the clear blue autumn sky.

秋の湖画家が捉える水の顔

> autumn lake — a painter captures the water's swell
>
> ポール　カルス/Paul Callus（マルタ/Malta）

秋の湖沈んだ葉には黒き魚

> autumn lake — small black fishes swim over sunk leaves in clear water
>
> アリアナ　ユハナ/Ariani Yuhana
>
> （インドネシア/Indonesia）

雲乗せて負荷のかかりて秋の湖

> nubi assembrate — sul lago autunnale un peso incombe
>
> クリスティーナ　プルビエンティ/Cristina Pulvirenti
>
> （イタリア/Italy）

オレンジの日の出に染まる秋の湖

> this morning an orange sunrise autumn lake aflame
>
> キム　オルムタック　ゴメス/Kim Olmtak Gomes
>
> （オランダ/Holland）

秋の湖月を映して静止せり

> immobile anche la luna riflessa lago d'autunno
> motionless even the moon reflected autumn lake
>
> ダニエラ　ミッソ/Daniela Misso（イタリア/Italy）

黒々と岬のかたち秋の潮

> black shape of cape autumn tide

中野千秋/Chiaki Nakano(日本/Japan)

秋の海【あきのうみ・akinoumi】
autumn sea / mer d'automne

The sea has turned deep in color and the waves have become a little higher in the fall.

移民者の舟の揉まれて秋の海

> autumn sea — boats of migrants at the mercy of the waves
> mare autunnale — barconi di migranti in balia delle onde

アンジェラ　ジオルダーノAngela Giordano
(イタリア/Italy)

秋の海波のワルツはゆつたりと

> mer d'automne — que des vagues qui valsent lentement

スアド　ハジリ/Souad Hajri(チュニジア/Tunisia)

秋の海凪いでささやくほどの波

> automne — le murmure des vagues meuble le silence de la mer

スアド　ハジリ/Souad Hajri(チュニジア/Tunisia)

秋の浜心模様が砂の上

> autumn beach — traces of my heart on the sand

ザヤ　ヨウクハンナ/Zaya youkhanna
(オーストラリア/Autaralia)

秋の海波の侵食受けた崖
> autumn sea — the cliffs eroded by the waves
> mare autunnale — le falesie erose dalle onde
>> アンジェラ　ジオルダーノAngela Giordano（イタリア/Italy）

秋の海あまねく波のシンフォニー
> mare d'autunno — la sinfonia d'onde nel gran silenzio
> autumn sea — symphony of waves in the great silence
>> クリスティーナ　プルビエンティ/Cristina Pulvirenti（イタリア/Italy）

秋の海足跡風に消えて行く
> mare autunnale — raffiche di vento cancellano le orme
>> テレサ　アンジオラ/Teresa Argiolas（イタリア/Italy）

秋の海浜に休める鷗たち
> mer d'automne — les mouettes se reposent sur le rivage
>> カルメン　バシキリ/Carmen Baschieri（イタリア/Italy）

足下にリーフのありて秋の海
> the reefs under my feet autumn sea
>> ナッキー　クリスティジーノ/Nuky Kristijno（インドネシア/Indonesia）

受け皿の水舐める猫秋の海
> autumn sea —the cat's lapping in the plant saucer
> mare d'autunno: il lappare del gatto nel sottovaso
>> マウリチオ　ブランカレオーニ/Maurizio Brancaleoni（イタリア/Italy）

秋の海島の先にも島があり
> autumn sea another island beyond the island
>> 中野千秋/Chiaki Nakano（日本/Japan）

水平線濃淡にして秋の潮

| nuance de l'horizon — mer d'automne

向瀬美音/Mine Mukose（日本/Japan）

> ### 秋の潮【あきのしお・akinoshio】
> autumn tides / marées d'automne
>
> Tides ebb and flow in the autumn sea. Autumn tides are deep in color and ebb and flow. The seaside is quiet after the bustle of summer has passed.

人生の流れのごとし秋の潮

| autumn tides — people come and go as life passes

キム　オルムタック　ゴメス/Kim Olmtak Gomes

（オランダ/Holland）

秋の潮持ち去る吾子の砂の城

| les marées d'automne — le château de sable de mon enfant emporté

向瀬美音/Mine Mukose（日本/Japan）

Kigo Gallery-2

七夕/the Star Festival …p268

新酒/new sake …p270（新酒と新米）

案山子/scarecrow …p275（稔田に立つ案山子）

生（せいかつ）活
(seikatsu)
life
vie

七夕【たなばた・tanabata】
the Star Festival / festival des étoiles

The night of the seventh day of the seventh lunar month, or the night of the festival. It is the night when Orihime and Hikoboshi are allowed to cross the Milky Way and meet once a year. On earth, people celebrate this night by decorating Tanabata bamboos with strips of paper with wishes written on them.

短冊や願ひの揺れる竹の先

tanzaku appesi — su ogni bambù ondeggia un desiderio

アンナ　リモンディ/Anna Rimondi（イタリア/Italy）

七夕や風にため息と願ひと

tanabata — desideri e sospiri mossi dal vento

アンナ　リモンディ/Anna Rimondi（イタリア/Italy）

紙吹雪の洪水の道星祭

un déluge de confettis dans la rue — tanabata

ベルナデット　クエン/Bernadette Couenne

（フランス/France）

七夕や願ひは糸に隠されて

tanabata — desideri nascosti appesi a un filo

アンジェラ　ジオルダーノ/Angela Giordano

（イタリア/Italy）

人知れず願ひの糸を掴みをり

tanabata — desideri nascosti appesi a un filo

アンジェラ　ジオルダーノ/Angela Giordano

（イタリア/Italy）

七夕やまだ織つている彼のもの
> tanabata — she is still finishing weaving souvenirs for her lover
>
> ザンザミ　イスマイル/Zamzami Ismail（インドネシア/Indonesia）

魔法使ひ再会したる星祭
> festival des étoiles — les premières retrouvailles des sorcières
>
> アブデラハイム　ベンサイド/Abderrahim Bensaïd
>
> （モロッコ/Morocco）

七夕や星もウィンクするらしき
> star festival — planets exchanging winks
>
> ザヤ　ヨウクハンナ/Zaya Youkhanna（オーストラリア/Australia）

愛と言ふ贈り物あり星祭
> the star festival — 'love is a many splendored' gift
>
> ポール　カルス/Paul Callus（マルタ/Malta）

星祭空の天蓋いと近き
> festival des étoiles — la voûte céleste si proche de moi
>
> アメル　ラドヒビ　ベント　チャディ/Amel Ladhibi Bent Chadly
>
> （チュニジア/Tunisia）

星祭スパンコールを纏ふ空
> festival des étoiles —le ciel s'habille en paillettes
>
> アメル　ラドヒビ　ベント　チャディ/Amel Ladhibi Bent Chadly
>
> （チュニジア/Tunisia）

七夕や湯浴みてよりの紅をさし
> star festival put on lipstick after bathing
>
> 中野千秋/Chiaki Nakano（日本/Japan）

新酒【しんしゅ・shinshu】
new sake / saké nouveau

Sake brewed with the new rice of the year. In the old days, sake was brewed as soon as the new rice was harvested, so the season was set in autumn, but nowadays cold brewing is the norm. However, the season is now dominated by cold brewing. Nevertheless, this season's word still includes the celebration of the harvest of new rice.

金毘羅や新酒を生める泉あり
> sanctuaire de Konpira — l'eau de source pour le saké nouveau
>> アンヌ-マリー　ジュベール-ガヤール/Anne-Marie Joubert-Gaillard
>>> (フランス/France)

鮮やかな夢の中なり新酒注ぐ
> sogni vividi — versare il nuovo saké
> vivid dreams — pouring new sake
>> ダニエラ　ミッソ/Daniela Misso(イタリア/Italy)

新酒酌み漱石の詩に酔ひにけり
> le saké nouveau — un recueil de Sôseki m'enivre
>> チュイリエ　フランソワーズ/Thuillier Françoise
>>> (フランス/France)

荒走り明日断食始めたる
> saké nouveau — demain commence le jeûne
>> ベルナデット　クエン/Bernadette Couenne(フランス/France)

荒走り呆然とした頭なり
> la tête étourdie de soleil — saké nouveau
>> ベルナデット　クエン/Bernadette Couenne(フランス/France)

荒走りラブストーリー始まりぬ

> le saké nouveau — histoire d'amour
>
> エウジェニア　パラシブ/EugéniaParaschiv
>
> (ルーマニア/Romania)

先祖よりの鉢に新酒を満たしけり

> ancestral set — serving new sake in a ceramic bowl
>
> クリスティーナ　チン/Christina Chin（マレーシア/Malaysia）

新酒酌む酔ひてだんだん異世界へ

> new sake — I am getting lost in the strange world
>
> タンポポ　アニス/Tanpopo Anis（インドネシア/Indonesia）

団欒の会話の続く新酒かな

> september walk — in the forest a mushrooms to mushrooms
> rujanska šetnja — u šumi gljiva do gljive
>
> ズデンカ　ムリナー/Zdenka Mlinar（クロアチア/Croatia）

新酒酌むひと口ずつに過去の疵

> sip by sip addressing past mistakes — new sake
>
> バーバラ　オルムタック/Barbara Olmtak（オランダ/Holland）

今年酒稚児の誕生喜びて

> nouveau saké — le nouveau-né fait la joie de route la famille
>
> カディジャ　エル　ブルカディ/Khadija El Bourkadi
>
> (モロッコMorocco)

新酒酌む気まずそうなる叔父とゐて

> new sake — uncle has something embarrassing
>
> アリアナ　ユハナ/Ariani Yuhana（インドネシア/Indonesia）

新酒酌むグラスを空にするなかれ
> new sake — don't let an empty glasses on the table
>> ザンザミ　イスマイル/Zamzami Ismail(インドネシア/Indonesia)

新酒酌む心の氷溶かしつつ
> new sake — melt the ice cliffs in his heart
>> ザンザミ　イスマイル/Zamzami Ismail(インドネシア/Indonesia)

新酒酌むどもりがちなる友の声
> new sake — my friend with his stammering voice
>> マフィズディン　チュードハリー/Mafizuddin Chowdhury(インド/India)

新酒飲む喉元にある恨みごと
> drowning grudges deep in the throat with new sake
> affogando i rancori in fondo alla gola col nuovo saké
>> アンジェラ　ジオルダーノ/Angela Giordano(イタリア/Italy)

新酒酌むひと啜りごと過去のこと
> sip by sip addressing past mistakes—new sake
>> バーバラ　オルムタック/Barbara Olmtak(オランダ/Holland)

過ぎた日の恨みを流し込む新酒
> with the new sake I push old grudges to the back of my throat
> col nuovo sakè caccio i vecchi rancori in fondo alla gola
>> アンジェラ　ジオルダーノ/Angela Giordano(イタリア/Italy)

新酒酌む君は昔の香りして
> nuovo saké — il profumo di allora sui tuoi vestiti
> new sake — the perfume of that time on your clothes
>> クリスティーナ　プルビエンティ/Cristina Pulvirenti(イタリア/Italy)

記紀の神にんげん臭し新酒酌む
> new sake — human like gods of Japanese mythology
>
> 中野千秋/Chiaki Nakano（日本/Japan）

唇に酔ひを乗せつつ新酒酌む
> buvant du saké nouveau — l'ivresse aux lèvres
>
> 向瀬美音/Mine Mukose（日本/Japan）

旅に出て二種の新酒を味はへり
> voyage—dégustation de deux sortes de saké nouveau
>
> 向瀬美音/Mine Mukose（日本/Japan）

やや薄き琥珀色なり今年酒
> légèrement ambré — saké nouveau
>
> 向瀬美音/Mine Mukose（日本/Japan）

新米【しんまい・shimmai】
new rice / nouveau riz

Rice harvested that year is available around October. This seasonal phrase expresses the joy of knowing that the rice one has spent so much time and effort to cultivate has been safely harvested again this year. Autumn festivals are held in each region to give thanks for the new rice harvest and to offer the new rice to the gods.

新米の香り寿ぐ感謝祭
> the scent of new rice — thanksgiving day at home
>
> タンポポ　アニス/Tanpopo Anis
> （インドネシア/Indonesia）

新米や妊娠したと告げられて
　　new rice — she announces her pregnancy
　　　　　　　　　　キム　オルムタック　ゴメス/Kim Olmtak Gomes
　　　　　　　　　　　　　　　　　　　　　　　（オランダ/Holland）

新米やその花の香を嗅ぎたくて
　　nouveau riz — envie de connaitre le parfum de sa fleur
　　　　　　　　　　　　　　　エレナ　ズアイン/Elena Zouain
　　　　　　　　　　　　　　　　　　　　　　　（ルーマニア/Romania）

新米や家族の会話弾みたる
　　lively conversation at the family table — new rice
　　　　　　　　　　キム　オルムタック　ゴメス/Kim Olmtak Gomes
　　　　　　　　　　　　　　　　　　　　　　　（オランダ/Holland）

新米や稚児の爪透明で
　　ongles du bébé presque transparents — nouveau riz
　　　　　　　　　　　　　　シュピー　モイサン/Choupie Moysan
　　　　　　　　　　　　　　　　　　　　　　　（フランス/France）

新米の一粒ずつの神気かな
　　new rice — god's blessing in each grain
　　　　　　　　　　　　　中野千秋/Chiaki Nakano（日本/Japan）

ふくよかな丸み持ちたる今年米
　　nouveau riz — un corps plein et arrondi
　　　　　　　　　　　　　向瀬美音/Mine Mukose（日本/Japan）

案山子【かがし・kagashi】
scarecrow / épouvantail

A doll erected in the rice paddy to protect the rice from birds. A kind of bird guard made of straw or other materials in the shape of a human being.
In the olden days, the heads of animals and fish were roasted and put on skewers and set up in the rice paddies or between rice fields to chase sparrows and other birds. This is where the word "snuffer" comes from.
The word "sniffing" is said to be derived from "sniffing".

稔田や案山子が役目全うし

> harvested rice field — scarecrow's kindness
>
> ザンザミ　イスマイル/Zamzami Ismail
> （インドネシア/Indonesia）

空き缶の騒音たてる案山子かな

> scarecrow — noisy sound of shaking gravel in cans
>
> アリアナ　ユハナ/Ariani Yuhana
> （インドネシア/Indonesia）

捨案山子雨の下に黒き帽子

> dans sa capeline noire sous la pluie — épouvantail d'automne
>
> アンヌ-マリー　ジュベール-ガヤール/Anne-Marie Joubert-Gaillard
> （フランス/France）

コロナウィルス追ひ払ふ捨案山子かな

> unique antidote for coronavirus — scarecrow tied to fence in front of house
>
> ザンザミ　イスマイル/Zamzami Ismail
> （インドネシア/Indonesia）

服脱いで案山子は棒に帰りけり

> undressed — the scarecrow is just a stick
>
> タンポポ　アニス/Tanpopo Anis（インドネシア/Indonesia）

真実を知らぬ人々案山子立つ

> scarecrow — thinking others don't know the truth
>
> アリアナ　ユハナ/Ariani Yuhana（インドネシア/Indonesia）

実り新た案山子は衣替へにけり

> new season — the scarecrow changes clothes
>
> nuova stagione — lo spaventapasseri cambia vestito
>
> アンジェラ　ジオルダーノ/Angela Giordano（イタリア/Italy）

案山子立ち鳥の国なる物語

> scarecrow — story of the land of the birds
>
> ザンザミ　イスマイル/Zamzami Ismail（インドネシア/Indonesia）

米つつく雀のそばの案山子かな

> scarecrow — sparrows peck a grain of rice
>
> アユング　ヘルマワン/Ayung Hermawan
>
> （インドネシア/Indonesia）

捨案山子涅槃の花に場所譲る

> épouvantail — il cède sa place à la fleur du nirvana
>
> オルファ　クチュク　ブハディダ/Olfa Kchouk Bouhadida
>
> （チュニジア/Tunisia）

馴染み合ひ鳥と案山子は共存す

> coexistence — birds and scarecrows adapt to one another
>
> ポール　カルス/Paul Callus（マルタ/Malta）

案山子立つ見かけによらぬこともあり
> scarecrow — looks can be deceiving
>
> ポール　カルス/Paul Callus（マルタ/Malta）

風受けて突然踊り出す案山子
> scarecrow — suddenly dance when the wind blows
>
> ナニ　マリアニ/Nani Mariani（オーストラリア/Australia）

案山子立つ四季の変化を楽しんで
> he's the only one who enjoys all seasons — scarecrow
>
> ザンザミ　イスマイル/Zamzami Ismail
> （インドネシア/Indonesia）

案山子立つ賞に輝くコメディアン
> the Scarecrow — he won the comedian competition
>
> ナニ　マリアニ/Nani Mariani（オーストラリア/Australia）

収穫や案山子無視する訪問者
> moissons — l'epouvantail semble ignorer les visiteurs
>
> カディジャ　エル　ブルカディ/Khadija El Bourkadi
> （モロッコ/Morocco）

鳥が来て見てみぬふりをする案山子
> birds pecking in the field — the scarecrow turns a blind eye
>
> ポール　カルス/Paul Callus（マルタ/Malta）

隼の嘴に骨案山子立つ
> scarecrow — a bit of bone between the beaks the falcon
>
> マフィズディン　チュードハリー/Mafizuddin Chowdhury
> （インド/India）

淡々と堂々として案山子かな
> scarecrow — simple but authoritative
>
> エル　ハミド/El Hamied（インドネシア/Indonesia）

一点を眺めて案山子立ちにけり
> scarecrow — his fixed stare
>
> キム　オルムタック　ゴメス/Kim Olmtak Gomes
> （オランダ/Holland）

収穫後案山子と鳥は和解せり
> after the harvest — the scarecrow and birds meet to make peace
>
> ポール　カルス/Paul Callus（マルタ/Malta）

案山子より挨拶されてウォーキング
> promenade — le bonjour de l'épouvantail
> walk — hello from the scarecrow
>
> マリー クレール　ブルゴ/marie-claire burgos
> （フランス/France）

収穫の影を見守る案山子かな
> l'épouvantail veille — ombres des récoltes
>
> エウジェヌ/Eugene（ロシア/Russia）

夕食時の父の寛ぎ捨案山子
> spaventapasseri — mio padre rilassato all'ora di cena
>
> アントニオ　ジラルディ/Antonio Girardi（イタリア/Italy）

案山子立つ人それぞれにある役目
> scarecrow standing — each person has a role
>
> 中野千秋/Chiaki Nakano（日本/Japan）

温め酒 【ぬくめざけ・nukumezake】
warm sake /saké chaud

On the ninth day of the ninth month of the lunar calendar, it was said that if you drank warm sake, you would not catch a cold. At this time of year, the cold weather starts to set in. It is also a good time to drink warm sake.

あつけなく終わるロマンス温め酒

> warm sake — the romance ended too soon
>
> ナッキー　クリスティジーノ/Nuky Kristijno
> （インドネシア/Indonesia）

温め酒今さら別の人なんて

> warm sake — after all I need you
>
> 中野千秋/Chiaki Nakano（日本/Japan）

傘寿の師あたため酒で祝ひけり

> anniversaire du maître de quatre vingts ans — saké chaud
>
> 向瀬美音/Mine Mukose（日本/Japan）

村芝居【むらしばい・murashibai】
village theater / théâtre villageois

A gathering of villagers to perform Kabuki and other entertainment. Often held as a festival after the harvest, it was a great pleasure for farmers in the old days when there was little entertainment.

村芝居観客は皆顔見知り
> théâtre villageois — tout le monde se connaît
>> オルファ　クチュック　ブハディダ/Olfa Kchouk Bouhadida
>>> (チュニジア/Tunisia)

手相見の女美し村芝居
> autumn raindrops — clearly the tinkling sound of shamisen
>> タンポポ　アニス/Tanpopo Anis(インドネシア/Indonesia)

甲高きオペラの歌や村芝居
> village theater — the shrill opera songs in high-pitched tones
>> クリスティーナ　チン/Christina Chin
>>> (マレーシア/Malaysia)

人混みに露店広がる村芝居
> village theatre — street vendors spread among viewers crowd
>> アリアニ　ユハナ/Ariani Yuhana
>>> (インドネシア/Indonesia)

自治体を批判している村芝居
> village theatre — criticism for local government
>> アリアニ　ユハナ/Ariani Yuhana
>>> (インドネシア/Indonesia)

観客の驚く顔や村芝居
> village theater — on the faces of the spectators the same astonishment
> teatro del villaggio — sul volto degli spettatori lo stesso stupore
>> アンジェラ　ジオルダーノ/Angela Giordano（イタリア/Italy）

村芝居まづは地元のコメディアン
> village theatre — the local comedian gets top billing
>> ポール　カルス/Paul Callus（マルタ/Malta）

即興に慌てる作家村芝居
> village theatre — the scriptwriter cringes at improvisation
>> ポール　カルス/Paul Callus（マルタ/Malta）

村芝居おのが歴史を語る家
> teatro del villaggio — ogni casa racconta la propria storia
> vllage theatre — every house tells its story
>> クリスティーナ　プルビエンティ/Cristina Pulvirenti（イタリア/Italy）

募りたる募金もありぬ村芝居
> l'appel de la quête — théâtre villageois
>> エウジェニア　パラシブ/EugéniaParaschiv（ルーマニア/Romania）

村芝居地元野菜の売られたる
> quails digging burrows in the tall grass — sand bathing
>> クリスティーナ　チン/Christina Chin（マレーシア/Malaysia）

笑ひ声響く広場や村芝居
> village theatre — laughter echoes in the main square
>> ポール　カルス/Paul Callus（マルタ/Malta）

音楽に合せ詩を読む村祭

> village festival — he reads poetry accompanied by traditional music
>
> ナニ　マリアニ/Nani Mariani
>
> (オーストラリア/AUstralia)

村芝居共に老うことの喜び

> théâtre de village — plaisir de vieillir ensemble
>
> エレナ　ズアイン/Elena Zouain
>
> (ルーマニア/Romania)

村芝居噂話の村社会

> village theatre — a tight-knit community full of gossip
>
> バーバラ　オルムタック/Barbara Olmtak
>
> (オランダ/Holland)

光る池鱒踊りたる秋祭

> ballet de truites dans la lumière du bassin — fête d'automne.
>
> ニリビ　ローラン/Nylybys Laurent
>
> (フランス/France)

終末の皆んな知つてる村芝居

> everyone knows how it ends — village theater
>
> 中野千秋/Chiaki Nakano(日本/Japan)

地酒とうに干して始まる村芝居

> théâtre de village — le saké local est déjà consommé
>
> 向瀬美音/Mine Mukose(日本/Japan)

秋思【しゅうし・shushi】
autumn sadness / tristesse d'automne

In autumn, it means to feel or think something in one's heart. In spring, it is called spring melancholy, and in autumn, it is called autumn thought. Compared to melancholy, thoughts have a dry feeling.

屑籠に葉、手紙、写真秋さびし
| feuilles, lettres et photos à la corbeille — l'automne à oublier
| ソニア　ベン　アマール/Sonia Ben Ammar
| (チュニジア/Tunisia)

秋さびし怖きヤモリはもういない
| solitude de l'automne — le gecko qui me faisait peur est mort
| ミュドハー　アリラキ/Mudher Aliraqi
| (イラク/Iraq)

秋寂しフロントガラスに葉の溜まる
| les feuilles d'arbres s'entassent sur les pare-brises — mélancolie d'automne
| アブデラヒム　ベンサイド/Abderrahim Bensaïd
| (モロッコ/Morocco)

新しき砂丘数える秋思かな
| mélancolie d'automne — je compte les nouvelles dunes
| アブダラ　ハジイ/Abdallah Hajji(モロッコ/Morocco)

さよならの涙溢るる秋思かな
| sorrow of autumn — the tears of our goodbye
| ポール　カルス/Paul Callus(マルタ/Malta)

ヴィオロンの小雨に添ふる秋思かな
> autumn melancholy — a violin accompanies the drizzling rain
>> ポール　カルス/Paul Callus（マルタ/Malta）

傷秋や妻の裏切り知つてより
> sorrow of autumn — knowing his wife betrayal
>> アリアナ　ユハナ/Ariani Yuhana
>> （インドネシア/Indonesia）

湖を渡る飛び石秋さびし
> autumn sorrow — skipping stones on the lake
> malinconia autunnale — far rimbalzare sassi sul lago
>> ダニエラ　ミッソ/Daniela Misso（イタリア/Italy）

旧友を亡くし雨恋ふ秋思かな
> nostalgie — tel un viel ami perdu
>> パトリック　ソンプル/Patric Somprou（フランス/France）

墓前には菊の花束ある秋思
> sorrow of autumn — a bunch of chrysanthemums on the grave
>> ポール　カルス/Paul Callus（マルタ/Malta）

秋さびし湖の澱みへ落つる雨
> pioggia d'autunno è un lago stagnante la malinconia
> autumn rain is a stagnant lake the melancholy
>> カルメン　バシキリ/Carmen Baschieri（イタリア/Italy）

秋さびし人生に三つの教訓
> malinconia — ricerco quei tre versi per questa vita
>> ミケーレ　ポチエロ/Michele Pochiero（イタリア/Italy）

燻る茶にゆっくり上る秋思かな
　un tè fumante — malinconia d'autunno che sale piano
　　　　　　　　アンナ　リモンディ/Anna Rimondi（イタリア/Italy）

空白のページを盗みたる秋思
　I steal a blank page from the night — autumn melancholy
　rubo alla notte una pagina bianca — malinconia d'autunno
　　　　　　　　アンジェラ　ジオルダーノ/Angela Giordano（イタリア/Italy）

紅く燃え金と輝く秋思かな
　reds and golds — the autumn mood of my heart
　　　　　　　　バリー　レビン/Barrie Levine（米国/United States）

共に居て雨音響く秋思かな
　the ticking of the rain for company — autumn melancholy
　il ticchettio della pioggia per compagnia — malinconia autunnale
　　　　　　　　アンジェラ　ジオルダーノ/Angela Giordano（イタリア/Italy）

少しずつ秋思に解けおさげ髪
　braided hair — autumn melancholy unfolds
　capelli intrecciati — si dipana la malinconia autunnale
　　　　　　　　アンジェラ　ジオルダーノ/Angela Giordano（イタリア/Italy）

墓の上に額縁写真ある秋思
　autumn sadness — framed photos on the graves
　　　　　　　　ポール　カルス/Paul Callus（マルタ/Malta）

憂愁の秋や小声で子守唄
　malinconia d'autunno — poi canta un'allodola
　　　　　　　　ガブリエラ　デ　マシ/Gabriella De Masi（イタリア/Italy）

秋さびし母のショールにラベンダーの香
> melancolie — parfumul de lavandă pe șalul mamei
> mélancolie — le parfum de la lavande sur le châle de la mère
>> マリン　ラダ/Marin Rada(ルーマニア/Romania)

秋のブルー遠くよりサクソフォーンの音
> blues d'autunno — il suono di un sax da lontano
>> ミレラ　イスター　ペノンヌ　マシ/Mirella Ester Pennone Masi
>> (イタリア/Italy)

秋さびし窓辺に休む黄色の葉
> solitude d'automne — une feuille jaune se pose sur la fenêtre
>> エレナ　ズアイン/Elena Zouain(ルーマニア/Romania)

秋寂し涙どの雲より来るの
> mélancolie d'automne — de quel nuage sont tombées ces larmes
>> ラシダ　ジェルビ/Rachida Jerbi(チュニジア/Tunisia)

村までの一人の道の秋思かな
> autumn sadness — the lonely road to the Village
>> ザヤ　ヨウクハンナ/Zaya youkhanna(オーストラリア/Australia)

虹出でて歩みの軽くなる秋思
> autumn gloomy — light my steps the rainbow
> cupo l'autunno — illumina i miei passi l'arcobaleno
>> アンジェラ　ジオルダーノ/Angela Giordano(イタリア/Italy)

姿見に秋思の部屋のありにけり
> autumn sadness — another room in the full length mirror
>> 中野千秋/Chiaki Nakano(日本/Japan)

憂愁の秋や眺める世界地図
　mélancolie d'automne — regarder la carte du monde
　　　　　　　　　　　　　向瀬美音/Mine Mukose（日本/Japan）

思ひ出の溢るる手紙秋寂し
　mélancolie d'automne — une lettre déborde de souvenirs
　　　　　　　　　　　　　向瀬美音/Mine Mukose（日本/Japan）

マリアにも菩薩にもある秋思かな
　statue de Marie statue de Bouddha — mélancolie d'automne
　　　　　　　　　　　　　向瀬美音/Mine Mukose（日本/Japan）

行事（ぎょうじ）

(gyoji)
event
ceremonie

聖人祭【せいじんさい・seijinsai】
all saints / la Toussaint

November 1st. There are many saints in the Christian faith, but it is not possible to celebrate each one individually, so a feast day is set aside to celebrate them all together. For Catholics, it is an important feast day representing autumn.

聖人の心よ天の梯子なり

> white heart — ladder to the sky all saints
> 　　　　　　　ザンザミ　イスマイル/Zamzami Ismail(インドネシア/Indonesia)

神とゆく聖人達の歩みかな

> all the saints — walk with his god
> 　　　　　　　ザンザミ　イスマイル/Zamzami Ismail(インドネシア/Indonesia)

万聖節捧げる菊の房豊か

> chrysanthèmes exposés pour la Toussaint, grosses boules
> 　　　　　　　マルセル　ペルチエ/Marcel Peltier(フランス/France)

万聖節君に触れたる残照よ

> reflets sur le marbre de Toussaint — mes doigts te parlent
> 　　　　　　　カリン　コシュト/Karine Cocheteux(フランス/France)

万聖節想ひ故郷に根を生やし

> premièr novembre — une pensée au sol natal enracinée
> 　　　　　　　カメル　メスレム/Kamel Meslem(アルジェリア/Algeria)

軋みたる歩の進む道万聖節

> primo novembre — i passi scricchiolanti turbano la via
> 　　　　　　　パトリチア　カバロ―ネ/Patrizia Cavallone(イタリア/Italy)

月のごと白菊墓に万聖節
| due novembre — sul crisantemo bianco spicchi di luna
ジナ　ボナセーラ/Gina Bonasera
(イタリア/Italy)

万聖節ひねもす菊の香りせり
| Toussaint — l'odeur des chrysanthèmes toute la journée
エレナ　ズアイン/Elena Zouain
(ルーマニア/Romania)

聖人祭小雨にけぶる坂の町
| all saint's day — hazy light rain town with many slopes
中野千秋/Chiaki Nakano(日本/Japan)

白菊のしばし華やぐ聖人祭
| chrysanthème blanc éclatant — Toussaint
向瀬美音/Mine Mukose(日本/Japan)

聖人の名を持つ子等や万聖節
| mes enfants ont tous un prénom de saint — Toussaint
向瀬美音/Mine Mukose(日本/Japan)

洗礼名マリアなりけり万聖節
| mon non de baptême 'Marie' — Toussant
向瀬美音/Mine Mukose(日本/Japan)

今生は通過点かや万聖節
| une vie est un point de passage — Toussant
向瀬美音/Mine Mukose(日本/Japan)

死後のこと少し心に万聖節

legers pensées de la vie après ma mort — Toussant

向瀬美音/Mine Mukose(日本/Japan)

子規忌【しきき・shikiki】

Shiki's memorial / anniversaire de la mort de Shiki

The anniversary of the death of Shiki Masaoka, haiku poet. Died of spinal caries on September 19, 1902. He was 35 years old.

瓢箪の赤き種落つ子規忌かな

Shiki's memorial — on the ground a red gourd seed

クリスティーナ　チン/Christina Chin

(マレーシア/Malaysia)

瓢箪の花満開の子規忌かな

Shiki's memorial — the gourd flowers blooming all over

ナニ　マリアニ/Nani Mariani(オーストラリア/Australia)

糸瓜忌や肺病といふのは夢かしら

anniversaire de la mort de Shiki — d'un malade du haiku serait-ce le rêve

フランソワーズ　チュイリエ/FrançoiseMarie Thuillier

(フランス/France)

糸瓜忌や彼の最後の俳句なり

last haiku — anniversary of Shiki's death

ultimo haiku — anniversario della morte di Shiki

アンジェラ　ジオルダーノ/Angela Giordano (イタリア/Italy)

子規の忌の花開きたる自然界
| anniversary of Shiki's death — nature blossoms
キム　オルムタック　ゴメス/Kim Olmtak Gomes
（オランダ/HOlland）

子規の忌や日本のランボー短命で
| anniversaire de la mort de Masaoka Shiki — si courte la vie du Rimbaud japonais
アンヌ-マリー ジュベール-ガヤール/Anne -Marie Joubert-Gaillard
（フランス/France）

悲しみも俳句に詠みて子規忌かな
| Shiki death anniversary — even sadness becomes a beautiful haiku
タンポポ　アニス/Tanpopo Anis（インドネシア/Indonesia）

小さきこと見くびるなかれ獺祭忌
| Shiki death anniversary — don't underestimate how small things can make a big impact
ザンザミ　イスマイル/Zamzami Ismail（インドネシア/Indonesia）

子規の忌や声に出しつつ俳句読み
| Shiki's memorial — voicing haiku with the breath of nature
キム　オルムタック　ゴメス/Kim Olmtak Gomes
（オランダ/Holland）

岩の上に赤き花ある子規忌かな
| red flowers on the rocks—Shiki's memorial
クリスティーナ　チン/Christina Chin（マレーシア/Malaysia）

柿見れば正岡子規をまづ思ふ

> Masaoka Shiki — enhanced by persimmons his memory

ポール　カルス/Paul Callus（マルタ/Malta）

皆触るへちまの丸み獺祭忌

> anniversaire de la mort de Shiki — tout le monde touche la rondeur de la gourde

向瀬美音/Mine Mukose（日本/Japan）

Kigo Gallery-3

鹿／deer …p296（奈良の鹿）

雁／wild goose …p318（夕暮れの雁）

鮭／salmon …p327（鮭の遡上）

赤蜻蛉／red dragonfly …p337

動物

(どうぶつ)

(dobutsu)

animals

animaux

鹿【しか・shika】
deer / cerf

Deer are a seasonal animal in autumn because of the melancholy sound they make when they cry out for their wives. Deer are kept in parks and other places, but in the wild, they can destroy fields, so traps are set and deer fences are erected to keep them away from human settlements.

遠き浜炎逃れる雌鹿ゐて
> rivage lointain — une biche fuit les flammes
>
> ベルナデット　クエン/Bernadette Couenne
> （フランス/France）

交差点鹿を危うく避けにけり
> deer crossing — a careless driver has a narrow escape
>
> ポール　カルス/Paul Callus（マルタ/Malta）

古き村雌鹿の食める墓地の傍
> vieux village — une biche broute autour du cimetière
>
> ナジャ　ナジャ/Naeja Naeja
> （フランス/France）

やはらかき雌鹿の目なり金の落暉
> la douceur de ses yeux de biche — crépuscule doré
>
> ラシダ　ジェルビ/Rachida Jerbi
> （チュニジア/Tunisia）

狩の季節鹿絶壁にかくれんぼ
> saison de chasse — le cerf joue à cache-cache dans les falaises
>
> イメルダ　セン/Imelda Senn
> （スイス/Switzerland）

鹿の眼にわれの姿のありにけり

> looking into the eyes of a deer i know he is with me
>
> キム　オルムタック　ゴメス/Kim Olmtak Gomes
>
> （オランダ/Holland）

月に向かひ鹿の悲しき声響く

> urlo di dolore — il bramito del cervo alla luna
>
> scream of sorrow — the roar of deer to the moon
>
> クリスティーナ　プルビエンティ/Cristina Pulvirenti
>
> （イタリア/Italy）

果樹園に小ざつぱりした鹿が来る

> well groomed visitors — deer at orchard
>
> クリスティーナ　チン/Christina Chin
>
> （マレーシア/Malaysia）

森の静寂月を待つ鹿の鳴き声

> silence de la forêt — le brame du cerf atteint la lune
>
> エレナ　ズアイン/Elena Zouain
>
> （ルーマニア/Romania）

秋さびし雌鹿のぴゆうと鳴きにけり

> automne triste — la biche brame
>
> 向瀬美音/Mine Mukose（日本/Japan）

秋されば切なき声の紅葉鳥

> automne — cri triste de la biche qui brame
>
> 向瀬美音/Mine Mukose（日本/Japan）

猪【いのしし・inoshishi】
wild boar / sanglier

A mammal of the even — toed ungulates. Its body is covered with brown fur and its neck is short and thick like a log. The name "Uribo" comes from the white vertical stripes on its body hair, like a gourd, which sometimes devour crops in the fields and cause damage to farming villages. They sometimes devour crops in the fields, causing damage to farming villages. It is the original species of pig, and is so tasty that it is called "mountain whale. It is eaten as sashimi or in boar stew.

猪の眠る茂みのマットレス

> warm mattress — wild boar sleeping beneath bushes
>
> ザンザミ　イスマイル/Zamzami Ismail
> （インドネシア/Indonesia）

猪や闘犬を見る村の衆

> wild boars — villagers watch trained dogs fighting
>
> アリアナ　ユハナ/Ariani Yuhana（インドネシア/Indonesia）

猪が掘り起こしたるさつまいも

> dug up sweet potatoes — wild boar
>
> クリスティーナ　チン/Christina Chin（マレーシア/Malaysia）

母のなき猪の子が草の上

> motherless — baby wild boars sleeping on the grass
>
> タンポポ　アニス/Tanpopo Anis（インドネシア/Indonesia）

猪や山の神社の奥に消ゆ

> wild boar — disappearing into mountain shrine
>
> 中野千秋/Chiaki Nakano（日本/Japan）

雉【きじ・kiji】
pheasant / faisan

Male pheasants are birds that call the female in spring with a "keen-kenken" call. They are more often seen walking than flying. The poem was composed as a symbol of female love.

物思ひ途切れ途切れに雉の声

ost in thought — the intermittent call of a pheasant

ダニエラ　ミッソ/Daniela Misso（イタリア/Italy）

雉子鳴いて山のフランス料理店

pheasant cry — french restaurant in the mountain

中野千秋/Chiaki Nakano（日本/Japan）

渡鳥【わたりどり・wataridori】
migratory birds / oiseaux migrateurs

Migratory birds include summer birds, winter birds, and itinerant birds. Summer birds spend the summer in Japan and engage in breeding activities. Summer birds spend the summer in Japan and are active in breeding. Major summer birds include the swallow, great bluebird, yellow — bellied flycatcher, time — warbler, and black thrush. Winter birds spend the winter in Japan and are mainly thrushes, mallards, swans, cranes, and geese. Traveling birds are birds that pass through Japan in the summer to breed in Siberia and other regions and overwinter in the south, such as the sandpiper and plover.

渡鳥風は飛翔を教えたる

le vent lui apprend à voler — oisillon migrateur

ラシダ　ジェルビ/Rachida Jerbi（チュニジア/Tunisia）

新学期に集ふ生徒ら渡鳥

> oiseaux migrateurs — les écoliers devant l'école le jour de la rentrée
>
> オルファ　クチュク　ブハディダ/Olfa Kchouk Bouhadida
>
> (チュニジア/Tunisia)

砂浜の夜明けに聞ける渡鳥

> oiseaux migrateurs — au crépuscule leurs chants sur la grève
>
> フランソワーズ　デニオ-ルリエーブル/Françoise Deniaud-Lelièvre
>
> (フランス/France)

渡鳥知らぬ大罪、温暖化

> oiseaux migrateurs — ni forfait ni changement climatique
>
> エウジェニア　パラシブ/EugéniaParaschiv
>
> (ルーマニア/Romania)

鳥渡る難民のゐるキャンプなり

> birds migrate — refugees stranded in reception camps
> migrano uccelli — i rifugiati bloccati nei campi di accoglienza
>
> アンジェラ　ジオルダーノ/Angela Giordano
>
> (イタリア/Italy)

籠の中に自由の歌や渡鳥

> oiseau migrateur — dans la cage le chant de la liberté
>
> アブダラ　ハジイ/Abdallah Hajji(モロッコ/Morocco)

残された巣より鳴き声渡鳥

> i hear a squeak in an abandoned nest — migratory bird
>
> ザンザミ　イスマイル/Zamzami Ismail
>
> (インドネシア/Indonesia)

渡鳥のリズムに雲変はる
> oiseaux migrateurs ― au rythme des oiseaux se déplacent les nuages
>
> アブデラヒム　ベンサイド/Abderrahim Bensaïd
>
> （モロッコ/Morocco）

雲間より白き羽落つ渡鳥
> oiseaux migrateurs ― d'un nuage descend une plume blanche
>
> ナディン　レオン/Nadine Léon（フランス/France）

渡鳥羽根の栞を日記の間に
> migratory birds ― a feather between two pages of my diary
>
> タンポポ　アニス/Tanpopo Anis（インドネシア/Indonesia）

渡鳥いつせいに翼羽ばたいて
> flapping of a hundred wings ― migratory birds
>
> バーバラ　オルムタック/Barbara Olmtak（オランダ/Holland）

新しき渡鳥木の皮剝がされて
> migrations nouvelles ― l'arbre déjà demi-déplumé
>
> フランソワーズ　ガブリエル/Francoise Gabriel
>
> （ベルギー/Belgium）

渡鳥空は我らのものと飛ぶ
> if you own the mainland, we are the sky owners ― migratory bird
>
> ザンザミ　イスマイル/Zamzami Ismail（インドネシア/Indonesia）

青空へ深く飛び込む渡鳥
> a plunge into the depth of sky's blue ― migratory bird
>
> バーバラ　オルムタック/Barbara Olmtak（オランダ/Holland）

渡鳥未知の世界を目指す旅
> migratory birds — the great trek to the unknown
>> キム　オルムタック　ゴメス/Kim Olmtak Gomes（オランダ/Holland）

広大な空に加はる渡鳥
> immense sky — migratory birds join the world
> cielo immense — gli uccelli migratori uniscono il mondo
>> クリスティーナ　プルビエンティ/Cristina Pulvirenti
>> （イタリア/Italy）

渡鳥翼に旅の旅程あり
> oiseau migrateur — sur ses ailes son itinéraire
>> アメル　ラディビ　ベント　シャディー/Amel Ladhibi Bent Chadly
>> （チュニジア/Tunisia）

羅針盤持たず到着渡鳥
> sans boussole arrivent à bon port — les oiseaux migrateurs
>> スアド　ハジリ/Souad Hajri（チュニジア/Tunisia）

南へと渡鳥羽広げたり
> ad ali spalancate migrando verso sud — un'aria nuova
>> アンナ　リモンディ/Anna Rimondi（イタリア/Italy）

南へと吹かるる音符渡鳥
> migratory birds　　musical notes blow south
>> キム　オルムタック　ゴメス/Kim Olmtak Gomes（オランダ/Holland）

青空に刻まれた道渡鳥
> migratory birds — a trail etched in a deep blue sky
>> キム　オルムタック　ゴメス/Kim Olmtak Gomes（オランダ/Holland）

気候変動ものともせずに渡鳥
> uccelli migratori — nessun cambiamento climatico
>
> アグネーゼ　ジアロンゴ/Agnese Giallongo
> (イタリア/Italy)

金星の宿る橅の木渡鳥
> oiseaux migrateurs — parmi le grand hêtre l'étoile du berger
>
> カメル　メスレム/Kamel Meslem(アルジェリア/Algeria)

渡鳥休暇明に北へ飛ぶ
> oiseau migrateur — de retour de vacances au grand nord
>
> イメルダ　セン/Imelda Senn(スイス/Switzerland)

渡鳥木々に静寂戻りたる
> migration des oiseaux — le calme s'installe dans l'arbre
>
> オルファ　クチュク　ブハディダ/Olfa Kchouk Bouhadida
> (チュニジア/Tunisia)

ひと気なき浜辺にわれと渡鳥
> keeping me company on a deserted beach — migratory birds
>
> ポール　カルス/Paul Callus(マルタ/Malta)

集団でV飛翔する渡鳥
> ils voyagent en V les oiseaux migrateurs — bande organisée
>
> スアド　ハジリ/Souad Hajri(チュニジア/Tunisia)

渡鳥ざわめき国境消しにけり
> migration — d'un murmure doux les oiseaux effacent les frontières
>
> エレナ　ズアイン/Elena Zouain(ルーマニア/Romania)

沼地には甲高き声渡鳥

> the wetland's piercing shrills — migratory birds
>
> クリスティーナ　チン/Christina Chin
>
> (マレーシア/Malaysia)

なんといふ重きしじまよ渡鳥

> départ des oiseaux — ce trop plein de silence me pèse
>
> カメル　メスレム/Kamel Meslem(アルジェリア/Algeria)

渡鳥日輪同じ道をゆく

> oiseau migrateur — le soleil suit le même chemin
>
> オルファ　クチュク　ブハディダ/Olfa Kchouk Bouhadida
>
> (チュニジア/Tunisia)

灰色の雲や南へ渡鳥

> nuvole grigie — uccelli migratori diretti a sud
> gray clouds — migratory birds southward
>
> ダニエラ　ミッソ/Daniela Misso(イタリア/Italy)

につぽんの芯に山あり渡鳥

> the core of Japan is mountains — migratory birds
>
> 中野千秋/Chiaki Nakano(日本/Japan)

俳諧は地球一周渡鳥

> oiseau migrateur — haiku fait le tour du monde
>
> 向瀬美音/Mine Mukose(日本/Japan)

人は皆海より生まれ渡鳥

> tout le monde est né de la mer — oiseau migrateur
>
> 向瀬美音/Mine Mukose(日本/Japan)

この先は太平洋か渡鳥
> au loin l'océan Pacifique — oiseau migrateur
>> 向瀬美音/Mine Mukose（日本/Japan）

小鳥【ことり・kotori】
bird coming / les oiseaux de retour

In autumn, they are birds that migrate to Japan or small birds that come down from the mountains to human settlements.

小鳥来る詩人の村に詩の暗唱
> poetic recital in the poet's home village — bird chirping
>> ズデンカ　ムリナー/Zdenka Mlinar（クロアチア/Croatia）

空の色変はり小鳥の戻り来る
> little bird is back — the sky changes color
>> ザンザミ　イスマイル/Zamzami Ismail（インドネシア/Indonesia）

ぽつぽつと空に斑点小鳥来る
> dots and speckles in the sky — little birds coming back
>> クリスティーナ　チン/Christina Chin（マレーシア/Malaysia）

小鳥来るあなたの家はここですよ
> little bird is back — where did your step go it's your house
>> ザンザミ　イスマイル/Zamzami Ismail（インドネシア/Indonesia）

小鳥来て歌の調子の変はりけり
> little birds coming back from the north — changing tunes
>> クリスティーナ　チン/Christina Chin（マレーシア/Malaysia）

商業施設に小さき図書館小鳥来る
> little bird coming back — small library inside the shopping center
>
> ナニ　マリアニ/Nani Mariani（オーストラリア/Australia）

小鳥来て大合唱の夕間暮
> evening trees birds flying back into the chorus
>
> プロビール　グプタ/Probir Gupta（インド/India）

鋸の音の真上に小鳥来る
> a bird comes — it's perpendicular to the sound of the saw
>
> マウリチオ　ブランカレオーニ/Maurizio Brancaleoni（イタリア/Italy）

風が止む第三チャクラ小鳥来る
> wind settles — in the tree's crown chakra a new song of birds
>
> バーバラ　オルムタック/Barbara Olmtak（オランダ/Holland）

小鳥来る熱き歌には秘密の愛
> rentrée des oiseaux — dans leur chant chaud notre amour secret
>
> フテン　フルチ/feten fourti（チュニジア/Tunisia）

湖に小さき砂浜小鳥来る
> little birds coming — small sandy shore at lake
>
> 中野千秋/Chiaki Nakano（日本/Japan）

燕帰る【つばめかえる・tsubamekaeru】
swallow comming away / retour d'hirondelle

Swallows that migrate in the spring return to the south in the fall. During the summer, they return with their chicks, and when they return in flocks around September, we are left with a sense of loneliness.

燕去ぬ我が根大地に定着し
> rondini in volo — ancorate alla terra le mie radici
>> アンジェラ　ジオルダーノ/Angela Giordano（イタリア/Italy）

燕去ぬ月の終着点求め
> vola una rondine — verso i confini di luna
>> アグネーゼ　ジアロンゴ/Agnese Giallongo（イタリア/Italy）

果てしなき空へ燕の去りにけり
> prêt pour le grand départ l'hirondeau — ciel sans limites
>> ラシダ　ジェルビ/Rachida Jerbi（チュニジア/Tunisia）

燕去ぬ修理をしたる古き小屋
> retour d'hirondelle — je répare mon ancienne cabane
>> アブダラ　ハジイ/Abdallah Haji（モロッコ/Morocco）

燕去る別れの日差し浴びながら
> swallow coming — farewell light from the sun
>> ザンザミ　イスマイル/Zamzami Ismael（インドネシ/Indonesia）

風に乗り空を撫でつつ帰燕かな
> rondine in volo sulle ali del vento carezza il cielo
> swallow flying on the wings of the wind caress the sky
>> パトリチア　カバローネ/Patrizia Cavallone（イタリア/Italy）

風立ちて燕の声の響きけり
> s'alza la brezza — il garrire di rondini nell'immensità
> the breeze rises — the roar of swallows in the immensity
>> パトリチア　カバローネ/Patrizia Cavallone
>>> （イタリア/Italy）

訪ねたる母校や秋の燕なり
> retour d'hirondelle — je visite mon ancienne école
>> アブダラ　ハジイ/Abdallah Hajji（モロッコ/Morocco）

終わりなきバレエのごとく帰燕かな
> ballet incessant — retour bruyant des hirondelles
>> カディジャ　エル　ブルカディ/Khadija El Bourkadi
>> （モロッコ/Morocco）

親切なしじまを持ちて帰燕かな
> un silence bienveillant — retour d'hirondelle
>> エウジェニア　パラシブ/Eugénia Paraschiv
>> （ルーマニア/Romania）

曇天や白き腹見せ燕去り
> nuages gris — le ventre blanc des hirondelles
>> イザベル　カルバロ　テール/Isabelle Carvalho Teles
>> （フランス/France）

ふるさとへ思ひ馳せつつ燕去る
> swallow coming — longing hometown
>> アリアニ　ユハナ/Ariani Yuhana（インドネシア/Indonesia）

燕去る羽をばたばた納屋の中
> return of swallows — fluttering in the barn
>> ポール　カルス/Paul Callus（マルタ/Malta）

薄暗く骨まで寒き帰燕かな
> faint light and the chill in bones — swallows coming
>> クリスティーナ　チン/Christina Chin（マレーシア/Malaysia）

天からの合唱のして帰燕かな
> partition céleste — sur les fils le retour des hirondelles
> celestial score — on the threads the swallows return
>
> イザベル　ラマン/Isa Lamant（フランス/France）

燕帰る祖母の伝える良きニュース
> hirondelle revient — ma grand-mère dit bonne nouvelle
>
> アブダラ　ハジイ/Abdallah Hajji（モロッコ/Morocco）

燕去る家族の絆取り戻し
> rekindling family bonds — swallows return
>
> バーバラ　オルムタック/Barbara Olmtak（オランダ/Holland）

ガザの秋燕と共に去る希望
> autunno a Gaza — insieme alle rondini va la speranza
>
> リタ　モアール/Rita Moar（イタリア/Italy）

刈りたての野原を発ちて帰燕かな
> freshly mowed grass — swallows leave the stubby field
>
> キム　オルムタック　ゴメス/Kim Olmtak Gomes（オランダ/Holland）

せつかちな翼を持ちて燕去る
> dernières hirondelles aux ailes impatientes
> the last swallows with impatient wings
>
> マリー クレール　ブルゴ/marie-claire burgos
> （フランス/France）

燕帰る屋上にある遊園地
> old amusement park on the rooftop — swallow coming away
>
> 中野千秋/Chiaki Nakano（日本/Japan）

捨てられぬドレスあれこれ秋燕

> beaucoup de robes que je ne peux pas abandonner — hirondelle d'automne

向瀬美音/Mine Mukose（日本/Japan）

栗鼠【りす・risu】
squirrel / écureuil

It is a autumn kigo. However, the Japanese giant flying squirrel (a mammal of the same squirrel family) is a seasonal word for winter.

黒き栗鼠葉の絨毯を駆ける昼

> soleil de midi — un écureuil noir court dans le tapis de feuilles

フランソワーズ　モリス/Francoise Maurice

（フランス/France）

葉の舞ひて泥棒栗鼠のゐたりけり

> crackling leaves fly around—thief squirrel

キム　オルムタック　ゴメス/Kim Olmtak Gomes

（オランダ/Holland）

はからずも階段に栗鼠の丸き瞳

> visite imprévue — les yeux ronds de l'écureuil sur le perron

ローラン　シビリン/Laurent Sybillin（フランス/France）

冬用意栗鼠はナッツを集めをり

> winter preparation — squirrels busy collecting nuts

キム　オルムタック　ゴメス/Kim Olmtak Gomes

（オランダ/Holland）

湖を覆ふ小枝に栗鼠がゐる

> squirrel — on the twigs covering lake
>
> 中野千秋/Chiaki Nakano(日本/Japan)

鵙【もず・mozu】
bull-headed shrike / pie-grieche

Shrikes make a sharp, squeaky, squeaky sound in the fall at the tops of trees. Although a small bird, it is a carnivore. The call is often associated with the clear autumn air, and is used in such phrases as "shrike day" and "shrike clear day.

残酷なひとことをつき鵙の鳴く

> your sadistic little mouth in seconds — shrike
>
> ザンザミ　イスマイル/Zamzami Ismail
>
> (インドネシア/Indonesia)

沈黙を満たし窓辺の鵙の声

> the song of the shrike on the windowsill fills the silence
> riempie il silenzio il canto dell'averla sul davanzale
>
> アグネーゼ　ジアロンゴ/Agnese Giallongo
>
> (イタリア/Italy)

鵙鳴いて夢の中には戻れない

> shrike singing — I can't return to my dream
>
> タンポポ　アニス/Tanpopo Anis(インドネシア/Indonesia)

鵙鳴いて山のホテルのアペリティフ

> aperitif of mountain hotel — call of bull-headed shrike
>
> 中野千秋/Chiaki Nakano(日本/Japan)

鶫【つぐみ・tsugumi】
thrush / merle

A bird of the thrush family. A winter bird that comes across the Sea of Japan in large flocks at the end of October. There are many species with blackish — brown spots on their breast. They spend the winter in mountain forests and rice paddies, and return to their breeding grounds in Siberia in the spring to replace the swallows.

秋の午後茶色の鶫歌ひ出す

après-midi d'automne — la grive brune chante à nouveau

イメルダ　セン/Imelda Senn（スイス/Switzerland）

楽しげな鶫よ森の広場なり

songs of bliss in the grassland forest — dusky thrush

クリスティーナ　チン/Christina Chin

（マレーシア/Malaysia）

鶫の飛翔空に丸ごと呑み込まれ

spiccano il volo i merli dal giardino — li inghiotte il cielo

アンナ　リモンディ/Anna Rimondi（イタリア/Italy）

深き影昏き水に飛び込む鶫

ombre profonde — il tuffo di un merlo nell'acqua scura

アントニオ　ジラルディ/Antonio Girardi

（イタリア/Italy）

鶫の嘴にまだ動きたるミミズゐて

sul becco del merlo si muove ancora—il vecchio verme

デニス　カンバロウ/Dennys Cambarau

（イタリア/Italy）

戸の外の鶫の声に目覚めけり
> risveglio — fuori dalla porta un tordo
> awakening — outside the door a dusky thrush
>
> ダニエラ　ミッソ/Daniela Misso（イタリア/Italy）

鶫鳴くクッキー缶のお針箱
> thrush chirping — empty cookie tin for sewing box
>
> 中野千秋/Chiaki Nakano（日本/Japan）

椋鳥【むくどり・mukudori】
white - cheeked starling / etourneau

This species breeds in the Tohoku and Hokkaido regions from spring to summer, and moves in flocks to the northwest of the Kanto region in autumn. It also feeds on the seeds of the Japanese bead tree, the Japanese bead tree, the Japanese bead tree, the Japanese persimmon, wild thorns, and the seeds of the Japanese knotweed. It is a beneficial bird.

落とし物残し椋鳥けたたまし
> noisy grey starlings in the city — leave behind droppings
>
> クリスティーナ　チン/Christina Chin（マレーシア/Malaysia）

椋の群れ雲間に羽を取られたる
> stormi di storni — non si impigliano le ali tra le nuvole
> troupeaux d'étourneaux — ils ne prennent pas leurs ailes dans les nuages
>
> デニス　カンバロウ/Dennys Cambarau（イタリア/Italy）

椋鳥の群のねじれて回転す
> a shifting cloud of starling — twists and turns
>
> クリスティーナ　チン/Christina Chin（マレーシア/Malaysia）

椋鳥や草の道よりクラクション

> grey starlings fly away — ringing the car horn on the grassy road
>
> タンポポ　アニス/Tanpopo Anis
>
> （インドネシア/Indonesia）

椋鳥の滑空したり休耕地　　　　　　　　　　　　　　　亜仁子

> starling — gliding the fallow land
>
> storno — scivolare terreno incolto
>
> アニコ　パップ/Anikó Papp（ハンガリー/Hungry）

黄昏や椋鳥装ふ枯れポプラ

> crépuscule — mis à nu le peuplier s'habille d'étourneaux
>
> ジェラール　ドユモン/Gerard Dumon
>
> （フランス/France）

椋鳥が空埋め尽くす夕間暮

> fill the sky at sunset — white-cheeked-starling
>
> 中野千秋/Chiaki Nakano（日本/Japan）

鵲【かささぎ・kasasagi】
magpie / pie

A bird that appears in the Tanabata legend. It is said that the bird builds a bridge with its wings for Orihime to cross the Milky Way. It looks like a crow, but its white belly distinguishes it from a crow.

鵲や日々幸せが増してくる

> magpie — day by day starting to feel happy
>
> ザンザミ　イスマイル/Zamzami Ismael（インドネシア/Indonesia）

屋根の上に鵲の鳴く夜明かな
> crows at dawn — magpie' songs fill the roof
>> クリスティーナ　チン/Christina Chin（マレーシア/Malaysia）

あかときや鵲胡桃摑みたる
> nouveau matin frais — la pie serre une noix sans pouvoir le dire
>> フランソワーズ　ガブリエル/Françoise Gabriel
>> （ベルギー/Belgium）

鵲や水のそばにも向こうにも
> near the water a magpie — metres away another hopping
>> キム　オルムタック　ゴメス/Kim Olmtak Gomes（オランダ/Holland）

悲しげに鵲歌ふ鳥籠よ
> chirp of magpie in a cage — beautiful sadness in the morning
>> タンポポ　アニス/Tanpopo Anis（インドネシア/Indonesia）

鵲や自然破壊を語りをり
> magpie — he told about damaged nature
>> エル　ハミド/El Hamied（インドネシア/Indonesia）

鵲のつつく光の欠片かな
> on the sliver of sun the little magpie pecks at the light
> sullo spicchio di sole la piccola gazza becca la luce
>> アンジェラ　ジオルダーノ/Angela Giordano（イタリア/Italy）

鵲の屋根で跳ねたる朝餉かな
> prima colazione — una gazza che saltella sul tetto
> breakfast — a magpie hopping on the roof
>> ダニエラ　ミッソ/Daniela Misso（イタリア/Italy）

鵲の止まつてをりぬ避雷針

| perching on the lightning bolt — magpie

中野千秋/Chiaki Nakano(日本/Japan)

鶉【うずら・uzura】
quail / caille

A bird of the Phasianidae family of the Galliformes order, about 20 cm in length. It hides in the grass on the riverbank and is not easily seen. Its distinctive call is a feature of the fall season. It is raised for food and eggs.

薮の底に野生の鶉隠れたり

| quail — the wild ones hide at the bottom of the bushes

アリアニ　ユハナ/Ariani Yuhana
(インドネシア/Indonesia)

砂浴びてさつぱりとして鶉かな

| quail—the freshness of sand bathing

エル　ハミド/El Hamied
(インドネシア/Indonesia)

里山に残る石垣鶉鳴く

| medieval stone wall in the mountain — quail song

中野千秋/Chiaki Nakano(日本/Japan)

啄木鳥【きつつき・kitsutsuki】
woodpecker / pivert

General name for birds of the woodpecker family, including small, red, and blue voles. A resident bird. The sound of woodpeckers tapping on trees as they forage for food and their conspicuous colors are striking in wooded areas in late autumn.

啄木鳥や木槌でノック裁判官

> woodpecker — knock the Judge's final decision of the case
>
> ナニ　マリアニ/Nani Mariani(オーストラリア/Australia)

啄木鳥や慣らしつつ履くハイヒール

> woodpecker — learn to wear high heels
>
> ナニ　マリアニ/Nani Mariani(オーストラリア/Australia)

木の上で狂ふ啄木鳥休暇の家

> un pivert se déchainer sur un arbre — maison de vacance
>
> エウジェニア　パラシブ/Eugénia Paraschiv
>
> (ルーマニア/Romania)

啄木鳥や誰がディナーに来るのだろう

> pivert — devine qui vient dîner?
>
> エウジェニア　パラシブ/Eugénia Paraschiv
>
> (ルーマニア/Romania)

啄木鳥や来客は扉の前に

> pivert au tronc — le visiteur devant la porte annonce son arrivée
>
> オルファ　クチュク　ブハディダ/Olfa Kchouk Bouhadida
>
> (チュニジア/Tunisia)

啄木鳥の嘴止まる金属音
> sound of metal — the woodpecker stops chiselling my home
>> クリスティナ　チン/Christina Chin（マレーシア/Malaysia）

啄木鳥や目覚時計など要らず
> woodpecker — I don't need an alarm clock
>> エル　ハミド/El Hamied（インドネシア/Indonesia）

啄木鳥に一瞬だけの間合かな
> woodpecker — a momentary break in diligent sound
>> 中野千秋/Chiaki Nakano（日本/Japan）

雁【かり・kari】
wild goose / oie sauvage

They arrive from the north in late fall and return in spring. The body is fat and grayish brown. They have long necks and short tails. They fly in a line in a pole — or hook — shaped formation, emitting a guang — guang call. The reason why the geese are called "karigane" is because many people have admired their call since ancient times.

曇天や雁は南方目指したる
> plumbeo cielo — le oche selvatiche dirette a sud
>> アンジェラ　ジオルダーノ/Angela Giordano
>> （イタリア/Italy）

雁渡る雲に加はる悲しみよ
> vol d'oies sauvages — ma tristesse rejoint les nuages
>> カディジャ　エル　ブルカディ/Khadija El Bourkadi
>> （モロッコ/Morocco）

避難民かりがね涙流しけり
> les oies sauvages pleurant — réfugiés
>> エウジェニア　パラシブ/EugéniaParaschi（ルーマニア/Romania）

空遠く雁の鳴き声こだまする
> del faggio rosso solo il profilo scuro — ultima luna
>> アンナ　リモンディ/Anna Rimondi（イタリア/Italy）

雁渡る青空へ飛ぶ白昼夢
> wild goose — daydreams fly to the blue sky
>> ナニ　マリアニ/Nani Mariani（オーストラリア/Australia）

鳴き声や雁は沼地に集まりぬ
> migration calls — wild geese assemble on the marsh
>> クリスティーナ　チン/Christina Chin（マレーシア/Malaysia）

旅立ちや夜に響ける雁の声
> una partenza — suono di oche selvatiche nella notte
> a departure — sound of wild geese in the night
>> ダニエラ　ミッソ/Daniela Misso（イタリア/Italy）

白き雁沼から沼へ渡りけり
> oie blanche — de marais en marais en migration
>> アンヌ-マリー　ジュベール-ガヤール/Anne-Marie Joubert-Gaillard
>> （フランス/France）

穏やかな湖面を崩し雁飛来
> spoil the eyes — small ripples from wild geese landing on a calm lake
>> ザンザミ　イスマイル/Zamzami Ismail（インドネシア/Indonesia）

雁渡る長々と待時間なり
> long wait — wild geese head south
> lunga attesa — le oche selvatiche si dirigono a sud
>> アンジェラ　ジオルダーノ/Angela Giordano（イタリア/Italy）

雁が来て茶色に染まる浅瀬かな
> wild goose — swimming in shallow pond the water turns into brown
>> アリアナ　ユハナ/Ariani Yuhana（インドネシア/Indonesia）

細波や水面の雲に雁の羽
> swamp ripple — goose feathers fall in the clouds
>> アユング　ヘルマワン/Ayung Hermawan（インドネシア/Indonesia）

秋空や日を目覚めさす雁の声
> autumn sky — wild geese sing the sun awake
>> マリリン アシユボ/Marilyn Ashbaugh（米国/United States）

雁渡る地平線まで青き空
> wild goose — the sky is so blue on the horizon
>> ナッキー　クリスティジーノ/Nuky Kristijno（インドネシア/Indonesia）

雁やＶの字を組む物語
> the story of V formation wild goose in the sky
>> ナッキー　クリスティジーノ/Nuky Kristijno（インドネシア/Indonesia）

南へと長き旅路や雁渡る
> the long journey of the wild geese towards the south
> verso sud il lungo viaggio delle oche selvatiche
>> アンジェラ　ジオルダーノ/Angela Giordano（イタリア/Italy）

雁や細波立てて羽ばたいて

> wild goose — lake water rippled of flapping wings
>
> ディア　ヌクスマ/Dyah Nkusuma（インドネシア/Indonesia）

しばらくは雁と並走ハイウェイ

> highway — running side by side with wild geese
>
> 中野千秋/Chiaki Nakano（日本/Japan）

地平線やや丸くして雁渡る

> vol d'oies sauvages — l'horizon est légèrement courbé
>
> 向瀬美音/Mine Mukose（日本/Japan）

鷹渡る【たかわたる・takawataru】
crossing hawk / vol d'un faucon

Eagle, a generic name for medium — sized birds of the hawk family, mainly dark brown in color. They have a strong, sharply curved bill and large, strong claws on their legs, which they use to attack and eat small animals. Giant hawks are mainly used for falconry. A "blue hawk" is a hawk that is three years old.

鷹渡る先祖は我ら見守りて

> crossing hawk — the ancestors are watching us
>
> ミレラ　ブライレーン/Mirela Brailean
>
> （ルーマニア/Romania）

鷹の飛翔雀怯へて散らばりぬ

> vol d'un faucon — du tremble se dispersent les passereaux
>
> フランソワーズ　デニオ-ルリエーブル/Françoise Deniaud-Lelièvre
>
> （フランス/France）

鷹渡る嵐の中に白と黒
> crossing hawk — the white and black ones fly with storm
>> アリアナ　ユハナ/Ariani Yuhana
>>> （インドネシア/Indonesia）

無くて七癖無限へと鷹渡る
> prisoner of habits — a hawk flies free into infinity
> prigioniera delle abitudini — un falco vola libero nell'infinito
>> アンジェラ　ジオルダーノ/Angela Giordano
>>> （イタリア/Italy）

鷹渡る慣れぬ言語の新生活
> peregrine falcon — a life in a new language
>> エウジェニア　パラシブ/EugéniaParaschiv
>>> （ルーマニア/Romania）

母鳥に隠れるひよこ鷹渡る
> crossing hawk — chick enters mother bird's wing
>> ザンザミ　イスマイル/Zamzami Ismail
>>> （インドネシア/Indonesia）

難民キャンプ鷹の無限の自由かな
> a free hawk in the infinite — refugee camp
> un falco libero nell'infinito — campo profughi
>> アンジェラ　ジオルダーノ/Angela Giordano
>>> （イタリア/Italy）

鷹渡る翼で叩く海や島
> migrating hawk — wings beat beyond the sea and island
>> ディア　ヌクスマ/Dyah Nkusuma（インドネシア/Indonesia）

鷹渡る山の天辺ぼんやりと
> crossing hawk — that elusive peak up there
>> クリスティーナ　プルビエンティ/Cristina Pulvirenti
>>> (イタリア/Italy)

鷹渡る雄大な景海の旅
> seaside trip — the majestic silhouette of a crossing hawk
> gita al mare — la maestosa sagoma di un falco che attraversa
>> ダニエラ　ミッソ/Daniela Misso
>>> (イタリア/Italy)

せめぎ合ふ自由と孤独鷹渡る
> crossing hawk — conflicting freedom and solitude
>> 中野千秋/Chiaki Nakano(日本/Japan)

鱸【すずき・suzuki】
sea bass / loup

A marine fish belonging to the sea bass family, it is widely distributed in coastal and inshore waters from Hokkaido to Kyushu. Like mullet, it changes its name as it grows, giving it the name of "successor fish. It is served as sashimi, sashimi raw, or grilled in salted water.

鱸釣る小さなものは逃しつつ
> catching sea bass — while release smaller ones
>> 中野千秋/Chiaki Nakano(日本/Japan)

秋鯖【あきさば・akisaba】
mackerel / maquereau

This term refers to mackerel caught in the fall. After spawning in the spring and early summer, mackerel fatten up during the summer and are at their most fatty in the fall.

秋鯖の昼餉の後の能楽堂

mackerel for lunch — then noh theater

中野千秋/Chiaki Nakano(日本/Japan)

鰯【いわし・iwashi】
sardine / sardine

The color of the ocean can change as large schools of these fish are swept into nearby waters by warm currents. They are caught in large numbers and are inexpensive. Its back is dark indigo and its belly is silvery white. It has a seven — star black spot on its body. It is in season in the fall and is served in ichimoku (raw fish) or grilled in salt.

卓の下鰯の骨は猫の手に

sardine bones remaining under the table — the cat licks its hands

タンポポ　アニス/Tanpopo Anis(インドネシア/Indonesia)

難民はキャンプの中で鰯缶

sardine — refugees crammed into camp

ナニ　マリアニ/Nani Mariani(オーストラリア/Australia)

鰯漁手の動く音聞こえたり

la pêche à la sardine — bruit des mains

エウジェニア　パラシブ/EugéniaParaschiv(ルーマニア/Romania)

サーディンに無垢の笑顔や戦禍の子
> sardine — laughter and innocent faces of children locked in war
>
> ナニ　マリアニ/Nani Mariani(オーストラリア/Australia)

野良猫の忙しく漁る鰯かな
> sardine — busy stray cat in the trash
>
> ナッキー　クリスティジーノ/Nuky Kristijno
>
> (インドネシア/Indonesia)

大海に銀の走れる鰯かな
> a skittering of silver in the ocean — sardine run
>
> クリスティーナ　チン/Christina Chin(マレーシア/Malaysia)

大きさに誇らしげなる鰯かな
> sardine — elle est fière de sa taille
>
> オルファ　クチュク　ブハディダ/Olfa Kchouk Bouhadida
>
> (チュニジア/Tunisia)

鰯のごと廃墟の草のぎつしりと
> packed like sardines — the weeds in the abandoned garden
>
> ポール　カルス/Paul Callus(マルタ/Malta)

細波の立ちて鰯の浅瀬かな
> shallow waves on the shore — shoals of sardines
>
> クリスティーナ　チン/Christina Chin(マレーシア/Malaysia)

今年また大群となる鰯かな
> again dense schools this year — sardines
>
> キム　オルムタック　ゴメス/Kim Olmtak Gomes
>
> (オランダ/Holland)

海の青鰯の銀がその先に
> beyond the ocean's blue the silver of sardines
>
> キム　オルムタック　ゴメス/Kim Olmtak Gomes
> (オランダ/Holland)

鰯缶クルーズの長き椅子の上
> sardines en boites sur des chaises longues en croisière
>
> イメルダ　セン/Imelda Senn
> (スイス/Swirzerland)

絶品の鰯マリネを手摑みで
> eaten by hand grilled marinated sardines — finger liking
>
> ポール　カルス/Paul Callus(マルタ/Malta)

魚市場不思議な歌の鰯売り
> à la criée — une douce chanson étrangère vend des sardines
>
> エレナ　ズアイン/Elena Zouain
> (ルーマニア/Romania)

のたうちて魚網をゆらす鰯かな
> wiggling sardine beats the fishing net
>
> キム　オルムタック　ゴメス/Kim Olmtak Gomes
> (オランダ/Holland)

猫たちが鰯を待つてゐる漁港
> fishing port — cats waiting sardines
>
> 中野千秋/Chiaki Nakano(日本/Japan)

> **鮭**【さけ・sake】
> salmon / saumon
>
> It is born in the river, grows up in the sea, and returns to the river to spawn again. It is used in a wide variety of dishes, such as salted salmon, salmon roe, and musuko (salmon roe or musuko). It is a favorite fish of the Japanese.

故郷の町への旅路鮭登る

> saumon — retour du voyageur dans sa ville natale
>
> アブダラ　ハジイ/Abdallah Hajji（モロッコ/Morocco）

鮭の皿オレンジ切りて添へらるる

> assiette de saumon — les quartiers d'orange dans un plateau
>
> オルファ　クチュク　ブハディダ/Olfa Kchouk Bouhadida
>
> （チュニジア/Tunisia）

鮭食べて骨スリッパに残りたる

> l'os dans son soulier — reste de saumon
>
> エウジェニア　パラシブ/Eugénia Paraschiv
>
> （ルーマニア/Romania）

釣り糸は旋回鮭の遡上かな

> swirling fishing reels — salmon filled river
>
> キム　オルムタック　ゴメス/Kim Olmtak Gomes（オランダ/Holland）

鮭泳ぐ潮に逆らう我が人生

> salmon — my life always against the tide
> salmoni — la mia vita sempre controcorren
>
> アンジェラ　ジオルダーノ/Angela Giordano
>
> （イタリア/Italy）

逆流に鮭もどりたる生家かな

> village natal — à contre-courant le retour du saumon
>
> アブダラ　ハジイ/Abdallah Hajji（モロッコ/Morocco）

鮭のぼる上流に待つ釣り師達

> salmon — anglers all waiting upstream
>
> キム　オルムタック　ゴメス/Kim Olmtak Gomes（オランダ/Holland）

産卵の鮭よ何かを絶叫し

> salmon spawning — screaming something
>
> 中野千秋/Chiaki Nakano（日本/Japan）

秋の蝶【あきのちょう・akinocho】
autumn butterfly / papillon d'automne

Butterflies seen after the first day of autumn. Compared to the butterflies of spring and summer, these butterflies look somewhat weak. As winter approaches, the number of butterflies becomes fewer and fewer.

灰色の世界彩る秋の蝶

> greyness everywhere — the colorful wings of an autumn butterfly
> grigiore ovunque — le ali variopinti di una farfalla autunnale
>
> アンジェラ　ジオルダーノ/Angela Giordano
> （イタリア/Italy）

秋蝶や透けるドレスをめくる風

> papillon d'automne — sa robe transparente soulevée par le vent
>
> ソニア　ベン　アマール/Sonia Ben Ammar
> （チュニジア/Tunisia）

秋蝶や今日も変はらずバレリーナ

> anche per oggi le farfalle d'autunno — le ballerine
>
> > ミケーレ　パチエロ/Michele Pochiero（イタリア/Italy）

秋蝶や壁画の花のありどころ

> murale a fiori — una farfalla in cerca di un giardino
>
> > アンナ　リモンディ/Anna Rimondi（イタリア/Italy）

もう飛べぬ秋蝶のゐる山の道

> papillon d'automne — sur le sentier de montagne incapable de voler
>
> > アブダラ　ハジイ/Abdallah Hajji（モロッコ/Morocco）

秋の蝶天に召された子の印

> papillon d'automne — le signe de son enfant parti au ciel
>
> > ベルナデット　クエン/Bernadette Couenne（フランス/France）

灰色の夜明の風に秋の蝶

> in the gray dawn an autumn butterfly colors the wind
> nell'alba grigia una farfalla autunnale colora il vento
>
> > アンジェラ　ジオルダーノ/Angela Giordano（イタリア/Italy）

秋の蝶羽が震へる花の前

> autumn butterfly — the wings tremble gently in front of the flower
>
> > エル　ハミド/El Hamied（インドネシア/Indonesia）

秋蝶や万華鏡へと還りゆく

> return to Kaleidoscope — autumn butterfly
>
> > 中野千秋/Chiaki Nakano（日本/Japan）

秋蝶のまぎれ込みたるブーケかな
> autumn butterfly — creep into the bouquet
>> 中野千秋/Chiaki Nakano（日本/Japan）

放たれて秋蝶終の飛翔かな
> liberté — le dernier vol du papillon d'automne
>> 向瀬美音/Mine Mukose（日本/Japan）

翅に傷負ひ秋の蝶高みへと
> papillon d'automne — aile cicatrisée vole vers les hauteurs
>> 向瀬美音/Mine Mukose（日本/Japan）

秋蝶や羽に乗せたる陽の名残
> papillon d'automne — un peu de soleil sur les ailes
>> 向瀬美音/Mine Mukose（日本/Japan）

澄みわたる青空目指す小灰蝶
>
>> 向瀬美音/Mine Mukose（日本/Japan）

小灰蝶かそけき背に秋日浴ぶ
>
>> 向瀬美音/Mine Mukose（日本/Japan）

手のひらに燐粉残ししじみ蝶
>
>> 向瀬美音/Mine Mukose（日本/Japan）

秋の蛇【あきのへび・akinohebi】
autumn snake / serpent d'automne

Snakes enter their burrows for hibernation. It is said that snakes enter their burrows on the autumnal equinox and leave them on the spring equinox, but this varies from region to region. Several to several dozen snakes gather in a single burrow to pass the winter.

蛇の皮進路変へたる風の中
| mue de serpent — dans le vent je change de voie
| アブダラ　ハジイ/Abdallah Hajji（モロッコ/Morocco）

秋の蛇枯葉の下の極楽に
| heaven under the dead leaves — autumn snake
| ザンザミ　イスマイル/Zamzami Ismail
| （インドネシア/Indonesia）

秋の蛇茶色き体葉の下に
| autumn snake — brown skin one creeps under dry leaves
| アリアニ　ユハナ/Ariani Yuhana
| （インドネシア/Indonesia）

秋の蛇インドの男歌ふ歌
| autumn snake — the Indian guy sings his song
| ナッキー　クリスティジーノ/Nuky Kristijno
| （インドネシア/Indonesia）

秋の蛇とぐろを巻いて未知の道
| sentiero sconosciuto — un serpente autunnale arrotolato
| unknown path — a coiled autumn snake
| ダニエラ　ミッソ/Daniela Misso（イタリア/Italy）

洞穴のところで止まる秋の蛇
　autumn snake — his journey ended in the cave
　　　　　　　ナッキー　クリスティジーノ/Nuky Kristijno（インドネシア/Indonesia）

ため息に気づく枯葉の下の蛇
　autumn snake — hissing breath under the dead leaves
　　　　　　　ザンザミ　イスマイル/Zamzami　Ismail（インドネシア/Indonesia）

秋の蛇薄暗き風の避難所
　serpent d'automne à l'abri du vent — pénombre
　　　　　　　エウジェニア　パラシブ/Eugénia Paraschiv
　　　　　　　　　　　　　　　　　　　　（ルーマニア/Romania）

緑の光螺旋状なる秋の蛇
　lumière verte — le serpent d'automne en spirale
　　　　　　　ベルナデット　クエン/Bernadette Couenne（フランス/France）

二股の舌を揺らして秋の蛇
　autumn snake — the black thin branched tongue's shaking
　　　　　　　アリアナ　ユハナ/Ariani Yuhana（インドネシア/Indonesia）

枝分かれする言の葉よ秋の蛇
　the words that came out of your mouth branched here and there
　— autumn snake
　　　　　　　ザンザミ　イスマイル/Zamzami　Ismail（インドネシア/Indonesia）

卵産む縞模様なる秋の蛇
　autumn snake — the dark yellow black stripes one lays on eggs in box
　　　　　　　アリアナ　ユハナ/Ariani Yuhana（インドネシア/Indonesia）

秋の蛇古代の遺跡守りたる
> protect ancient ruins — autumn snake
>
> イスニ　ヘルヤント/Isni Heryanto（インドネシア/Indonesia）

秋の蛇岩を動かす庭師をり
> autumn snake — gardener removing the rocks
>
> キム　オルムタック　ゴメス/Kim Olmtak Gomes（オランダ/Holland）

岩にまだ熱き蛇の皮松林
> forêt de pins sur le rocher encore chaud mue du serpent
>
> アブダラ　ハジイ/Abdallah Hajji（モロッコ/Morocco）

ジグザグに晴舞台まで秋の蛇
> autumn snake — zig zag route of the rally special stage
>
> ナッキー　クリスティジーノ/Nuky Kristijno
> （インドネシア/Indonesia）

廃屋や塀にくねつた蛇の痕
> maison en ruines — suivant le muret les traces sinueuses du serpent
>
> ラシダ　ジェルビ/Rachida Jerbi（チュニジア/Tunisia）

円錐のフェンスが遮断秋の蛇
> sharp circular fence keeps autumn snakes out of my yard
>
> ナッキー　クリスティジーノ/Nuky Kristijno
> （インドネシア/Indonesia）

秋の蛇やつと道路を渡り切る
> autumn snake — finally cross the road
>
> 中野千秋/Chiaki Nakano（日本/Japan）

蜻蛉【とんぼ・tombo】
dragonfly / libellule

Oni yanma, salty dragonfly, general name for insects belonging to the order of dragonfly fishing dragonflies. Also called akitsu, yanma, etc. The abdomen is elongated and cylindrical. It flies with two pairs of transparent wings and has large compound eyes. The name "Akitsushima," which refers to Japan, comes from a legend that it resembles the shape of a dragonfly with its tail in its mouth.

湖の風蜻蛉の翅の煌めきて

vento di lago ― il luccichio delle ali di libellule
lake wind ― glittering of dragonflies wings

ダニエラ　ミッソ/Daniela Misso（イタリア/Italy）

エッチングのごとき翅なり赤蜻蛉

red dragonfly ― the wing veins etched in glass

マリリン　アッシュボ/Marilyn Ashbaugh
（米国/United States）

とんぼの止まる場所には澄んだ水

autumn indicator ― where the dragonfly lands there is clean water

ザンザミ　イスマイル/Zamzami Ismail
（インドネシア/Indonesia）

水鏡水面に不動の蜻蛉ゐて

la libellula immobile sull'acqua ― forse si specchia

アンナ　リモンディ/Anna Rimondi
（イタリア/Italy）

枯枝の蜻蛉の翅を接写する
> close up — the needle dragonfly's wings land on dry branch
>
> ザンザミ　イスマイル/Zamzami Ismail
>
> （インドネシア/Indonesia）

とんぼうやダンサーの手の細つそりと
> dragonfly — the dancer's hands are very slender
>
> ナニ　マリアニ/Nani Mariani（オーストラリア/Australia）

すきとほる羽広げたる蜻蛉かな
> transparence — la libellule déploie ses ailes
>
> ベルナデット　クエン/Bernadette Couenne（フランス/France）

苔茂る小さき池に大きな蜻蛉
> petit bassin — dans la mousse pond la grande libellule
>
> フランソワーズ　デニオ-ルリエーブル/Françoise Deniaud-Lelièvre
>
> （フランス/France）

蜻蛉舞ふその束の間の儚くて
> il breve volo di una libellula — dopo piu nulla
>
> マリア　ビアンカ/Maria Bianca（イタリア/Italy）

蜻蛉来て絹のドレスの煌めきぬ
> libellule — le chatoiement de sa robe de soie
>
> カディジャ　エル　ブルカディ/Khadija El Bourkadi
>
> （モロッコ/Morocco）

夜のしじま蜻蛉空の鏡たたむ
> silence du soir — la libellule plie le miroir du ciel
>
> エレナ　ズアイン/Elena Zouain（ルーマニア/Romania）

蜻蛉の青き羽越しなる世界
> libellula attraverso ali blu il mondo
> dragonfly through blue wings the world
>> ナザレナ　ランピニ/Nazarena Rampini（イタリア/Italy）

とんぼうの羽音の撒いてゐる光
> vrombissement la libellule à mon oreille sème sa lumière
> humming the dragonfly in my ear sows its light
>> マリー-クレール　ブルゴ/marie-claire burgos
>> （フランス/France）

蜻蛉の羽を透かして陽の光
> dragonfly zooms by ― I catch the sun through its wings
>> キム　オルムタック　ゴメス/Kim Olmtak Gomes
>> （オランダ/Holland）

ホバリング蜻蛉何か囁けり
> vol stationnaire ― le murmure d'une libellule
>> エレナ　ズアイン/Elena Zouain（ルーマニア/Romania）

目で追ひて蜻蛉の道の長さかな
> long le cheminement de la libellule ― mon regard suit son vol
> long the path of the dragonfly ― my gaze follows its flight
>> ミュールバッハ　アキツ/F.Mühlebach akitsu
>> （フランス/France）

蜻蛉が風に乗りたる水の上
> on the stagnant waters the dragonfly rides the wind
> sulle acque stagnanti la libellula cavalca il vento
>> アンジェラ　ジオルダーノ/Angela Giordano（イタリア/Italy）

蜻蛉の国を通してもらひけり

> let me through — the land of dragonfly

中野千秋/Chiaki Nakano（日本/Japan）

赤蜻蛉【あかとんぼ・akatombo】
red dragonfly / libellule rouge

The red dragonfly is a common name for the red damselflies. The larva lives in paddy fields and other stagnant water. The adult emerges in early summer and migrates to high mountains shortly after hatching. In early autumn, they return to the plains to lay eggs. The larvae can be seen until around November.

古池の朝の波紋や赤とんぼ　　　　　　　　　　　亜仁寿（自訳）

> red dragonfly — morning ripples on the old pond

タンポポ　アニス/Tanpopo Anis（インドネシア/Indonesia）

赤蜻蛉硝子の翅に刻む脈

> red dragonfly — the wing veins etched in glass

マリリン　アッシュボフ/Marilyn Ashbaugh（米国/United States）

曇天や池に輝く赤蜻蛉

> plumbeo cielo — una libellula rossa si specchia nello stagno

アンジェラ　ジオルダーノ/Angela Giordano
（イタリア/Italy）

ゴンドラや水面と陽の間の赤蜻蛉

> la libellule rouge entre l'eau et le soleil — balancelle

エウジェニア　パラシブ/EugéniaParaschiv
（ルーマニア/Romania）

忘れえぬ休暇なりけり赤蜻蛉

> la libellule rouge — un souvenir de vacances inoubliable
>
> イメルダ　セン/Imelda Senn（スイス/Switzerland）

赤蜻蛉淀む水面を往復す

> une libellule rouge — vol aller retour au-dessus de l'eau stagnante
>
> イメルダ　セン/Imelda Senn（スイス/Switzerland）

山の風湖面の波に赤蜻蛉

> mountain wind — red dragonfly floating on the rippling lake
>
> アユング　ヘルマワン/Ayung Hermawan
>
> （インドネシア/Indonesia）

水の音山を染めたる赤蜻蛉

> the sound of water — red dragonflies dyeing the mountain
>
> タンポポ　アニス/Tanpopo Anis
>
> （インドネシア/Indonesia）

赤蜻蛉ローカル列車長く待ち　　　　　　　　亜仁寿（自訳）

> red dragonfly — the long wait for local train
>
> タンポポ　アニス/Tanpopo Anis（インドネシア/Indonesia）

赤蜻蛉年を重ねて丸くなる石

> libellule rouge — un galet arrondi par ses années
>
> エレナ　ズアイン/Elena Zouain
>
> （ルーマニア/Romania）

赤蜻蛉水に尻尾をつけてみよ

> red dragonfly — dip its tail into the water
>
> エル　ハミド/El Hamied（インドネシア/Indonesia）

保育所や児の前髪に赤蜻蛉　　　　　　　　　　　　　　亜仁寿

> nursey school — a red dragonfly on the kid's bangs
>
> 　　　　　　　　　タンポポ　アニス/Tanpopo Anis
> 　　　　　　　　　　　　　　　　（インドネシア/Indonesia）

自転車にとまつたままの赤蜻蛉

> red dragonfly — still perch on my bike
>
> 　　　　　　　中野千秋/Chiaki Nakano（日本/Japan）

蟋蟀【こおろぎ・korogi】
cricket / grillon

There are many species of autumn insect, the cricket. They are mainly dark brown in color and chirp in grassy areas, dark places, or in the corners of houses. When I hear the cricket chirping, I feel a sense of loneliness, and the autumnal atmosphere is deeply felt. The old name of this species was Kirigirisu.

蟋蟀や近くに寄れば声の止み

> cricket — stop singing when I step closely
>
> 　　　　　アリアナ　ユハナ/Ariani Yuhan（インドネシア/Indonesia）

夕暮れや夜の蟋蟀鳴き始め

> tombée de la nuit — le cri nocturne du grillon commence
>
> 　　　　　カメル　メルレム/Kamel Meslem（アルジェリア/Algeria）

蟋蟀の声柔らかくなる静寂（しじま）

> the song of the cricket ever softer — autumn stillness
> il canto del grillo sempre più lieve — quiete autunnale
>
> 　　　　アンジェラ　ジオルダーノ/Angela Giordano（イタリア/Italy）

蟋蟀や今宵少女の靴の中
> grillons — rendez-vous le soir dans la bottine de la fillette
>> アブデライム　ベンサイド/Abderrahim Bensaïd
>>> (モロッコ/Morocco)

そよ風や小屋の後に鳴く蟋蟀
> soft breeze — the sound of crickets sounds sweet behind the old hut
>> アユング　ヘルマワン/Ayung Hermawan
>>> (インドネシア/Indonesia)

蟋蟀の告白室で鳴いてゐる
> crying in the confessional — cricket
>> イシ　ヘルヤント/Isni Heryanto
>>> (インドネシア/Indonesia)

蟬の声夜明けの雲のごとく湧く
> cicadas voice — dawn clouds crawl in the silence
>> タンポポ　アニス/Tanpopo Anis
>>> (インドネシア/Indonesia)

怖がりて洗濯ばさみで摑む蟋蟀
> la peur au ventre — elle prend un criquet pour un pince à linge
>> スアド　ハジリ/Souad Hajri (チュニジア/Tunisia)

ちちろ鳴く短期滞在なる宿舎
> breve soggiorno in una locanda — grilli
> brief stay in an inn — crickets
>> ダニエラ　ミッソ/Daniela Misso (イタリア/Italy)

幼年の頃の思ひ出ちちろ鳴く

> cricket sound — childhood memories fill the void
> tiếng dế — ký ức tuổi thơ lấp đầy khoảng trống
>> ディン　ニュグエン/Dinh Nguyen（ベトナム/Vietnam）

蟋蟀の大合唱の闇の中

> ombra fitta nel canto forte dei grilli nel canto forte dei grilli
> a thick shadow in the loud singing of crickets sweet idleness
>> ディミトリー/Dimitrij Škrk
>> （スロベニア/Slovenia）

蟋蟀やふと湧き上がる里心

> sound of crickets makes me miss home
>> ナッキー　クリスティジーノ/Nuky Kristijno
>> （インドネシア/Indonesia）

蟋蟀や夜明の雲の広がりて

> cricket — dawn clouds crawl in the silence
>> タンポポ　アニス/Tanpopo Anis
>> （インドネシア/Indonesia）

蟋蟀や思ひ一つの音となり

> cricket—our longing in one note
>> エル　ハミド/El Hamied（インドネシア/Indonesia）

蟋蟀や地面の下の活断層

> cricket — active faults under the ground
>> 中野千秋/Chiaki Nakano（日本/Japan）

鈴虫 【すずむし・suzumushi】
bell cricket, grillon / le chant Evoque un grelot

In the past, bell insects were called pine insects, and pine insects were called bell bugs, and vice versa. They have also been loved in the world of waka poetry as a Japanese word for "wagging a bell," "going through," "getting old," "falling," and so on. Many people enjoy the sound of bell bugs because they can be artificially bred.

鈴虫や少年はまだ外にゐる

> bell cricket — bell cricket
>
> ナッキー　クリスティジーノ/Nuky Kristijno
> （インドネシア/Indonesia）

鈴虫や眠りを覚ます雨の音

> bell cricket—sound of heavy down pour wakes my sleep
>
> ナッキー　クリスティジーノ/Kristijno
> （インドネシア/Indonesia）

傷ついた心の叫び月鈴子

> bell cricket—the scream of a wounded heart
>
> エル　ハミド/El Hamied（インドネシア/Indonesia）

鈴虫や少し失敗する手品

> bell cricket — magic tricks go a little wrong
>
> 中野千秋/Chiaki Nakano（日本/Japan）

蟷螂【かまきり・kamakiri】
praying mantis / mante

An insect of the order Mantis. Head triangular, forelimbs as sickle — shaped captive limbs, which catch and feed on other insects. Green or brown in color. After mating, the female may devour the male.

蟷螂や落ち葉の下で洗顔中
> the praying mantis cleans its face — a red leaf falls
>> クリスティーナ　チン/Christina Chin(マレーシア/Malaysia)

蟷螂やグァバの葉つぱに止まりたる
> praying mantises — perch on green guava leaves
>> アリアナ　ユハナ/Ariani Yuhana(インドネシア/Indonesia)

蟷螂やかちりと蜘蛛の巣にかかる
> caught in a web — the praying mantis clicks a maracas sound
>> クリスティーナ　チン/Christina Chin(マレーシア/Malaysia)

蟷螂や秋と同じ色を持ちて
> la mantide — il medesimo colore dell'autunno
>> ガブリエル　デ　マシ/Gabriella De Masi(イタリア/Italy)

蟷螂を乗せ晩禱の修道士
> vesper — on the cloister' threshold a praying mantis
>> ミレラ　ブライレーン/Mirela Brailean(ルーマニア/Romania)

挑戦か事実か蟷螂と睨めつこ
> dare or truth — the praying mantis and I stare each other out
>> ポール　カルス/Paul Callus(マルタ/Malta)

蟷螂や膝まづきたる肖像画
praying mantis — before his father's picture my son on his knees
キム　オルムタック　ゴメス/Kim Olmtak Gomes
（オランダ/Holland）

蟷螂や祈りの後に餌を食む
praying mantis — he prays before eating
エル　ハミド/El Hamied（インドネシア/Indonesia）

蟷螂や手の中に数珠持つ朝
réveillée à l'aube chapelet en mains — mante religieuse
ラシダ　ジェルビ/Rachida Jerbi
（チュニジア/Tunisia）

蟷螂や風のごとくに太極拳
tai chi steps swift as the wind — praying mantis
バーバラ　オルムタック/Barbara Olmtak（オランダ/Holland）

蟷螂の罪を告白する姿　　　　　　　　　　亜仁寿（自訳）
praying mantis — is he confessing his sins to God?
タンポポ　アニス/Tanpopo Anis
（インドネシア/Indonesia）

蟷螂の顔をはみ出す目玉かな
praying mantis — eyeballs protruding from the face
中野千秋/Chiaki Nakano（日本/Japan）

Kigo Gallery-4

柿/Japanese persimmon …p359(安曇野の柿・長野県)

紅葉/autumn leaves …p382(平泉の紅葉・岩手県)

朝顔／morning glory …p402

菊／chrysanthemum …p408

植(しょくぶつ)物

(shokubutsu)

plant

plante

秋薔薇【あきそうび・akisobi】
autumn rose / rose d'automne

A rose that blooms in the fall. They are small in size but deep in color. Most of them bloom in all seasons and do not have the vigor of summer roses.

秋薔薇微笑む君の温かさ
| autumn rose — the warm of her smile
| マリリン　アッシュボウ/Marilyn Ashbaugh
| （米国/United States）

秋薔薇風に香りの振りまかれ
| autumn rose — wind blows the fragrant around
| アリアニ　ユハナ/Ariani Yuhana
| （インドネシア/Indonesia）

しわくちゃの祖母の手にキス秋薔薇
| rose d'automne — un baiser sur les mains fripées de grand-mère
| ラシダ　ジェルビ/Rachida Jerbi（チュニジア/Tunisia）

秋薔薇祖母より知らぬ物語
| rosa d'autunno — racconti della nonna che non ricordo
| ミケーレ　ポッチエロ/Michele Pochiero
| （イタリア/Italy）

秋薔薇写真の中の祖母の手よ
| trandafiri de toamnă — mâinile bunicii într-o fotografie
| roses d'automne — les mains de grand-mère dans une photo
| マリン　ラダ/Marin Rada（ルーマニア/Romania）

秋薔薇異国の香り肌に匂ひ

> rosa autunnale — il profumo esotico della tua pelle
>
> アンジェラ　ジオルダーノ/Angela Giordano(イタリア/Italy)

秋薔薇ピアノの楽譜色褪せて

> rose d'autunno — note di un pianoforte in dissolvenza
>
> autumn roses — fading notes of a piano
>
> ダニエラ　ミッソ/Daniela Misso(イタリア/Italy)

秋薔薇水浴のいと楽しくて

> rosée d'automne — le plaisir de baignade
>
> エウジェニア　パラシブ/Eugénia Paraschiv(ルーマニア/Romania)

秋薔薇亀裂の間にも香は匂ふ

> rose d'automne — les racines parfumées entre les fissures
>
> アブダラ　ハジイ/Abdallah Hajji(モロッコ/Morocco)

秋薔薇の甘き香りが雨の中

> sweet floral notes in the rain — autumn rose
>
> クリスティーナ　チン/Christina Chin(マレーシア/Malaysia)

秋薔薇野生のエキス持ちにけり

> toute la quintessence des parfums sauvages — rose d'automne
>
> カディジャ　エル　ブルカディ/Khadija El Bourkadi
>
> (モロッコ/Morocco)

秋薔薇静かなる目に瞑想す

> rose d'automne — dans ses yeux je contemple la sérénité
>
> アブデラヒム　ベンサイド/Abderrahim Bensaïd
>
> (モロッコ/Morocco)

秋の薔薇鏡の中の少女は誰
> rose d'automne — qui est la fille dans le miroir
> autumn rose — who is the girl in the mirror
>> クリスティーナ SNG/Christina Sng(シンガポール/Singapore)

秋薔薇その無限なる美しさ
> autumn roses — the timeless beauty
>> ミレラ　ブライレーン/Mirela Brailean(ルーマニア/Romania)

秋薔薇頬を赤く染めたる陽よ
> rose d'automne — le rayon de soleil empourpe ses belles joues
>> カメル　メスレム/Kamel Meslem(アルジェリア/Algeria)

秋の蝶壁画の花のありどころ
> murale a fiori — una farfalla in cerca di un giardino
>> アンナ　リモンディ/Anna Rimondi（イタリア/Italy)

てつぺんの秋薔薇つひに枯れにけり
> in cima al gambo la rosa che non colsi — ora è appassita
>> アンナ　リモンディ/Anna Rimondi（イタリア/Italy)

秋薔薇花弁の雫落ちにけり
> rose d'automne — au sol gisent ses pétales emperlés
>> フランソワーズ　デニオ-ルリエーブル/Françoise Deniaud-Lelièvre
>> (フランス/France)

窓辺には新たな匂ひ秋薔薇
> autumn rose — a new scent on the windowsill
> rosa autunnale — un nuovo profumo sul davanzale
>> アンジェラ　ジオルダーノ/Angela Giordano(イタリア/Italy)

秋薔薇ふたりの心成熟す
> autumn roses — our mature awareness
> rose autunnali — la nostra matura consapevolezza
>> アンジェラ　ジオルダーノ/Angela Giordano（イタリア/Italy）

アンコール二つ答へて秋薔薇
> autumn roses — response to two encores
>> タンポポ　アニス/Tanpopo Anis（インドネシア/Indonesia）

まだ続く夢ありけり秋の薔薇
> autumn rose — a dream that goes on
> rosa d'autunno — un sogno che continua
>> ローザマリア　ディ　サルバトーレ/Rosa Maria Di Salvatore
>> （イタリア/Italy）

秋の薔薇もの憂げに聴くバイオリン
> autumn rose — the melancholic sound of the violin
>> ナッキー　クリスティジーノ/Nuky Kristijno
>> （インドネシア/Indonesia）

秋の薔薇懐かしきもの漂よはせ
> with autumn roses in the air an essence of nostalgia
> autunnali nell'aria una essenza di nostagia con le rose autunnali
> nell'aria una essenza di nostagia
>> アンジェラ　ジオルダーノ/Angela Giordano
>> （イタリア/Italy）

心境の変化の中に秋薔薇
> amidst a change of heart — autumn rose
>> クリスティーナ　チン/Christina Chin（マレーシア/Malaysia）

秋薔薇黄昏へ向かふ道のあり

rose d'autunno — strada rivolta al crepuscolo

リタ　モアール/Rita Moar（イタリア/Italy）

秋の薔薇静かな愛を育てつつ　　　　　　　亜仁寿（自訳）

autumn roses — growing up a quiet love

タンポポ　アニス/Tanpopo Anis
（インドネシア/Indonesia）

秋薔薇彼女の肌に匂ひたる

rose d'automne — reste sur sa peau nue le parfum d'un châle
autumn rose — remains on her naked skin the scent of a shawl

イザベル　ラマン/Isa Lamant（フランス/France）

秋薔薇壁にもたれて泣いており

rose d'automne — s'appuyant contre le mur elle pleure

アンヌ-マリー　ジュベール-ガヤール/Anne-Marie Joubert-Gaillard
（フランス/France）

金木犀【きんもくせい・kimmokusei】
fragrant olive tree / olivier odorant

The golden osmanthus has orange — yellow flowers. Silver rhinoceros has white flowers. It flowers in September around mid — autumn. Its flowers are small but highly fragrant, and it is widely used as a garden tree. The fragrance of the golden rhinoceros is stronger than that of the silver rhinoceros. The fragrance wafting in a fresh breeze tells us that autumn is deepening

金木犀風の流れに匂ひ添ひ

> olivier odorant — la valse avec le vent
>
> アメル　ラディビ　ベント　シャディ/AmelLadhibi Bent Chadly
>
> （チュニジア/Tunisia）

金木犀紅茶に杏子の混じるやう

> un soupçon d'abricot dans le thé aux fleurs — olivier odorant
>
> ラシダ　ジェルビ/Rachida Jerbi（チュニジア/Tunisia）

早朝の空気の中の金木犀

> mattina presto — un soffio di osmanto nell'aria
> early morning — a waft of osmanthus in the air
>
> ダニエラ　ミッソ/Daniela Misso（イタリア/Italy）

図書館の窓より香る金木犀

> osmanthus fragrant in the breeze — open library window
>
> タンポポ　アニス/Tanpopo Anis（インドネシア/Indonesia）

地中海の風心地良き金木犀

> fragrant olive tree — charm of the mediterranean sea wind
>
> キム　オルムタック　ゴメス/Kim Olmtak Gomes
>
> （オランダ/Holland）

そよ風が金木犀を吹き抜ける

> light wind swishing through — fragrant olive tree
>
> クリスティーナ　チン/Christina Chin（マレーシア/Malaysia）

銀輪に金木犀の香を乗せて

> fragrant olive — carry the scent by bike
>
> 中野千秋/Chiaki Nakano（日本/Japan）

どの家も金木犀の香る今朝

chaque maison embaumée d'olivier odorant — matin d'automne

向瀬美音/Mine Mukose（日本/Japan）

木槿【むくげ・mukuge】
rose of sharon / rose chamallow

A deciduous shrub of the mallow family native to China, India, and Asia Minor. It grows to about 3 meters. It is planted as a garden tree or hedge, and produces five — petaled flowers that are mainly reddish — purple, white, or wilted. It blooms in the morning and withers at dusk. It is also used as a metaphor for something transient.

花木槿イコンの聖の涙なり

rose de sharon — les incroyables larmes de l'icône

エウジェニア　パラシブ/Eugénia Paraschiv

（ルーマニア/Romania）

花槿腰の周りにバスタオル

rose chamallow — sa serviette de bains autour des hanches

アンヌ-マリー　ジュベール-ガヤール/Anne-Marie Joubert-Gaillard

（フランス/France）

芙蓉咲く夜は濃くなる花の色

cotton rose malow — pinky flowers turned dark red at night

アリアナ　ユハナ/Ariani Yuhana（インドネシア/Indonesia）

花木槿甘き香りが部屋に満ち

a read leaf — caught by the crescent moon

マリリン　アッシュボ/Marilyn Ashbaugh（米国/United States）

花木槿散つた辺りを歩きけり

> rose of sharon — she steps around a fallen petal
>
> バリー　レビン/Barrie Levine（米国/United States）

蜜蜂は花粉に塗れ花木槿

> the bumble bee buzzes a pollen bed — rose of sharon
>
> クリステーナ　チン/Christina Chin（マレーシア/Malaysia）

花木槿浜に祭のドレスの娘

> à la plage dans sa petite robe des fêtes — rose de sharon
>
> ラシダ　ジェルビ/Rachida Jerbi（チュニジア/Tunisia）

花木槿聖なる書物なりにけり

> rose de sharon — les livres sacrés
>
> エウジェニア　パラシブ/Eugénia Paraschiv
>
> （ルーマニア/Romania）

回廊に朝日の差して花木槿

> rose di sharon — la prima luce nel silenzio del chiostro
> rose of sharon — first light in the silence of cloister
>
> クリスティーナ　プルビエンティ/Cristina Pulvirenti（イタリア/Italy）

芙蓉咲く年を経るほど美しく

> confederate rose — the older the more beautiful
>
> ザンザミ　イスマイル/Zamzami（インドネシア/Indonesia）

芙蓉咲くカーテン揺れるその先に

> rosa confederata — le tende ondeggiano dolcemente
> cotton rose mallow — the curtains gently swaying
>
> ダニエラ　ミッソ/Daniela Misso（イタリア/Italy）

芙蓉咲く鏡の中の瞳かな

confederate rose — the beauty in the mirror of her eyes

ミレラ　ブライレーン/Mirela Brailean

(ルーマニア/Romania)

艶やかに木槿の花を髪にさす

fragrance of a woman — the rose of sharon pinned on her hair

クリスティーナ　チン/Christina Chin

(マレーシア/Malaysia)

手の甲に軽くくちづけ花木槿

rose of sharon — his gentle kiss on my hand

ナッキー　クリスティジーノ/Nuky Kristijno

(インドネシア/Indonesia)

旅終はる閉ぢたフェンスに花木槿

the end of my journey — rose of sharon on the fence closed up tightly

タンポポ　アニス/Tanpopo Anis

(インドネシア/Indonesia)

花木槿いつも晴れてる地中海

rose of sharon — always sunny on the mediterranean coast

キム　オルムタック　ゴメス/Kim Olmtak Gomes

(オランダ/Holland)

花木槿ピンクの影のアイシャドウ

ose of sharon — the pink shade of her eyeshadow

ナッキー　クリスティジーノ/Nuky Kristijno

(インドネシア/Indonesia)

花木槿のパステルカラー蜂鳥来

| rose of sharon lured by pastel blossoms hummingbirds

ポール　カルス/Paul Callus（マルタ/Malta）

空へ向く家より高き花木槿

| rose of Sharon faces the sky — higher than my house

タンポポ　アニス/Tanpopo Anis
（インドネシア/Indonesia）

底紅や少女の羽化の秘めやかに

| rose de sharon — le secret de l'éclosion d'une fille

向瀬美音/Mine Mukose（日本/Japan）

芙蓉 【ふよう・fuyo】
confererate rose / cotton rose mallow

Deciduous shrub of the mallow family. The height is 1.5 to 3 meters. It produces white or light red five — petaled flowers from August to October, which fade in the evening. After blooming, it produces light green, bud — like fruits. It is planted in gardens and other places as an ornamental.

芙蓉咲き美しき日の始まりぬ

| cotton rose blooming one by one — beautiful day begins

タンポポ　アニス/Tanpopo Anis（インドネシア/Indonesia）

蠟燭に花の匂ひや芙蓉咲き

| cotton rose mallow — the aromatic scent of your candle

ナッキー　クリスティジーノ/Nuky Kristijno
（インドネシア/Indonesia）

花芙蓉誰にも会はぬ日を化粧ふ
> cotton rose mallow ― makeup on the day I don't see anyone
>
> 中野千秋/Chiaki Nakano（日本/Japan）

後れ毛の目立つシニヨン木槿咲く
> chignon with loose back hair ― rose of sharon
>
> 中野千秋/Chiaki Nakano（日本/Japan）

桃【もも・momo】
peach / peche

Peach seeds came from China and have been cultivated since the Nara period (710 ― 794). Many varieties of peaches have been cultivated since the mizu ― mitsume peach. Early peaches are shipped from late June, while mizu ― mitsume peaches and white peaches are shipped in mid ― August. Flower is a seasonal word in spring.

桃のジャム庭に瓶など並べたり
> confitures de pêches ― le jardin en pot
>
> イザベル　カルバロ　テール/Isabelle Carvalho Teles
> （フランス/France）

桃の実や干からびてゐる祖母の肌
> uicy peaches ― the skin of the grandmother more and more dry
> pesche succose ― la pelle della nonna sempre più secca
>
> アンジェラ　ジオルダーノ/Angela Giordano（イタリア/Italy）

熟れた桃菜園の匂ひの台所
> pesche mature ― il profumo dell'orto entra in cucina
>
> リタ　モアール/Rita Moar（イタリア/Italia）

ボクサーも優しき指で桃を剝く　　　　　　　亜仁寿（自訳）
　boxers also peel peaches with gentle fingers
　　　　　　　　　　　　　タンポポ　アニス/Tanpopo Anis
　　　　　　　　　　　　　　　　　　（インドネシア/Indonesia）

白桃の故郷の香を届けけり　　　　　　　　　亜仁寿（自訳）
　white peach — bringing the scent of hometown
　　　　　　　　　　　　　タンポポ　アニス/Tanpopo Anis
　　　　　　　　　　　　　　　　　　（インドネシア/Indonesia）

桃の実やジャンプのたびに跳ねるチュチュ
　peach — tutu bounces with her jump
　　　　　　　　　　　ナッキー　クリスティジーノ/Nuky Kristijno
　　　　　　　　　　　　　　　　　　（インドネシア/Indonesia）

箱詰の桃の匂へる無人店　　　　　　　　　　亜仁寿（自訳）
　unmanned store — filled with the smell of boxed peaches
　　　　　　　　　　　　　タンポポ　アニス/Tanpopo Anis
　　　　　　　　　　　　　　　　　　（インドネシア/Indonesia）

桃を食ぶさてもう一度恋をせん
　eat a peach — now fall in love again
　　　　　　　　　　　　　中野千秋/Chiaki Nakano（日本/Japan）

惜しみなく捧げるからだ水蜜桃
　sans hésiter de donner mon corps — pêche juteuse
　　　　　　　　　　　　　向瀬美音/Mine Mukose（日本/Japan）

梨【なし・nashi】
pear / poire / poirier

One of the most representative fruits of autumn. There are many varieties, including Chojuro (red pears) and Nijusseiki (green pears). They are rich in moisture, sweet, and have a refreshing taste.

梨一つ落ちて子供の歩む音
> une poire tombe — le bruit de pas d'enfant
>
> エレナ　ズアイン/Elena Zouain
>
> (ルーマニア/Romania)

新しきことは苦手よ梨を剝く
> peeling a pear — not good at new things
>
> 中野千秋/Chiaki Nakano(日本/Japan)

山間の香り閉じ込めラフランス
> les poires — condensé de parfum de la montagne
>
> 向瀬美音/Mine Mukose(日本/Japan)

画布に乗る色食べ頃のラフランス
> couleur sur la toile — poire prête à manger
>
> 向瀬美音/Mine Mukose(日本/Japan)

柿【かき・kaki】

Japanese persimmon / plaquemine kaki

A deciduous tree of the family Oysteraceae. Endemic to the temperate regions of East Asia, the fruits are edible. The stiff leaves are glossy. It is dioecious. Sweet persimmons, such as Fuyu, Gosho, and Jirō persimmons, turn from yellow to red when ripe and are eaten as they are. Dried astringent persimmons become sweet. The green astringent persimmon yields persimmon tannin, which is used for waterproofing and preserving persimmon.

幾百の柿の花実はいくつかしら

des centaines de fleurs de plaqueminier — combien y aura-t-il de kakis?

イメルダ　セン/Imelda Senn(スイス/Switzerland)

待ち侘びた甘き柿なる贈り物

Japanese persimmon — a sweet gift for those who wait

ポール　カルス/Paul Callus(マルタ/Malta)

柿を食ぶ記憶の中の旅の味

Japanese persimmons — the taste of an unforgettable travel

ミレラ　ブライレーン/Mirela Brailean(ルーマニア/Romania)

故郷のその明るさよ柿すだれ　　　　　　　　　　亜仁寿（自訳）

persimmons hung to dry — the brightness of my hometown

タンポポ　アニス/Tanpopo Anis(インドネシア/Indonesia)

柿実るオレンジ色の地平線

persimmons — orange colouring on the horizon

キム　オルムタック　ゴメス/Kim Olmtak Gomes(オランダ/Holland)

359

丘の上を煌めく日差し柿熟れる
ripe persimmons — flashes of sunshine on the hill
cachi maturi — sprazzi di sole sulla collina
アンジェラ　ジオルダーノ/Angela Giordano
(イタリア/Italy)

日蝕に柿実りたる輝きよ
éclipse solaire — sur le plaquemier un kaki plus lumineux que tous les autres
ラシダ　ジェルビ/Rachida Jerbi(チュニジア/Tunisia)

鐘鳴りて柿の実落ちる悲しさよ
tristi rintocchi suonano le campane — cadono i cachi
ミケーレ　ポッチエロ/Michele Pochiero
(イタリア/Italy)

黄昏の壁画めきたる柿簾
curtains of kaki caught in the sunset — a mural is painted
バーバラ　オルムタック/Barbara Olmtak
(オランダ/Holland)

丸窓に夜明けの光柿匂ふ
dawn's first light through the marumado — the scent of persimmon
バーバラ　オルムタック/Barbara Olmtak
(オランダ/Holland)

柿落ちて蝙蝠赤き警報を
sui cachi caduti bubola il gufo — allerta rossa
アンナ　メダ/Anna Meda(イタリア/Italy)

柿をもぐ籠いっぱいに鳥の歌
> picking persimmons — my basket is full of bird sounds
> hái quả h4ng — trong giỏ của tôi đầy tiếng chim
>> ディン　ニュグエン/Dinh Nguyen(ベトナム/Vietnam)

彼方まで旧街道の柿の秋
> persimmon grow — as far as the end of old road
>> 中野千秋/Chiaki Nakano(日本/Japan)

熟柿【じゅくし・jukushi】
ripe persimmons

A red, ripe persimmon. Sometimes astringent persimmons are eaten as ripe persimmons. The flesh is jelly — like and has a strong sweet taste.

くちびるに秋の味なる熟柿かな
> ripe persimmon — the taste of autumn on the lips
>> ディン　ニュグエン/Dinh Nguyen(ベトナム/Vietnam)

熟す柿犬は小蠅を追い払ひ
> cachi maturi — tra i moscerini il cane scuote la testa
>> ガブリエル　デ　マシ/Gabriella De Masi(イタリア/Italy)

黄金のランタンのごと柿実る
> lanterns' golden glow — persimmons
>> キム　オルムタック　ゴメス/Kim Olmtak Gomes(オランダ/Holland)

木の上に鳥の国あり熟柿かな
> country of birds in the tree — ripe persimmons
>> 中野千秋/Chiaki Nakano(日本/Japan)

林檎【りんご・ringo】
apple / pomme

Rosaceae. Originates from Europe. One of the most popular autumn fruits. There are many varieties such as Fuji, Benitama, Ohorin, Tsugaru, and Golden Delicious. Aomori and Nagano are the most famous production areas.

林檎狩恋愛小説読むやうに
> un romanzo d'amore — tonfo di mele in giardino
> a romance book — thud of apples in the garden
>> ダニエラ　ミッソ/Daniela Misso（イタリア/Italy）

林檎狩旬のジュースのいと甘き
> cueillette — le jus sucré de la première pomme
>> イザベラ　カルバロ　テール/Isabelle Carvalho Teles
>> （フランス/France）

幼少の庭には古き林檎の木
> vieux pommier — retour vers le jardin de mon enfance
>> ベルナデット　クエン/Bernadette Couenne
>> （フランス/France）

子供の日カラメル色の林檎食べ
> fête des enfants — pommes caramélisées
>> ベルナデット　クエン/Bernadette Couenne
>> （フランス/France）

齧りたるところ変色する林檎
> bite marks are slightly brown — apple
>> ザンザミ　イスマイル/Zamzami Ismail（インドネシア/Indonesia）

風に落ち収穫時期となる林檎

> windfall — apples ready for picking
>
> ポール　カルス/Paul Callus（マルタ/Malta）

林檎畑娘生まれし故郷よ

> champ de pommiers — c'est bien là que la petite est née
>
> カディジャ　エル　ブルカディ/Khadija El Bourkadi
（モロッコ/Morocco）

禁断の林檎を持ちて誘惑す

> apple — she tempts with forbidden fruit
>
> ポール　カルス/Paul Callus（マルタ/Malta）

祖父植えし林檎に秋の陽の優し

> sole d'autunno — una carezza al melo che piantò il nonno
>
> ガブリエラ　デ　マシ/Gabriella De Masi
（イタリア/Italy）

秋のパイまづは林檎のスライスを

> slicing apples on a wooden board — first autumn pie
>
> バリー　レビン/Barrie Levine（米国/United States）

デザートに甘き林檎を収穫す

> sweet culinary apples ready to pick — autumn desserts
>
> クリスティーナ　チン/Christina Chin
（マレーシア/Malaysia）

短日や林檎を突つく灰鴉

> courte journée — le corbeau picore les pommes tombées
>
> イメルダ　セン/Imelda Senn（スイス/Switzerland）

林檎捥ぐ君の最初の詩歌の本
　　cueillette de pommes — son premier carnet de chants
　　　　　　　　　　　カリン　コシュト/Karine Cocheteux（フランス/France）

林檎熟し毎年のラブストーリー
　　mele succose — tutte le storie d'autunno di anno in anno
　　　　　　　　　　　フランシー　ゼタ/Francy Zeta（イタリア/Italy）

焼き林檎祖父の果樹園から来る
　　baked green apples — from granddad's orchard
　　　　　　　　　　　クリスティーナ　チン/Christina Chin（マレーシア/Malaysia）

その種を蒔いてみたる赤き林檎
　　la couleur des pommes — je jette un pépin au hasard
　　the color of apples — I throw a seed at random
　　　　　　　　　　　ミュールバッハ　アキツ/F.Mühlebach akitsu
　　　　　　　　　　　　　　　　　（フランス/France）

雨の日の林檎の匂ふ部屋の中
　　it's raining — room smells of apples
　　dežuje — v sobi dišijo jabolka
　　　　　　　　　　　ディミトリー/Dimitrij Škrk（スロベニア/Slovenia）

重力のレッスン林檎の木を揺らす
　　leçon de gravité — le professeur secoue le pommier
　　　　　　　　　　　アブダラ　ハジイ/Abdallah Hajji（モロッコ/Moroco）

林檎剝くふるさとの夜を持て余し
　　peel an apple — bored night in my hometown
　　　　　　　　　　　中野千秋/Chiaki Nakano（日本/Japan）

紅玉を箱ごと買ふも冬支度
| qcheter des caisses de pommes ― préparation pour l'hiver

向瀬美音/Mine Mukose（日本/Japan）

キッチンに香るシナモン林檎焼く
| la cannelle embaume dans la cuisine ― pommes cuites

向瀬美音/Mine Mukose（日本/Japan）

青林檎乳歯の歯形くつきりと
| pommes vertes ― marque des dents d'un petit enfant

向瀬美音/Mine Mukose（日本/Japan）

葡萄【ぶどう・budo】
grapes / raisin

Vine family. Vining, growing rapidly. Leaves are heart ― shaped and jagged. It produces green granular flowers. Fruits ripen from August to October and are used for food, jam, wine, etc.

黒葡萄水彩の子の頬の色
| trugurii negri ― pe obrajii copiilor acuarele
| raisins noirs ― sur les joues des enfants des aquarelles

マリン　ラダ/Marin Rada

（ルーマニア/Romania）

黄昏や収穫の葡萄みな金色
| soleil couchant ― tout dorés les petits grains de la vendange

フロ　ファブリス　ファルク/Flo Fabrice Farque

（フランス/France）

黄金に輝く葡萄摘む夜明け
　alba di canti ― raccolto nei vigneti l'uva dorata
　　　　　　　　　　　アグネーゼ　ジアロンゴ/Agnese Giallongo
　　　　　　　　　　　　　　　　　　　　　　　（イタリア/Italy）

葡萄の葉抱き合ひ秋の色づきぬ
　feuilles de vignes enlacées ― l'automne défile ses couleurs
　　　　　　　アメルラディヒビ　ベント　シャディー/AmelLadhibi Bent Chadly
　　　　　　　　　　　　　　　　　　　　　　　（チュニジア/Tunisia）

マルメロを砂糖煮にして葡萄畑
　quinces compote ― autumn works in the vineyard
　kompot od dunja ― jesenski radovi u vinogradu
　　　　　　　　　　　　ズデンカ　ムリナー/Zdenka Mlinar
　　　　　　　　　　　　　　　　　　　　　　　（クロアチア/Croatia）

太陽はルビーの色に葡萄畑
　blurred valley ― in the vineyard a sun the color of rubies
　zamagljena dolina ― u vinogradu sunce boje rubina
　　　　　　　　　　　　ズデンカ　ムリナー/Zdenka Mlinar
　　　　　　　　　　　　　　　　　　　　　　　（クロアチア/Croatia）

黒葡萄摘んで紫色の空
　purple sky ― picking Black Pinot
　ljubičasto nebo ― branje Crnog pinota
　　　　　　　　　　ズデンカ　ムリナー/Zdenka Mlinar（クロアチア/Croatoa）

寛容な年なり葡萄豊作に
　une année généreuse ― quelle récolte de raisin à profusion
　　　　　　　　　　　イメルダ　セン/Imelda Senn（スイス/Switzerland）

活気づく斜面や葡萄収穫し

> harvesting grapes — mountain slopes teem with activity
>
> ポール　カルス/Paul Callus(マルタ/Malta)

ワイン飲む夕日に染まる葡萄畑

> red vines in the sunset — sipping wine
>
> クリスティーナ　チン/Christina Chin(マレーシア/Malaysia)

黄葡萄や我が唇に蜂蜜を

> struguri galbeni — pe buzele tale picături de miere
> yellow grapes — drops of honey on your lips
>
> ダニエラ　トピルシーン/Daniela Topîrcean(ルーマニア/Romania)

葡萄採る昔の歌が丘の上

> on the hill the grape harvest — ancient songs
> sulla collina la raccolta dell'uva — antichi canti
>
> アンジェラ　ジオルダーノ/Angela Giordano(イタリア/Italy)

葡萄の木薫る暑き夜青き月

> lune bleue — l'odeur des vignes dans la nuit chaude.
>
> ナタシャ　カール　ベズソノフ/Natacha Karl Bezsonoff(フランス/France)

白葡萄嚙みて人生ほろ苦し

> croquer du raisin blanc — amertume de la vie
> biting into white grapes — bitterness of life
>
> ミュールバッハ　アキツ/F.Mühlebach akitsu(フランス/France)

収穫の葡萄の列に農夫の歌

> raccolto d'uva — il canto contadino tra i filari tra i filari
>
> アグネーゼ　ジアロンゴ/Agnese Giallongo(イタリア/Italy)

幼子は舌を見せてつつ葡萄食ぶ
> grape — little son shows his red tongue
>
> アリアナ　ユハナ/Ariani Yuhana
>
> (インドネシア/Indonesia)

収穫後終の葡萄は鶫へと
> fin des vendanges — les dernières grappes pour le merle
>
> エレナ　ズアイン/Elena Zouain(ルーマニア/Romania)

赤らみてロビンの帰り待つ葡萄
> la vigne roussit dans l'attente du retour du rouge-gorge
>
> ナディン　レオン/Nadine Léon(フランス/France)

雀等の来ては去りては葡萄狩
> grape harvest — the sparrows come and go
> vendemmia — i passeri vanno e vengono
>
> アンジェラ　ジオルダーノ/Angela Giordano
>
> (イタリア/Italy)

葡萄食ぶ一粒ごとに違ふ味
> grape — i found a different taste in each grain
>
> エル　ハミド/El Hamied(インドネシア/Indonesia)

黒葡萄いつも正装令夫人
> black grapes — a lady always in formal attire
>
> 中野千秋/Chiaki Nakano(日本/Japan)

みはるかす葡萄畑やブルゴーニュ
> Bourgogne — vignobles sans fin à perte de vue
>
> 向瀬美音/Mine Mukose(日本/Japan)

一粒ごと光の雫マスカット

> muscat — une goutte de lumière luit sur chaque grain
>
> 向瀬美音/Mine Mukose（日本/Japan）

頬赤き農夫と樽の葡萄園

> un paysan aux joues rouges — du vin dans un tonneau
>
> 向瀬美音/Mine Mukose（日本/Japan）

くろがねの葡萄の重み蛇笏の忌

> poids des raisins noirs — anniversaire de la mort de 'Dakotsu'
>
> 向瀬美音/Mine Mukose（日本/Japan）

栗【くり・kuri】

chestnut / marron, chataignier

Fagaceae. The fruit grows in a ball of dense thorns. It grows wild in the mountains and the berries have been used as food since ancient times. It produces strongly fragrant flowers around June. The wood is moisture — resistant and durable, and has been used for house foundations, sleepers, piles, etc.

足元に最初の栗や森の散歩

> promenade en forêt — les premières châtaignes sous mes pas
>
> アンヌ-マリー　ジュベール-ガヤール/Anne-Marie Joubert-Gaillard
>
> （フランス/France）

栗の毬落つる音秋の便りかな

> suoni d'autunno i ricci che cadono — nuovi messaggi
>
> ミケーレ　ポチエロ/Michele Pochiero
>
> （イタリア/Italy）

焼栗の匂ひや曲がり角の先
> smell of roasted chestnut as I turn to the end of street
>
> ナッキー　クリスティジーノ/Nuky Kristijno
>
> (インドネシア/Indonesia)

焼栗やいくつか温かき言葉
> roasted chestnuts — a few warm words
>
> アンナ　イリナ/Ana Irina（ルーマニア/Romania)

焼栗の匂ひのしたる君の髪
> the smell of burnt chestnut on her hair
>
> ナッキー　クリスティジーノ/Nuky Kristijno
>
> (インドネシア/Indonesia)

毬栗やもうじき母が巡礼に
> vertes les bogues des châtaignes — bientôt le pèlerinage de ma mère
>
> green the chestnut burrs — soon my mother's pilgrimage
>
> ミュールバッハ　アキツ/F.Mühlebach akitsu
>
> (フランス/France)

栗を剝き指を怪我した幼き日
> childhood memories — peeled chestnuts and wound on my fingers
>
> タンポポ　アニス/Tanpopo Anis（インドネシア/Indonesia)

栗剝いて親子の会話はじまりぬ　　　　　　亜仁寿（自訳）
> peeling chestnuts — the conversation between parent and child begins
>
> タンポポ　アニス/Tanpopo Anis（インドネシア/Indonesia)

焼栗や昔の暖炉懐かしき
> roasted chestnuts — childhood memories by the fireplace
> caldarroste — i ricordi d'infanzia accanto al camino
>> アンジェラ　ジオルダーノ/Angela Giordano（イタリア/Italy）

突然に音たて栗の落下かな
> chestnuts — a sudden thud on the ground
> castagne — un tonfo improvviso sul terreno
>> アンジェラ　ジオルダーノ/Angela Giordano（イタリア/Italy）

もぐら塚埋めたる栗の園庭よ
> jardin habité une châtaigne enfouie dans la taupinière
>> フランソワーズ　デニオ-ルリエーブル/Françoise Deniaud-Lelièvre
>> （フランス/France）

四苦八苦しながら栗を剝いてをり
> she is having a hard time opening the chestnut
>> ナッキー　クリスティジーノ/Nuky Kristijno（インドネシア/Indonesia）

登校も下校も栗を見つけたる
> both going to school and leaving school — find chestnuts
>> 中野千秋/Chiaki Nakano（日本/Japan）

焼き栗の香り漂ふセーヌ沿ひ
> qrôme de châtaignes grillées — le long de la Seine
>> 向瀬美音/Mine Mukose（日本/Japan）

焼き栗売り声高らかにセーヌ川
> marrons grillés — vendus gaiement le long de la Seine
>> 向瀬美音/Mine Mukose（日本/Japan）

焼き栗や心にぬくし京言葉

> marrons grillés — douceur du dialecte de Kyoto
>
> 向瀬美音/Mine Mukose（日本/Japan）

ポケットに転がす栗やまだぬくき

> marrons roulés dans ma poche — encore chauds
>
> 向瀬美音/Mine Mukose（日本/Japan）

柘榴【ざくろ・zakuro】
pomegranate / grenades

Deciduous tree native to Central Asia. Fruits in autumn. The tough, hard rind is cracked open to reveal a jewel — like mass of small, dark red, lush, fresh berries. It is used for viewing, eating, and medicinal purposes. It has a sweet and sour taste with a hint of bitterness.

天高く我が家の柘榴黄に熟す

> la mia casa — il giallo dell'autunno sul melograno
>
> ジオバンナ　ジオイア/Giovanna Gioia（イタリア/Italy）

石榴の種老婆ロザリオ磨きをり

> chicchi di melograno — la vecchia signora sgrana il suo rosario
>
> アンジェラ　ジオルダーノ/Angela Giordano
> （イタリア/Italy）

びつしりと赤き宝石柘榴割る

> glitter and glamour of gems — pomegranates
>
> バーバラ　オルムタック/Barbara Olmtak
> （オランダ/Holland）

柘榴の木ルビーの杯の震へけり
> sur le grenadier coupes de rubis frémissantes —ses fruits
>> アメル　ラディビ　ベント　シャディー/Amel Ladhibi Bent Chadly
>>> （チュニジア/Tunisia）

熟したる柘榴抱へる農夫かな
> contadini colgono — melograni maturi in ceste piene
>> アグネーゼ　ジアロンゴ/Agnese Giallongo（イタリア/Italy）

小雨降る夜は柘榴の匂ひして
> scroscio di pioggia — la notte profuma di melograno
>> ガブリエラ　デ　マシ/Gabriella De Masi
>>> （イタリア/Italy）

柘榴の実ルビーはキロで売られたり
> grenades — vente de rubis aux kilos
>> スアド　ハジリ/Souad Hajri（チュニジア/Tunisia）

雨に濡れ柘榴は赤く反射せり
> le melagrane — sulle gocce di pioggia riflessi rossi
>> アルベルタ　カテリナ　マトリ/Alberta Caterina Mattoli（イタリア/Italy）

実柘榴のかくも重くて瑞々し
> how heavy the pomegranate — juicy
>> キム　オルムタック　ゴメス/Kim Olmtak Gomes
>>> （オランダ/Holland）

柘榴の実傷口開き血の垂れる
> grenades éclatées d'automne — tout ce sang répandu
>> シュピー　モイサン/Choupie Moysan（フランス/France）

変るだろう我も柘榴の色のやうに
> sta cambiando il colore del melograno — io sono già diversa
>
> ジオバンナ　ジオイア/Giovanna Gioia
> （イタリア/Italy）

唇の赤さよ柘榴熟れにけり
> red lips — the pomegranates are ripe now
>
> ローザ　マリア　ディ　サルバトーレ/Rosa Maria Di Salvatore
> （イタリア/Italy）

実柘榴や輝く種のびつしりと
> seeds tightly packed glistening in your hands — pomegranate
>
> プロビール　ギュプタ/Probir Gupta（インド/India）

柘榴割れ騙されさうな赤き色
> ripe pomegranate — murmures de l'automne
>
> キム　オルムタック　ゴメス/Kim Olmtak Gomes
> （オランダ/Holland）

初めてのトルコ旅行や柘榴の実
> pomegranate — my first trip to Turkey
>
> アンナ　イリナ/Ana Irina（ルーマニア/Romania）

柘榴の実ルージュをさして白き肌
> pomegranate — rouge on her pale skin
>
> ポール　カルス/Paul Callus（マルタ/Malta）

柘榴の実宝探しのごとく割る
> pomegranate — splitting it was like finding treasure
>
> エル　ハミド/El Hamied（インドネシア/Indonesia）

柘榴の実DNAの赤き糸
> pomegranate — the red thread of my dna
>
> バーバラ　オルムタック/Barbara Olmtak
>
> (オランダ/Holland)

柘榴の実ゴーギャンの描く女達
> pomegranate — women painted by Gauguin
>
> 中野千秋/Chiaki Nakano(日本/Japan)

退廃の艶を放ちて柘榴の実
> grenades — lustre aux reflets de décadence.
>
> 向瀬美音/Mine Mukose(日本/Japan)

無花果【いちじく・ichijiku】
figue / figuier

A small deciduous tree of the mulberry family that is cultivated throughout Japan. It appears to bear fruit without flowers, hence the name "fig," but in fact, numerous white flowers bloom inside a flower sac from spring to summer, which ripen into dark purple fruit in the fall.

通学路に幼少よりの無花果の木
> chemin de l'école toujours là le figuier de mon enfance
>
> カディジャ　エル　ブルカディ/Khadija El Bourkadi
>
> (モロッコ/Morocco)

無花果や甘き香放つ村の道
> allen figs — sweet scent along the village road
>
> タンポポ　アニス/Tanpopo Anis
>
> (インドネシア/Indonesia)

新学期子らは無花果の木の影に

> retour à l'école — les enfants à l'ombre du figuier
>
> アブダラ　ハジイ/Abdallah Hajji（モロッコ/Morocco）

無花果に死ぬ蜂愛の唇よ

> lèvres amoureuses — la guêpe du figuier meurt à l'intérieur
>
> エウジェニア　パラシブ/Eugénia Paraschiv
>
> （ルーマニア/Romania）

無花果の傷んで蟻のご馳走に

> figues pourries — le régal des fourmis
>
> オルファ　クチュク　ブハディダ/Olfa Kchouk Bouhadida
>
> （チュニジア/Tunisia）

収穫の月無花果の落ちにけり

> lune des moissons — des figues oubliées par terre
>
> イメルダ　セン/Imelda Senn（スイス/Switzerland）

無花果の甘き香に来る雀蜂

> ripe figs — wasps enticed by sweet aroma
>
> ポール　カルス/Paul Callus（マルタ/Malta）

胡桃【くるみ・kurumi】
walnut, walnut tree / noix, noyer

The fruit of a deciduous tree of the walnut family. The onion walnut grows wild in Japan. The fruit is almost spherical, about 3 cm in diameter. It is densely covered with fine hairs and the shell is extremely hard. Inside is a fatty pulp with white cotyledons, which is used in salad, confectionery, and other dishes.

指先に幼少の香や胡桃の簞笥

> commode en noyer — les effluves de mon enfance sur les doigts
>
> アンヌ-マリー　ジュベール-ガヤール/Anne-Marie Joubert-Gaillard
>
> (フランス/France)

屋根裏部屋に胡桃広げて乾かせり

> vecchia soffitta — le noci distese ad asciugare
>
> アンジェラ　ジオルダーノ/Angela Giordano(イタリア/Italy)

胡桃の木後ろに手を組む子どもゐて

> walnut tree — child hides his hands behind his back
>
> ミレラ　ブライレーン/Mirela Brailean(ルーマニア/Romania)

静寂を破る胡桃の落つる音

> falling walnuts — the soft sound breaks the silence
>
> クリスティーナ　チン/Christina Chin(マレーシア/Malaysia)

現在と過去を繋いで胡桃の木

> linking the present to the past — a black walnut tree
>
> ポール　カルス/Paul Callus(マルタ/Malta)

胡桃割るジョークを言つて笑ひつつ

> together we crack a few jokes and laugh — walnuts
>
> バーバラ　オルムタック/Barbara Olmtak
>
> (オランダ/Holland)

胡桃の実祖父の記憶の曖昧に

> walnut kernels — grandfather's memory begins to falter
>
> gherigli di noce — la memoria del nonno inizia a vacillare
>
> アンジェラ　ジオルダーノ/Angela Giordano(イタリア/Italy)

その殻に知恵を収めてゐる胡桃
> walnut — wisdom encased in a shell
>
> ポール　カルス/Paul Callus（マルタ/Malta）

胡桃の木二人の名前刻まれて
> our names still engraved on the walnut tree
>
> ナッキー　クリスティジーノ/Nuky Kristijno（インドネシア/Indonesia）

手に籠や胡桃を狙ふカケスゐて
> mon panier à la main au noyer les geais sonnent l'alerte
>
> フランソワーズ　デニオ-ルリエーブル/Françoise Deniaud-Lelièvre
>
> （フランス/France）

テーブルに胡桃転がる静けき夜
> silent night — the sounds of rolling walnuts on the wooden table
>
> タンポポ　アニス/Tanpopo Anis（インドネシア/Indonesia）

どのやうにしても割れない胡桃かな
> walnut no matter what I try it won't crack
>
> 中野千秋/Chiaki Nakano（日本/Japan）

青蜜柑【あおみかん・aomikan】

green mandarin / mandarin vert / green orange / orange vert

A general term for citrus fruits in the mandarin orange family that belong to the mandarin orange genus. They are grown in warm regions such as Shizuoka, Wakayama and Ehime, and although they start out green, they turn yellow in late autumn. They are sweet and sour and are eaten. Some are sold in stores with their outer skin still blue.

剝けなくて守りの固い青蜜柑

> defensible hard to peel — green mandarin
>
> 中野千秋/Chiaki Nakano（日本/Japan）

> **オリーブの実**【おりーぶのみ・oribunomi】
>
> green olive / olive verte
>
> An evergreen tree of the Moraceae family. Native to the Mediterranean region, it is cultivated in Japan on Shodoshima Island and elsewhere. It produces flowers in early summer, followed by blue berries. It is used to make olive oil, and the blue berries are used in pickles.

オリーブの古木や父の声のして

> antico uliveto — nel vento risuona la voce di mio padre
>
> アンジェラ　ジオルダーノ/Angela Giordano（イタリア/Italy）

身籠もりて青きオリーブむさぼりぬ

> pregnancy — munching a full jar of green olives
>
> ナッキー　クリスティジーノ/Nuky Kristijno
>
> （インドネシア/Indonesia）

宝島川に囲まれオリーブ畑

> île au trésor — le champ d'oliviers entouré d'une rivière
>
> オルファ　クチュク　ブハディダ/Olfa Kchouk Bouhadida
>
> （チュニジア/Tunisia）

オリーブの下に結婚誓ひけり

> outdoor terrace — under the olive tree wedding vows
>
> キム　オルムタック　ゴメス/Kim Olmtak Gomes
>
> （オランダ/Holland）

オリーブ摘む昔のことを語りつつ
| raccolta delle olive parlando di vecchi tempi
| olive picking — talking about old times

ダニエラ　ミッソ/Daniela Misso（イタリア/Italy）

オリーブの実のなる島へ上陸す
| land on the island — where olive is growing

中野千秋/Chiaki Nakano（日本/Japan）

> ### 檸檬【れもん・remon】
> **lemon, citron / citronnier**
>
> It produces flowers in summer and oval fruits in autumn. The fruits are bright yellow and have a strong sour taste and aroma. In addition to cooking, the pulp can be squeezed to make juice or sliced to add to tea.

夢の庭ミントのそばに檸檬の木
| her dream garden — a lemon tree near the spearmint patch

バリー　レビン/Barrie Levine（米国/United States）

檸檬の香良きアイディアの浮かびたり
| village theater — farmer's vegetables are very fresh and cheap

ナニ　マリアニ/Nani Mariani
（オーストラリア/Australia）

檸檬の木いと芳しき香を放つ
| parfum des citronniers — une sacrée surprise

エウジェニア　パラシブ/Eugénia Paraschiv
（ルーマニア/Romania）

檸檬摘み牡蠣いつぱいの皿並べ
> assiettes remplies d'huîtres — assiettes remplies d'huîtres je cueille un citron
>
> フランソワーズ　デニオ-ルリエーブル/Françoise Deniaud-Lelièvre
>
> （フランス/France）

檸檬切るボウルの中に笑みあまた
> lemon wedges — many smiles in the bowl
>
> バリー　レビン/Barrie Levine（米国/United States）

太陽に赤くなる顔檸檬の木
> citronnier — son visage rougit sous les rayons de soleil
>
> アブデラヒム　ベンサイド/Abderrahim Bensaïd
>
> （モロッコ/Morocco）

檸檬嚙む別れの苦さ引きずつて
> lemon — the bitterness of parting is still felt
>
> ナニ　マリアニ/Nani Mariani
>
> （オーストラリア/Australia）

檸檬の木太陽がまた近くなる
> lemon tree — the sunlight so close again
>
> アンナ　イリナ/Ana Irina
>
> （ルーマニア/Romania）

檸檬の花庭師の帽子唸る蜂
> fleurs de citronnier sur le chapeau du jardinier — les abeilles bourdonnent
>
> アブダラ　ハジイ/Abdallah Hajji
>
> （モロッコ/Morocco）

自転車のベルの音して檸檬の香
> limoni — il suono dei campanelli delle biciclette
> lemons — the sound of bicycle bells
>> ダニエラ　ミッソ/Daniela Misso(イタリア/Italy)

贈り物檸檬もぎ取り木は揺れる
> don du citron cueilli la branche vibre encore
>> マルレーヌ　アレクサ/Marlene Alexa
>> (フランス/France)

葉の間に日の光あり青き檸檬
> raggi di sole brillano fra le foglie — limoni acerbi
>> ナザレナ　ランピニ/Nazarena Rampini(イタリア/Italy)

あの頃のわたしにひとつ檸檬投ぐ
> to me at that time — throw a lemon
>> 中野千秋/Chiaki Nakano(日本/Japan)

紅葉【もみじ・momiji】
autumn leaves, fall lovage, maple / feuilles de l'érable rouge

The leaves of deciduous trees turn red and yellow to decorate autumn in the fields and mountains. When we speak of autumn leaves, we are mainly referring to maple trees. It is said that the custom of admiring the autumn leaves originated in the Heian period (794 — 1185).

抱擁は紅葉の中の車道かな
> carezze — foglie d'acero rosse sul vialetto
> caresses — red maple leaves on the driveway
>> ダニエラ　ミッソ/Daniela Misso(イタリア/Italy)

全山を風に抱かるる紅葉かな
> riflessi d'oro — su mille foglie rosse la carezza del vento
>
> アンジェラ　ジオルダーノ/Angela Giordano（イタリア/Italy）

血族や水の音に紅葉浮きて
> feuille d'érable rouge au bruit frais d'eau — filiation
>
> エウジェニア　パラシブ/Eugénia Paraschiv
>
> （ルーマニア/Romania）

紅葉映ゆ園のベンチの老夫婦
> autumn leaves on a park bench — the old couple
>
> ダニエラ　ロディ/Daniela Rodi（フィンランド/Finland）

陰鬱に通りを覆ふ散紅葉
> gloomy melancholy — the red and yellow leaves color the avenue
> cupa malinconia — le foglie rosse e gialle colorano il viale
>
> アンジェラ　ジオルダーノ/Angela Giordano（イタリア/Italy）

言の葉の間に架かる枯紅葉
> hanging between two worlds a withered maple leaf
>
> ダニエラ　ロディ/Daniela Rodi（フィンランド/Finland）

照紅葉時を待ちつつ色づいて
> waiting for time autumn leaves
>
> ザンザミ　イスマイル/Zamzami Ismail
>
> （インドネシア/Indonesia）

くちびるにシロップ楓紅葉かな
> red maple tree — the taste of syrup lingers on my lips
>
> ポール　カルス/Paul Callus（マルタ/Malta）

紅葉して新しくした髪の色
> red maples my new hair color
> aceri rossi il mio nuovo colore di capelli

アンジェラ　ジオルダーノ/Angela Giordano（イタリア/Italy）

紅葉して扇の裏の化粧顔
> behind her handfan a painted smile red maple leaf

バーバラ　オルムタック/Barbara Olmtak
（オランダ/Holland）

紅葉見て旅の帰りも同じ道
> momiji — I take the same path for the journey and return

タンポポ　アニス/Tanpopo Anis（インドネシア/Indonesia）

印象派の絵画となりて散紅葉　　　　　　　　亜仁寿（自訳）
> scattered maple leaves — an impressionist art painting

タンポポ　アニス/Tanpopo Anis（インドネシア/Indonesia）

秋風に舞へる紅葉は万華鏡
> autumn wind kaleidoscopic fluttering of leaves

キム　オルムタック　ゴメス/Kim Olmtak Gomes（オランダ/Holland）

緋の紅葉秋は優しく絵となりぬ
> ceri rossi — l'autunno cosi' dolce sembra un quadro

モルガン　マリオ/Morgan Mario（イタリア/Italy）

緋の紅葉風に吹かれる広葉樹
> érable rouge d'automne — l'arbre feuillu au souffle du vent

オルファ　クチュク　ブハディダ/Olfa Kchouk Bouhadida
（チュニジア/Tunisia）

紅葉燃ゆどんな言葉も尽くし得ず
> foglie d'autunno — tutte le parole che sapevo
>
> ガブリエラ　デ　マシ/Gabriella De Masi（イタリア/Italy）

グラスワイン紅葉は風に揺れてゐる
> verre de vin les — feuilles rouge d'automne titubent dans le vent
>
> フランソワーズ　モリス/Francoise Maurice（フランス/France）

紅葉山最後は赤きドレスのやう
> l'ultima foglia con il vestito rosso — acero spoglio
>
> アンナ　リモンディ/Anna Rimondi（イタリア/Italy）

紅葉してわれの思ひ出われのもの
> red autumn maple tree my memories are mine
>
> ナニ　マリアニ/Nani Mariani（オーストラリア/Australia）

君の髪紅葉のやうな色をして
> rosse fiammelle le foglie autunnali tremanti al vento
>
> アルベルタ　カテリナ　マトリ/Alberta Caterina Mattoli（イタリア/Italy）

緋の紅葉ぬくき登校路となりぬ
> érable rouge d'automne — sur l'allée une rentrée scolaire chaleureuse
>
> オルファ　クチュク　ブハディダ/Olfa Kchouk Bouhadida
>
> （チュニジア/Tunisia）

暁の紅葉琥珀の花のごと
> frunze de toamnă — în lumina zorilor flori de chilhlimbar autumn leaves — amber flowers in the light of dawn
>
> ダニエラ　トピルシーン/Daniela Topîrcean（ルーマニア/Romania）

紅葉して昔話の厚き本
> foglie d'autunno — quante pagine colme di vecchie storie
>> ミケーレ　ポチエロ/Michele Pochiero（イタリア/Italy）

紅葉映ゆスクールバスの窓ガラス
> the colored leaves on glass school bus
>> ナニ　マリアニ/Nani Mariani（オーストラリア/Australia）

秋の陽や紅葉の葉脈赤きこと
> nervures au soleil d'automne l'érable rougeoyant
>> フランソワーズ　デニオ-ルリエーブル/Françoise Deniaud-Lelièvre
>> （フランス/France）

紅葉して風の息吹の匂ひたり
> acero rosso — nel respiro del vento la sua essenza
> red maple — in the breath of the wind its essence
>> パトリチア　カルヴァローネ/Patrizia Cavallone（イタリア/Italy）

前触れもなく色を変へ紅葉川
> without warning the river changes color — red maples
> senza preavviso cambia colore il fiume — aceri rossi
>> アンジェラ　ジオルダーノ/Angela Giordano（イタリア/Italy）

散る前の安らぎの色照紅葉
> at ease with its colours just before flying autumn leaves
>> バーバラ　オルムタック/Barbara Olmtak（オランダ/Holland）

校長の退職の日の照紅葉
> headmaster of the school retiring — maple leaf reddens
>> プロビール　ギュプタ/Probir Gupta（インド/India）

紅葉してゆつくり変はる川の彩
> with the red maples the river slowly changes color
> con gli aceri rossi il fiume lentamente cambia colore
>> アンジェラ　ジオルダーノ/Angela Giordano（イタリア/Italy）

紅葉且つ散る人生に分れ道
> autumn leaves in the wind — life takes us in different directions
>> キム　オルムタック　ゴメス/Kim Olmtak Gomes（オランダ/Holland）

秋風の吹くままに紅葉狩をせり
> que soufflent les vents d'automne — momiji gari
>> ジャンリュック　ヴェルパン/jean luc werpin（ベルギー/Belgium）

紅葉狩赤くなりたる頬を持つ
> momiji gari — un leggero rossore sulle sue guance
>> ダニエラ　ミッソ/Daniela Misso（イタリア/Italy）

天と地の短き旅なり散紅葉
> foglie d'autunno — dal cielo alla terra un breve viaggio
> autumn leaves — from sky to earth a short journey
>> マリア　パテルリーニ/Maria Paterlini（イタリア/Italy）

「ちゃん」付けで語り合ひつつ紅葉狩
> autumn leaves viewing — calling by the childhood name while chatting
>> タンポポ　アニス/Tanpopo Anis（インドネシア/Indonesia）

初紅葉朝の挨拶届けけり　　　　　　　　　　　亜仁寿（自訳）
> the first momiji — sending a morning greeting
>> タンポポ　アニス/Tanpopo Anis（インドネシア/Indonesia）

紅葉狩時間の道を見失ふ
> momijigari — loosing mountainous tracks of time
>
> キム　オルムタック　ゴメス/Kim Olmtak Gomes
> （オランダ/Holland）

紅葉狩ひと夜に重き旅鞄
> autumn leaves viewing — heavy bag for overnight trip
>
> 中野千秋/Chiaki Nakano（日本/Japan）

魂の触れ合ふ距離に初紅葉
> les âmes sont proches — momiji legerment rouges
>
> 向瀬美音/Mine Mukose（日本/Japan）

初紅葉長きトンネル抜けてより
> sortir dun long tunnel — momiji légèrement rouge
>
> 向瀬美音/Mine Mukose（日本/Japan）

紅葉狩はちみつ色の陽の中を
> momijigari — marche dans le soleil de couleur de miel
>
> 向瀬美音/Mine Mukose（日本/Japan）

晩年の恋の未知数薄紅葉
> inconnue de l'amour vers la fin de sa vie — érable légèrement rouge
>
> 向瀬美音/Mine Mukose（日本/Japan）

黄葉【こうよう・koyo】

leaves turn yellow / feuilles jaunes

The leaves of trees turn yellow. It refers to the yellow leaves of ginkgo, sawtooth oak, and zelkova. In ancient times, all deciduous trees turning red or yellow in late autumn were written as "yellow leaves", and the word "momiji" was used

眠る川ベットを覆ふ黄葉なり

> sonnecchia il fiume — sul letto una coperta gialla di foglie
>
> リットリア　ガンドルフィ/Littoria Gandolfi
>
> （イタリア/Italy）

黄葉やすべて金色なる世界

> out of the tree all of the gold — autumn leaves
>
> バリー　レビン/Barrie Levine（米国/United States）

屋外の木の食卓へ散る黄葉

> foglie gialle sul tavolo di legno — pranzo all'aperto
>
> yellow leaves on the wooden table — outdoor dining
>
> ダニエラ　ミッソ/Daniela Misso（イタリア/Italy）

黄葉や水面に鴨の通り道

> feuilles jaunes — dans l'étang le sentier des canards
>
> アブダラ　ハジイ/Abdallah Hajji（モロッコ/Morocco）

黄葉や風の腕輪に抱かれて

> yellow leaves — wind bracelet last hug
>
> lá vàng — vòng tay gió cái ôm cuối cùng
>
> ディン　ニュグエン/Dinh Nguyen – Vietnam
>
> （ベトナム/Vietnam）

黄葉やラジオに古き歌流れ

| autumn leaves — old song on the radio

キム　オルムタック　ゴメス/Kim Olmtak Gomes
（オランダ/Holland）

黄葉や樫の影なお明るみて

| feuilles jaunes — l'ombre du chêne plus lumineuse

エレナ　ズアイン/Elena Zouain
（ルーマニア/Romania）

流れ行く川底に光る黄葉

| sul fondo brilla una foglia ingiallita corre il ruscello

ナザレナ　ランピニ/Nazarena Rampini
（イタリア/Italy）

黄葉と日差しの作り出す炎

| l'autunno giallo di foglie e di sole — fiamme di luce
| the yellow autumn of leaves and sun — flames of light

マリア　パテルリーニ/Maria Paterlini
（イタリア/Italy）

風に乗り風に吹かれてゐる黄葉

| volano via nel vento le foglie gialle
| the yellow leaves fly away in the wind

ローザ　マリア　ディ　サルバトーレ/Rosa Maria Di Salvatore
（イタリア/Italy）

飛ぶ時を待ちて黄葉のハート型

| leaves turn yellow — its heart shape

中野千秋/Chiaki Nakano（日本/Japan）

黄落【こうらく・koraku】
yellowing and falling of broadleaf trees

The yellowing and falling of broadleaf trees. The sight of zelkova, yunugi, beech, gingko, and other trees falling in the sun is beautiful.

黄落や仏陀の足に日の差して

> ginko leaves — at the foot of the Buddha the sun stops
> foglie di ginko — ai piedi del Budda si ferma il sole
>
> アンジェラ　ジオルダーノ/Angela Giordano
> (イタリア/Italy)

黄落や芝生に模様つけながら

> foglie ungiallite — colorano il prato a una a una
>
> マリア　ビアンカ/Maria Bianca
> (イタリア/Italy)

黄落や優美に散つてゆくばかり

> falling ginkgo leaves — waiver's grace
>
> ミレラ　ブライレーン/Mirela Brailean
> (ルーマニア/Romania)

ウォーキングシューズの合はず黄落期

> yellow leaves — bad mood of wearing wrong walking shoes
>
> ナッキー　クリスティジーノ/Nuky Kristijno
> (インドネシア/Indonesia)

黄葉やもの憂きときのハーブティー

> falling.yellow leaves — herb tea for my melancholy
>
> 中野千秋/Chiaki Nakano(日本/Japan)

楓【かえで・kaede】
maple / l'érable

Maples are especially beautiful and representative among the colorful trees. Its leaves resemble the hands of a frog, hence the old name "kaerude" ("frog's hand"). The greenery in spring is beautiful as well as in fall.

緋の楓われのドレスの深き色

> red maple — the deep colors of my fall dresses
>> バリー　レビン/Barrie Levine（米国/United States）

秋の葉や楓の上にロビンゐて

> feuille d'automne sur l'érable se pose un rouge — gorge
>> ジェラール　ドユモン/Gérard Dumon（フランス/France）

樹皮滑り古き楓の声を聞く

> j'écoute les vieux érables—ta main glisse sur l'écorce.
>> エリック　デスピエール/Eric Despierre（フランス/France）

夕楓小舟で向かふ今日の宿

> maple in the twilight — today's lodge going by boat
>> 中野千秋/Chiaki Nakano（日本/Japan）

桐一葉【きりひとは・kirihitoha】
one paulownia leaf

The falling of paulownia leaves in autumn. It is called "kiri hitoha (one paulownia leaf) or ihitoha" (one paulownia leaf). The original name "paulownia" refers to the family of the Japanese Paulownia trees, but the name "paulownia" also includes the family of the Gomanoideae.

桐一葉故郷の色変はりけり　　　　　　　　　　　　　　　亜仁寿

> paulownia — the color of my hometown is changing
>
> 　　　　　　　タンポポ　アニス/Tanpopo Anis（インドネシア/Indonesia）

桐一葉過去のどこかに落ちてゆく

> one paulownia leaf — falling somewhere in the past
>
> 　　　　　　　　　　　中野千秋/Chiaki Nakano（日本/Japan）

> ### 銀杏散る【いちょうちる・ichochiru】
> falling ginkgo leaves / la chute des feuilles de ginkgo
>
> ---
>
> This is the falling of the yellow colored ginkgo leaves. It is a spectacular sight to see the leaves fall and the ground becomes a yellowish color.

銀杏散る未知なる島に旅出せり

> la chute des feuilles de ginkgo — voyage à l'île inconnue
>
> 　　　　エウジェニア　パラシブ/Eugénia Paraschiv（ルーマニア/Romania）

夜通しの嵐に銀杏落葉かな

> tempesta notturna –foglie giallo brillante sul marciapiede
> overnight storm –bright yellow leaves on the sidewalk
>
> 　　　　　　　ダニエラ　ミッソ/Daniela Misso（イタリア/Italy）

銀杏散る栗鼠はまあるくなりにけり

> les écureuils en boule — chute des feuilles de ginkgo
>
> 　　　　　ベルナデット　クエン/Bernadette Couenne（フランス/France）

銀杏散る樹々の震へはおさまらず

> chute des feuilles de gingko — les arbres frissonnent
>
> 　　　　　ベルナデット　クエン/Bernadette Couenne（フランス/France）

夕闇を灯して銀杏黄葉かな

golden ginkgo leaves — the brightness of darkness scattered at dusk

タンポポ　アニス/Tanpopo Anis

（インドネシア/Indonesia）

金の羽飛ばして銀杏落葉かな

fly golden feathers — falling ginkgo leaves

中野千秋/Chiaki Nakano（日本/Japan）

銀杏散る大きな人に抱かれて

la chute des feuilles de ginkgo — embrassée par un bel homme

向瀬美音/Mine Mukose（日本/Japan）

銀杏【いちょう・icho】
yellow autumn ginkgo / ginkgo jaune d'automne

Round fruits that ripen yellow on female plants when ginkgo leaves turn yellow. They fall off, emit an odor, and may cause a rash when touched. Inside the pulp is a hard seed, which is taken out and used for food.

金色の日差に銀杏黄葉かな

even the sun shines golden ginkgo yellow tree

ザンザミ　イスマイル/Zamzami Ismail

（インドネシア/Indonesia）

黄葉の銀杏に黙る太陽も

yellow autumn ginkgo — the sun is lost for words

ポール　カルス/Paul Callus（マルタ/Malta）

神が美を託せし銀杏黄葉かな

ginkgo — this is where your god entrusts beauty

ザンザミ　イスマイル/Zamzami Ismail

（インドネシア/Indonesia）

金髪の女の子立つ銀杏の木

sous le gingko biloba — la fille aux cheveux d'or

イザベル　カルバロ　テール/Isabelle Carvalho Teles

（フランス/France）

銀杏黄葉金色の雲に変貌す

trasformazioni — il gynkgo tra poco una nuvola d'oro

ステファニア　アンドレオニ/Stefania Andreoni

（イタリア/Italy）

屋外の木の食卓へ銀杏紅葉

foglie gialle sul tavolo di legno — pranzo all'aperto

yellow leaves on the wooden table — outdoor dining

ダニエラ　ミッソ/Daniela Misso（イタリア/Italy）

飛行船過ぎゆく銀杏並木かな

airship flying — over yellow ginkgo trees

中野千秋/Chiaki Nakano（日本/Japan）

銀杏【ぎんなん・ginnan】
ginkgo nut / noix de ginkgo

When the ginkgo trees turn yellow, the female trees produce round yellow fruits. When they fall, they give off a strong odor, and touching them can cause a rash. The hard seeds inside the flesh are edible.

湖や銀杏一つ落つる音　　　　　　　　　　　　　　亜仁寿（自訳）

> clear lake — the sound of one ginkgo nut falling
> 　　　　　タンポポ　アニス/Tanpopo Anis（インドネシア/Indonesia）

銀杏や賢者の語る言葉あり

> ginkgo nuts — the wise man's words
> 　　　　　ミレラ　ブライレーン/Mirela Brailean（ルーマニア/Romania）

銀杏や決して終はらぬ物語

> ginkgo — this story will never end
> 　　　　　ザンザミ　イスマイル/Zamzami Ismail（インドネシア/Indonesia）

銀杏の地雷を踏んでしまいけり

> landmine — stepping on the ginkgo nut
> 　　　　　中野千秋/Chiaki Nakano（日本/Japan）

蔦【つた・tsuta】
ivy / lierre

It is a vine that crawls rapidly on things. It grows wild in the mountains and fields, but can also be seen on exterior walls and stone walls in towns. In late fall, its leaves turn red and stain trees and buildings red. Blue ivy is a summer season word.

廃屋の梯子を蔦の覆ひけり

> casa abbandonata — una vecchia scala ricoperta di edera
> abandoned house — an old ladder ivy covered
>
> ダニエラ　ミッソ/Daniela Misso（イタリア/Italy）

蔦茂るシーツの下に絡み合ふ

> ivy — the two of us entwined under the sheet
> edera — noi due avvinghiati sotto il lenzuolo
>
> アンジェラ　ジオルダーノ/Angela Giordano（イタリア/Italy）

蔦覆ふチャペルの尼僧微笑みて

> ivy covered the old chapel wall — young nun's smile
>
> タンポポ　アニス/Tanpopo Anis（インドネシア/Indonesia）

燭台と蔦の抱擁に秘密の園

> jardin secret l'étreinte du lierre et du vieux bougeoir
> secret garden et du vieux bougeoir and the old candlestick
>
> イザベル　ラマン　ムニエ/Isabelle Lamant Meunier
> （フランス/France）

蔦剝がれ生家に新しき住人

> lierres arrachés — de nouveaux habitants dans la maison d'enfance
>
> ベルナデット　クエン/Bernadette Couenne
> （フランス/France）

壁に蔦絵描きは構図変へにけり

> lierre sur le mur — le peintre change de programme
>
> オルファ　クチュク　ブハディダ/Olfa Kchouk Bouhadida
> （チュニジア/Tunisia）

月滑る蔦に覆はれた壁の上
> sur le mur cascade de lierre — la lune coule dessus
>> シュピー　モイサン/Choupie Moysan
>>> （フランス/France）

藤蔓の庭の壁よりなだれ来る
> cascading from garden walls — invasive wisteria
>> ポール　カルス/Paul Callus（マルタ/Malta）

青空にしがみつく蔦朝の光
> lumière du matin — le lierre s'accroche au bleu du ciel
>> エレナ　ズアイン/Elena Zouain
>>> （ルーマニア/Romania）

蔦の這ふ赤いトタンの牛舎かな
> covered in lvy — red tin barn
>> 中野千秋/Chiaki Nakano（日本/Japan）

白壁をまた探しては蔦かづら
> le lierre monte encore et encore — à la recherche d'un mur blanc
>> 向瀬美音/Mine Mukose（日本/Japan）

蔦かずら日々求め合ふ二人かな
> lierre — deux personnes se découvrent jour après jour
>> 向瀬美音/Mine Mukose（日本/Japan）

カンナ【かんな・kanna】
canna

A perennial of the Canna family. The tallest plants grow to about 2 meters in height, and both the leaves and flowers are so large that they are noticeable from a distance. It has a long flowering season, blooming from summer to early winter. The flowers are red, yellow, orange, etc., and are showy and conspicuous.

カンナ咲く色鉛筆を尖らせて
> canna — all colored pencils sharpened
>
> ミレラ　ブライレーン/Mirela Brailean
> (ルーマニア/Romania)

赤カンナ舞台を揺らすフラメンコ　　　　　　亜仁寿（自訳）
> red canna — flamenco dance shakes the stage
>
> タンポポ　アニス/Tanpopo Anis（インドネシア/Indonesia）

花カンナくちづけ交はす海辺かな
> fiori di canna — un bacio davanti al mare
> canna flowers — a kiss in front of the sea
>
> ダニエラ　ミッソ/Daniela Misso（イタリア/Italy）

花カンナ微熱のやうに過去のこと
> canna — the past comes up like slight fever
>
> 中野千秋/Chiaki Nakano（日本/Japan）

カンナ咲く一途といふはうとましき
> canna — la sincérité est parfois pesante
>
> 向瀬美音/Mine Mukose（日本/Japan）

蘭【らん・ran】
oriental orchids / orchidées

There are Western orchids and Oriental orchids. Oriental orchids such as spring orchids and cold orchids began to be cultivated in the Kamakura period (1185 — 1333), while Western orchids such as cattleyas and butterfly orchids were introduced from the West after the Meiji period (1868 — 1912).

東洋の蘭に着物の少女かな

oriental orchids in bloom — girls with kimono

ミレラ　ブライレーン/Mirela Brailean

(ルーマニア/Romania)

愛し合ふとき東洋の蘭香る

united in love — oriental orchids in a vase

ポール　カルス/Paul Callus(マルタ/Malta)

蘭強く香れる母の誕生日

mother's birthday — the titillating scent of wild pigeon orchids

クリスティーナ　チン/Christina Chin

(マレーシア/Malaysia)

蘭咲いて日当たりの良きバルコニー

sunny side of the balcony — flowering oriental orchid

クリスティーナ　チン/Christina Chin

(マレーシア/Malaysia)

蘭の花書斎を兼ねて応接間

oriental orchid — drawing room as well as study

中野千秋/Chiaki Nakano(日本/Japan)

ダリア【だりあ・daria】
dahlia

Compositae. A perennial plant native to Mexico. The bulbs are planted in spring and the flowers bloom in summer. There is a wide variety of shapes and colors, including pompon-shaped flowers and tongue-shaped flowers.

筆の跡ダリアの束は黄昏色

traces de pinceau — le bouquet de dahlias aux couleurs du crépuscule

エレナ　ズアイン/Elena Zouain

(ルーマニア/Romania)

ダリア咲くその艶やかな夢広げ

dahlias unfold layers of bold burning hues petals scatter dreams

ラシュミ/Rashmi Mohapatra(インド/India)

とりどりのダリアをいけて貴賓室

colorful dahlias in the vase — vip room

中野千秋/Chiaki Nakano(日本/Japan)

声もまたエロスのひとつ蘭の花

voix est aussi érotique — orchidée

向瀬美音/Mine Mukose(日本/Japan)

朝顔 【あさがお・asagao】
morning glory / volubilis

Morning glories are flowers that herald the arrival of autumn. They open at dawn and wilt by noon. Japanese people have long felt the arrival of autumn with this flower. It was brought to Japan as a medicine during the Nara period (710 — 794) by Japanese envoys to the Tang Dynasty (710 — 794). In the Edo period (1603 — 1867), it came to be cultivated as an ornamental flower. It is also called kengyuhana because it blooms around Tanabata, the seventh month of the lunar calendar (late August in the new calendar).

朝顔やまたの日の出に感謝して

> morning glory — thankful for yet another sunrise
>
> ポール　カルス/Paul Callus（マルタ/Malta）

朝顔や青を極めているところ

> sunning on her vine — thankful for yet another sunrise
>
> バリー　レビン/Barrie Levine（米国/United States）

あかときや新しき朝顔三つ

> nuit évaporée — trois nouvelles fleurs au volubilis
>
> フランソワーズ　デニオ-ルリエーブル/Françoise Deniaud-Lelièvre
>
> （フランス/France）

朝顔や昨日と同じ美しさ

> morning glory — as beauty as yesterday morning
>
> イワン　セティアワン/Iwan Setiawan（インドネシア/Indonesia）

朝顔や紫色の過去の恋

> morning glory — the purple color reminds of his romance
>
> ディア　ヌクスマ/Dyah Nkusuma（インドネシア/Indonesia）

朝顔や私の庭の青き空

> morning glory — a blue sky is climbing in my garden
>
> キム　オルムタック　ゴメス/Kim Olmtak Gomes
>
> (オランダ/Holland)

朝顔や壁を這ひたる陽の光

> volubilis — sur le mur un rayon de soleil grimpe
>
> アブダラ　ハジイ/Abdallah Hajji
>
> (モロッコ/Morocco)

朝顔や君の笑顔を探したる

> morning glory — I search for your smile
>
> アンナ　イリナ/Ana Irina (ルーマニア/Romania)

朝顔や捉へきれない愛求め

> morning glory — searching for elusive love
>
> ポール　カルス/Paul Callus (マルタ/Malta)

夜が明けて森の朝顔 ビロードの青

> si apre al mattino velluto blu nel bosco — è l'ipomea
>
> ダニエラ　フォンタナ/Daniela Fontana
>
> (イタリア/Italy)

マラソンの訓練始め牽牛花

> morning glory — my first training for the marathon
>
> ナッキー　クリスティジーノ/Nuky Kristijno (インドネシア/Indonesia)

朝顔の芯の真白き奈落かな

> in the heart of morning glory — pure white abyss
>
> 中野千秋/Chiaki Nakano (日本/Japan)

コスモス【こすもす・kosumosu】
cosmos / cosmos

Annual herb of the Asteraceae family. It grows to about 2 meters tall. The leaves are finely lobed and the stems grow spindly. It produces white or pink flowers from September to October. It is also called "autumn cherry blossom" because its petals resemble cherry blossoms.

コスモスや真摯な瞳信じてる

> uno sguardo sincero — fiori di cosmos
> a sincere look — cosmos flowers
>
> ダニエラ　ミッソ/Daniela Misso（イタリア/Italy）

コスモスや熱情あつけなく冷めて

> cosmos flowers — our passion fades quickly
> fiori di cosmo. — appassisce in fretta la nostra passione
>
> アンジェラ　ジオルダーノ/Angela Giordano（イタリア/Italy）

コスモスより広大無辺の空を見て

> fermare il tempo — sguardo al cielo infinito dal micro — cosmo
> stopping time — glance to infinitive sky from tiny cosmos
>
> クリスティーナ　プルビエンティ/Cristina Pulvirenti
> （イタリア/Italy）

秋桜はかなき煙螺旋状

> éphémères cosmos — volutes de fumées
>
> ベルナデット　クエン/Bernadette Couenne（フランス/France）

コスモスや寒さ暑さの中間に

> cosmos flower — striking a balance between cold and hot
>
> ポール　カルス/Paul Callus（マルタ/Malta）

コスモスの重き一鉢風に揺れ
> les cosmos se balancent au vent — déjà de lourdes potées de chrysanthèmes
>> シュピー　モイサン/Choupie Moysan(フランス/France)

初めての子の言葉「あさがお咲いた」
> toddler's first word — morning glory unfolds
>> キム　オルムタック　ゴメス/Kim Olmtak Gomes(オランダ/Holland)

暗闇の風コスモスの種運ぶ
> temps sombres le vent emporte au loin des graines de cosmos
> dark times the wind carries away seeds of cosmos
>> イザベル　ラマン　ムニエ/Isabelle Lamant Meunier(フランス/France)

コスモスを持ちて少女が道をゆく
> steli di cosmos — si diverte una bimba lungo i sentieri
> stems of cosmos — a little girl is having fun along the paths
>> パトリチア　カバローネ/Patrizia Cavallone(イタリア/Italy)

コスモスや世界を見やる新生児
> cosmos — newborn opens her eyes to the world
>> キム　オルムタック　ゴメス/Kim Olmtak Gomes(オランダ/Holland)

コスモスやあまたなる可能な世界
> cosmos — so many possible worlds
>> アンナ　イリナ/Ana Irina(ルーマニア/Romania)

コスモスや人の繋がり求めたる
> cosmos — always feel homesick wherever I go
>> キム　オルムタック　ゴメス/Kim Olmtak Gomes(オランダ/Holland)

限りなき夢を持ちたり秋桜
> cosmos — rêves sans limites

エレナ　ズアイン/Elena Zouain
（ルーマニア/Romania）

コスモスや小さき幸せ揺らしたる
> es cosmos balancent leur beauté dans la brise — petit bonheur
> cosmos sway their beauty in the breeze — little happiness

マリー　クレール　ブルグ/Maria-claire burgos
（フランス/France）

コスモスや切望したる青き空
> cosmos — I am longing for the blue sky

ナッキー　クリスティジーノ/Nuky Kristijno
（インドネシア/Indonesia）

コスモスや君の揺らぎと吾の揺らぎ
> cosmos — your fluctuation and my fluctuation

中野千秋/Chiaki Nakano（日本/Japan）

求めらる方に傾く秋桜
> cosmos — penché vers un homme qui me désire

向瀬美音/Mine Mukose（日本/Japan）

青空を揺らすごと秋桜かな
> cosmos — le ciel bleu se balance

向瀬美音/Mine Mukose（日本/Japan）

草の花【くさのはな・kusanohana】
grass flower

The flowers of the grasses that bloom in the fall. I often think of them as having bloomed well. From there, one can think of them as being wistful, pretty, plain, and fragile, but there is no denying the impression that they are also stubborn.

草の花初恋の日に指輪かな　　　　　　　　　　　　亜仁寿（自訳）

| grass flower — the ring on the first love day

　　　　　　　　　　　　　　　　タンポポ　アニス/Tanpopo Anis

　　　　　　　　　　　　　　　　　　　　　（インドネシア/Indonesia）

その中に蝶の止まれる草の花

| among the wildflowers autumn butterflies perch

　　　　　　　　　　　　　　ナッキー　クリスティジーノ/Nuky Kristijno

　　　　　　　　　　　　　　　　　　　　　（インドネシア/Indonesia）

草の花ちさき幸せ賜りぬ

| wild flowers worthy creation nature brings small happiness

　　　　　　　　　　　　　　　　プリヤ　モハンティー/Priya Mohanty

　　　　　　　　　　　　　　　　　　　　　（米国/United States）

草の花その中にある玉簾

| rain lilies among grass flowers — the road divider

　　　　　　　　　　　　　　　クリスティーナ　チン/Christina Chin

　　　　　　　　　　　　　　　　　　　　　（マレーシア/Malaysia）

鬼灯【ほおずき・hozuki】
thud of apples

The hohzuki is believed to be native to Asia, but its native habitat is not clear. In Japan, it is cultivated in parks and gardens for horticultural purposes. (Masanori Fujiyoshi, author)

鬼灯や居酒屋の灯が雨の中

> golden berry — lantern of izakaya on rainy day
>
> タンポポ　アニス/Tanpopo Anis
>
> (インドネシア/Indonesia)

鬼灯や魂ひとつ殻のなか

> chinese lantern plant — one soul in the shell
>
> 中野千秋/Chiaki Nakano(日本/Japan)

菊【きく・kiku】
chrysanthemum / chrysantheme

Perennial herb of the Asteraceae family. Native to China. It came to Japan in the Nara period (710 — 794). In the Edo period (1603 — 1867), the production of chrysanthemums for ornamental purposes became popular. Fragrant and beautiful to look at. It is also edible. It is one of the four representative flowers of autumn (plum, bamboo, orchid, and chrysanthemum).

葬送の風に吹かれて菊香る

> uneral — the scent of chrysanthemums blowing in the wind
>
> タンポポ　アニス/Tanpopo Anis
>
> (インドネシア/Indonesia)

太陽の色の黄菊を籠に盛る
> raggio di sole ― crisantemi gialli in una cesta
> ray of sun ― yellow chrysanthemums in a bask
>> ダニエラ　ミッソ/Daniela Misso（イタリア/Italy）

白菊や貞淑な髪の銀色に
> chrysanthèmes ― les cheveux argentés de la sagesse
>> イメルダ　セン/Imelda Senn（スイス/Switzerland）

菊を挿し秋の匂ひの立ち込める
> autumn smell ― a few chrysanthemums in a vase
>> ミレラ　ブライレーン/Mirela Brailean（ルーマニア/Romania）

彼の墓希望の菊に囲まれぬ
> chrysanthemums ― hope blooms around his grave
>> ポール　カルス/Paul Callus（マルタ/Malta）

白菊や玄関先の月明り
> pot of white mums ― moonglow on my front stoop
>> バリー　レビン/Barrie Levine（米国/United States）

菊香る女王の在位七十年
> haiku u čast kraljice Elizabete II ― prijevod na japanski
> seventy years of queen Elizabeth II's reign ― the smell of chrysanthemums
>> ズデンカ　ムリナー/Zdenka Mlinar（クロアチア/Croatia）

最後の視線墓香らせる菊の花
> dernier regard ― les chrysanthèmes parfument la tombe
>> カメル　メスレム/Kamel Meslem（アルジェリア/Algeria）

菊咲きて夜がだんだん長くなる
> nights getting longer — chrysanthemums in bloom
>> キム　オルムタック　ゴメス/Kim Olmtak Gomes（オランダ/Holland）

白菊や父の墓石を見守りて
> chrysanthème — un compagnon devant la tombe de mon père
>> オルファ　クチュク　ブハディダ/Olfa Kchouk Bouhadida
>>> （チュニジア/Tunisia）

初めての水墨画なり菊を描く
> first black and white drawing — chrysanthemums
>> キム　オルムタック　ゴメス/Kim Olmtak Gomes（オランダ/Holland）

花嫁が選ぶブーケは菊の花
> autunno — la sposa sceglie un bouquet di crisantemi
>> ガブリエラ　デ　マシ/Gabriella De Masi（イタリア/Italy）

満開の菊に豊作祈りたり
> may the harvest be full in bloom chrysanthemum
>> キム　オルムタック　ゴメス/Kim Olmtak Gomes（オランダ/Holland）

色彩の語る言葉よ菊花展
> expoziție de crizanteme — limbajul culorilor
> chrysanthemum exhibit — color language
>> ミレラ　ブライレーン/Mirela Brailean
>>> （ルーマニア/Romania）

菊の花翡翠の壺に生けにけり
> vase de jade — un bouquet de chrysanthèmes
>> エリック　デスピエール/Eric Despierre（フランス/France）

墓石に菊を供へて君の笑み

> white gravestones — chrysanthemums light up your smile
> bianche lapidi — i crisantemi illuminano il tuo sorriso
>> アンジェラ　ジオルダーノ/Angela Giordano（イタリア/Italy）

ちさき菊震へる大理石の墓

> tombeaux de marbre — le petit chrysanthème tremble au soleil
>> キャロル　ディウゼイド/Carole Dieuzeide（フランス/France）

黄菊咲き光よ届け愛する人へ

> una luce nuova per i nostri cari che sono altrove — crisantemi gialli
>> ローザ　マリア　ディ　サルバトーレ/Rosa Maria Di Salvatore
>>> （イタリア/Italy）

秋の陽に菊の香りの漂へり

> sole d'autunno — crisantemi gialli
> soleil d'automne — si doux le parfum des chrysanthèmes
>> カルメン　バシキリ/Carmen Baschieri（イタリア/Italy）

生と死の間に菊の咲きにけり

> i crisantemi tra la vita e la morte — la processione
> chrysanthemums between life and death — procession
>> クリスティーヌ　プルビエンティ/Cristina Pulvirenti（イタリア/Italy）

岩の間に黄菊の咲いてゐる廃墟

> abandoned wall blooming from the crevices of rocks yellow chrysanthemums
> bức tường bỏ hoang nở từ kẽ đá những hoa cúc vàng
>> ディン　ニュグエン/Dinh Nguyen（ベトナム/Vietnam）

苦々し記憶よ菊の匂ふ墓

> in bitter memories scented chrysanthemums on your tombstone
> nei ricordi amari crisantemi profumati sulla tua lapide
>
> アンジェラ　ジオルダーノ/Angela Giordano
>
> (イタリア/Italy)

白菊が土を覆ひて冬の墓地

> white chrysanthemums flaking the black soil — winter in the cemetery
>
> キム　オルムタック　ゴメス/Kim Olmtak Gomes
>
> (オランダ/Holland)

菊の花血は涙へと変はりたり

> crisantemi — il sangue muta in lacrime per quel ricordo
> chrysanthemum — blood turns in tears for that memory
>
> クリスティーヌ　プルビエンティ/Cristina Pulvirenti
>
> (イタリア/Italy)

菊が香や風に漂ふ無縁墓

> unrelated grave — the scent of chrysanthemum flying in the wind
>
> タンポポ　アニス/Tanpopo Anis(インドネシア/Indonesia)

いつぺんに小菊が咲ける誕生日

> small chrysanthemums blooming all at once
>
> タンポポ　アニス/Tanpopo Anis(インドネシア/Indonesia)

快晴のひと日に菊を摘んでをり

> plucking chrysanthemums — a perfect sunny day
>
> キム　オルムタック　ゴメス/Kim Olmtak Gomes
>
> (オランダ/Holland)

日差し受け籠いっぱいの黄菊かな
> raggio di sole — crisantemi gialli in una cesta
> ray of sun — yellow chrysanthemums in a basket
>> ダニエラ　ミッソ/Daniela Misso（イタリア/Italy）

あかときの重さ囁く菊の上
> murmure — sur les chrysanthèmes le poids de l'aube
>> エレナ　ズアイン/Elena Zouain（ルーマニア/Romania）

白菊や墓に十月の優しさ
> chrysanthèmes blancs — un peu de douceur d'octobre sur la tombe
>> アンヌ　デアルベルテルト/Anne Dealbertert（フランス/France）

白菊の中の視線や空の影
> ombre nel cielo — tra crisantemi bianchi gli sguardi muti
> shadows in the sky — among white chrysanthemums the silent glances
>> マリア　パテルリーニ/Maria Paterlini（イタリア/Italy）

菊の花褪せた写真をそっと撫で
> crisantemi — una carezza sulla foto sbiadita
>> ガブリエラ　デ　マシ/Gabriella De Masi（イタリア/Italy）

花弁となる記憶の抱擁菊の花
> crisantemi — l'abbraccio dei ricordi si fa petalo
>> アントニオ　ジラルディ/Antonio Girardi（イタリア/Italy）

君の墓に光溢れる白き菊
> sulla tua tomba — i crisantemi bianchi pieni di luce
>> アグネーゼ　ジアロンゴ/Agnese Giallongo（イタリア/Italy）

大菊の丈を貫く力かな 千秋

large flowered chrysanthemum — the power to penetrate its hight

中野千秋/Chiaki Nakano（日本/Japan）

敗荷【やれはす・yarehasu】
fading lotus / lotus fané

The lotus leaves, which were tossed in the wind at the beginning of autumn, fade away day by day and are torn by the wind and rain. This is the lonely and dreary autumnal scene itself.

破蓮栄華の過去を漂はせ

shades of a flourishing past—wilted lotuses

バーバラ　オルムタック/Barbara Olmtak

（オランダ/Holland）

破蓮や化粧に頼ること増えて

fading lotus — her dependence on makeup increases

ポール　カルス/Paul Callus（マルタ/Malta）

敗荷や小川の水の乾きたる

lotus fané — la rivière manque d'eau

オルファ　クチュク　ブハディダ/Olfa Kchouk Bouhadida

（チュニジア/Tunisia）

敗蓮や沼の迷路に月明かり　　　　　　　　亜仁寿（自訳）

fading lotus — moonlight on the swamp maze

タンポポ　アニス/Tanpopo Anis（インドネシア/Indonesia）

敗荷や再生の種宿したる

> remaining the seeds for rebirth — fading lotus
>
> タンポポ　アニス/Tanpopo Anis（インドネシア/Indonesia）

破蓮赤子の肌のすべすべと

> withered lotus — the smooth skin of the little baby
>
> loto appassito — la pelle liscia del piccolo neonato
>
> アンジェラ　ジオルダーノ/Angela Giordano（イタリア/Italy）

破蓮国家をあげて喪に服す

> lotus fading — a declaration of mourning in the country
>
> ザヤ　ヨウクハンナ/Zaya youkhanna（オーストラリア/Australia）

枯蓮や彼の若さも長くない

> fading lotus — his youthful look doesn't last long
>
> ナッキー　クリスティジーノ/Nuky Kristijno
>
> （インドネシア/Indonesia）

天と沼に敗荷の実を任せたる　　　　　　　　　　亜仁寿（自訳）

> entrusting the seeds of fading lotus — to the sky and the swamp
>
> タンポポ　アニス/Tanpopo Anis（インドネシア/Indonesia）

破蓮虚空を満たす匂ひかな

> fading lotus — in the void fill with fragrance
>
> hoa sen tàn — trong khoảng trống lấp đầy hương thơm
>
> ディン　ニュグエン/Dinh Nguyen（ベトナム/Vietnam）

美術館の通路に沿つて破蓮

> fading lotus — along the corridor of art museum
>
> 中野千秋/Chiaki Nakano（日本/Japan）

敗荷の奥に潜める浄土かな

| lotus fané — la terre pure cachée derrière

向瀬美音/Mine Mukose（日本/Japan）

南瓜【かぼちゃ・kabocha】
pumpkin / citrouilles

The robust stems grow to crawl across the ground during the summer. After bearing large yellow flowers, it bears fruit in the fall. It is somewhat humorous to see a human head — sized plant lying around in the field. The skin is very tough. It is widely used for boiled vegetables, soups, sweets, etc.

フォーク刺す月のやうなるパンプキンパイ

| pumpkin pie — my fork sinks into the sweet side of the moon

バリー　レビン/Barrie Levine（米国/United States）

秋の収穫積み上げられた南瓜あり

| récolte d'automne — une statue de citrouilles empilées

イメルダ　セン/Imelda Senn（スイス/Switzerland）

大南瓜座禅を組める夕間暮

| big pumpkins in the field — zazen under the twilight sky

タンポポ　アニス/Tanpopo Anis

（インドネシア/Indonesia）

どの子にも南瓜スープの行き渡る

| warm soup — a pumpkin smile on each child

マリリン　アッシュボ/Marilyn Ashbaugh

（米国/United States）

大きさと形を競ふ南瓜かな
> farmer's market — the shapes and sizes of pumpkins
>
> クリスティーナ　チン/Christina Chin（マレーシア/Malaysia）

奇怪な顔の南瓜畑に満ち溢れ
> volti spettrali — zucche bitorzolute in tutto il campo
>
> アンナ　リモンディ/Anna Rimondi（イタリア/Italy）

おおいなる南瓜や庭は野菜祭り
> zucche giganti — nell'orto una festa d'ortaggi
>
> シルビア　ビストッチ/Silvia Bistocchi（イタリア/Italy）

ひとめぼれ同じかぼちやを選ぶとは
> we choose the same pumpkin — love at first sight
>
> ザンザミ　イスマイル/Zamzami Ismail
> （インドネシア/Indonesia）

大南瓜馬車になるのを待つ子かな
> giant pumpkin — the niece waits for it to turn into a carriage
> zucca gigante — la nipote aspetta che si trasformi in carrozza
>
> アンジェラ　ジオルダーノ/Angela Giordano
> （イタリア/Italy）

南瓜切る太陽の色皿の上
> cutted pumpkin — the color of the sun on my plate
>
> タンポポ　アニス/Tanpopo Anis（インドネシア/Indonesia）

丁寧に掘られて笑ふ南瓜かな
> a pumpkin carved with care — autumn's playful grin
>
> エウジェヌ/Eugene（ロシア/Russia）

五通りの使い道あり大南瓜

> five different recipes — giant pumpkin

中野千秋/Chiaki Nakano(日本/Japan)

秋茄子【あきなす・akinasu】
autumn eggplant / aubergine d'automne

Eggplants that are harvested in the fall. Even if sown at the same time of the year, there is a time difference and some eggplants are harvested in autumn. The eggplants are smaller in size, but the fruits are tighter and deeper in color.

秋茄子や苦労の色に母の愛　　　　　　　　　　　亜仁寿（自訳）

> autumn eggplant — my mother's love in the color of struggle life

タンポポ　アニス/Tanpopo Anis(インドネシア/Indonesia)

エプロンを広げ秋茄子貰ひけり

> spread my apron — get autumn eggplants

中野千秋/Chiaki Nakano(日本/Japan)

落穂【おちぼ・ochibo】
gleaning / glanage

The ears that fall in the rice fields, between rice fields, and under the rice racks after harvesting. Picking up fallen ears is an important task, as we do not want to waste even a single grain of rice.

雀と女落ち穂拾ひをする夜明け

> morning light — women and sparrows are mingling in gleaning

タンポポ　アニス/Tanpopo Anis(インドネシア/Indonesia)

落穂拾ひ蟻は忙(せわ)しく運動会

> gleaning — busy ants have a field day
>
> ポール　カルス/Paul Callus(マルタ/Malta)

烏来て落穂拾ひの手を早め

> crows on the wires — the gleaner speeds up the work
> corvi sui fili — la spigolatrice accellera il lavoro
>
> アンジェラ　ジオルダーノ/Angela Giordano(イタリア/Italy)

子ども等の鳩に与へる落穂かな

> gleaning day — children share grains for doves
>
> タンポポ　アニス/Tanpopo Anis(インドネシア/Indonesia)

芒【すすき・susuki】

Japanese pampas grass / herbes des pampas

Perennial herb of the grass family. A typical autumn plant used as a tsukimi (moon — viewing) offering. It is also one of the seven autumn flowers. The young ears are moist and look like they have been drenched in oil. It is a spectacular sight to see the silvery ears fluttering all at once in places such as Sengokuhara in Hakone.

芒野や牛の耕す影のあり

> forked horns moving in the reeds waves — field of pink miscanthus
>
> ザンザミ　イスマイル/Zamzami Ismail(インドネシア/Indonesia)

パンパスグラス美容師の髪の色

> pampas grass plumes — my coiffeuse's hair tints
>
> クリスティーナ　チン/Christina Chin(マレーシア/Malaysia)

芒揺れビールの瓶とマリア像

> miscanto al vento: dietro la Madonna bottiglie di birra
> miscanthus in the wind — behind Our Lady bottles of beer
>
> マウリチオ　ブランカレオーニ/Maurizio Brancaleoni
> (イタリア/Italy)

芒原海の唸りを聞きにけり

> herbes des pampas — j'entends le rugissement de la mer
>
> アブダラ　ハジイ/Abdallah Hajji(モロッコ/Morocco)

赤くなる海原を待つ芒原

> herbes des pampas — j'entends le rugissement de la mer
>
> アブダラ　ハジイ/Abdallah Hajji(モロッコ/Morocco)

一歩ずつ選択のあり芒原

> l'herbe de la pampa — à chaque pas, le choix de nos directions
> pampas grass — with every step, the choice of our directions
>
> ミュールバッハ　アキツ/F.Mühlebach akitsu(フランス/France)

種飛ばす風の吹きゆく芒原

> Japanese pampas grass — the wind blows the seed away
>
> アリアナ　ユハナ/Ariani Yuhana(インドネシア/Indonesia)

芒原黄色めきたる山の道

> Japanese pampas grass — yellow sight of the mountain path
>
> ナッキー　クリスティジーノ/Nuky Kristijno(インドネシア/Indonesia)

鉄路まだ形を留め芒原

> pampas grass field — abandoned rail road still have shape
>
> 中野千秋/Chiaki Nakano(日本/Japan)

あるがまま溺れてみたき芒原
  le champ de pampas — j'ai envie de m'y noyer
向瀬美音/Mine Mukose（日本/Japan）

月宿しひそと輝く尾花かな
  lune — scintille discrètement dans les herbes des pampas
向瀬美音/Mine Mukose（日本/Japan）

露を帯び微かな光花芒
  herbes de pampas — lueur sur la rosée
向瀬美音/Mine Mukose（日本/Japan）

桔梗【ききょう・kikyo】
Japanese bellflower / campanule

The sharp contours and the neatly folded shape of the flowers have a dignified elegance. Although purple is the main color, the white bellflower has its own charm. The morning glories that were mentioned in the poem "Kikyo" by Yamakami Mimura were Kikyo. It is one of the seven autumnal flowers.

桔梗咲く慈愛に満ちた贈り物
  Japanese bellflower — gifted with affection
ポール　カルス/Paul Callus（マルタ/Malta）

りんりんと桔梗の花が風に鳴る
  bellflowers blowing in the wind — my ears are ringing
ザンザミ　イスマイル/Zamzami Ismail（インドネシア/Indonesia）

桔梗咲く恋に年齢などはなく

> Japanese bellflower — never too late to fall in love
>
> シウホング　イレーヌ　タン/Siu Hong — Irene Tan
>
> （インドネシア/Indonesia）

ぶんぶんと蜜蜂の音桔梗咲く

> Japanese bellflower — sound of bee buzzing
>
> ナッキー　クリスティジーノ/Nuky Kristijno
>
> （インドネシア/Indonesia）

桔梗咲く二人の愛にゆるぎなく

> bellflower — our steadfast eternal love
>
> ザヤ　ヨウクハンナ/Zaya youkhanna
>
> （オーストラリア/Australia）

水牛の首輪の音や桔梗咲く

> Japanese bellflower — buffalo wood necklace sound
>
> アリアナ　ユハナ/Ariani Yuhana（インドネシア/Indonesia）

祖父の忌にゆたかに桔梗供へけり　　　　　　亜仁寿（自訳）

> grandfather death anniversary — giving plenty of bellflowers
>
> タンポポ　アニス/Tanpopo Anis（インドネシア/Indonesia）

桔梗咲く皆聞き覚えある言葉

> Japanese bellflower — it all sounds familiar
>
> アンナ　イリナ/Ana Irina（ルーマニア/Romania）

産声や白き桔梗に雨の粒　　　　　　　　　　亜仁寿（自訳）

> the first cry of birth — raindrops on a white bellflower
>
> タンポポ　アニス/Tanpopo Anis（インドネシア/Indonesia）

桔梗咲く路地に響いて下駄の音

> Japanese bell flower — noisy wooden clogs in the alley
>
> > ナッキー　クリスティジーノ/Nuky Kristijno（インドネシア/Indonesia）

白桔梗小さな秘密持ちて生く

> white bellflower — life with little secret
>
> > 中野千秋/Chiaki Nakano（日本/Japan）

竜胆【りんどう・rindo】
gentian / gentian

A perennial herb in the Gentian family. It grows wild in the mountains and fields of Honshu, Shikoku and Kyushu. The plant grows to a height of 20 cm to 1 m. The leaves are opposite, with rough edges. The leaves grow in opposite pairs and have rough edges. Blue — purple flowers bloom at the tips of stems and leaf axils from September to October. The rhizome is used for medicinal purposes. The rhizome is used for medicinal purposes.

竜胆や北国の青空届き　　　　　　　　　　　　　　　亜仁寿（自訳）

> gentian — the sky of northern country reaching me
>
> > タンポポ　アニス/Tanpopo Anis（インドネシア/Indonesia）

竜胆の種の無数が風の中

> split — hundreds of gentian tiny seeds scattered by the wind
>
> > ザンザミ　イスマイル/Zamzami Ismail（インドネシア/Indonesia）

青空や竜胆鼻をアルプスに

> un ciel bleu intense — les gentianes pointent leur nez à l'alpage
>
> > イメルダ　セン/Imelda Senn（スイス/Switzerland）

竜胆や空の深き色を見つけ
> gentian — finding the colour of the sky
>> アンナ　イリナ/Ana Irina（ルーマニア/Romania）

君の眼よりも蒼きアルプスの竜胆
> plus bleues que tes yeux — les gentianes des Alpes
>> アンヌ-マリー　ジュベール-ガヤール/Anne-Marie Joubert-Gaillard
>> （フランス/France）

竜胆の色の深さや親孝行　　　　　　　　　　　亜仁寿（自訳）
> filial piety — the colour depth of gentian flower
>> タンポポ　アニス/Tanpopo Anis（インドネシア/Indonesia）

住み慣れし古家の庭に咲く竜胆　　　　　　　　亜仁寿（自訳）
> gentian blooming in my old house garden
>> タンポポ　アニス/Tanpopo Anis（インドネシア/Indonesia）

竜胆や優しき気持ちくれる君
> gentian flower — she offers me compassion in moments of sadness
>> ポール　カルス/Paul Callus（マルタ/Malta）

竜胆や帽子をとりて挨拶し
> gentian — the stranger lifts up his hat to salute
>> ナッキー　クリスティジーノ/Nuky Kristijno（インドネシア/Indonesia）

竜胆を宇宙の色と思ひけり
> gentian — feel like the color of the universe
>> 中野千秋/Chiaki Nakano（日本/Japan）

竜胆の藍の深さの恋に落つ

> les gentianes indigo — je tombe dans un profond amour

向瀬美音/Mine Mukose（日本/Japan）

茸【きのこ・kinoko】
mushroom / champignon

A common name for a large fungus that grows in swamps and decaying wood in mountain forests in late autumn. There are many varieties in the form of umbrellas, and some poisonous mushrooms with beautiful colors. Shiitake, maitake, shimeji, and enoki mushrooms have a good taste and can be artificially cultivated and shipped to the market.

雨宿りする蟻のゐる茸かな

> a tiny mushroom — ants take shelter from the rain

タンポポ　アニス/Tanpopo Anis（インドネシア/Indonesia）

キャンプして最初の場所に茸かな

> camping — sur notre emplacement les premiers champignons

フランソワーズ　デニオ-ルリエーブル/Françoise Deniaud-Lelièvre（フランス/France）

本に住む妖精赤き茸かな

> funghi rossi — un libro di gnomi e folletti
> red mushrooms — a book of dwarves and elves

ダニエラ　ミッソ/Daniela Misso（イタリア/Italy）

様々と森の茸は風に告ぐ

> parole al vento — ogni bosco profuma dei suoi funghi

ミケーレ　ポチエロ/Michele Pochiero（イタリア/Italy）

雨上がり茶色の耳を出す茸

> mushroom — the brown like ears grow over decayed wood after raining
>
> アリアナ　ユハナ/Ariani Yuhana（インドネシア/Indonesia）

木の穴を埋め尽くしたる茸かな

> hollow fruit tree — mushrooms fill the emptiness
>
> マリリン　アッシュボ/Marilyn Ashbaugh（米国/United States）

森ゆけば茸の香り溢れたる

> les sous-bois parfumés d'une odeur de champignons — balade en forêt
>
> イメルダ　セン/Imelda Senn（スイス/Switzerland）

大理石隠す子供や庭の茸

> champignons au jardin — l'endroit où l'enfant cache ses billes
>
> オルファ　クチュク　ブハディダ/Olfa Kchouk Bouhadida
> （チュニジア/Tunisia）

茸生え闇の中さへ消えぬ愛

> mushroom — love survives even in the dark
>
> ポール　カルス/Paul Callus（マルタ/Malta）

茸狩白き斑点頬にあり

> mushrooming — white patches on your cheeks
>
> ザンザミ　イスマイル/Zamzami Ismail（インドネシア/Indonesia）

茸生えヴァカンス村の趣よ

> une colonie de vacances — armillaires.
>
> マルセル　ペルティエ/Marcel Peltier（フランス/France）

森の茸薄つすら土に繋がつて
> funghi del bosco connessioni sottili sotto la terra
>
> mushrooms of the wood — thin connections under earth
>
> クリスティーナ　プルビエンティ/Cristina Pulvirenti
>
> (イタリア/Italy)

暗闇に光る真っ赤な毒菌　　　　　　　　　　亜仁寿（自訳）
> glowing in the dark—bright red poisonous mushroom
>
> タンポポ　アニス/Tanpopo Anis
>
> (インドネシア/Indonesia)

茸狩玉虫色の森の中
> cueillette des champignons — la forêt aux couleurs chatoyantes
>
> ベルナデット　クエン/Bernadette Couenne
>
> (フランス/France)

森の散歩松のくぼみに赤き茸
> promenade en forêt — enfoui dans le creux du pin un champignon rouge
>
> ラシダ　ジェルビ/Rachida Jerbi（チュニジア/Tunisia）

茸生え不思議の国のアリスかな
> mushrooms — I dream of Alice in Wonderland
>
> アンナ　イリナ/Ana Irina（ルーマニア/Romania）

採れたての茸の匂ふ無人駅
> unmanned station — smell of freshly picked mushrooms flowing in the wind
>
> タンポポ　アニス/Tanpopo Anis
>
> (インドネシア/Indonesia)

切り株の茸や葉に雨のざわめき
> champignons sur une souche — murmure de la pluie sur le tapis de feuilles
>
> エレナ　ズアイン/Elena Zouain
>
> （ルーマニア/Romania）

雨上り祖父と一緒の茸狩
> after the rain — mushroom picking with grandpa
> dopo la pioggia — la raccolta dei funghi insieme al nonno
>
> アンジェラ　ジオルダーノ/Angela Giordano
>
> （イタリア/Italy）

橅の香や犬はトリュフを見つけたる
> odeur terreuse de la hêtraie—le chien trouve sa première truffe.
>
> シュピー　モイサン/Choupie Moysan
>
> （フランス/France）

朝早く野生のきのこ探しけり
> early autumn mornings — foraging for wild mushrooms
>
> ポール　カルス/Paul Callus（マルタ/Malta）

妖精の本の真つ赤な茸かな
> funghi rossi — un libro di gnomi e folletti
> red mushrooms — a book of dwarves and elves
>
> ダニエラ　ミッソ/Daniela Misso（イタリア/Italy）

モリーユ(茸)や大事な秘密隠れたる
> ce petit coin de morilles — notre secret bien gardé
>
> アンヌ-マリー　ジュベール-ガヤール/Anne-Marie Joubert-Gaillard
>
> （フランス/France）

茸生ゆ少しの毒を持ちて生く
mushroom — my life having a little poison

中野千秋/Chiaki Nakano(日本/Japan)

解説 「国際俳句」の多様な可能性を世界に広げた人
―― 向瀬美音編著『国際俳句歳時記　秋
国境を越えた魂の震撼』に寄せて

　　　　　　　　　　詩人・批評家　**鈴木比佐雄**

1

　向瀬美音氏が主宰する国際俳句グループ「俳句ガーデン」で発表された俳句を読んでいると、外国人には俳句の季語などはたぶん理解できないという、日本人の閉鎖的な俳句観がすぐに打ち砕かれるだろう。そんな先入観から自由になった日本人たちは、俳句が抱えていた底知れぬ本質的な世界文学の可能性に驚かされる。そして世界の人びとが俳句の最小の言葉で世界の本質を摑み取り、暮らしの場所から自由な想像力を駆使して俳句を創作していることに気付かされ、国境を越えて深く感動するだろう。

　向瀬美音氏は、2024年新春に編著『パンデミック時代における国際俳句の苦闘と想像力　2020.1―2021.1』を刊行した。その内容は2020年1月から始まったパンデミック時代の1年間を、毎週一人で合計で約50人の俳人がその週に寄稿された作品の中から優れた作品を評論させたものだった。それから一年後の2025年春に『国際俳句歳時記　秋　国境を越えた魂の震撼』を編集・刊行された。本書は以前から刊行を計画していた『国際俳句歳時記』の「春」・「夏」・「冬」に次ぎ最後に執筆された歳時記であり、量的にも前の3冊よりも倍ほどの頁数がある。但し「夏」に関しては他社の刊行が遅れているようで、本書の「秋」が先に刊行された。

　向瀬氏は『パンデミック時代における国際俳句の苦闘と想像力』の「序文」において、現在の「俳句ガーデン」の俳句に向かっていったプロセスを次のように語っている。

《私は俳句ガーデンという国際俳句グループの主宰を務めている。／このグループは7年前に俳句の海外交流を目的として立ち上げたものである。／当初は、国際俳句の饒舌な三行詩に疑問を持ち二行詩、取り合わせを試みた。／また七つの規則、1．切れ、2．省略、3．具体的なものに託す、4．今の瞬間を切り取る、5．季語、6．用言はできるだけ少なくする、7．取り合わせ、を示し、だんだん、全体的に短く簡潔になり、説明的な句は無くなってきた。／グループ結成当初はメンバーは100人にも満たなかったが、今では3,200人を超えている。一日の投稿数も50句から100句に及ぶ。国籍も30は超えるだろう。／初めは、キーワードとして、水、光、匂い、香りなどでまとめていた。そして2年目から季語を導入した。季節のない国もあるから季語は無理だろうと考えていたが大きな間違いであった。季語の中には、時候、天文、生活、植物、動物の中から世界の俳人と共有できる季語はたくさんある。季語の持つ深い大意を理解してもらうのは時として難しいが、植物、動物、天文、時候のいくつは十分分かち合える。私は今まで500近くの季語を紹介して、歳時記も作ってきたが、季語というのは世界の俳人を魅了するものだと確信した。》

この時から1年が経ち、8年目の現在の会員数は300人増えて3,500人に達していると聞いている。向瀬氏の独創的なところは、「当初は、国際俳句の饒舌な三行詩に疑問を持ち二行詩、取り合わせを試みた」と言い、さらに実践的に英語を初めとする世界の言語であっても一行詩にした方が、俳句の簡潔さと省略を担うに相応しいのではないかと考えたのだろう。そして「七つの規則、1．切れ、2．省略、3．具体的なものに託す、4．今の瞬間を切り取る、5．季語、6．用言はできるだけ少なくする、7．取

り合わせ、を示し、だんだん、全体的に短く簡潔になり、説明的な句は無くなってきた」と、海外の俳句を創作する人びとに七つの基本的な創作ルールを提示していった。また2年目には海外向けの季語を提示して、それを入れた俳句作りを促していった。その結果として会員が七つの規則や季語の使用に共感を示して3,500人の投稿者になっていったのだろう。

　かつて私は親しかった米国の詩人たちとメールで交流する際に、初めに三行詩を送ると「俳句をありがとう」と返信があったものだった。それが今では、二行詩でも一行詩でも俳句とみなされてきた。向瀬氏の一行詩俳句は、国際俳句の創作において、多用な方法の一つとして、新たな可能性を広めていると言えるだろう。

　因みにイタリアでは「mono-haike」という一行詩俳句が増えてきていると聞いている。

2

「序」によると今回の『国際俳句歳時記　秋』には、当初はこの何年分かでも約4,000句の候補作があったが、最終的には約100名による約2,160句が収録された。向瀬氏の「序」の後には、3,500人の中から5人の俳句評論が収録されている。この5人の中からナディン・レオン氏の「私が考える俳句とは」を紹介したい。次のように俳句の精神性を簡潔で思索的な言葉で語っている。

《俳句は伝統とモダニズムが融合した日本の美学であり、その基本原則の3つは象徴性、節制、空虚である。具体的で、地味で、単純で、日常的で、自発的なものすべてを好むことによって、暗黙のうちに感情を伝え、雰囲気を描くのが作者の技術である。この繊細な芸術は、物事のはかなさを感じさせたり（もののあわれ）、はかなさや不完全さに美を感じさせたり（わびさび）、神秘

的で不可解なものに美を感じさせたり（幽玄）、繊細さを感じさせたり（しおり）、ユーモアに軽妙さを感じさせたり（かるみ）することができる。俳句では、安定と進化という相反する2つの原理が共存している。安定は季語の使い方にあり、進化は作者のものの見方にある。》

　ナディン・レオン氏は、俳句の重層的な精神性を深く理解し、それらを咀嚼して自分の言葉で語っている。俳句の定義を「俳句は伝統とモダニズムが融合した日本の美学であり、その基本原則の3つは象徴性、節制、空白である」と簡潔に語っている。俳句を「繊細な芸術」であり、「安定と進化という相反する2つの原理が共存している」という俳句の「相反する2つの原理」の力学が生み出す奇跡の詩的瞬間を想定しているかのようだ。俳句が生まれ出てくる時空間には、伝統と現代、安定と進化、永遠と瞬間など異なる次元の二物衝撃のエネルギーが引き合い、激突し、未知の存在を生み出そうとする一行詩俳句の創作の精神性が宿るのだろう。ナディン・レオン氏は次のようにフランスの俳句への高い志を最後に紹介している。

《一般的に、フランスの俳句は、子規が提唱した季語や5・7・5のリズムのような、任意となった特定のルールから解放されている。俳句の特徴は、「まこと」、自発性、信憑性、そして通常最終行にある驚きの効果である。「私」は一人称で行動や感情を表現するのに使われる。しかし、共感の効果によって、何よりも「普遍的な私」になる。》

　ナディン・レオン氏を含めてフランスの俳人たちは、芭蕉の禅への関心を現在にも引き継ぎ、俳句に「まこと」の精神を追い求

めている。「私」の行動や感情を自覚的に振り返るが、他者や自然などへの「共感」によって、本来的な「普遍的な私」に至る遍歴の旅を俳句の創作に求めているのかも知れない。この俳句評論を読んでいると、デカルトの「良識」やメルロー・ポンティの『知覚の現象学』などを思索した伝統のある国の末裔だと感じさせてくれる。たぶんその他の世界の俳人たちも芭蕉の禅的精神性を多様な国の伝統を踏まえて現代に生かそうと試みているのだろう。芭蕉の俳句の原点に立ち還り、それを鏡として自らの現実から国際俳句が、向瀬美音氏の「俳句ガーデン」で生み出されているのだと私は考えている。

3

　本書は一般的な歳時記の分類に則り、時候、天文、地理、生活、行事、動物、植物の七つに分けられている。季語はその七つ合わせて134が収録されている。

　初めの時候には19の季語に分類されて402句が収録されている。19の季語は、「立秋、秋初め、九月、残暑、秋分、十月、秋の朝、秋の昼、秋の暮、秋の夜、夜長、秋澄む、冷やか、爽やか、秋麗、秋深し、行く秋、晩秋、秋惜しむ」であり、その言葉の意味が紹介された後に、日本語に翻訳された俳句と原文である英語、フランス語、イタリア語など2か国か3か国語で表現されている。立秋の俳句を紹介したい。

立秋や南瓜スープを嬰が食み
pumpkin soup —— a baby tastes the first autumn
タンポポ　アニス/Tanpopo Anis（インドネシア/Indonesia）

インドネシアのタンポポ　アニス氏の句は、家族詠でありなが

らも、秋の初めと命を得た赤子が南瓜スープを飲むという取り合わせが、絶妙な効果をあげていて読者の心を温かくしてくれる。

秋めきて蒼白になる移民の顔
retour d'automne ── les visages pâles des immigrés
ソニア　ベン　アマール/Sonia Ben Ammar(チュニジア/Tunisia)

チュニジアのソニア　ベン　アマール氏は、イタリアまで150kmの浜辺から様々な理由で地中海を横断して移民を試みる人びとの「蒼白な顔」を記す。その顔は遭難する恐れのある人びとの恐怖の顔を暗示しているようだ。美しい秋が到来しても世界の難民の悲劇が続いていて、その悲しみを伝えてくれる優れた社会詠になっている。

山頂の色づき秋のラプソディ
a burst of colours on the mountain peak ── autumn rhapsody
バーバラ　オルムタック/Barbara Olmtak(オランダ/Holland)

秋の紅葉を愛でる作品は数多くあると思われるが、その光景を「秋のラプソディ/狂詩曲」という音楽に喩えていることに驚かされる。オランダのバーバラ　オルムタック氏は赤や黄の多彩な紅葉の山を登って行ったのだろう。その感動的な山の光景を見た時空間を作曲家のように「秋のラプソディ」と名付けたのだ。

空つぽのベンチに秋が座してゐる
an empty bench autumn sits quietly on it
prazna klop nanjo tiho seda jesen
ディミトリー　シュクルク/Dimitrij Škrk（スロベニア/Slovenia）

スロベニアのディミトリー　シュクルク氏の句は、秋という季節感が激しかった夏の高揚感を一度「空っぽ」にし、冷静になって新たに生き直すような時間の始まりだと暗示しているかのようだ。「ベンチに秋が座してゐる」とは禅の瞑想の境地を幻視している。実存主義的であり存在論的な思索詠だと思われる。

　ガザの秋少女の瞼永遠に閉づ
　autunno a Gaza —— la bimba copre gli occhi la bimba copre gli occhi
　ガブリエラ　デ　マシ/Gabriella De Masi（イタリア/Italy）

イタリアのガブリエラ　デ　マシ氏はガザの空爆などで命を亡くした少女たちの存在から目を背けずに、決して忘れてはならないと言う。そしてガブリエル氏は少女の死は民間人を無差別に殺戮してはならないという、国際法の精神が崩壊していることに起因し、人類の科学技術文明が未来の地球の担い手である子供たちの瞼を閉ざしてしまう恐るべき兵器になっていることを危惧している。

　最後に「時候」に収録されている向瀬美音氏の俳句を２句引用したい。

　果てしなき雲の広がり秋告げる
　une étendue infinie de nuages —— l'automne

　混沌は混沌を呼び秋暑し
　chaos sur chaos —— dernière chaleurs de l'été

向瀬美音/Mine Mukose（日本/Japan）

　向瀬美音氏にとって「果てしなき雲」とは「果てしなき国際俳句」なのだろうと私には感じられる。そして気候変動や海面水温上昇などによって「秋暑し」であるのは、人類もそのような破滅に向かう「混沌」に加担しているからだろうと危惧している。向瀬氏は本来的な「混沌」はもっと多様性や他者と共生していくものなのだが、人類はどこか間違えているのではないかという思いを込めているようだ。そして「秋暑し」という季語には、人類の環境破壊に対して批判的な意味を込めているようだ。向瀬氏は国際俳句の道標として一行詩俳句や七つの規則を提案し、世界の俳人たちの創作の背中を押してきた。それは「混沌」の中の一筋の光明であったに違いない。収録された約2,160句の中から論じたい句は数多く存在する。この30カ国を越える国々の俳人たちの国際俳句の試みは、伝統と進化を融合させる世界文学の新たな可能性に寄与し続けるだろうと、私は考えている。

Commentary
The person who spread the diverse possibilities of 'International Haiku' around the world.
- International Haiku Saijiki Autumn : The Souls Shaking Across Borders, edited by Mine Mukose.

Poet & Critic Hisao Suzuki

1

Reading the haiku published in the international haiku group Haiku Garden, which Ms. Mine Mukose presides over, you will immediately shatter the closed Japanese view of haiku, that foreigners cannot possibly understand the seasonal words in haiku. Free from such preconceptions, the Japanese will be surprised at the unfathomable and essential world literary potential of haiku. And they will be deeply moved beyond national borders to realise that people around the world are grasping the essence of the world in the smallest words of haiku and creating haiku from the places where they live, using their free imagination.

Ms. Mine Mukose published her edited volume 'The Struggle and Imagination of International Haiku in the Age of Pandemics 2020.1-2021.1' in the new spring of 2024. The content of the book was a critique of the year-long pandemic era that began in January 2020 by one haiku poet each week, for a total of about 50 haiku poets, who critiqued outstanding works from among those contributed that week. A year later, in the spring of 2025, she edited and published International Haiku Saijiki [Autumn]: The Shaking of Souls Across Borders. This is the last of the International Haiku Saijiki, following Spring, Summer and Winter, which had been planned for publication for some time, and has twice as many pages as the previous three volumes. However, the publication of 'Summer' seems to have been delayed by other companies, and this book, 'Autumn', was published first.

In the 'Preface' to 'The Struggle and Imagination of International Haiku in the Age of Pandemics', Ms. Mukose describes the process that led to the current 'Haiku Garden' haiku as follows.

> I am the president of an international haiku group called Haiku Garden.
>
> This group started seven years ago for the purpose of international haiku exchange.
>
> In the beginning, I questioned the talkative three-line poetry of international haiku and tried two-line poetry and toriawase of the two.
>
> The seven rules of haiku are: 1) cut, 2) omission 3) use something concrete, 4) capture the present moment, 5) use seasonal words, 6) use as few verbs as possible, and 7) toriawase
>
> When the group was formed, there were less than 100 members. Now there are more than 3,200 members. The number of daily submissions ranges from 50 to 100 haikus. The number of nationalities is probably more than 30.
>
> In the beginning, I used keywords like water, light, smell, and fragrance, but in the second year, I introduced seasonal words. I thought it would be impossible to use seasonal words because some countries do not have seasons, but it was a mistake. There are many seasonal words from season, astronomy, life, plants, and

animals that can be shared with haiku poets around the world. It is sometimes difficult to get people to understand the deeper meaning of a seasonal word, but plants, animals, astronomy, and some seasonal words can be shared with haiku poets all over the world. I have introduced nearly 500 seasonal words and have written saijiki spring, winter and new year. I am convinced that seasonal words attract haiku poets from all over the world.

A year has passed since then, and now, in its eighth year, the number of members has increased by 300 to 3,500, I am told. Ms. Mukose's originality lies in the fact that she says, 'At first, I had doubts about the talkative three-line haiku of international haiku and tried two-line poetry, or a toriawase,' and then, more practically, she thought that one-line poetry, even in English and other world languages, would be more suitable for haiku's brevity and abbreviation. She also presented seven basic rules for haiku to overseas haiku composers: 'The seven rules are: 1. brevity; 2. omission; 3. concrete objects; 4. cutting out the present moment; 5. season words; 6. use as few words as possible; 7. toriawase, and gradually, the haiku became shorter and more concise overall, with no more explanatory phrases. In the second year, she presented the seven basic rules of haiku creation to overseas haiku creators. In the second year, she also presented a set of seasonal words for overseas haiku and encouraged them to write haiku that included them. The result may have been that members became sympathetic to the seven rules and the use of seasonal words, and the number of contributors grew to 3,500.

In the past, when I would email my close US poets, I would first send them a three-line poem and they would reply, 'Thanks for the haiku'. Nowadays, a two-line haiku or a one-line haiku is considered a haiku. Ms. Mukose's one-line haiku is one of the many methods used in the creation of international haiku, and are opening up new possibilities. Incidentally, I have heard that "mono-haike" one-line haiku are on the rise in Italy.

2

According to the 'Preface', the International Haiku Saijiki [Autumn] initially contained approximately 4,000 candidate haiku from the past few years, but in the end it contained approximately 2,160 haiku by about 100 authors. After Ms. Mukose's 'Foreword', five haiku critics from among the 3,500 are included. From among these five, I would like to introduce Ms. Nadine Léon 'What I think of haiku'. She describes the spirituality of haiku in concise and thoughtful terms as follows.

'Haiku is a Japanese aesthetic that combines tradition and modernism, and its three basic principles are symbolism, moderation and blankness. By favouring all that is concrete, sober, simple, everyday and spontaneous, the author's skill is to implicitly convey emotion and portray atmosphere. This subtle art can evoke a sense of the transience of things (mono no aware), beauty in transience and imperfection (wabi sabi), beauty in the mysterious and inexplicable (yugen), delicacy (shiori) or lightness in humour (karumi). In haiku, two contradictory principles coexist: stability and evolution. Stability lies in the use of seasonal words, while evolution lies in the

's way of seeing things.

Ms. Nadine Léon has a deep understanding of the multi-layered spirituality of haiku and has digested them and spoken about them in her own words. She defines haiku succinctly as 'haiku is a Japanese aesthetic that combines tradition and modernism, and its three basic principles are symbolism, moderation and blankness'. She seems to envisage haiku as a 'delicate art' and the miraculous poetic moments created by the dynamics of the 'two conflicting principles' of haiku, where 'stability and evolution coexist'. The time-space in which haiku emerges may be inhabited by the spirituality of the creation of one-line haiku, in which the energies of the impact of two different dimensions - tradition and modernity, stability and evolution, eternity and the moment - attract and collide, trying to give birth to an unknown entity. Ms. Nadine Léon concludes her introduction to the high aspirations of French haiku as follows.

'In general, French haiku is free from certain rules that have become arbitrary, such as the seasonal words and the 5-7-5 rhythm advocated by Shiki. Haiku is characterised by 'makoto', spontaneity, authenticity and the effect of surprise, usually in the final line. 'I' is used to describe actions and feelings in the first person. But the effect of empathy makes it, above all, 'the universal I.'

French haiku poets, including Ms. Nadine Léon, have taken over Basho's interest in Zen to the present day, pursuing the spirit of 'makoto' in their haiku. They look back consciously on the actions and feelings of the 'I', but through empathy with others and nature, they may be seeking in their haiku creation an itinerant journey to the original 'universal I'. Reading this haiku review makes me feel that they are descendants of a country with a tradition of contemplating Descartes' Decency and Merleau-Ponty's Phenomenology of Perception. Perhaps haiku poets from the rest of the world are also attempting to bring Basho's Zen spirituality to life today in the context of diverse national traditions. I believe that international haiku is being produced in Ms. Mine Mukose's 'Haiku Garden' by returning to the origins of Basho's haiku and using them as a mirror for her own reality.

3

This book is divided into seven categories according to the general chronological classification: time, astronomy, geography, life, events, animals and plants. There are 134 entries for each of these seven categories.

The first section contains 402 haiku, classified according to 19 seasonal words: 'Risshū, early autumn, September, lingering summer, autumn equinox, October, autumn morning, autumn afternoon, autumn evening, autumn night, autumn long night, autumn clear, cool, fresh, autumn beautiful, autumn deep, autumn going, autumn late, autumn regret', after which the meaning of each word is introduced, The haiku are translated into Japanese and the original text is expressed in two or three languages, including English, French and Italian. I would like to introduce the haiku of Risshū.

立秋や南瓜スープを嬰が食み
pumpkin soup —— a baby tastes the first autumn
タンポポ　アニス/Tanpopo Anis（インドネシア/Indonesia）

This haiku by Ms. Tanpopo Anis from Indonesia is a family poem, but the combination of the beginning of autumn and a baby coming to life drinking pumpkin soup has an exquisite effect and warms the reader's heart.

秋めきて蒼白になる移民の顔
retour d'automne —— les visages pâles des immigrés
ソニア　ベン　アマール/Sonia Ben Ammar（チュニジア/Tunisia）

Ms. Sonia Ben Ammar from Tunisia describes the 'pale faces' of those who attempt to emigrate across the Mediterranean for various reasons from the 150 km beach to Italy. The faces seem to suggest the faces of fear of those who are in danger of being lost. The tragedy of the world's refugees continues even as the beautiful autumn arrives, making this an excellent social poem that conveys the sadness of the situation.

山頂の色づき秋のラプソディ
a burst of colours on the mountain peak —— autumn rhapsody
バーバラ　オルムタック/barbara olmtak（オランダ/Holland）

There may be many works of art that admire the autumn leaves, but it is surprising that the scene is likened to the music of an 'autumn rhapsody/rhapsody'. Ms. Barbara Olmtack from the Netherlands must have climbed the mountains with their variety of red and yellow autumn leaves. Like the composer, she named the time and space in which she saw this inspiring mountain scene 'Autumn Rhapsody'.

空つぽのベンチに秋が座してゐる
an empty bench autumn sits quietly on it
prazna klop nanjo tiho seda jesen
ディミトリー　シュクルク/Dimitrij Škrk(スロベニア/Slovenia)

Slovenian Ms. Dimitri Škulc's haiku seems to suggest that autumn is the beginning of a time when the seasonality of the summer is 'emptied' of its intense exuberance and a time to cool down and start living anew. The phrase 'Autumn is sitting on the bench' evokes the meditative state of Zen. It seems to be an existentialist and ontological contemplative poem.

ガザの秋少女の瞼永遠に閉づ
autunno a Gaza —— la bimba copre gli occhi la bimba copre gli occhi
ガブリエラ　デ　マシ/Gabriella De Masi（イタリア/Italy）

Italy's Ms. Gabriella De Masi says that we must not turn away from the girls who have lost their lives, including in the bombing of Gaza, and that we must never forget them. And Ms. Gabriella fears that the deaths of the girls are due to a breakdown in the spirit of international law, which prohibits the indiscriminate killing of civilians, and that human technological civilisation has become a terrible weapon that shuts the eyelids of children, who are the future bearers of the earth.

Finally, I would like to quote two haiku by Ms. Mine Mukose from 'Jikkou'.

果てしなき雲の広がり秋告げる
une étendue infinie de nuages —— l'automne

混沌は混沌を呼び秋暑し
chaos sur chaos —— dernière chaleurs de l'été
向瀬美音/Mine Mukose（日本/Japan）

For Ms. Mine Mukose, 'endless clouds' are, I feel, 'endless international haiku'. And I fear that the reason it is 'hot in autumn' due to climate change and rising sea-surface temperatures is because humanity is part of the 'chaos' that is heading towards such destruction. Ms. Mukose believes that the essential 'chaos' is more about diversity and living in harmony with others, but she seems to think that humankind has made a mistake. And the seasonal phrase 'autumn heat' seems to be critical of mankind's environmental destruction. Ms. Mukose has proposed the one-line haiku and the Seven Rules as a guidepost for international haiku, and has pushed haiku poets around the world to create more. It must have been a ray of light in the midst of 'chaos'. There are many haiku to discuss from the approximately 2,160 haiku in the collection. I believe that this international haiku experiment by haiku poets from over 30 countries will continue to contribute to new possibilities for world literature that fuse tradition and evolution.

あとがき

向瀬美音

　今回は春夏秋冬の最後の「秋」の歳時記を出すことにした。「秋」は他の季節に比べて厚くなってしまった。

　これは世界の俳人がますます季語に関心を持ってきたということと、秋には海外の人と共有できる季語が多いからだと思う。

　海外の俳人は天文が大好きで、特に月、星、銀漢、流星には多くの句が寄せられた。月を見て思うことは万国共通であり、星を見て煌めく心も同じであるのだろう。

　年々投稿量が膨大になり、私一人ではもうどうしようもなくなってきたのだが、「ひろそ火」の同人で、日英バイリンガルの中野千秋氏が、五年前からずっと、一日も休まず、英語の俳句に関しては完璧に訳、選句をこなしてくれているので、どうにか続けられている。彼女とは同じ志を持って活動している。海外の俳人と同じ沼に浸かって切磋琢磨していることである。

　こちらから提供できるとことは紹介し、海外から、吹いてくる新鮮な風に感性を揺すぶられることである。

　この歳時記「秋」は2022,2023,2024年の投句を保存してまとめたものであるが当時は長井美佐子氏にとても助けられた。現在では、林淳子氏にフランス語の訳をほとんどお願いしている。

　みんなに深く感謝している。

　またこの活動は完全にボランティアなのだが、毎週の秀句鑑賞を始め今回は内容の濃いエッセイを寄せてくれた外国の俳人にも深く感謝している。全てがこのグループの俳人達の信頼、善意、向上心に基づいてると思う。

またこの大変な作業を短期間でまとめてくれたコールサック社の皆様にも深く感謝している。

Afterword

Mine Mukose

This time I decided to publish a chronicle of 'autumn', the last of the spring, summer, autumn and winter seasons.

'Autumn' has become thicker than the other seasons.

I think this is because haiku poets around the world are increasingly interested in seasonal words, and because autumn has many seasonal words that can be shared with people abroad.

Haiku poets abroad love astronomy, and many haiku were written especially about the moon, stars, silver halves and meteors. The thoughts of the moon are the same all over the world, and the hearts that twinkle at the sight of the stars must be the same.

The volume of submissions has grown so large over the years that I have been unable to handle it on my own, but I am somehow able to keep going because Chiaki Nakano, a Japanese-English bilingual haiku writer who has been a member of HIROSOBI for five years now, has never missed a day of work and is perfectly capable of handling the task of writing haiku in English. She and I are working with the same ambition. It is a friendly competition, immersed in the same swamp as haiku poets from abroad.

We introduce what we can offer, and are shaken to our senses by the fresh winds blowing in from abroad.

This Chronicle of Autumn is a compilation of the poems submitted in 2022, 2023 and 2024, which were saved and compiled by Misako Nagai, who was a great help at the time. Nowadays, I ask Junko Hayashi to do most of the French translations.

I am deeply grateful to all of them.

Although this activity is completely voluntary, we are also deeply grateful to the foreign haiku poets who have contributed essays, including a weekly appreciation of excellent haiku, which this time was very rich in content. I believe that everything is based on the trust, goodwill and ambition of the haiku poets in this group.

I am also deeply grateful to the call sackers who have put together this difficult task in such a short time.

Postface

Mine Mukose

Cette fois, j'ai décidé de publier une chronique de l'automne, la dernière des saisons printemps, été, automne et hiver.

L'« automne » est devenu plus épais que les autres saisons.

Je pense que cela est dû au fait que les poètes de haïku du monde entier s'intéressent de plus en plus aux mots saisonniers et que l'automne contient de nombreux mots saisonniers qui peuvent être partagés avec des personnes à l'étranger.

Les poètes de haïku à l'étranger aiment l'astronomie, et de nombreux haïkus ont été écrits sur la lune, les étoiles, les moitiés d'argent et les météores. Les pensées de la lune sont les mêmes partout dans le monde, et les cœurs qui scintillent à la vue des étoiles doivent être les mêmes.

Au fil des ans, le volume des soumissions est devenu si important que je n'ai pas pu y faire face seule, mais j'ai réussi à continuer parce que Chiaki Nakano, une écrivaine de haïkus bilingue japonais-anglais, membre HIROSOBI depuis cinq ans, n'a jamais manqué un seul jour de travail et est parfaitement capable de s'acquitter de la tâche d'écrire des haïkus en anglais. Elle et moi travaillons avec la même ambition. Il s'agit d'une compétition amicale, plongée dans le même marécage que les poètes de haïku de l'étranger.

Nous présentons ce que nous pouvons offrir, et nous sommes secoués par les vents frais qui soufflent de l'étranger.

Cette Chronique d'automne est une compilation des poèmes soumis en 2022, 2023 et 2024, qui ont été sauvegardés et compilés par Misako Nagai, qui m'a été d'une grande aide à l'époque. Aujourd'hui, je demande à Junko Hayashi de faire la plupart des traductions en français.

Je leur suis profondément reconnaissant.

Bien que cette activité soit entièrement bénévole, nous sommes également très reconnaissants aux poètes de haïku étrangers qui ont contribué à la rédaction d'essais, y compris une appréciation hebdomadaire d'excellents haïkus, qui cette fois-ci a été très riche en contenu. Je pense que tout repose sur la confiance, la bonne volonté et l'ambition des poètes de haïku de ce groupe.

Je suis également très reconnaissante aux personnes qui ont répondu à l'appel et qui ont mené à bien cette tâche difficile en si peu de temps.

著者略歴

向瀬美音（むこうせ　みね）

1960年、東京生まれ。上智大学外国語学部卒業。

日本ペンクラブ会員、日本文藝家協会会員

2013年頃から作句を始め、大輪靖宏、山西雅子、櫂未知子から俳句の指導を受ける。2019年、第一句集「詩の欠片」上梓。2020年、国際歳時記「春」。現在、「HAIKU ガーデン」主宰。俳句大学機関誌「HAIKU」Vol1 ［世界の俳人55人が集うアンソロジー］Vol5［世界の俳人150人が集うアンソロジー］の編集長兼発行人。2020年　Vol6「世界の俳人90人が集うアンソロジー」。2022年、国際歳時記「冬、新年」 2022年、第二句集「カシオペア」上梓。2024年「パンデミック時代における国際俳句の苦闘と想像力 2020·1―2021·1」

日本伝統俳句協会、俳人協会、国際俳句協会、フランス語圏俳句協会AFH,上智句会、「舞」会員、「群青」購読会員。

Profile

Mine Mukose

Born in Tokyo, 1960. Graduated from Sophia University, Faculty of Foreign languages.

Member of Japan Pen Club and Japan Literary Association.

Started writing haiku around 2013, receiving haiku instruction from Yasuhiro Owawa, Masako Yamanishi, and Michiko Kai. 2019, published her first collection of haiku, "pieces of Poetry"; 2020, International saijiki "Spring".

Currently, she preside at "HAIKU Garden". Editor-in-Chief and Publisher of "HAIKU" Vol1 [anthology of 55 haiku poets from around the world] Vol5 [anthology of 150 haiku poets from around the world], 2020 Vol6 [anthology of 90 haiku poets from around the world], 2022, International saijiki "Winter, New Year", 2022, Second collection of haiku "Cassiopeia",

Member of Japan Traditional Haiku Association, Haiku Poets Association, International Haiku Association, French-speaking Haiku Association AFH,

Sophia Haiku Association, member of "Mai", and "Gunjo" reader.
The Struggle and Imagination of International Haiku in the Age of Pandemics 2020.1-2021.1

Profil

Mine Mukose

Née à Tokyo en 1960. Diplômée de l'université Sophia, faculté des langues étrangères.
Membre du Pen Club japonais et de l'Association littéraire japonaise.
A commencé à écrire des haïkus vers 2013, en suivant les cours de Yasuhiro Owawa, Masako Yamanishi et Michiko Kai. En 2019, elle a publié son premier recueil de haïkus, "pieces of Poetry" ; en 2020, elle a publié le saijiki international "Spring".
Actuellement, elle préside la "Garden HAIKU". Rédactrice en chef et éditrice de "HAIKU" Vol1 [anthologie de 55 poètes de haïku du monde entier] Vol5 [anthologie de 150 poètes de haïku du monde entier], 2020 Vol6 [anthologie de 90 poètes de haïku du monde entier], 2022, saijiki international "Hiver, Nouvel An", 2022, deuxième recueil de haïku "Cassiopée",
Membre de l'Association japonaise du haïku traditionnel, de l'Association des poètes du haïku, de l'Association internationale du haïku, de l'Association francophone du haïku (AFH), de l'Association du haïku de Sophia, membre de "Mai" et lecteur "Gunjo".
The Struggle and Imagination of International Haiku in the Age of Pandemics 2020.1-2021.1

現住所

〒160-0011　東京都新宿区若葉1-21-4-405
address
1-21-4-405 Wakaba Shinjyuku-ku Tokyo Japan 160-0011
MAIL　mine.mukose@me.com

国際俳句歳時記　秋 ——国境を越えた魂の震撼

International Saijiki : Autumn ——The Shaking Souls Across Borders

2025 年 3 月 25 日初版発行
企画・編集　　　向瀬美音
翻訳　　　　　　向瀬美音・中野千秋
編集・発行者　　鈴木比佐雄
発行所　　株式会社 コールサック社
〒 173-0004　東京都板橋区板橋 2-63-4-209
電話 03-5944-3258　FAX 03-5944-3238
suzuki@coal-sack.com　http://www.coal-sack.com
郵便振替　00180-4-741802
印刷管理　（株）コールサック社　制作部

装幀　松本菜央

落丁本・乱丁本はお取り替えいたします。
ISBN978-4-86435-647-3　C0092　￥2500E

title

Copyright © 2025 by Mukose Mine
Published by Coal Sack Publishing Company

Coal Sack Publishing Company
2-63-4-209 Itabashi Itabashi-ku Tokyo 173-0004 Japan
Tel: (03)5944-3258 / Fax: (03)5944-3238
suzuki@coal-sack.com　http://www.coal-sack.com
President: Hisao Suzuki

Photos of Haiku Authors

Attalah Abdellatif
アタラ　アドベラティフ
アルジェリア

Tanpopo Anis
タンポポ　アニス
インドネシア

Teresa Argiolas
テレサ　アルジオラ
イタリア

Gavril Bâle
ガブリル　バル
ルーマニア

Mohammed Benfares
モハメド　ベンファレス
モロッコ

Abderrahim Bensaïd
アブデラヒム　ベンサイド
モロッコ

Michel Berthelin
ミシェル　ベルトラン
フランス

Natacha Karl Bezsonoff
ナタシャ　カール　ベズソノフ
フランス

Najet Bokr
ナジェ　ボクリ
チュニジア

Gina Bonasera
ジナ　ボナセーラ
イタリア

Mallika Bouzidi
マリカ　ブジディ
モロッコ

Mirela Brailean
ミレラ　ブライレーン
ルーマニア

Maurizio Brancaleoni
マウリチオ　ブランカレオーニ
イタリア

Paul Callus
ポール　カルス
マルタ

Dennys Cambarau
デニー　カンバロウ
イタリア

Isabelle Carvalho Tele
イザベル　カルバロ　テール
フランス

Partizia Cavallone
パトリチア　カバローネ
イタリア

Patrizia Cenci
パトリチア　センシ
イタリア

AmelLadhibi Bent Chadly
アメルラディヒビ　ベント　チャディ
チュニジア

Jeanine Chalmeton
ジャニン　シャルメトン
フランス

Christina Chin
クリスティーナ　チン
マレーシア

Mafizuddin Chowdhury
マフィズディン　チュードハリー
インド

Jean-Hughes Chuix
ジャン　ユーグ　シュイ
フランス

Karine Cocheteux
カリン　コシュト
フランス

Vittoria Colucci
ビットリア　コルッチ
イタリア

Bernadette Couenne
ベルナデット　クエン
フランス

Py Daniel
ピイ　ダニエル
フランス

Anne Dealbert
アンヌ　デアルベルト
フランス

Eric Despierre
エリック　デスピエール
フランス

Carole Dieuzeide
キャロル　デイウゼイド
フランス

Feten Fourti
フテン　フルチ
チュニジア

Françoise Gabriel
フランソワーズ　ガブリエル
ベルギー

Barbara Anna Gaiardoni
バーバラ　ガイアルドーニ
イタリア

Agnese Giallongo
アグネーゼ　ジアロンゴ
イタリア

Giovanna Gioia
ジオバンナ　ジオイア
イタリア

Angela Giordano
アンジェラ　ジオルダーノ
イタリア

Antonio Girardi
アントニオ　ジラルディ
イタリア

Probir Gupta
プロビール　ギュプタ
インド

Souad Hajri
スアド　ハジリ
チュニジア

El Hamied
エル　ハミド
インドネシア

Ana Irina
アナ　イリナ
ルーマニア

Rachida Jerbi
ラシダ　ジェルビ
チュニジア

Anne-Marie Joubert-Gaillard
アンヌ・マリー　ジュベール・ガヤール
フランス

Olfa Kchouk Bouhadida
オルファ　クチュク ブハディダ
チュニジア

Eugene Khvalkov
エウジェヌ　カルコフ
ロシア

Nuky Kristijono
ナッキー　クリスティジーノ
インドネシア

Mihaela Lenutas
ミハエラ　レニュタス
ルーマニア

Nadine Leon
ナディン　レオン
フランス

Barrie Levine
バリー　レビン
米国

Larbi Limi
ラルビ　リミ
モロッコ

Nani Mariani
ナニ　マリアニ
オーストラリア

Burgos Marie-Claire
ブルゴ　マリー-クレール
フランス

Alberta Caterina Mattoli
アルベルタ　カテリナ　マトリ
イタリア

Francoise Maurice
フランソワーズ　モリス
フランス

Anna Meda
アンナ　メダ
イタリア

Jacque Michonnet
ジャック　ミショネ
フランス

Daniela Misso
ダニエラ　ミッソ
イタリア

Zdenka Mlinar
ズデンカ　ムリナー
クロアチア

Rita Moar
リタ　モアール
イタリア

Rashmi Mohapatra
ラシュミ　モハパトラ
インド

Brigitte Monloubou
ブリジット　モンルブー
フランス

Florence Muhlnbach
フローランス　ミューンバッハ
フランス

Mine Mukose
向瀬美音
日本

Chiaki Nakano
中野千秋
日本

Đinh Nguyễn
ディン　ニュグエン
ヴェトナム

Dyah Nkusuma
ディア　ヌクスマ
インドネシア

Barbara Olmtak
バーバラ　オルムタック
オランダ

Kim Olmtak
キム　オルムタック
オランダ

Aniko Papp
アニコ　パップ
ハンガリー

Eugénia Paraschiv
エウジェニア　パラシブ
ルーマニア

Maria Paterlini
マリア　パテルリーニ
イタリア

Mirella Ester Pennone Masi
ミレラ エステル ペノンヌ　マシ
イタリア

Michele Pochiero
ミケーレ　ポチエロ
イタリア

Cristina Pulvirenti
クリスティーナ　プルビエンティ
イタリア

Marin Rada
マリン　ラダ
ルーマニア

Christina Sng
クリスティーナ　SNG
シンガポール

Imelda Senn
イメルダ　セン
スイス

Patrick Somprou
パトリック　ソンプル
フランス

Laurent Sybillin
ローラン　シビリン
フランス

Zohra Nabil Tabet
ゾラ　ナブリ　タベ
チュニジア

Tounès Thabet
トウーン　チャベ
チュニジア

Daniela Topîrcean
ダニエラ　トピルセーン
ルーマニア

Francisco Palladino
フランチェスコ　パラディノ
イタリア

Paola Trevisson
パオラ　トレビッセン
イタリア

Zaya Youkhanna
ザヤ　ヨウクハンナ
オーストラリア

Ariani Yuhana
アリアナ　ユハナ
インドネシア

Francy Zeta
フランシー　ゼタ
イタリア

Elena Zouain
エレナ　ズアイン
ルーマニア